THE CORPSE BLOOM

BRYAN WIGGINS

with LEE THIBODEAU, MD

ISBN: 979-8-9895720-0-7

For Danna,

*who has always shown me that the best way to
serve those we love is to serve the wider world.*

Table of Contents

The Need to Feed

THE HUNTER WAS hungry.

As the days shortened, the osprey's appetite grew. Each morning, he soared along the coast of Maine in search of food to fuel his flight to Mexico.

Today at dawn, after several slow circles, he spotted what he'd sought: the silver flicker of a school.

He tipped his head, and with wings fixed fast, he fell until the silence was split by an engine's roar. He broke and veered from a red car that left the pine-lined road and headed toward the shore.

As the raptor rose, the car sailed too, as silently as the bird, arcing through the air and into the surf below.

From high above, the osprey spied a plume of white that bloomed against the gray. It settled to show a slab of pipes and struts that bobbed and winked before it slipped into the sea.

This time the osprey dived straight and true through the icy froth to pierce his prize. With wings spread wide, he churned and sprayed till he broke free from the waves. A talon's twist snapped the fish's spine as the bird began to climb.

He rose to race the rising sun and his prey's soul into the endless sky.

Chapter One

Early Exit

THE CALL THAT changed Dr. Bradley Baker's future came from his past. In the first few seconds of his rise from sleep, Brad was a child again, listening to the voice of the friend he'd drifted so far from.

"Brad? It's Sam. They found a kidney for me—almost a perfect match. Can you come?"

+

No mistakes…no mistakes…

Brad's mantra played in his head as he pushed his BMW up to ninety through the empty lanes of Storrow Drive. The two-word dictum normally began when he stepped into the operating room, but this morning had already veered far from Brad's plan for the day. He'd expected to walk onto a jet, not race into surgery. Everything changed with Sam's two a.m. call.

Now childhood memories of his friend blurred with the white lights of the Boston skyline whizzing by. Scouting forest trails, racing through cornfields, diving into the churning waters of the cold Maine sea—they all came back in a flash, like the flickering frames of a movie of their days spent exploring the woods and coast near the Baker family farm.

Brad saw the red light too late and hit the brakes. He turned the wheel to correct his skid over a patch of ice. With the car's nose poking into the empty intersection, he waited for his pulse to settle. Glancing to either side, he punched the pedal and ran the light. Time was an enemy now. Every second lost increased the chance that the waiting kidney would fail his friend.

Five minutes later, Brad screeched to a stop in his parking spot at Boston General Hospital. He slammed the door, sprinted inside, and weaved past the residents and attendings making their early morning rounds in the quiet halls. He changed into scrubs in the surgeons' locker room and put on a mask.

"How we looking, Bonnie?" Brad asked his circulating nurse when he walked into OR 19, noting the lock of hair peeking out of Bonnie's surgical cap that revealed the color of her latest dye job (blond). He glanced at the patient on the table in the center of the sterile white room.

Sam Kirby was fully anesthetized and lying on his back, his body draped in sheets the same robin's-egg blue as the scrubs worn by the surgical team.

"*We're* looking good, Doctor," Bonnie replied. "I only hope my kids are when they walk out the door. The last time Tom got them off to school, Kelly came home with her skirt inside out, and Robbie had two different shoes on his feet."

"At least you got this crew in order," Brad said, glad to see the familiar faces of his team. "Thanks for rounding up the usual suspects."

"With one addition," Bonnie said as the door behind them swung open. Brad turned to see a rail-thin kid wiping at his steamy glasses with the sleeve of his scrubs. Bonnie walked over and pinched the bridge of the young man's mask tight over his nose.

"That should help cut the fog," she said. "Dr. Baker, this is Ryan Turner. He's a fourth-year med student. I'm not quite sure how he found his way into our OR this morning."

Brad nodded at Ryan, thankful that his own mask concealed his frown. He had approved Ryan's attendance at Brad's next living-donor transplant, an operation that would have been a lot less hurried than the cadaver transplant he had rushed in to perform today. Someone in administration must have screwed up and called Ryan to come in.

While Brad relished his role in training the next generation of healers, this morning he planned on putting his full focus on his friend. But his next thought was about the nature of that man and how Sam would have responded to the earnest young face turned toward Brad now.

"No matter," Brad said, crinkling his eyes so the kid could infer Brad's smile. "I assume you did your homework this morning?"

"Homework?" asked Ryan, his eyes widening.

"Did you do a preoperative evaluation of our patient?"

"Oh, yes. Of course."

"Tell me about the lab values."

"His hemoglobin was low, and his potassium was high."

"Why?"

"His failing kidneys are responsible for both. They're no longer able to remove potassium or make the erythropoietin that produces red blood cells."

"Right on both counts. We've got two units of blood cross-matched and ready to go to provide the latter when the clamps come off at the end of this procedure. Now let me introduce you to the crew," Brad said, turning to the staff around him. "You're in luck, Ryan. You've got the A-team here today.

"That long drink of water is our surgical tech, Logan Carter," Brad said, pointing to the young man at the foot of the operating table. "And the guy standing over our patient who looks like Tom Brady is Miles Riker. Miles only has about six months left in his fellowship before he heads up a transplant team of his own."

"Five months," Miles said. "And you know I hate football."

"Heresy," Brad said, walking around the OR's perimeter for a quick survey of the preparations being made before moving to the drape separating the sterile operating field from the upper portion of his patient's body.

The rest of the room was in motion as well. Logan was laying out scalpels, hemostats, retractors, and clamps on the instrument table. Nurses were connecting suction tubes to pumps and aspirators. Miles hovered over Sam's abdomen, positioning the transparent drape that would maintain the sterile field, and the anesthesiologist pivoted back and forth as she scanned her screens.

"Dr. Eva Patel here just put our patient under," Brad said to Ryan, giving a nod to the woman almost entirely hidden by the bulk of her anesthesia machine. "How's he doing, Dr. Patel?"

"A few PVCs, Doctor, but he's stable."

Brad turned to Ryan. "What did she just tell me?"

"Uh, premature ventricular contractions?"

"You asking or telling?"

"Telling, Doctor."

"Good, yes. But his heart couldn't be in better hands," Brad said, tipping his head at Eva again. "Did you notice anything unusual about the way she answered me?"

"Not really..."

"She never looked up from her screen. Why?"

"She was busy monitoring the patient, I guess."

"No guessing about it. We call it *practicing* surgery because our goal is the orderly repetition of tasks in exactly the same way, from first slice to final stitch. To do that, the patient must remain stable. Now, tell me what an anesthesiologist has to do to maintain that condition."

"Control the drugs that keep the patient anesthetized," Ryan answered.

"*Powerful* drugs," Brad said, "an entire cocktail of sedatives, opioids, hypnotics, muscle relaxants, and paralytics. The only way to do it without killing the patient is to track every single bodily function those drugs control. Dr. Patel will monitor our patient's heart rate, blood pressure, hemoglobin levels, pulmonary function, and brain activity. She'll tweak whatever meds are needed to keep his vital signs stable. It's a delicate dance between pharmacology and physiology that lets us do the work we're here for—"

"You mean the plumbing," Miles broke in.

"Why don't you explain that to Ryan," Brad said.

"The main focus of this procedure," Miles said, "are the anastomoses we'll perform to connect the pipes that put the new kidney in place. Once we suture the donor's renal artery to the recipient's external iliac artery, and the donor's renal vein to the recipient's external iliac vein, we'll connect the ureter to the recipient's bladder, and our patient here should be good to go."

"Literally," Brad said, "although a cadaveric kidney like the one we'll be using today can take longer than a living donor's organ to output urine."

Another swing of the OR's door announced the entrance of the team's last member, the only one whose scrubs were not a shade of blue. The woman adjusted a bright pink surgical cap festooned with Disney cartoon characters.

"Ryan Turner," Brad said, "may I introduce Dr. Jill Delaney."

"Welcome," the attending nephrologist replied, giving Ryan a nod.

"Don't let those cartoons on her head fool you," Brad said. "The brain underneath them holds just about everything you need to know about the organ we're transplanting today."

Brad took a moment to survey his crew, murmured a quick "Follow me" to Ryan, then led him out of OR 19 to the substerile room to scrub in. Brad usually used this three-minute period to clear his mind as he prepared for the hours of concentrated focus required ahead. But with an eager med student shadowing him, this was the best time to give Ryan an overview of the nature of his team.

"Everyone in that room we just left has a critical role," Brad told him, as he began to wash his hands and forearms in the surgical scrub sink. "A good surgical team operates in the same manner as the body it serves. Like the organs within it, each team member is responsible for a particular task. I've worked with this crew for a long time. I trust each one of them to do the job they trained for. Staying focused on their tasks while keeping tuned to the entire team is the best way to reduce the chance for errors *and* increase the odds for our patient's best outcome."

"But you're the one who orchestrates it all," said Ryan.

"That's a good word for it," answered Brad, as he continued to scrub. "There are a lot of moving parts that need to work in complete harmony. But the legal view of my role isn't conductor, it's captain of the ship. I'm the one ultimately responsible for my team's actions and our patient's care."

He finished his scrub and led Ryan back into the operating room, where Logan was waiting to gown and glove him. When Brad was fully attired, he addressed his staff. "Let's do a quick time-out," he said as the team turned their attention to him.

"We're here this morning to perform a right iliac fossa cadaveric renal transplant on Reverend Sam Kirby to address his end-stage renal disease. Are we all on the same page?"

Brad waited until all team members voiced their assent, then turned to Ryan.

"You get a different question. Diabetes is the leading cause of renal failure. What are the next two major causes?"

"High blood pressure, and…"

Brad and the team waited. Dr. Delaney finally decided to help the kid out. "Glomerulonephritis," she said.

"I told you about that brain," Brad said, wagging a gloved finger at Jill. "You've got one more shot, Ryan. Can you describe that disease?"

"Inflammation of the glomeruli," Ryan said immediately, "the tiny filters in the kidney that remove waste products from the blood."

"Excellent," Brad responded. "You made the cut. Speaking of which," he said as he approached the table where Miles and Logan now waited, "shall we begin?"

+

It went like clockwork. The mood in the room stayed focused but relaxed; Miles assisted while Brad took the lead with the scalpel. Even Ryan seemed to tap into the room's flow, asking questions only in those short gaps that came between one part of the procedure and the next. When Miles removed the clamps from Brad's final anastomoses, the connection between the ureter and bladder proved as leak-free as the arterial and venous anastomoses that had preceded it.

"Take a look at that running suture," Miles said to Ryan with a wave at Brad's handiwork. "You won't find a better-looking one in your surgical textbook." Then Eva announced the only hiccup to their work so far.

"More PVCs, Doctor," she said.

Brad and Miles paused with their gloved hands in midair and traded a long glance. The silence in the room stretched for the next few seconds while the team waited. A moment later, a single word from the anesthesiologist put the world right again.

"Stable," Eva said.

The performance of the newly transplanted kidney was the day's best surprise. The organ pinked up almost immediately. Brad and Miles shared a thumbs-up when it did, agreeing that the quick way it had perfused meant there was a good chance it would start making urine soon.

In just over three hours, the job was almost done. "Don't you have a plane to catch?" Miles asked Brad. "Logan can assist while I close."

"I wasn't counting on an early exit," Brad said. "I didn't think there was any way I was going to make that flight. I already called Catherine to let her know I'd be delayed a day."

"She must have loved that," Miles said. "But I guess she'll still have the thrill of listening to you deliver your paper to the other type A docs at your conference."

"That's not quite the scene I shared when I pitched a Cancún vacation to her and Grace."

"Grace probably didn't need any selling. She's tall enough to pass for eighteen."

"Why does that matter?" Brad asked.

Miles shook his head as he held out his hand to accept a pair of forceps from Logan. "That's the drinking age down there, Dad."

Brad's eyes flicked to the clock on the wall just as Bonnie drew close to his side.

"You may want to take him up on that offer, Doctor," she said, dropping her voice to a whisper. "That nurse who ducked in a few minutes ago had me step out to take a call from your wife." Brad waited for Bonnie to say more, but the look in her eyes told him this was a conversation best held outside.

She continued the instant the OR door closed behind them. "First, Grace is okay."

Brad froze.

"She was horseback riding on the resort's beach," Bonnie said quickly. "She took a fall and hit her head but—"

"Tell me she was wearing a helmet."

"She was, but she was knocked out—"

"For how long?"

"I'm not sure. Catherine was pretty upset. She said Grace is conscious now, but then the call was dropped. I'm guessing cell reception may not be the best in Mexico."

Brad's eyes raced over the tiles on the floor, as if the answers he sought lay somewhere between the grid of lines at his feet. "Thanks," he said over his shoulder as he hurried to the locker room.

He called Catherine on his cell, hit the speaker icon, and placed the phone on the bench in front of his locker while he changed. A moment later, he heard his wife's voice-mail message play and cursed softly.

He snatched up the phone and jammed it in his pocket as he left, running straight into the orderly mopping the hall. They traded apologies as Brad made for the elevator. His mind started moving as fast as his legs while he searched for a way he could skip going home and head straight to the airport.

In front of the elevator, as he eyed the line of lights over the door, Brad had the nagging feeling that he'd left something undone. Then the face of the woman in the surgical waiting room he'd neglected to check in with flashed in his mind. He shook his head and turned around to go tell Sam Kirby's wife, Faye, just how bright her husband's future looked.

He flew back down the hall, careful to steer clear of the orderly, oblivious to the announcement that crackled over the hospital's ancient PA. But the second time that tinny voice blared, Brad heard its message loud and clear:

"Code blue, OR nineteen."

Chapter Two

Lost Lesson

THE OPERATING ROOM LOOKED like a crash site—which was exactly what it was. The six team members Brad had left to finish their flawless operation were now joined by a dozen more. Doctors, nurses, and techs bustled among the tables, monitors, and machines, trampling the bloody bandages and surgical drapes littering the floor.

Brad could barely see his patient in the middle of the melee. He moved around the crowd and got a view of the open wound, now packed with lap sponges. The rest of Sam's torso was covered by a sea of blue-gloved hands adjusting IV lines and EKG leads.

One of the techs felt for Sam's carotid artery and announced, "No pulse." Miles moved in the middle of the crowd, placing one hand over the other to deliver CPR. It took a hell of a push to depress the sternum the two inches needed to force the blood through the body until the heart could take over again. It was easy to break a rib when performing the maneuver, but that was the least of the worries for the man lying on the table now.

Brad's first reaction was relief at seeing his big colleague at the center of the action. His second was regret that he wasn't standing in Miles's place.

Brad caught Bonnie's eye and waved her over. "Why didn't you come get me?" he asked, keeping his voice low, though there was little risk he'd be heard over the room's din.

"It happened too fast," she whispered back. "A minute after we transfused the second unit of blood, Miles got ready to close. The next thing we knew, the guy's in V-fib. He—"

"Quiet!"

Eva was usually the quietest person in the room. But her single shout now brought the silence needed for her next command to be heard: "Give him another milligram of epi."

A nurse injected the epi into a peripheral IV. "Epi given." Brad kept his eyes on Eva, who had hers pinned to her monitor.

"Hold CPR," Eva said. Every head turned to the monitor. "Fine V-fib. Shock him."

"'Charging," a nurse said. "Everybody clear." After everyone stepped back, she hit the button on the machine.

Sam Kirby's body rose in a quick convulsion before falling still on the table again. "Resume CPR and change compressors," Eva said. Brad searched Eva's face and clenched his jaw when he saw her brow furrow.

Logan took over from Miles before Brad had a chance to move in. "Prepare another round of epi," Eva said.

Brad looked over the shoulder of the nurse recording the code's events, then turned to check out the cardiac monitor's rhythm strip indicating the progression of degenerating electrical signals from Sam's heart.

Earlier, Brad had quizzed Ryan on Sam's PVCs, seeing them as nothing more than an opportunity for a teaching moment. But Sam had had another run of PVCs. Looking at the V-tach and V-fib sequences that had followed, Brad realized this might turn into a very different kind of lesson for the young med student.

"Classic pattern," Brad heard someone say behind him. He turned to meet the gray eyes that he knew so well. They were framed by the thick black glasses that his mentor had started wearing when he'd left the OR and confined his role as chief of surgery to administrative duties alone.

Dr. Peter Webb was considered something of a white-haired wizard around Boston General. His flawless record inspired whispers about his surgical gifts and the source that had sustained those powers for so long. Brad had always turned a deaf ear to the latter out of appreciation for how generously Webb had shared the former with him.

"He was stable, Peter. I don't—" Brad began, but his voice was drowned out by Eva's next string of commands.

Over the next several minutes, the team rotated through another round of epi, defib, and CPR. However, after the last round of CPR, Eva didn't call for the defibrillator. Brad knew that meant one of two things: either the patient's heart had started again, or it was in asystole. In asystole, the heart had no electrical activity, so the defibrillator would be useless.

After several more cycles of CPR, Eva said, "Hold compressions." She checked for a pulse again, looked at the monitor, and finally made the call: "Time of death, ten thirty-two."

Logan's soft panting was the only sound in the OR.

Brad stood there, stunned. Death was a risk in any major operation, but when things went wrong with a kidney-transplant patient, it was almost always after the procedure: a blood clot, a stroke, or some other post-op complication. For transplant patients, the ICU was usually the way station between this world and the next.

Peter Webb gave Brad a pat on the shoulder and turned to answer questions from some of the colleagues who were analyzing what had happened as they walked away from the chaos of the room. Logan and Bonnie began cleaning the body to prepare it for its trip downstairs to the morgue.

The conversations around Brad began to fade as he stood in a corner going over the code notes, searching for something in the history of the morning's events that would tell him what he had missed, what he could have done to save his friend.

After almost twenty years of performing thousands of operations, Brad was more amazed than ever at the human body's power. Every day, he sliced them open and stitched them back together, trusting in their ability to not only survive but thrive and function better after the ordeal.

But there were limits to how far you could push flesh, blood, and bone. Every surgeon knew that you spent the first ten years learning *how* to operate, the next ten learning *when* to operate, and the last ten learning when *not* to operate. But even though Brad knew Sam's only chance for a longer life lay in the procedure he'd just performed; its outcome left him feeling like he missed that last lesson today.

"Sorry, Brad," Miles said, startling him. "But the guy was on dialysis for the past three years and developed resistant hypertension at, what, age twenty-one? You're not responsible for the fact that his heart's been working overtime because of the damage his kidneys have done for the past twenty years."

Brad looked up from the code report. "I should have taken those PVCs more seriously."

"A couple of early beats don't mean anything," Miles said.

Brad lowered the clipboard and tipped his head to where Logan was drawing a sheet over Sam. "I'm not sure my friend there would agree."

Chapter Three

Planting Promises

BRAD SAT AT his kitchen table stirring his coffee long after the single shot of cream had disappeared, still lost in the day before. He'd played phone tag with Catherine for hours, finally making a spotty connection with her when he got home. After a couple of minutes of their staccato exchange, he understood that Grace was fine but had been admitted to the hospital for observation. Once Brad knew his daughter was out of immediate danger, his next thought was whether this delay meant he'd be unable to give his speech at the conference. He was smart enough not to share that concern with Catherine.

His wife alternated between sympathizing with Brad over Sam's death and being frustrated with him for his absence while foreign doctors tended to their daughter. Their conversation quickly deteriorated, and not just because of the static on the line.

Brad had hung up and gone to bed, but after a few hours of twisting in the sheets, he'd showered and gone back downstairs. The ghost of his friend had haunted his sleep, but now, as the steam rose from his mug, that image was replaced by the face of the wife that his friend had left behind.

Bonnie told him that when Faye Kirby heard the code called in the OR, she'd tried to enter the surgical suite and had to be physically restrained. Brad found Faye later, sitting motionless in the middle of the empty waiting room.

"He's dead, isn't he?" Faye asked when Brad took a seat beside her. While he detailed the events that had led to her husband's death, she stared straight ahead, not once glancing at him. Faye's eyes streamed with tears, but she didn't make a sound.

✦

Brad found his eyes resting on a gift Sam had sent him more than a dozen years before. Brad had unwrapped the tiny wooden cross and put it on the kitchen counter then, right next to the trash bin he planned to dump it in. But Catherine had come in, picked it up, and looked at the one-line note it rested on: *You are blessed.* "You are, you know," she said, "to have a friend like that who still cares after all this time."

He'd waited for her to make yet another bid for him to reconcile with Sam. She stayed silent, but later, he found the cross hung on the wall between the cupboard and kitchen sink. Every time he saw it, he was tempted to remove it—but never did.

Catherine might have regarded the gift as an olive branch, but Brad saw the thing's straight intersecting lines as a symbol of the crossroads where their friendship had split.

The bond he and Sam formed in childhood grew even stronger in high school. As Sam's medical issues grew, Brad encouraged his friend's fierce determination to outrun his diabetes, joining him on every team that kept them racing across a court or field. But when they reached college, the shared passion for academia that had distinguished the pair from their peers began to set them apart from each other as well. With each passing year, Brad's quest to find life's meaning in medicine took him farther away from Sam's search for it in the halls of Harvard Divinity School. The intellectual jousts they'd always enjoyed turned into increasingly heated arguments.

The breaking point came on a rainy night in a dank basement pub near Harvard Square. Brad could never recall how the argument started, but he would always remember the words they'd traded at its end.

"You're a cliché," Sam said as he stood up and pushed his chair back, "the doctor drunk on playing God."

"Better than a fool," Brad said as Sam walked away, "who worships a god that's not there."

It took more than two decades for them to find each other again. When Brad discovered Sam in his waiting room at Boston General Hospital, he saw it as Sam's admission that Brad had selected the right path; after devoting his entire life to doing God's work as an Episcopalian priest, Sam, it seemed, realized that in the end, science, not faith, held the key to his salvation.

The long-lost friend Brad found waiting outside his office was almost as lean and wiry at forty-five as he had been at twenty-five. But when he looked at Sam's face, Brad saw the full weight of the disease Sam had carried for so long. At Sam's side sat the woman who'd helped her husband shoulder that burden for years.

Faye Kirby took quick control of that first meeting. She rattled off Sam's entire medical history, then revealed why she'd steered Sam to Brad's door. "We've been waiting over three years," Faye said. "You know better than anyone that a transplant's his only option now. We're hoping there's something thing you can do to get him to the head of the line."

"Faye," Sam began, "I thought we agreed—" Faye stopped her husband with a clutch of his arm and another round of questions for Brad.

"My position doesn't grant me any power to change Sam's status, Mrs. Kirby," Brad said. He watched as the woman's bright green eyes grew darker and her lips thinned. "Over three thousand patients are added to the kidney-transplant waiting list each month, a list that has well over a hundred thousand names on it. Not even a transplant surgeon has the power to jump that line. But I promise," Brad continued, looking Faye straight in the eye, "when"—*or if,* he thought—"a donor organ becomes available, I'll drop what I'm doing and call in my team, and they're the best you can get."

You are blessed, Brad thought now, a lump rising in his throat. He winced at the words but knew they were true. He walked over to the window and peered at the cold February morning dawning outside. His thoughts turned to Grace. His daughter was in the hospital, but unlike Sam, she was in a warm bed surrounded by those charged with her care—not on a steel slab in the morgue.

He took a last sip of his coffee and dumped the rest in the sink. It had grown bitter and cold. Then he left the house and went to the one place where he could always see life's brighter side.

✦

An hour later, he forced his fingers into the dirt, feeling for the bulb. He'd tried the same maneuver with a hand trowel the year before, but he'd nicked the edge of the plant's big corm. That single slip had turned months of preparation into his third straight failure. Overwatering had produced the fungus that led to the first. The nematodes he'd found invading other pots in his greenhouse came second. Three strikes might have convinced another man to try an easier plant to raise, but easy had never been Brad Baker's style.

Trying to grow what was commonly known as "the tallest flower in the world" was certainly not easy. The begonias, African violets, and orchids Brad first tinkered with flourished around him, but the joy he'd found in nurturing them had faded long ago. The *"Amorphophallus titanium"* (more commonly known as the *"titan arum"*) before him presented a far greater challenge. Growing this most famous of all "corpse flowers" required the same acuity, dexterity, and discipline that had made Brad one of the top transplant surgeons in Boston, perhaps even the world. And although the flower's bloom was magnificent, its scent of rotting meat, designed to deceive carrion-feeding insects into pollinating the plant, wasn't the kind of feature most home gardeners were looking for.

Catherine thought he was crazy. When he told her of his plan for creating the space the plant needed, her mouth fell open, and it took a few seconds before she found her voice. "You're trashing a perfectly good greenhouse just to build one that's tall enough for a flower that will take, what, ten years to bloom?"

"It's an inflorescence, not a flower," Brad answered. "Really, a cluster of flowers arranged on a stem that—"

"Spare me the anatomy lesson, Doctor," Catherine said, rolling her eyes.

Botany lesson, Brad thought but didn't say. Instead, he gave Catherine a kiss and a smile, then took her to her favorite restaurant in Boston's North End, thankful that his wife had the good grace to pretend to forget the conversation that had brought them there.

His daughter, however, was on board immediately. She was seventeen, and the family's three-bedroom Victorian in

Belmont was no longer the center of her world. Her absences removed a leg of the tripod that had supported the family for so long. That left Brad and Catherine wavering between trying to rediscover the young couple who'd first met on Tufts University's sunny quad, and drifting away toward the other people and interests in their lives.

When the big flatbed truck delivered Brad's new toy, Grace spent the entire weekend working with him on designing the greenhouse's interior while the contractors banged the big structure together outside. Catherine knew better than to argue. Though she and her daughter shared a lot, when there was a split decision in the Baker family, Grace usually cast her vote for whatever her father wanted.

As usual, Catherine had taken comfort in the one family member who loved her above the rest. In the greenhouse now, Brad looked up from his work and chuckled when he saw where his wife's best friend lay. He'd bought the golden retriever fifteen years ago and named him Murray in honor of the Nobel Prize–winning Boston physician who'd performed the first successful kidney transplant. The pup had been a Christmas present for his wife and three-year-old daughter. At the time, it had been an extravagant purchase since dog food was a luxury for a young father still making his way through his surgery residency.

The dog, however, wasn't quite living up to his namesake's august reputation now. Murray lay corkscrewed on his back, with his pink tongue lolling over a white-whiskered jaw, his big belly exposed, paws in the air, fast asleep. The old pooch had discovered a prime spot for his nap. He lay sprawled in the only corner of the greenhouse lit by the winter sun. Brad shook his head and smiled as Murray snored away.

Brad looked up and caught his reflection in the building's glass wall to see that Murray wasn't the only one showing his age. The face staring back at him had changed a lot since the day he'd brought Murray home. His forehead had grown larger with the retreat of his hairline, though the locks left were still as dark as his deep-set eyes and held no traces of the white wisps he erased from his chin with his razor each morning. The nose he'd always thought a bit too big looked larger too. But it was the feature Catherine told him she loved best. Half her kisses always seemed to land on its slightly bulbous tip.

Brad turned back to his work; he pressed his hands together gently, raised the ball of earth, and carried it over to the sink at the end of the potting table. He began rinsing away the soil, his pulse quickening slightly at the sight of the cream-colored form emerging. He'd felt the same excitement as a small boy in Maine, kneeling by his father to pull potatoes from the stony soil of their farm. Brad could still see the smile that split his father's dirt-stained face as he held a spud out to his son. "Didn't I promise you it'd be worth it when we planted this field last spring?"

"It's just a potato, Dad," Brad had answered, but his smile had been just as wide. The father's joy in the simple miracles of the natural world had taken root in his son as well.

When the corm was clean, Brad stooped to position it in the big pot of soil resting on the dolly nearby. As he laid the bulb's smooth oval form into that close cavity, he was struck by the familiarity of the act, almost identical to what he'd done yesterday and so many times before. It mirrored the movement of laying a kidney in the hollow of the iliac fossa before suturing the final vein and artery that would allow the recipient's body to claim the new organ as its own.

With the transplant complete, Brad rolled the pot to its location in the sparkling structure's center, then climbed a stepladder to adjust the woven plastic netting fastened to the inside of the roof's glass panes. That sun shield was just one of the additions he'd made; others included the bank of full-spectrum fluorescent lights beneath it, half a dozen radiant heat lamps, and the array of oscillating fans that gave the greenhouse its soothing hum.

He'd waited six weeks after the space was set up before putting it to its intended use. Each evening he'd find time to fiddle with a new piece of equipment, then record specs in the little green notebook he kept on the potting table. Only after a month of noting consistent 75-degree temperatures and 80 percent humidity did Brad allow himself to order his first corm.

Such a strict protocol reflected the actions of a man who always took the long view. Nobody looking for a quick trip to the top would have signed up for the twenty years it had taken Brad to achieve his status as BG's top transplant surgeon. He tried to console himself with that broad perspective now as he thought back to what he'd told Faye Kirby just before he'd headed into the OR: "I've never lost a patient," he'd said.

He smacked his dirty hands on his thighs, gave the soil a final spritz of water, and whistled for Murray. It took the dog a full minute to rise, stretch his arthritic legs, and walk past his master. Brad closed the greenhouse door and followed him, trying to keep thoughts of the day before away with visions of what might blossom a decade ahead. Perhaps only someone like Brad, intimate with the thin veil separating life and death, could fully appreciate the connection between the thing he'd just buried and what it would become.

As the morning sun rose behind him, he envisioned that nighttime bloom. On that distant evening, the plant's four-foot-wide purple spathe would unfurl, warming to the temperature of the human body as it filled the air with its noxious scent. Then, out of the night, the carrion feeders would crawl, lured by the fake perfume of decayed flesh into pollinating the flower. The fruit of ten years' promise lay within a blossom that would open, deceive its prey, and die within a single day.

Chapter Four

Postmortem

THE SAME MAN who could name all 206 bones in the human body could never remember to charge his cell phone at night. The next morning, Brad's foot hit the top step just as the tinny blare of music drifted from where he'd just plugged the stupid thing in by his bed. It took another few seconds for him to realize that Grace must have once again taken his phone and changed the ringtone to yet another song with a medical theme. This time it was the Bee Gees' "Staying Alive."

"They want to discharge her," Catherine said when Brad picked up.

"Good morning to you too," Brad replied.

"I'm serious, Brad. I have no idea if these doctors know what they're doing. Their English is as bad as your Spanish. When do you get in?"

"Not till eleven p.m. your time."

"Why so late? We need you."

"Schools are on winter break here, remember? I was lucky to get a flight with three layovers."

Catherine stayed silent long enough for Brad to get the message.

"I'll go to Logan Airport after breakfast, Cat. Maybe I can fly standby earlier."

"Thanks, Doc," Catherine said.

Brad smiled when he put the phone down. It'd been a long time since Catherine had called him by that nickname. She'd first used it in the same two-word sentence she'd just signed off with.

"Thanks, Doc," Catherine had said on that early autumn afternoon as they sat on the curb in front of Trinity Church, her bare foot in Brad's lap. The picture of that day came back in a flash: Catherine dressed in one of the grunge outfits she sported through all her college years, so at odds with Brad's buttoned-up style. He could still see her round face flushed under its crown of auburn curls, her red plaid shirt, and her torn jeans with one leg rolled up to reveal the slender ankle Brad cradled in his hands.

"I think it's just a sprain," Brad said, reaching over to untie the laces of the roller skate on her other foot. "But we'll be rolling in a cab from here."

The nickname stuck, and even though Brad had heard it from thousands of patients since then, it never touched him the way it did when it came from Catherine's lips.

He was halfway down the stairs when the Bee Gees crooned again; Catherine must have forgotten to tell him something. He took the steps two at a time, picked up the phone, and, inspired by the memory of that roller-skate date, said, "Listen, honey, I'm gonna move heaven and earth to get to you."

There was a long pause before Peter Webb replied. "Gee, Brad, I thought we agreed to keep things professional."

Brad laughed for the first time in twenty-four hours.

"How's Catherine doing?" Peter asked. "And Grace?"

"Both fine, I think. Though I'm not sure Catherine believes anyone outside Boston's city limits should be granted a medical license."

"She's been spoiled by the best," Peter said.

"I'm not exactly feeling like the best this morning."

"I know, but I went over what happened with your team. They're called heart attacks for a reason, Brad. You know you can't predict them. Kirby's hit fast. And hard. You—"

"I should have stayed till we closed," Brad said. He waited, but it was a long time before Peter replied.

"I wouldn't share that sentiment with anyone else if I were you," he said.

"Why not?"

This time, the silence stretched even longer before Peter answered. "Listen, I wasn't going to tell you this, but given what you just said, it's probably best you know. Faye Kirby called yesterday. Several times, actually. She wants an autopsy."

"So?" Brad answered. "Do it. Unless I miss my guess, one look at the coronary artery will show the blockage that led to Sam's death."

"Probably, but there's also a chance she'll change her mind. She's still in shock from losing her husband. She might have second thoughts about opening him up, unless word gets out that you had misgivings about leaving the OR."

"I'll keep my thoughts to myself," Brad said, "but that doesn't change them."

"Good. Now I can tell you why I really called. I spoke to the conference coordinator in Cancún. She's willing to shuffle the schedule so you can still present your paper, but you have to contact her as soon as you get in to make that happen."

"I'll have to check in on Grace first."

"I thought you said she was okay."

"Well, she is, I think. But Catherine's not."

Peter was quiet for so long this time that Brad looked at his cell screen to see if the call had been dropped.

"Do you remember what you said when I hired you?" Peter asked.

"'Thanks?'"

"You said a bit more than that. You said, 'Thanks, Dr. Webb. I'll do everything I can to reward your faith in me.' Well, guess what? Now's the time to do it, for me *and* the hospital that's sponsored your research. You've seen the speakers list for this conference. The surgical techniques and drug therapies they're presenting are small breakthroughs, at best. None of those advances will grab the kind of attention we will. When the press writes the story of this event, your paper will be its headline, especially after you tell your audience it's about to be published in the *New England Journal of Medicine.*"

"I didn't spend the last three years working on a drug that extends the working life of cadaveric kidneys just to make headlines."

"Don't be naive—of course you did. You might not be looking for fame, but you're certainly looking for more funding. Those headlines are just what we need to win the grants we've been gunning for."

This time, Peter was the one who had to wait for a reply.

"You're asking me to put my job before my family," Brad said.

"You're a doctor, Brad," Peter said right before he hung up. "Of course I am."

Brad shook his head and made his way back downstairs. He had just whistled for Murray on the bottom step when the Bee Gees started screeching again. The old dog's hearing was mostly gone, but he usually responded to a high-pitched call. But no long, golden nose came poking around the kitchen doorway. Brad overrode his urge to ignore the phone and returned to take what he hoped would be the morning's last call.

He didn't recognize the number on his screen and was tempted to let it ring but picked it up anyway.

"Hello, BB," a woman said, her voice breaking and dissolving into sobs.

"BB" was the only other nickname Brad Baker had ever been given, and it was used solely by the person who'd bestowed it on him when he was six years old.

"Hey, Barb," Brad said as the woman continued to sob. "Shhh. It's okay, Barb. It's gonna be okay."

"He loved you, you know," Sam's sister, Barb Kirby, said after a huge gulp of breath. "I know you guys weren't exactly close these days, but he talked about you, Brad. He talked about you all the time…"

Brad bit his lip and waited for Barb to stop crying. After a minute, she blew her nose so loudly that they both laughed. A few seconds later, she started crying again.

"I'm sorry," she said.

"It's okay."

"I didn't cry when I first found out. It's just that, hearing your voice, well, you know. We were like the Three Musketeers back then."

"More like the Three Stooges," Brad said. Barb laughed, and he waited to see if she'd start crying again, but this time the laugh ended with a sigh.

"We used to get into *so* much trouble," Brad continued, "but you were the one who always got us out."

"Do you remember the time," Barb said, her voice quiet now, but under control, "when we stole those lobsters from Mr. Queeney's back porch?"

"You and Sam stole them," Brad said.

"Well, you helped cook them," Barb shot back. "Or you tried to, with that stupid camp stove. You almost burned down your father's field."

"Did we even eat them?" Brad asked.

"Sam wouldn't let us. He felt guilty, don't you remember?"

"No."

"Well, I do. He hung his head for a week. Then he took all the money he'd been saving from his paper route, stuffed it in a coffee can, and left it on Queeney's porch. Guess it's no wonder he ended up as a priest."

Brad kept quiet but had to agree. Sam's moral compass seemed to be firmly set long before his young peers had any sense of such a thing.

"I miss him," Barb continued, "and I know he missed you. You should be there when we say goodbye. His funeral is the day after tomorrow. That's why I called. I want you to come."

"I'm not sure Faye would want me there."

"Faye wasn't his sister," Barb said quickly, and by the sound of her voice, Brad could tell that Barb didn't think of Faye as *her* sister either.

"And I'm leaving for Mexico. Today, actually, to join Catherine and Grace there."

"Oh. Well, okay," Barb said, her voice breaking again. "I'll tell him you said goodbye."

By the time the lump in Brad's throat had settled to allow him to thank Barb for calling, the line was dead.

He sat and stared at the thick gray carpeting under his feet, listening to the faint flicks of sleet pelting the windows at the far end of the room. It was a long time before the chime from the grandfather clock in the living room roused him from his trance and drew him back down the stairs.

He whistled for Murray again at the bottom landing, then went into the kitchen to urge the dog from his bed. Brad had followed the directions Catherine left him for the dog's care and parked the big stuffed pad against the toe-kick heater under the kitchen sink the night before. But when he circled the granite-topped island, he saw Murray wasn't there.

It took him a while to make a full tour of the first floor of the empty house. When he finally found Murray sleeping by the back door, he laughed in surprise. "What are you doing there, boy?" he asked as he approached. But the smile faded from his lips when he knelt and saw the strange angle of the animal's head.

The moment he touched the dog, the memories came: the Christmas morning Catherine and their toddler laughed as the puppy yipped and jumped at their feet; the summer afternoon the dog launched himself three feet in the air to catch a Frisbee flicked from Grace's hand; the autumn evening Brad raked around the edges of the last leaf pile Murray sat on, watching his tail wag each time he passed by. Those scenes and others passed in a bittersweet parade. Brad savored each one as he stroked the cold head of the second friend he'd lost in two days.

Chapter Five

Paper Power

THE TIME-SHARE SALESMEN were circling like sharks. Brad tightened his grip on the handle of his rolling suitcase after he cleared customs and pushed past the throng milling in the corridor. He looked up only once to locate the airport exit, then picked up his pace and rushed to the glass doors. When they opened, the wall of heat that hit him almost brought him to his knees. The thermometer outside his kitchen window had read 18 degrees that morning. It felt like 90 now.

In the few seconds it took him to recover, a porter made a grab for his bag. Brad shook him off and didn't stop again until he'd collapsed into the back of a taxi.

"Plaza Paraiso, por favor," Brad told the driver, then he sent Catherine a text to let her know he'd landed. He waited, but when no reply came, he sat back and closed his eyes. After a few minutes, the traffic noise faded under the sound of the cab's wheels. The gentle hum finally coaxed Brad to sit up and take stock of the scene he was rolling by.

The glance he'd given to the route map in the back of his in-flight magazine didn't begin to tell the story of where he'd landed. For the first time, he got a sense of the seventeen hundred miles he'd traveled to reach the tip of the Yucatán Peninsula. As usual, when Brad finally turned his attention from the world inside the human body to the one outside it, the first things to capture his attention were green.

He scooted closer to the cab's window and craned his neck to inspect what towered above. His eyes followed the gray columns of royal palm trunks up to their emerald crowns. Below and behind them shimmered other verdant shapes and shades—sage spikes of agave, lime lobes of prickly pear cactus, and chartreuse fans of dwarf palmettos were studded among shrubs dotted with brilliant bursts of blooms. Blue morning glories, red hibiscus, orange marigolds, and golden trumpet flowers flashed by in a kaleidoscope of colors almost too rich for Brad to take in with his winter-weary eyes.

Finally, the cab slowed and passed through the gates of the Plaza Paraiso Resort. In the thirty seconds it took Brad to pay the driver, a bellhop in a burgundy cap and matching jacket with gold buttons had popped the trunk, grabbed his suitcase, and positioned himself at the curb.

"Un momento, por favor," Brad told him, turning from the resort's huge glass doors to face a snow-white strip of beach bordering a sparkling turquoise sea. He watched a line of pelicans soaring behind a stand of yellow beach umbrellas, then closed his eyes. After taking a long, slow breath, he heard the cries of laughing gulls carried by the salt-scented breeze.

Throughout the past three days, Brad's mind had been running the show. But once he got a look at that beach, his body was ready to claim the rest it needed. That's what he'd promised Catherine when he'd first mentioned this trip: a long, relaxing break under the tropical sun for all three of them.

He took a last look at the shore and saw a pair of horse-back riders trotting down the line between sand and sea. He thought of Catherine's concern over the competency of Grace's doctors. He'd assumed his wife's anxiety was due to the same ignorance of medicine that fed most laypeople's fears. Now he realized that he'd believed his daughter was out of danger because he'd *wanted* to believe that; it cleared both his conscience and schedule so he could present the paper that would finally reveal his work to the world.

Brad checked his watch. He had less than an hour before he was scheduled to speak. That was enough time to check into his suite to see for himself how Grace was doing. But it was also enough time to get into another argument with Catherine about the cost their family paid to support Brad's career.

Brad turned to the bellhop. "Take my bags to the front desk and have them hold them for me, please," he said. "I'll pick them up later."

✦

When Brad introduced himself to the conference coordinator, he thought she might cry. As soon as he gave her his name, the older Latina sitting at the registration table let out a shriek that turned the heads of those nearby. She slipped around the table and hugged Brad, crushing him to her burgundy-uniformed chest in a hug. Then she turned and said something in Spanish to a waitress carrying a tray of canapés that sent her scurrying out of the room.

"*Justo a tiempo*—eh, just in time, Doctor, you make it just in time!" the coordinator said. She hugged him again, then released him from her embrace and looked at her watch. "We hold one last speaker spot for you. It is in fifty-five—no, fifty minute!"

She spun around, grabbed one of the few manila envelopes on the long table, dug out a lanyard with a conference pass on it, and slipped it around Brad's neck. Then she wrapped an arm around him again and steered him through the crowds in the hall while Brad tried to keep up.

She deposited him in a large, empty conference room, said, "You prepare," turned on her heels, and left. Brad made his way to the lectern to pull his notes from his briefcase. Another burgundy-clad hotel worker, this one looking like he was still in his teens, popped in to fiddle with a projector at the back of the room. A minute later, he approached Brad with a small remote in his hand.

"All set, Dr. Baker," he said, clicking the remote at the giant screen behind Brad before handing the device to him. Brad turned to see the first slide of his PowerPoint presentation fill the screen.

Brad studied his notes and ignored the Spanish voice he heard over the PA until he recognized his name. The announcement of his presentation was repeated in English. Just as he finished reviewing his speech, attendees began filing into the room. He did a quick count of the number of chairs in a row and multiplied that by the number of rows in the space. By the time a fellow transplant surgeon he knew only through e-mail exchanges came to the front of the room and introduced him with a long, embarrassing speech, most of the three hundred chairs were filled.

Catherine had been a willing audience for Brad's first forays into public speaking. As executive director of the nonprofit Boston's Best, she'd become an expert at making a case to a crowd. Her ability to rattle off her hunger-relief organization's stats played well with the corporate and major donor philanthropists she cultivated. That skill had helped her double the nonprofit's annual budget in her first year on the job.

But it was Grace who told Brad that his talent for reeling off statistics could work against him when he was trying to win over an audience. She taught her father all the tricks she'd learned since her first role: playing Tinker Bell in a middle-school production of *Peter Pan*. "You need to find your light," she told him. "And make it personal, Dad. The slides will sell the data. *You* have to sell the story of why it matters. Drop that professional distance you're so careful about maintaining. I know that's risky territory for you, but that's where you need to go. Open up. A little vulnerability can bring your audience a lot closer to you."

Now Brad scanned the crowd before him as his pulse quickened. He took three deep breaths, stepped up to the lectern, and began.

"Every morning when my feet hit the floor, I tell myself a lie. The lie is this: I have time."

He checked a few expressions. One face looked curious, another surprised, a third wore the start of a smile.

"That I have time to do the work I care about," Brad continued. "Time to relax when it's done. Time to share all life has to offer with the people I love.

"And behind that deception lies a bigger one. It's the lie I think we *all* tell ourselves to make it through the day. The lie is this: I won't die."

Now more than one face showed the slight confusion Brad was looking for. He didn't have all of life's answers, but he had an insider's view of what came next.

"We pretend Death is a character in the story of *other* people's lives. Until one day, we find it standing in our own.

"Before that day arrives, the best we can do is make the most of what time we have. But when Death came for my closest childhood friend three days ago, a friend I'd let drift—no, a friend I'd *pushed* away, I discovered just how badly I failed.

I thought I'd have time to fix our friendship, and since he needed a new kidney, I just had to fix him first. Problem was, I couldn't."

Brad paused to let the words sink in. Making a public statement of his failure stung, but that was why it held the attention of the faces he scanned. And in that instant, Brad recognized his admission as something more—a confession.

"You, the people in this room, know better than anyone why my friend died. You know the toll a lifetime of diabetes takes on a pair of kidneys. And a body. A person. A family. Our job, our sacred duty, is to give those patients the one thing so precious to us all—a little more time.

"The research my partners and I have done at Boston General over the past few years has yielded a discovery that promises to do just that. As you know, most transplanted cadaveric kidneys last only around twelve years. Our perfusion solution can extend the working life of one of those kidneys by as much as five years. We named it ReNovus, a portmanteau of the Latin words for 'kidney' and 'new,' because those rejuvenated organs will grant their hosts that additional time.

"Five years might not seem like a lot to the average person. But the patients you and I have shepherded through their illnesses aren't average. They're the ones who don't have the luxury of lying to themselves at the start of each day. And that may make them better than anyone else at making the very most of whatever time they have."

Brad waited a moment before pulling up the first of the slides that shared the technical details of his work. Every face was turned toward him, and more than one pair of eyes were shining.

Grace had been right about the slides. He'd taken her advice and weeded out the ones featuring the complex details that would be revealed in the published paper. The slides that were left hit the highlights of his research and told a better story.

After his last click, there were three or four scary seconds of silence before the audience turned their attention from the Boston General Hospital logo on the screen to Brad. After that, it took only a single clap to ignite the entire room with a barrage of applause. When a few people got to their feet, the rest of the room followed quickly.

The scheduled ten-minute Q-and-A stretched to thirty minutes. After that, it took almost another hour before Brad could make his way through everyone who'd lined up to speak to him. He fielded their questions and asked his own about their work, collecting a stack of business cards he planned to dump in the middle of Peter Webb's desk.

In the back of the room, he glimpsed a pair of tortoise-shell sunglasses perched atop a woman's head. They looked just like the pair he'd presented to Catherine when he'd surprised her with this trip, reminding him that it was well past time to check in with his family.

But those who'd waited for him the longest seemed to have the most to say. Just as Brad was talking to the last person in line—a retired nephrologist who looked like Santa Claus and insisted on sharing tales of his glory days—a dark-haired Hispanic man with a neatly trimmed beard in a pin-striped suit came up and stood behind the nephrologist.

Santa finally left, and Brad began to follow him out the door. "I'm sorry," he said to the Hispanic man as he passed him, "but my wife and daughter are waiting for me."

"Of course, Doctor," he heard the man say behind him in a voice as deep and smooth as the man's silk tie. "I'm sure Catherine will feel better once you've examined Grace to check her recovery from her fall."

Brad froze, then spun around to take a long look at the man's face. His coffee-colored eyes didn't blink once, but they were tempered by the hint of a smile. The man's round face softened his stare as well. His body was solid, but the way he held himself told Brad that he was carrying more muscle than fat.

"You know my family?" Brad asked.

The man's smile widened, revealing a row of even white teeth that seemed to glow against his skin. He extended a hand to Brad. "Carlos Cardoza," he said. "I am your host here."

"You run the resort?"

"No, the conference. And as you are our most prestigious speaker, of course I took an interest in your family's welfare."

"Are you a physician?"

"No, but I met with the one who cared for your daughter. Dr. Juarez assured me that Grace's memory and her verbal and motor responses were all fine. I insisted on an MRI anyway. When it came back clear, I asked him to discharge her."

"But you're not a doctor."

"I know a bit of medicine and a lot about hospitals. That's why I'd like to talk to you, if you'd allow me to detain you just a bit longer. Perhaps you'd permit me to buy you a drink?"

Brad's eyes flicked to the doorway he'd been trying to slip through for the past hour. But the concern over his daughter's condition that had compelled his desire to escape had completely evaporated, and the man responsible for easing those fears now stood waiting for his reply.

One drink turned into three palomas: ice-cold tequila cocktails mixed with grapefruit soda and lime. After those marvelous concoctions, Brad found it easy to accept an invitation to dinner from his genial host. During a bathroom break before the meal, Brad took out his phone to text Catherine that he'd been delayed, only to find that his battery was dead.

He thought about excusing himself to check in with her, but Carlos took him by the arm as soon as he came out of the restroom, asking Brad questions about his work at Boston General while leading him to a private dining room with frescoed walls and a table set with bone china and white linen napkins. It was a far cry from the crowded banquet hall they passed where the rest of the conference attendees dined. One of the resort's waiters stood in the corner of the room during the entire meal, clearing each dish as it was finished and immediately bringing the next.

Just after the lobster bisque but before they dug into their tuna carnitas, Carlos got to the reason for the meal. "My partners and I arranged this conference," he told Brad, "to celebrate the start of our own work in your field. We're opening a new kidney transplant center here. It's called Nueva Vida."

"'New Life'?" asked Brad.

"Exactly," Carlos said, sliding over a green business card with gold lettering and a circular logo of a silhouette of a kidney nestled within a glowing sun. Brad picked it up and read Carlos's name above the title of executive director.

"Nueva Vida will do much more than help patients here. We're creating a transplant model that can be scaled up to provide hope for new life to the ten percent of the global population affected by chronic kidney disease."

Brad put down his fork and turned his face to his host. "How?"

"By concentrating almost exclusively on cadaveric kidneys."

"Not living donors?" Brad asked.

"No."

"But why?"

"Because medical, legislative, and technical advances make cadaveric kidneys our best chance for saving the millions who die each year due to a lack of affordable treatment and donor organs. You hold the key to the medical part of that equation, Doctor."

"ReNovus?"

"Of course." Carlos waved away the waiter approaching to top off their water glasses and leaned closer to Brad. "The advance copy of your paper that you provided us with mentioned that your solution could extend the life of a transplanted cadaveric kidney to match the twenty years or more that a living-donor organ lasts."

"Potentially," Brad said carefully.

"If it does, that is the *medical* piece of the cadaveric puzzle that ReNovus can solve. But the legislative and technical issues have already been addressed."

"Sounds like you've been busy."

Carlos smiled. "On the technical side, yes. The Mexican government provided the legislative action needed to make Nueva Vida feasible in 2018. They passed a law that automatically makes any deceased adult a potential donor."

"Wow."

"Yes, wow. With a single flick of a pen, our supply problem was solved."

"What about transport time for the organs? Cadaveric kidneys last only forty-eight to seventy-two hours."

"And even longer with your perfusion drug."

"Not that much longer. Yet."

"Long enough. We have two helicopters that put Nueva Vida within two hours of nine hospitals in the Yucatán, and there are other medical clinics we're exploring as well."

Brad chewed on his lip for a moment. "But how do you coordinate that potential donor pool with your patients' needs?"

"Ah, yes. *That* is the technical problem," Carlos answered. "It took us two years of IT work and many meetings with state and government officials to solve that. Did you know that Mexico has no national donor registry, nothing like your country's Organ Procurement and Transplantation Network?"

"No."

"Nueva Vida is building one for the Yucatán to meet our local needs. It may one day serve as the model for a national network."

When Brad's eyebrows rose in response, Carlos laughed. "Perhaps 'wow' again?" he asked.

"Yes. Wow again."

By the time they'd finished their chocolate churros, Carlos had outlined the rest of Nueva Vida's business plan. Then he signaled the waiter, who came over a moment later with two round snifters filled with a dark brown liquid pooled around ice cubes. The waiter set them down along with two small cups of espresso, and Carlos gave him another nod.

"Have you tried our carajillo?" Carlos asked. Brad shook his head. "Then you're in for a treat. I'll show you." He picked up the cup of espresso, poured it over the icy concoction, and gave it a stir with his spoon. Brad did the same. When he sampled it, his eyebrows rose, sparking Carlos's deep laugh.

"It's bitter *and* sweet at the same time," Brad said.

"Like life, no?"

"Yes, like life."

Brad took another sip. Carlos reached into his suit jacket pocket and withdrew a green envelope the same color as the Nueva Vida business card. When he placed the envelope on the table, Brad saw his name printed on it.

"What's this?" Brad asked, leaving the envelope where it lay.

"An offer," Carlos said. "We're looking for someone to serve as chief of staff for Nueva Vida, my friend. Someone exactly like you."

Brad smiled and shook his head. "I'm honored, Carlos. But I have a job and a whole life back in Boston."

"Of course. It would take a lot to give that up. A *riesgo*—eh, a risk, no? But sometimes, the biggest risk is not taking one at all. In any event, please take this with you," Carlos said, picking up the envelope. "This offer doesn't expire. You're who we want, Dr. Baker. If we hire someone else and you decide to accept later, you'll assume the position at that time." His dark eyes stayed on Brad's until Brad finally took the envelope from his hand and tucked it into his jacket.

"Good!" said Carlos, raising his glass. "A toast, then, to the future, whatever it may hold."

Brad clinked his glass and sipped. "Ah, so good," he whispered.

"And the perfect drink for this occasion. Carajillo has a history dating back to when Cuba was a Spanish province. It was given to the troops for the one thing we all need when we're uncertain of our fate."

"And that is?" asked Brad.

Carlos flashed his smile again, drained his glass, and set it on the table with a thump.

"Courage," he said.

Chapter Six

For Better, for Worse

"WHERE ARE *YOU* going?" Catherine asked.

"For a run," Grace replied.

"You can't."

"Watch me."

Brad heard the last words grow louder, just as the hotel door flew open before Grace ran into him, Catherine right behind.

"Thank God," both women said in unison.

Brad stared, taken aback yet again by the fact that he now faced his daughter eye to eye.

Grace's recent growth spurt seemed to confirm the adult status she'd been angling for in the Baker family ever since she was a child. But her face told a different story. It was the same oval shape as her father's but with her mother's wide-set hazel eyes. Those eyes were always moving, searching for the answers to the question she called her life.

"Can you tell her I'm okay?" Grace asked, moving aside to let her father into the spacious suite before closing the door behind him.

"Are you?" Brad asked.

"No running for a week," Catherine said. "That's what Dr. Juarez said."

"Now he's Dr. Juarez?" Grace asked with a wave of her hand. "What happened to Dr. Pato?"

Brad frowned.

"It's Spanish for 'duck,'" Grace explained. "Mom thinks he's a quack."

"Your turn," Catherine said, waving her hand with the same gesture her daughter had just used.

"Kind of late for a run," Brad said, putting a finger under Grace's chin. He tipped it up gently. "Let's take it slow." When Grace met his gaze, Brad looked from one eye to the other to verify that his daughter's pupils were the same size. "Maybe we can take a long walk on the beach together in the morning instead?"

Now it was Brad whom Grace mirrored, chewing on the corner of her lip in the same way he did when he puzzled over a problem. "Can we go somewhere else? I met a girl at the pool who told me about a tour she took of some Mayan ruins. She got to climb a pyramid."

Brad glanced over Grace's shoulder and saw Catherine shrug.

"Deal," he said. Grace gave him a kiss.

The three turned at the sound of a knock on the door. Brad opened it to find a bellhop. The man cradled an ice bucket holding a magnum of champagne and clutched two flutes in his other hand.

"I didn't order this," Brad said.

"A gift," the bellhop responded with a grin, spinning the bottle to show Brad the card taped to its side. Brad waved him in, and the man placed the bucket on the marble coffee table. The bellhop's smile widened at the tip Brad gave him. "Gracias, señor," he said, then left.

Brad pulled the card from the bottle and read its two-word message penned over a single initial: *To courage! —C.*

"Who's it from?" Grace asked.

"Our host," Brad said.

Catherine moved closer and tipped her head to read the label on the champagne. "It's Cristal. I'm guessing a two-hundred-dollar bottle doesn't come standard with the room?"

"I met him."

"Met who?"

"The man sponsoring the conference. His name is Carlos."

Catherine's brow furrowed. "When did you meet him? I thought you just got in."

"I texted you when I landed."

"I never got it."

"Actually," Brad said slowly, "I've been here a while."

"What?" Catherine said, her voice growing sharper. Grace turned and slipped down the hall to her room, leaving her parents alone.

"I checked in at the conference before coming here."

"How long ago?"

"How about a drink?" Brad asked, pulling the bottle from the bucket and offering Catherine one of the flutes.

"Nice try," she said, not moving an inch.

Brad put the bottle back and collapsed with a sigh on the couch that curved around the table. "I gave my speech. Carlos ambushed me with dinner afterward."

Catherine laughed and shook her head. "Poor baby."

"Catherine, I—"

"Yeah, I, I, I. Me, me, me. It's all about you, Brad, as usual, while your doting wife and injured daughter wait like fools for you to show up."

"Grace is okay."

"How would you know?"

"Carlos had her checked out."

Catherine laughed again. "Well, then, I guess that if the— the what, the hotel concierge you met a couple of hours ago says that your daughter's concussion has healed, we can all relax."

"He's not the con—"

"Unbelievable," Catherine said.

Then she said a lot more, but Brad had heard most of it before.

✦

She came to him later, swimming across the silk sheets on the big king bed, spooning against Brad's back, and whispering him awake with her apology. Brad turned to slip an arm under Catherine to offer his own. Twenty-three years of marriage had taught him the value of apologizing after a fight, even when he had no idea how he'd offended her. He'd watched the marriages of scores of his peers fall apart, casualties of their careers. Brad had bitten his tongue when Peter Webb expressed his amazement that his wife had decided to leave him. Nobody but Peter was surprised.

It was easy to see the mistakes those other doctors made, but Brad suspected he was probably blind to his own failures as well. So he stroked Catherine's head while she whispered all the fears and frustrations she'd suffered over the past few days. After a while, they let their bodies do the talking instead.

✦

He got up at five, as usual, made coffee, and went out to the suite's living room. At six, Catherine joined him on the couch with a novel and her own mug. Brad pecked away on his laptop, and by the time Grace walked by them to grab the coffeepot in the kitchen, he had a plan for the day.

"Ixmoja!" Brad said as he closed his laptop's lid.

"Gesundheit," Grace replied.

Catherine looked up from her paperback with her eyebrows raised.

"It's the tallest pyramid on the Yucatán," Brad explained, "in the ancient Mayan city of Coba. It's tucked deep in the jungle, surrounded by a maze of white plaster roads marked by sculpted stone pillars."

"I thought Chichén Itzá was the big draw here," Catherine said. "That's where the hotel tours go."

"That's where *everybody* goes," Brad said. "This will be so much better."

Catherine frowned and dropped her book in her lap. "Why do you always have to do the hard thing?"

"C'mon," Brad said, sliding over and wrapping an arm around his wife. "It'll be a *real* adventure. We'll rent a car—no, a jeep! We'll be like Indiana Jones in *Raiders of the Lost Ark*."

"More like the *Temple of Doom*," Catherine said, still frowning.

"It *does* sound kinda cool, Mom," Grace said.

And that was that.

✦

The AC quit an hour into the ride. It was hotter inland, and though Brad had arranged the trip to Coba quickly, he was trying to get to the ruins before noon, pushing the Toyota 4Runner he'd rented to eighty on Highway 109 through Nuevo Durango.

"I hope you brought plenty of cash," Catherine said quietly from the passenger seat.

"Admission to the ruins is seventy-five pesos," Brad said. "I think I can cover it."

"You're going to need more than that to pay off the cop who pulls you over for speeding."

"We'll be cooler if we keep the air moving faster," Brad said.

"Really, Dad," Grace said, leaning forward between her parents, "it's worse here in the back. That last pothole sent me airborne."

"Okay, okay," Brad said, easing up on the accelerator. "Hand me a water bottle, will you, Grace? Pass your mom one too."

"I'm not thirsty," Catherine said.

"You're going to be once we start walking," Brad said. "By the time you're thirsty, it'll be too late."

"Too late for what?"

"You should have eight to sixteen ounces in you *before* you start exercising."

"He's right, Mom," Grace said quietly, reaching forward with a water bottle. She held it there for four or five long seconds before Catherine finally took it.

The sun was directly overhead when they pulled into the dusty parking lot in Coba. Brad went to buy the tickets at one of the thatched-roof buildings in front of the green wall of jungle growth while Catherine and Grace got their daypacks out of the car. After studying the map he received with his tickets, Brad led his family down one of the white trails that disappeared into the jungle.

They wound through the green world around them for the next few minutes, looking at stone ruins shrouded by the dense foliage that threatened to swallow them again.

"What's this?" Grace asked when Brad stopped in the middle of a long rectangular amphitheater framed by two high, angled walls on either side. Projecting from the top of each was a giant stone ring.

"I read about this this morning," Brad said. "It's a court for an ancient game called pok-a-tok. The Mayans used a heavy rubber ball to play it. The two teams could only hit it with their knees, hips, and elbows. The goal was to get it through the hoop."

"What did you get if you won?" Grace asked.

"The question was," Brad said, "what did you *lose* if you won?"

"I'll bite," Catherine said. "What?"

"Your head."

"The winners were decapitated?" Catherine asked with a grimace.

"The captain of the winning team was," Brad replied.

"For *winning?*" Grace said.

"It was considered an honor," Brad said. "They'd have a priest do it as a tribute to their gods."

"Pretty savage gods," whispered Catherine.

"No more savage than the one I was raised to believe in," Brad said.

"C'mon, Dad," said Grace. "You were raised Christian."

"Catholic," Brad said. "Father Doyle preached a lot of homilies about the Crucifixion. Is cutting off someone's head more barbaric than nailing them to a cross? It's less so, actually. Decapitation is a quick death. The sudden loss of blood to the brain would probably cause the subject to lose consciousness in two, maybe three seconds at most. In the Gospel According to Mark, Jesus was on the cross for six hours."

"Sometimes I really wish you weren't a doctor," Catherine said.

"But that's different," Grace said. "Jesus died for other people's sins."

"That's my point," Brad said. "Jesus made the sacrifice that others claim as their ticket to salvation. That always seemed way too easy for me." Brad pointed to the stone rings above his wife and daughter as he continued. "There's something you have to admire about the guys trying to put a ball through that hoop. They weren't asking anyone to make a sacrifice for their god on their behalf. They played this game ready to make it themselves."

"Where's the pyramid?" Catherine asked.

"Less than a mile. We just walk back to the main trail and take a left."

"I could have missed this particular tourist attraction," Catherine said under her breath as she led them away.

They had the trail almost entirely to themselves. They grew quiet as they walked, the sounds of the jungle replacing their banter. The foliage kept them cooler than they'd been in the car, but the background buzz of insects and chatter of birds kept Brad watchful as he trailed the family.

When they finally broke through the trees to see Ixmoja, they stopped to take the pyramid in. "Looks pretty big," Catherine said. "Those people at the top look like ants."

"It's the context of the jungle that makes it look big," Brad said. "We'll be at its peak in ten minutes, tops."

"Wonder how many steps," Grace said.

"One hundred and twenty," Brad answered.

"Now, why am I not surprised you knew that?" Catherine asked.

Brad trailed Catherine as they stuck close to the rope going up the center of the pyramid's wide staircase. Grace didn't bother with the rope and quickly outpaced her parents, but Catherine kept her hand on it with every step.

Brad had been right about the climb; it was short but taxing. When he and Catherine joined Grace at the top, all three dug their bottles from their packs and drank.

Catherine closed her eyes after a long sip and said, "Thank God for this breeze." As the women talked, Brad walked away from the stone hut at the top of the pyramid to stand at the structure's edge. As he stared down at the carpet of green, he thought of the evenings he'd crawl from his bedroom window, sit on the roof, and take in the view of the Atlantic from his father's farm.

The flat blue plane of the sea Brad saw then granted him the same sense of peace he felt now. The cool breeze had cleared the chaos of the past three days, giving Brad a glimpse of his ordered world again. His eyes traced the trees from the pyramid's base and beyond, boughs merging into the green cluster of canopies that softened to an emerald field before fading into a white horizon barely distinguishable from the bleached-blue edge of the Yucatán sky. He stared into that slim space for a long time before asking himself what—or who—he was looking for. When Catherine came over and took his hand, he kissed hers but made no mention of Sam.

✦

"Can we stop? I need to pee," Grace said two hours later. Brad had the pedal down on the 4Runner again, eager to get them all back to the hotel for cool showers and a change of clothes.

"Not much around here," he said, slowing down to survey the scrubby trees that lined the desolate road.

"There's something up ahead," Catherine said. "Maybe a town?"

It was nothing more than a collection of tin-roofed shacks, but one had a small stand out front with two large baskets of oranges on either side. Brad walked with Catherine and Grace to the stand, which he saw held a collection of embroidered fabrics, worn leather goods, and wood carvings.

A small dark-haired boy with a moon-shaped face sat on a faded yellow beach chair parked next to one of the baskets of fruit. He was stroking the head of a rail-thin dog curled at his feet. When Brad approached, the boy returned his smile but kept his seat.

"*Buenos días,*" Brad said. "Would you happen to have a bathroom?"

"Buy something, Dad!" Grace whispered fiercely. The slap of a screen door announced the arrival of a woman from the shack behind the stand. She had the same round face and dark eyes as the boy.

"*Cuánto?*" asked Catherine, lifting one of the strips of embroidered fabric from the stand. She unspooled it to reveal a long, slender shawl. The woman eyed her, but Catherine spoke before she could respond. "Perhaps this will be enough?" She walked over to the woman and handed her the two five-hundred-peso notes she'd slipped from the bag on her shoulder. When the woman's eyebrows rose, Catherine added, "*Y el baño por favor?*"

The woman took the bills, nodded, and waved for Catherine to come with her into the shack. Catherine motioned to Grace, who followed the woman inside. Catherine slipped the shawl around her shoulders and went over to kneel by the boy. When she reached down to pet the dog, the animal rolled over on his back to expose his belly, making them both laugh.

"*Es tan flaco,*" Catherine said.

"*Sí, siempre tiene hambre,*" said the boy, smiling. Then he said softly, as the smile faded, "*Siempre tengo hambre también.*"

Catherine reached into her bag again, rummaged through its contents, pulled out a granola bar, and offered it to the boy. He froze for a few seconds, then took it gingerly from her hand, unwrapped it, and devoured it in three quick bites. He gave Catherine a sheepish smile and handed the empty wrapper back to her.

She stayed next to him for the next few minutes, talking to him softly in Spanish while the two worked the dog's matted fur from snout to tail. After a while, Grace slipped out of the shack followed by the woman; she whispered a quick "Gracias" and led her parents back to the car.

"I think you're supposed to haggle when you make a purchase down here," Brad told Catherine when they were under way again. "You paid more than fifty dollars for that shawl."

"I know the exchange rate," Catherine said. "You saw how they lived."

"I know," Brad said, "but giving them a few extra pesos isn't going to change that."

"I gave some of my time too. You just stood there like a statue while I spoke to that boy."

"You know I don't speak Spanish."

"You don't speak poor."

"What's that supposed to mean?"

"I mean I'm surprised you have a problem with me giving a few extra pesos to that family. That's the form *your* charity takes. You talked about your respect for sacrifices back there in the jungle, but really, you'd rather write a check than sacrifice any of your time. I can't remember the last shift you worked at the food bank with me."

Brad held his tongue for a moment before responding. "I don't hear any complaining when Boston's Best deposits those checks," he said. "And every couple of years when you ask me to increase our pledge, you seem pretty pleased with them too."

Catherine opened her mouth, then shut it again. Brad glanced in the rearview mirror and caught Grace's eye for a moment before his daughter looked away.

"Those people at the food bank need their spirits nour-ished as much as their bodies," Catherine continued. "That doesn't take money. It takes time."

They rolled on in silence for the next few minutes. The air blowing in through the open windows did nothing but move the heat around the car. After a while, Catherine reached for Brad's hand. "I do appreciate those checks, Doc," she said quietly. "And the few pesos we were able to leave for that family. When I men-tioned how skinny that mutt was, the kid said his dog was always hungry. Then he said he was always hungry too. I couldn't help but think about the buffet we feasted on at the hotel and our full fridge at home. I think Murray eats better than that boy does."

A moment later Brad pulled the 4Runner to the side of the road.

"Why are you stopping?" Catherine asked.

Brad felt her eyes on his face but looked out the wind-shield while he replied. "Murray. I didn't want to tell you over the phone," Brad said, "then, after all that happened last night, I didn't want to spoil today…"

Grace said softly from the back seat, "Did Murray die?"

"I'm sorry," Brad answered, and Grace began to cry.

Catherine pursed her lips and released a long sigh. She turned to Brad and reached back to take Grace's hand. "How did he go?" she asked.

"In his sleep," Brad said, though he didn't really know if that was true. The image of the dog lying with his head bent sharply against the back door appeared again in his mind.

"Let's go back," Catherine said.

"We'll be at the hotel in less than an hour," Brad said, turning the key.

"I mean back to Boston," Catherine said. She turned around to speak to Grace. "If I can get us on a flight, would you mind leaving earlier?" she asked.

"Not really," Grace replied.

"But we've still got two days left," Brad said.

"Sorry, Dad," Grace said, "but I think Mom's right. It's time to go home."

Chapter Seven

Plaintiff Problems

THE BIG MAN in seat 37B wasn't helping the problem. Brad had known the man, Jamie, was a talker the moment he squeezed past him and dropped into the window seat. Jamie had started by sharing the details of his job as a manager of a pet supply store, then moved on to his divorce and his weekend gigs playing bass for a heavy metal cover band. All Brad wanted was some peace and quiet so he could figure out what was wrong with his laptop, but the guy just wouldn't shut up.

When the plane was somewhere over Georgia, Jamie's third rum and Coke kicked in and he finally fell asleep. It took Brad all of five seconds to diagnose his neighbor's sleep apnea. Most of the people around them probably could too, since Jamie's snoring was louder than the roar of the engines in the back of the plane.

"You two can have the seats up front," Brad had told Catherine and Grace before they boarded. It had taken Catherine an hour online and two calls to Delta to get them all on the same flight, but only two of the tickets were first class. Brad offered to crowd in with the rest of the herd in coach. He thought Grace might argue with him, but his daughter turned the full beam of her smile on him, gave him a quick hug, and chirped "Thanks, Dad!"

Brad wished Grace was here now so he could hand her his laptop. His technophobia was a family joke. For some reason, the intuitive skills that guided him while navigating the human body were useless when he was trying to find his way around a hard drive. Now, after rebooting the stupid machine twice and checking his connection to the plane's internet for the third time, he still saw nothing under his name on Boston General's electronic scheduling system but a blank string of empty boxes.

Normally, those squares held items to be clicked on for each day, every hour assigned to the clinical, research, or administrative duties that defined Brad's working life. He'd been trying to pull up the patient records for his next scheduled surgery so he could review them during the flight. But no amount of clicking could get him past the blank screen.

He was about to close the laptop when he thought to check Miles's schedule. He clicked on Miles's name, and his full calendar popped into view. Brad clicked each square, and the rest of the team members' names appeared. The only name missing was his.

✦

Nobody at Boston General knocked on Peter Webb's door before noon. When the hospital board finally pried Webb out of the OR at age seventy-two, they'd done everything they could to make him feel welcome in the corner office on the seventeenth floor. That included hanging the full-scale, five-foot-wide reproduction of Edward Hopper's *Nighthawks* painting that dominated the wall behind the chief of surgery's massive mahogany desk. Brad had heard more than one person remark that the guy behind the counter in the painting was Webb's doppelgänger. But it was the work's title, not the subject, that had inspired the board to buy it.

They knew Webb shone brightest when the sun was down. Toward the end of his surgical career, he was one of the few surgeons on the BG staff with the clout to refuse to operate before noon. Working under him as a resident certainly didn't afford Brad that luxury. Brad was on the floor making rounds every morning by five a.m. Then he hustled to keep up with Peter at the other end of the day, trying to hang on until his boss finally sent him home around ten p.m. Even at that hour, Webb ran at full steam. The running joke in the doctors' lounge was that if Peter Webb could've found a willing gas-passer to keep his patients under, he would've operated all night long.

Peter certainly *looked* like he'd been up all night when Brad showed up at his office the following afternoon. Brad knocked twice on the open door, but Peter remained at his desk, staring out the window. His cheeks appeared to have hollowed even more in the short time Brad had been away.

Brad's third knock finally broke the old man out of his trance. Peter turned to him, his eyes and mouth so wide that Brad could only laugh.

"Sorry," Brad said. His boss's expression didn't change. "Peter?"

"Sorry, yes," Peter replied. He frowned, then instantly switched to a quizzical smile. "I thought you weren't due back till Monday."

"Change of plans," Brad said. "Speaking of changes, I have a problem with my schedule. It's empty."

"Have a seat," Peter said, motioning to one of the two leather armchairs that Brad stood between.

"What about the schedule?" Brad asked, still standing.

"First things first. The conference. How'd it go?"

Brad held Peter's gaze for a long moment. He reached into his jacket pocket, pulled out the stack of business cards he'd collected, and placed them on Peter's desk "Well," Brad said.

"Brad…"

"It went well, Peter," Brad said, finally taking a seat with a sigh. "I was pretty much mobbed after I spoke."

"Was there press?"

"I saw a camera in the room."

"No interviews?"

"With doctors, not reporters. There might have been some there, but I got shanghaied by the conference director into having dinner after that."

"How'd *that* go?"

Brad didn't answer for a moment. Peter stayed silent too, but the white wisps of his eyebrows rose. "Strange. Good, I guess," Brad said. "He was cordial, warm, even. He's opening a transplant center."

"Yes, I heard about that. Did he give you any details?"

"Some. I'm not sure he's got the staff to meet his ambitions, which are huge. They're concentrating their efforts on cadaveric transplants, choppering in kidneys from Yucatán hospitals."

Peter frowned. "You're kidding."

"I'm not. He almost makes it sound possible. Looks like he's got plenty of cash to build a state-of-the-art facility. Seems like his biggest issue will be finding the staff that can live up to his promises. I'm not sure about the standard of care down there.

"Now," Brad said, shifting in his chair, "can we talk about my schedule? I thought there was a computer glitch, but I can tell from the way you changed the subject that there's not."

Peter's eyes flicked to the documents scattered across his desk. He sat back in his chair, picked up his reading glasses, gave them a wipe, and put them on. After shuffling through a few of the papers, he pushed a stapled stack of them across the desk to Brad. "You don't have a software problem," Peter said.

"What kind of problem do I have?" Brad asked, ignoring the papers.

"Legal."

"Legal?"

"Faye Kirby."

Brad sat back and shook his head.

"I still think it'll all blow over," Peter said.

"Just tell me, Peter."

"Well, you know the four Ds of any malpractice suit as well as I do: duty, deviation, damages, and direct cause. Mrs. Kirby is claiming that you failed to meet your duty as Sam's physician by deviating from your place in the OR. She thinks the damage—Sam's death—was a direct cause of your absence when he coded."

"She said that?"

"The sharks at Cooper, Cutter, and Lowe did," Peter said, tilting his head toward the documents in front of Brad.

"Jesus."

"Yeah, not exactly a bush-league law firm."

"What about the autopsy results?"

"Partial blockage of the coronary artery. Guess the sharks at Cooper are focusing on the 'partial' part. But listen, like I said, it's early. I just need you to lay low while I work on things from my end."

"How long?"

"Let's start with a couple of weeks. Take a bit of time off."

"I just got back from vacation."

"Oh, really? You were gone, what, all of three days? And you were in a conference room for one of them. I'm guessing that didn't leave much time for fun in the sun. You look as pale as you did when you left."

"Last time we spoke, you weren't that interested in my tan. You wanted me at a podium, not on a beach."

"See? You deserve a *real* vacation. How 'bout that beach house of yours in Maine?"

"It's February, Peter."

"Then spend some time with the girls."

"Grace is in school. Catherine is at work, which is where I should be. What about the lab? Am I banned from there too?"

"You're not banned from anywhere. Nothing's official yet."

"Yet," Brad said.

"Spend some time in that greenhouse of yours," Peter said. "How long till that thing of yours blooms anyway?"

"Years. I don't how many. Listen, maybe I should talk to Faye."

"No way," Peter answered, bringing his arms onto the desk to lean closer to Brad, "and that comes directly from Cindy Butler. She's got the rest of legal on this. We've got your back, Brad."

Brad got out of his chair and went over to the window. Far below him, the evening commute was already beginning; cars whizzed by on either side of the Charles River. Along the edge of that silver ribbon's frozen surface, he could see a few ice skaters making the most of the short winter day. A moment later, Peter rose to join him. He draped an arm around Brad's shoulders before he spoke. "Brad, do you trust me?"

"Of course."

"Then let me do my thing. I didn't get to be this old or reach this position without earning a few favors along the way.

But I can't control how this story goes if you're trying to work it too."

"Is that what this is, a *story*? I thought we'd just tell the truth."

"The truth *is* a story. But when it's shared in a courtroom, it comes down to which side has the most convincing version."

"Spoken just like a lawyer."

"Good. Now you understand. The lawyers are the ones we need to speak for us now. So no calls, no e-mails, no contact with the team," Peter said. He turned Brad from the window and began walking him out of his office. "If you've got questions, they come only to me."

When they got to the doorway, Peter took out his phone and flicked away at its screen. "A week, that's all I'll need," he said. He slipped the phone into his pocket and stuck out his hand. "I'll see you back here at, say, three p.m. on Monday, March second, but I need you to steer clear of here till then. Is it a deal?"

Brad shook Webb's hand and his own head. "A pretty raw one," he said.

Chapter Eight

A Test at School

THE PIZZA SITTING on the kitchen island spelled trouble. Nobody knew better than a surgeon just how much damage junk food could do to a body. But Brad's healthy diet paled in comparison to his wife's. She'd serve him a steak or burger for special occasions, only. The only time he got pizza was when he grabbed a slice downtown. Catherine had the numbers of three vegetarian restaurants on speed-dial on her cell, so even on the nights she worked late, Brad and Grace could feast on whatever box of cooked greens and grains the takeout driver delivered to their door.

Tonight, however, her blue Prius had been parked in its usual spot next to Brad's beat-up pickup truck when he pulled into the family's four-car garage. He went upstairs to find Catherine sitting on the edge of their king-size bed. She was still dressed in her work clothes—a navy-blue skirt and blazer—massaging one stockinged foot while the other remained sheathed in its black high heel. Grace lay flat on her stomach in the middle of the bed, dressed in sweats, pecking away at her laptop. The only thing left on the paper plate next to it was a strip of crust and crumbs.

"I knew it was a stupid idea to schedule one trip right after another," Catherine said to Grace, raising a hand to wiggle her fingers in a quick hello as Brad entered the room.

"We talked about this, Mom," Grace answered, her eyes still on her screen. "Two trips, one reentry, remember? I got most of the assignments for the classes I'm missing done already."

"Well, unfortunately, it looks like I didn't get *my* homework done," Catherine said. "I thought I had Healthy Harvest locked in for three years. How am I supposed to fly to Buffalo and take you to visit the schools in Maine you've applied to at the same time?"

"Healthy Harvest is pulling out?" Brad asked.

"I think they're about to," Catherine said. "They're our second-largest grocery donor. If they bail, there's no way we'll make budget. Even with them," Catherine said with a sheepish smile, "I was already drafting a letter to persuade our top donors to increase their pledges."

"I'll do it," Brad said.

"Increase our pledge?" asked Catherine.

"That's another discussion. I mean I'll take Grace on her college tour."

Grace finally looked up at her father, her mouth open.

When Brad saw the same expression on Catherine's face, he laughed. "It'll be fun," he said.

"It'll be fun?" Catherine repeated.

"Yeah," Brad said, "why not?"

"What about work?"

Brad went over to the walk-in closet to take off his suit jacket and raised his voice to be heard as he slipped inside. "Peter kept my surgical schedule pretty light for my return. I can push a few dates, get coverage if I need to."

When he came out of the closet, Catherine was frowning and watching him through narrowed eyes.

"What's up?" she asked.

"What do you mean, what's up?"

"Why would you do this?"

"Like Grace said, two trips, one reentry. I only poked my head in to work today, I'm not back in the groove yet."

"You can't even make it through a weekend without thinking about work," Catherine said.

Brad shrugged. "You guys need help. You can't take her. I will."

Catherine's eyebrows rose as she stared at her husband. A moment later, her eyes began to fill. She opened her arms, and Brad moved in to accept her hug. The embrace kept him from meeting his wife's gaze, but he couldn't escape his daughter's eyes.

✦

It was a quick trip. After tagging behind Grace for the first of the two campus tours they took in as many days, Brad wasn't surprised when she finally asked if he'd mind if she did the last one alone. He'd kept his mouth shut about the artsy vibe he got from the Bates College campus in Lewiston. He knew it was just the type of school Catherine would have loved and encouraged their daughter to explore. But he was careful not to prejudice Grace's impression of the place. He knew she had an eye on medicine but loved theater as well. As worried as he was about how she'd ever make a living in front of the footlights, he was determined to let his daughter find her future for herself.

He had the opposite reaction to Colby College the following morning but kept his lips zipped for the same reason. With its beautiful collection of classic New England buildings perched high upon a hill, miles away from town, it was the kind of academic island Brad could see himself thriving in. Its location farther north was another plus. It put the school less than two hours away from the family's Down East coastal cottage, the sanctuary Brad built on the foundation of the farmhouse that had been his childhood home.

Now he sat in a coffee shop in Brunswick where he'd promised to stay until Grace returned from the Bowdoin College tour. He could already tell from Grace's bright chatter this morning that the small town cradling the network of pines and paths of the Bowdoin campus made her feel completely at home.

When they'd left the city at the start of this trip, Brad put thoughts of Boston General behind him as well. Now, however, he flipped open his laptop to check his schedule, sighed, and took a long, warm slug of his dark roast Sumatra to console himself; his calendar was still empty. He stared out the shop's big plate-glass window and considered whether to prod Peter Webb with an e-mail to try to get his life back on track again.

Through the window, he saw a kid on a bike. It had to be a Maine kid since no one else would wear shorts in February with half a foot of new snow on the ground. And of course, he wasn't wearing a helmet; only the black hood of his sweatshirt covered his head. One long tangle of dyed red hair streamed out behind him as he whizzed by the coffee shop.

In the next instant, the kid turned the bike's wheel, and his body went flying. He sailed over the handlebars toward the busy intersection he'd turned to avoid. Brad was glad to see the boy tuck his head down before he hit the ground. Still, he landed hard on his shoulder, right in the middle of the road. The metallic crash of his bike was followed by the screech of tires and long honk of a horn.

Brad was out the door seconds later. The guy in the green Volvo who'd almost creamed the kid got out of his car and started to yell. Brad ignored him and rushed to the boy, who was rolling back and forth and moaning while cradling his arm.

"I'm a doctor," Brad said. "Can you tell me your name?"

"Jody," the kid said through gritted teeth. The man in the Volvo got tired of yelling, slammed his door, and took off with a screech.

"Do you think you can get up, Jody?" Brad asked.

"My legs are okay," Jody said, staggering as he rose. "But my shoulder…"

Brad helped him to his feet, walked him back to the coffee shop, and steered him to a chair. He unzipped the boy's sweatshirt and slowly slipped it off him. Even through the thin fabric of the T-shirt, Brad could see that Jody's shoulder was dislocated.

"Shall I get an ambulance?" the woman at the counter called out.

"I'm not going to the hospital," Jody said.

"But Jody—" Brad said.

"Forget it," Jody said, wincing as he made a move to grab his sweatshirt from the table. "I gotta fix my bike."

"We need to fix *you* first," Brad said.

Brad ran his hand over Jody's shoulder to feel the deformity. When the bell over the shop's door tinkled, he looked up and saw Grace. She moved behind Brad immediately, positioning herself for anything he might need.

"That's my daughter, Nurse Grace, behind me," Brad said. Jody laughed, then winced again.

"I need you to relax, Jody. Take a few deep breaths, then try to sit up with your shoulders back and chest out."

Jody did as he was told. Brad did a quick neurological exam and found sensation and motor function intact. "Jody, this really should be done in a hospital," he said.

"No way. My mom will kill me if she finds out I wrecked my bike again."

Brad sighed and went behind the boy. "Grace, hold his arm out and push slightly against his chest, the way I taught you that time." Grace moved into position. Brad pressed his hands against the boy's scapula and gently manipulated it until the humerus popped back into place. The boy smiled. "Magic," he said.

"Nope," Brad answered. "Medicine."

✦

The BMW's heated seats were a blessing.

Yesterday, after finally convincing Jody that he really did need to go to the ER, Grace and Brad took him and his mangled bike to the Mid Coast Hospital and waited until Jody's mother arrived. Then they ditched their parkas to enjoy an unseasonably warm day exploring the Bowdoin campus and town.

But today the cold front that had been predicted hit hard, making them wince against the winter wind as they raced from the hotel lobby to the warmth of Brad's car.

An hour later as they topped the Piscataquis River bridge, Brad let out a sigh.

"What's wrong?" Grace asked, her eyes still pinned to the pages of a Bowdoin brochure.

"Nothing. I guess I just miss Maine. My dad used to say God put it so far east so the best part of the country could get a jump start on the day."

"What was he like?"

"Your grandfather? Well, now, that's a question. 'Perry the Paradox,' that's what your grandmother called him."

"What was *she* like?"

"I guess you were too young to remember her?"

Grace looked up from the brochure and stared out the window before she replied. "I remember sitting next to her someplace. Someplace quiet. Maybe church? And I remember she always smelled like lemons."

Brad laughed. "That's a pretty good description of my mother. When she wasn't helping my father on the farm, she was in church. And she made that lemon soap herself. She wouldn't think of buying a bar of Ivory. She could squeeze a nickel even tighter than my father, and that's saying something."

"Why'd she call him a paradox?"

"Because he was. Your grandpa never made it past high school, but he had a hungry mind. He was up at five every morning, and he must have been exhausted at the end of the day, but he'd still reserve an hour, sometimes two, every night to read."

"Read what?"

"Anything. Everything. He knew so much, and not just about farming. He knew about the stars, the sea, history, politics. And no matter the subject, he was never satisfied with seeing it only one way. He was a fiscal conservative but a social liberal. He set a high standard for honesty and loyalty for his family and friends, but he was the first to forgive them when they fell short. And, unlike your grandma, he set foot in a church only when someone died. But I think he might have been the most *spiritual* man I ever knew."

"He died of a heart attack, right?"

"Yep. Doing what he loved best—working on his farm. Though I'm not sure he would have chosen to go out stuck under that damned tractor with a wrench in his hand."

"How did Grandma die?"

"In her sleep, of natural causes, about three years after him. But I think she just decided she was done with life after your grandfather was gone."

"I wish I could've known them."

"Me too. They would've been so proud of you, Grace, getting ready to go to college. Neither of them went, but they made sure I did."

Grace tossed the brochure onto the back seat. "But how did you decide where to go? All of the schools we just saw had things I liked, and there are others I still have to look at."

"Guess it was easier for me. No way I was going to college without a scholarship. Tufts offered the biggest one, though I wasn't exactly excited about it. I was a hick at heart, just like your grandfather. I had no interest in life in the big city. In med school, I did an eight-week rotation in upstate clinics here, everywhere from Bangor to Fort Kent. My plan then was to come back and practice rural medicine in Maine."

"Do you ever wish you did? You were pretty cool yesterday, Dad, the way you helped that boy. I know you still help people, but they're usually unconscious when you do. And the rest of the time you're in the lab. If I do go into medicine, it won't be research. That path makes the whole idea of helping people feel so, I don't know, so abstract."

They settled into a comfortable silence for the next hour. After a while, Grace drifted off to sleep, and the traffic grew thicker. Brad didn't say anything else until he saw the bright jumble of skyscrapers of the Boston skyline from the Tobin Bridge.

"Find the work you love and hold on to it," he said softly to his sleeping daughter. "It's so easy to lose your way."

Chapter Nine

Stuck in Neutral

AFTER HALF AN hour on the treadmill, Brad still couldn't outrun the thoughts that had chased him out of bed. The big TV he jogged in front of in his basement gym only made matters worse. Every stock market report underscored just how easy it was to lose your money, and the news was full of stories of people jockeying for more.

After a shower and another fruitless check of his empty surgical schedule, he found the next distraction he needed in the room off the kitchen. Just a glance at its faded carpet and blanket-covered couch tugged at his heart. Catherine tried to spruce the space up whenever company was coming, but it was hard to hide what it had become. Even with Murray gone, it still had the look, smell, and feel of the family's dog den.

Brad spent an hour clearing out and cleaning the room; when he was done, he carted Murray's toys and dog bed to the garage and loaded them into his pickup truck. He punched the remote clipped to the truck's sun visor to open the garage door, got into the vehicle, took a deep breath, and grabbed the stick shift.

Catherine had not been happy when he'd first driven the truck home. The 1999 Ford F150 looked every year of its age, with more primer than paint covering its faded gray body. It was dimpled with dents and stamped with a long, jagged crease that ran down the entire driver's side. But when Brad told Catherine it reminded him of his father's truck on the farm, she rolled her eyes, kissed the tip of his nose, and didn't mention it again.

Now the vehicle was performing its favorite trick, refusing to let Brad coax it out of neutral and into reverse. He'd been wrestling with it for weeks, always meaning to find a Saturday to fix it himself. He kept his hand light, trying to use the same finger sensitivity that allowed him to suture a new kidney in place to finesse the balky clutch so he could slip the stick home. The longer he tried, the harder the job became; the garage filled with smoke and echoed with the clacks of the ancient engine's worn valves.

When he looked in his rearview mirror and saw Catherine's Prius pull up through the haze, he shut the truck off and got out, waving the white cloud around him away. "Welcome home," he said.

"Thanks," she answered with a cough and a wince. "Glad you found time to play with your toy."

"Stick's stuck."

"Now there's something new," Catherine said, her eyes flicking to the pickup's bed. She leaned in to accept Brad's kiss. "Where are you taking that?" Catherine asked, tilting her head at the dog bed.

"Goodwill. I figured somebody could use it."

She walked around and looked over the relics of Murray's life that Brad had packed around the bed. Her eyes drifted over a half-empty bag of kibble, the big blue food bowl the dog always pushed around the floor with his nose when it was empty, and the collection of stuffed animals and tennis balls. She reached in, grabbed Murray's worn red collar, and rubbed the gold name tag that hung from it between her fingers over and over again.

When Catherine lowered her head, Brad thought she was inspecting one of the dog's toys. Then her arms came up to rest on the gate; she buried her face in them and started to cry.

He went over to stand behind her and kissed the side of her neck, whispering as he breathed in the sandalwood smell of her Chanel Number 5. "He was old, Cat," he said. "It was his time."

"It wasn't *my* time. I didn't even get to say goodb—" she began, but her sobs swallowed her words. He held her until she turned to hug him back, then made her laugh when he brushed at the twin streaks of mascara streaming from her eyes.

"Guess you didn't exactly come home to the girl of your dreams," she said.

"Sure I did," he answered, fishing a handkerchief out of his pocket and handing it to her. "Was Healthy Harvest as knocked out by you as I am?"

Catherine wiped at her face with the handkerchief. "Not quite. Bob Thompson greeted me so warmly that I thought he'd reconsidered. I spent an hour at lunch going over our strategic plan to let them know just how many people their donations would feed. Then I found out they had their own plan—to consolidate corporate giving. They're supporting only in-state charities now.

"So," she continued with a sigh, "I've got to make the rounds around town again. Speaking of which, what do you think about upping what we give?"

"We should probably keep it level this year," Brad said. "We've got tuition coming up."

Catherine laughed. "So? We've been planning for that. Are you telling me we really can't afford to bump up our pledge?"

"I just want to be careful right now," Brad said. He walked over to shut the Prius's door. When he turned back to Catherine, she had the same expression on her face she'd had when Brad told her he'd take Grace on her college tour.

"Why aren't you at work?" she asked.

"I'm going in on Monday."

Catherine kept her eyes fixed on him.

"Listen, I didn't want to worry you," Brad said.

"Well, you're worrying me now."

"There's been a bit of trouble from Sam's wife."

Catherine's sharp mind had been the first thing Brad fell in love with, but he wasn't exactly adoring her ability to figure things out so quickly right now. He could actually see her do it, watched her eyes flick from the house to the BMW to the pickup, then back to Brad. She took her time on him, scanning the jeans and plaid flannel shirt he was wearing now, the Saturday clothes he was so uncharacteristically dressed in on this Thursday afternoon.

"She's suing you."

"She's making noise about suing the hospital, not me. But it's a bogus case. It'll never even make it to the tribunal."

"The what?"

"They have a special hearing in Massachusetts for malpractice cases, just to see if they're worth taking to trial. This one isn't. There's no—"

Brad's words were cut short by a bang so loud that it made him cringe until its echo finally faded from the big garage. It took him a second to realize that it had come from the bed of the truck that his wife had just smacked with the palm of her hand.

"You lied to me!" Catherine said.

"How did I lie?"

"You said Peter kept your surgical schedule light when you got back."

"He did!"

"How light?"

"What do you mean?"

"Just how many surgeries did you have to push back to take Grace on that trip?"

Brad chewed his lip. Catherine shook her head.

"Cat, I—"

"How long can we make it?"

Brad blinked. "What do you mean?"

"I mean, if you lose your job, how long can we make it until you find another?"

"You're catastrophizing."

Catherine folded her arms across her chest and studied Brad for a moment. As she did, Brad flashed to the memory of his first visit to a research lab as a medical student. An image from that day appeared crystal clear in his mind: the pink eyes and twitching nose of the mouse pressed against the glass of the gas chamber, just seconds before the lab tech turned the valve.

"Will you answer my question?" Catherine asked.

"I don't know how long," Brad said, raking his hand through his hair before facing the garage's open doorway. "Three months. Four, maybe, before we eat into retirement."

"That's all? With what *you* make?"

"It goes in a lot of directions, Catherine. The mortgage for this place," Brad said with a wave of his hand. "The equity loan for the work we did on the house in Maine. The condo at Sugarloaf. Your mother's condo *and* medical bills. And, like I said, now college too. That'll be three hundred grand, easy. And you know better than anyone how much goes to Boston's Best."

"I should never have agreed to let you take over the bills," Catherine said.

Brad laughed. "If you think you can manage them better, be my guest."

"Why didn't you just tell me about all this, Brad?" Catherine asked in a voice so broken that Brad wished she'd go back to yelling.

"Because I'm handling things."

Catherine walked over to her Prius, popped the trunk, grabbed her suitcase from it, and slammed it shut.

"I sure wish *I* wasn't one of those things," she said.

He stood in the garage for a long time after she left, watching the everyday rituals of his neighborhood, a view he rarely saw. The mailman came. A UPS truck drove by. The school bus unloaded a line of kids who laughed and chattered their way up the sidewalk before disappearing into the neighborhood's other three-car-garage, four-bedroom homes.

This was just the kind of scene Brad had envisioned when he bought this house—the quiet, comfortable life he wanted to provide for his family while he went off each morning to secure their future in an uncertain world.

Now here he stood, spinning his wheels at home while that world went right on by. By the time he punched the button on the wall and watched the garage door rumble down to close his view of the day, Brad had a new vision for what he was going to do with the next one.

Chapter Ten

Internal Affairs

HE TIMED IT perfectly. Brad walked into the doctors' lounge to find three members of his surgical team sitting on the couch, doubled over with laughter. But the fun ended the moment Brad opened the door. In the quiet seconds that followed, he scanned the faces turned toward him, looking for clues to what had happened while he was away.

Bonnie recovered quickest. "Hey, Brad!" the nurse said brightly as she rose. Brad's eyes widened at Bonnie's latest change in hair color as he accepted her hug.

"I like the red," he said.

"Yeah, I went with Paprika," Bonnie said, flicking the tresses at her neck. "I was gonna go with Black Cherry. It was a lot more subtle. But then I figured, what the hell."

Brad turned to Miles. "How's Mrs. Benton?" he asked, referring to the patient he had noticed on Miles's schedule, the same patient whose transplant the team had just performed.

The team's anesthesiologist beat Miles to the answer. "Vitals looked good," Eva said.

"The kidney we replaced sure didn't," Miles said. "But the new one pinked up immediately. Porter credited ReNovus. Said the cadaveric organ looked as good as a donor kidney, that the solution's ability to mop up inflammatory proteins was amazing."

"Where is he?" Brad asked, though he wasn't surprised to find Porter gone. The surgeon had earned a nickname for his habit of skipping post-op debriefings: Dr. Cut and Run.

"Just left," Miles said. "He let me run the show."

"No reason not to," Brad said. "You've been ready for center stage for a while now. Though," Brad continued, turning his back on the group and walking over to the coffeepot in the corner of the lounge, "that spotlight can get pretty hot sometimes."

No one said a thing. Brad blew across the top of his filled mug, walked over to a chair in the corner, set the cup down on a table, and spread his hands. "So, gang," he said, "what's been going on?"

"Maybe we should talk privately, Brad," Miles said.

"Why?" Brad asked, flashing a smile. "We're all pals here, right?"

"Sorry, Brad," Eva said, rising to leave. "I've got another case to prep for."

"C'mon, Brad," Miles said, getting up as well. "Let's go talk in my office."

"It's okay," Bonnie said, "you can have the room."

"So?" Brad said once he and Miles were alone.

"So, what did you expect," Miles answered with a frown, "ambushing us like this?"

"Is that what I did?"

"Listen, I'm not even supposed to be talking to you."

"Says who?"

Miles looked at his shoes.

"Who *are* you supposed to be talking to?" Brad asked. "Cindy Butler?"

"Of course."

"And what have you told her?"

Miles looked up to meet Brad's gaze. "I told her what happened."

"And what was that?"

"You were there."

"I was there when it happened, but I wasn't there when Legal started asking questions."

Miles took a couple of steps away, spun around, and crossed his arms. "Talking to you could cost me my job."

"You mean the job I've been training you to do for the past two years?"

"What are you worried about, anyway?" Miles said. "You know the suit's bullshit."

"Is that what Cindy Butler said?"

"Legal doesn't have an opinion yet. They're just trying to get a handle on what happened."

"They're circling the wagons," Brad said, "and I'm on the outside."

✦

It was a long walk to the far side of the Boston General lot where Brad's car was parked in its reserved space. But as soon as he left the building, he could tell who was waiting by his BMW by her red hairdo.

He heard Bonnie whisper a soft "Shit" when she saw him approaching. She dropped her cigarette on the snowy ground and stamped it out with a quick twist of her foot.

"Thought you'd stopped," Brad said as he clicked his key fob to unlock the car.

"I did. I only do it when I'm nervous."

"Keep doing it and you'll have plenty to be nervous about."

"Buy me a cup of coffee, Doctor?" Bonnie asked.

"In the cafeteria?" Brad answered, tilting his head to the building behind them.

"Someplace in town," she said.

✦

Twenty minutes later, they were parked in a booth at the back of a busy café on Boylston Street. The two waitresses bustling through the place passed by without so much as a glance, but given how Bonnie was shredding the napkin in front of her, Brad wasn't sure she needed any more caffeine.

"First thing I asked them was if you'd had a chance to review the case with them," Bonnie said.

"Asked who?"

"Legal, when they called us in for statements. Dr. Webb was there, but Cindy Butler ran the show, and she said *she* would be the one asking the questions, that this was a legal matter now and that you weren't in charge. Then the little bitch had the nerve to ask me if I liked working at BG."

"Take a breath, Bonnie. And listen, I do appreciate your talking to me, but maybe you should think twice. I don't know what's going on, but I don't want you to lose your job over this."

"Screw 'em," Bonnie said. "I like my job, but the best part of it has been working with you. If they're not going to stand by you, I'll take my talents elsewhere." She pushed the remnants of her shredded napkin into a pile and then apparently decided to leave the mess alone. "Anyway, the questions started out pretty routine. But somewhere along the way,

Butler shifted her focus. It was only later that I realized that she did and how good she was at changing the conversation without me even realizing it."

"What do you mean?"

"She started out asking about the case, Kirby's condition and all, but then the questions were all about you."

"What kinds of questions?"

"'How did Dr. Baker react to the PVCs? Did he seem concerned? Distracted?' That kind of thing. Then she asked if you'd asked Dr. Patel any follow-up questions. I tried to tell her that there was no reason to, but every time I said something like that, she just cut me off. It's funny," Bonnie said, flashing a sad smile while shaking her head. "Webb began the conversation by saying it was just an informal inquiry. But when Butler started talking, it sure didn't feel like that. I felt like I was already on the witness stand."

✦

The weekend was anything but relaxing. Brad and Catherine were civil to each other, but in their three-person family, any distance between two of its members was impossible to hide from the third. Grace spent most of the time bouncing between her friends' homes or up in her room with her earbuds plugged into her phone.

When Monday morning came, Brad dressed for work as usual but spent the day hopping from one coffee shop to another until it was finally time for his three p.m. meeting with Peter Webb.

Unlike last time, the senior surgeon was anything but foggy when Brad appeared at his office door. Peter stayed seated when Brad entered. His gray eyes were wide open, but his thin lips stayed shut. He motioned to one of the empty chairs on the other side of his desk and waited for Brad to sit down.

"I heard about your little post-op visit Friday," Peter said. "What happened to our deal?"

"And I heard about your interrogation of my staff. What happened to having my back?" Brad replied.

"It's *my* staff, not yours, and it's Legal's show, at least for now." Peter held Brad's gaze for a second, drummed his polished desk with his long fingers twice, and sighed. "Brad, I can't fix this if we're not on the same page."

"You said you needed a week to fix it."

"It's going to take longer."

"How much longer?"

"Listen, if Kirby doesn't drop it and it does go to the tribunal, I still have no doubt it'll die there."

"How long to reach the tribunal?"

"Maybe a year."

Brad closed his eyes. "I can't afford to be out of work for a year, Peter."

"Brad, my hands are tied till this thing goes away."

Brad stood up. "So that's it? Boston General's done with me?"

"Of course not. Sit down. We'll figure something out. I can probably get you a post as a consultant. Maybe secure a teaching position for you somewhere."

Peter waited, but Brad stayed on his feet, then shook his head and laughed. "Great. Those sound like great options for polishing my LinkedIn résumé."

"You got a better idea?"

Brad looked at the chair he'd vacated for a moment before he finally sat down again. He could feel Peter's eyes on him, but he let him wait as he studied the *Nighthawks* reproduction behind Peter's desk.

His eyes usually settled on the cook behind the counter in the painting, the one who looked so much like his boss. This time, however, he was drawn to the man and woman sitting at the counter. The man was looking at the cook, but the woman's attention was fixed on something Brad had never noticed before. Her dark eyes were pinned to the small book of matches she held in one hand. Its cover was the same shade of green as the envelope that lay tucked in Brad's top dresser drawer.

"Maybe I do," Brad finally replied. "Cardoza offered me a job."

Peter frowned. "Guess you forgot to tell me that."

"I had no intention of taking it."

Peter sat back in his chair and crossed his long legs. He stared at Brad for so long that Brad finally turned away.

"Tell me more about Nueva Vida," Peter said.

Brad did. As he talked, he watched Peter's eyes shift to the window, as if Peter could see the details Brad provided about the clinic materializing in the world outside. When he was finished, Peter kept staring at the Boston skyline.

"I think you should take it," Peter finally said.

"You're kidding."

"It could be the best thing for you. And for BG," Peter said, straightening in his seat and talking faster. "You said yourself that the staff was the thing he was missing. If you help him set it up, it could do wonders for us. Mayo, Johns Hopkins, UCLA, they're all focused on their domestic programs. This could be our chance to make the kind of international reputation that fuels our funding for years."

"What about *my* reputation?"

"What about it? The board only cares about money. They'll be delighted to hear that Nueva Vida's footing the bill while their top transplant surgeon creates a new beachhead for the BG brand. Our PR department would have a field day telling the world how we're bringing state-of-the-art transplant care to a developing country."

For as long as Brad had known Peter, they'd shared the same passion for facts. Facts, not feelings, determined the course of their work. Brad had developed that mindset years before when he'd trained himself to park the messy mix of emotions that could interfere with his work outside the OR. Now he took a moment to study the pattern in the Persian carpet under his feet while he considered the logic of his boss's plan.

"I'll think about it," Brad said when he finally looked up. Peter smiled.

Brad didn't, and walked out the door.

Chapter Eleven

Going South

BRAD KEPT WALKING.

He hadn't dressed for the weather but didn't care. He strolled right past his car in the BG lot, stuck his hands in the pockets of his trench coat and picked up his pace to ward off the late-afternoon chill.

Ten minutes later, he looked up to find that his feet had followed the path they'd taken so often years before. He crossed the Longfellow Bridge, made a left, and settled into his old run route along the Charles.

When a couple in matching tracksuits ran past him, Brad was tempted to start jogging too. He would have if he'd been wearing anything other than a pair of wingtips on his feet. His treadmill had become a poor substitute for the runs he'd taken here during his medical school days.

He threw his head back and took a deep breath, then let it out slowly as he surrendered to the winter day's spell. The sky was already dimming to a cobalt blue against the golden glow of the city night's first lights, and the breeze brushing his face made his nose wrinkle with the promise of coming snow.

Brad walked and walked—through space and time—following Memorial Drive through a tour of his city and his past.

He caught sight of the Kendall Hotel tower and thought about the stay he'd splurged on there to celebrate Catherine's thirtieth birthday. They'd made the most of that first weekend alone since Grace had been born the year before. Brad's mother had driven down from Maine to camp out with the baby in their cramped apartment in West Roxbury while he and Cat ordered room service and went back and forth between their suite's jacuzzi and four-poster bed.

A few minutes later, he passed the pub where he and Peter celebrated the first big research grant they'd scored. Peter had been ecstatic when they'd entered the bar that day, buying a round for the house to celebrate their win. Brad was the one who was always in the weeds with his clinical work. Peter never wanted to be bothered with the small advances Brad made along the way. So Brad had waited until there was no doubt about the results of his preclinical research on ReNovus, applied for the grant himself, and surprised Peter with the win.

In the next instant, he felt a stab of regret for the way he'd just turned his back on the man who'd been his champion for so long. "Friends make mistakes too," his father had told him once after Brad complained to him about some slight from Sam he couldn't even remember now. "But the best ones get over them," his father added. "Nothing builds a bond better than forgiveness."

Despite the differences between Brad and Peter in their years, positions, and temperaments, Brad had always thought of him as a friend. Now he considered everything that had happened and, for the first time, tried to see Peter's perspective on the mess Brad was in. From that vantage, Peter was doing his best to protect Brad and the hospital that kept both of them employed.

Other scenes came and went as Brad made his way through the city. After a while, he looked up to realize that his feet were no longer leading him; he was following his ears. The peal of a bell had lured him, its hollow echoes calling over the snatches of conversation from other pedestrians he caught between the whoosh of passing cars.

After a couple of blocks, he discovered the sound's source. The bell hung at the base of a tapered steel spire perched atop a small, cylindrical building set in an open field. Brad circled the walkway around it but couldn't find a single window cut into its curved brick face. When he saw the long, covered passage that led inside, he was so transfixed by the structure's shape that he missed the sign by its door.

He was disoriented when he entered the dimly lit space. The sole source of illumination was a skylight at its far end. It shone on a small sea of silver rectangles hanging on a screen of threads stretching from ceiling to floor. Brad followed the mobile down to the huge marble block below it and realized he'd found his way into a church.

That glimpse of the white altar glowing in the dark, silent space sparked the memory he buried years before. Brad had been in churches a handful of times since that day, but those funerals and weddings had all been communal affairs. The quiet he now found in this sacred place was the same one he'd welcomed often as a ten-year-old boy when he and Tommy Lapierre helped Father Doyle prepare for Mass.

Brad and his mother had attended St. Andrew's Catholic Church every Sunday. He could still remember searching his father's face at dinner on the evening that his mother first suggested that Brad become an altar boy. But as usual, on any matter concerning the religion that Brad's mother clung to so fiercely, his father held his tongue, so Brad agreed.

It was Palm Sunday when it happened, the first spring morning warm enough for Brad to convince his mother to let him put his bike in the back of their pickup so he could ride it home when he finished his duties after church. When they arrived at St. Andrew's, Brad discovered that Tommy had decided to skip Mass again. Brad tried not to smile in the sacristy as he and Father Doyle were preparing the elements when the priest muttered that the chubby boy was probably at home trying to figure out where his parents hid his Easter candy.

Like most high holy days, the church swelled for the service. At its height, Brad waved his palm frond along with the crowd as they sang "Hosanna" and swayed in time with the hymn. After the service, he said goodbye to his mother and walked between the pews to collect the discarded programs.

As much as he enjoyed his role in front of the congregation, he looked forward to this time the most. When asked by his mother or a priest, he would always give the answers about their Heavenly Father that he knew were expected of him. But the only time that he could ever imagine that God might be real was when he was alone in the place where so many gathered to worship Him.

After collecting the programs, Brad went to the cloakroom off the sanctuary to hang up his white cassock. He was still struggling with the garment's collar when Father Doyle appeared. Brad looked up to see the priest's frame filling the doorway. The big man's face was lost in shadow, but the outline of his white hair and beard glowed, creating a corona around his head illuminated by the light spilling in from outside.

Father Doyle laughed softly as Brad fumbled with the button at his neck. "Need some help?" the priest asked, then moved in to take the cassock's collar in his hands. Brad thanked him quietly as the cassock was slipped over his head. Father Doyle's hands came to rest on Brad's shoulders.

"You did well today, Brad," he said quietly. "Don't tell Tommy I said this, but you're much sharper than he is. You may very well be the best altar boy I've ever had." Brad thanked him, and Father Doyle bent forward and kissed him on his head. A moment later, the priest bent down again, but this time, he kissed Brad on the mouth. Brad froze as the man's hands slid down his back, then went lower as he drew the boy to him.

The only memory Brad could ever conjure of the next few minutes was the view framed beyond the cloakroom's door—so similar to the one he saw now. On that distant day, he'd kept his eyes locked on the altar's smooth white surface, barely breathing, while the sound of rushing blood pulsed in his ears; he forced himself to keep his unblinking eyes open long after they'd begun to sting, welcoming the hot white pain of the tears streaming down his face that took him far away from Father Doyle's busy hands.

Brad spent years torturing himself with the same question about the time he spent in that dark room. Over and over, it played in his mind: Why, oh, why had it taken him so long to run?

But run he did, surprising the priest with a twist and bolting from the man's embrace so quickly that it sent Father Doyle spinning to the floor.

Brad burst from the cloakroom and ran to the church door; he slammed it so hard with his two palms that it flew open and hit the stone wall behind it with a crack that echoed across the churchyard as he raced for his bike. He struggled with the kickstand, banging at it with his heel for a few seconds that seemed to stretch to an eternity before risking a single terrified look at the doorway behind him. Still empty.

Brad kicked the stand once. Then hard. Then harder. The thing shrieked a rusty creak and moved. He hopped on his bike and pedaled home madly, weeping the whole way.

The following Saturday night at dinner, Brad told his mother he was done being an altar boy. In fact, he said as her eyes went wide, he didn't want to go to church at all anymore. As his mother began to protest, Brad turned to watch his father's response. "Perhaps," his father told his mother quietly, "our boy's old enough to make this decision for himself."

And though his mother often asked him about it, Brad never shared the reason for that choice with her—or anyone.

The coming snow he'd sensed during his walk to the MIT chapel arrived and left Boston buried for two weeks. Now, as the roar of jet engines filled Brad's ears and shook his body while the plane taxied down the runway at Logan, he thought back to the end of that long day. By the time he'd gotten to his car, he'd made his decision; he sent Carlos Cardoza an e-mail before even driving home. Once he got there, he found Grace and Catherine had already eaten dinner, and Grace had gone to bed.

He stood at one end of the kitchen island while Catherine sat on a stool at the other, nursing a glass of wine. Brad put a few bites of the veggie lasagna she'd left out in his mouth as Catherine watched him wordlessly. Then he put his fork down and told her everything that had happened to threaten all they'd worked for.

Catherine stayed motionless until he broke the news of his new job to her. Then she bit her lip and walked around the huge granite slab to stand beside him. She paused, then gave Brad a hug so strong it took his breath away.

Now, as the wheels left the ground and the plane ascended into a leaden sky, Brad thought about that embrace. He looked down on the city dissolving below, trying to decide what inspired that hug. Was it Catherine's relief over his rescue of their family or her sorrow over his departure? As the gray world beyond his window grew darker, he wondered if the difference between those two reasons really mattered at all.

Chapter Twelve

Public Relations

THE CHETUMAL AIRPORT was only a couple hundred miles south of Cancún, but it felt like the end of the world to Brad. His first flight to Mexico had been a five-hour nonstop. This one took three planes, two layovers, and twenty-two hours.

There was no sea of time-share salesmen circling when he cleared customs this time. But one person was waiting for him. The suit that was stretched tight across the small man's barrel chest was the same color as his thick gray hair. He stood even shorter than Brad and held a cardboard sign bearing Brad's name.

When Brad introduced himself, the man lifted his aviator sunglasses and offered a nod, but no smile. Brad saw his eyes for only a second before the man dropped his shades again. It was the only glimpse Brad would get that day. But the sunglasses couldn't hide the feature that really caught Brad's attention: the entire lobe of the man's right ear was gone.

"Luis?" Brad asked, using the name that Carlos had mentioned in his e-mail.

"Sí, Dr. Baker," Luis said in a voice so soft that Brad almost missed the reply. "My way, please."

Brad followed him to baggage claim, where Luis stopped and turned to face the luggage carousel without saying a word. Brad wondered if the man's thick accent was a sign that he spoke little English.

Brad slipped his cell from his pocket and pecked an English phrase into the translation app on his phone. *"Qué tan lejos está de* Nueva Vida?" Brad asked, wondering just how badly he'd mangled his accent.

Luis made a chuffing noise. Later, Brad would discover that it was Luis's laugh.

"No need to use your phone," Luis said. "My English okay. And your phone do not work where we go."

"How far is it to Campeche?"

"Campeche is big state," Luis said, still not turning from the carousel. "Only one hour, little more, to border. *Much* longer to Nueva Vida. But we stop one time."

The carousel rumbled to life. A minute later, Brad's two big suitcases appeared. When he made a move to grab them, Luis cut him off with a soft "I take." Brad offered to carry one, but Luis ignored him and hefted them both; still managing to outpace Brad as he led him out of the terminal. The black SUV Luis stopped at was parked right in front of the airport's door with its engine idling.

The hot day disappeared as soon as Brad ducked behind the darkly tinted windows of the air-conditioned car. A moment later, he lost his view of the back of Luis's head as well. "Long ride. You rest," Luis said, just before a dark glass wall slipped up soundlessly between them.

A rest sounded good, but Brad's mind was busy doing what it always did: analyzing the situation, weighing options against outcomes before diving in to cut to the heart of the matter. But while that protocol worked well in the OR in Boston, Brad was far from that world now.

✦

He had no idea how long he slept; Brad only knew that the view out his window was very different from the glimpse of the highway he'd gotten when they'd left Chetumal. Now there was nothing but a wall of green foliage on either side of the car. He leaned forward and knocked on the glass partition. It slid down immediately, but Luis didn't say a word.

"Why'd we stop?" Brad asked, grabbing the full water bottle he found next to his seat.

"*Un pavo,*" Luis said, pointing to the road ahead.

"*Pavo?*" Brad repeated, leaning forward for a better look.

"Turkey," Luis said, but the bird Brad saw parked in the road didn't look like any turkey he'd ever seen.

It was the right size and shape, but the colors it sported came straight out of some hallucinogenic dream. The bird's pink legs were topped by a body that sparkled with a rainbow of hues. Its wings had black and white markings on their tips, a scarlet band in the middle, and turquoise shoulders that flashed with a metallic sheen. Its cyan tail feathers were striped with bright tangerine bands. The turkey's breast shaded from dark navy at the bottom to a shimmering aquamarine at the top. A robin's-egg blue colored its neck and head. Crowning the latter was a cluster of yellow and orange beads sparkling above the jet-black eye that stared straight at the car. It disappeared once under a cherry-red lid that flashed as the big bird blinked.

Luis gunned the engine, but the turkey didn't flinch.

"Adiós, pavo," Luis said softly as he hit the gas.

"Stop!" Brad yelled, then braced himself for a bump under the wheels that never came.

"Is okay, Doctor," Luis said, chuffing his soft laugh as they sped away. "They do this. Is animals you *not* see in jungle to be afraid. We go to Calakmul, place *inside* of Campeche. You know name of this place, what it means?"

"No," Brad said, still sitting forward in his seat.

"Is Maya name. Is kingdom of snake."

They drove on. Brad peered at the same leafy view for mile after bumpy mile, wondering what else might lay within that endless green world.

Somehow, he managed to asleep again. The next time he woke, Luis had stopped for something other than a bird. Brad rubbed a hand across his face as Luis held the back door of the SUV open until Brad finally got the message and exited the car.

From the shrieks and laughter he heard, he thought they'd arrived at a party. But as Brad's eyes adjusted to the white heat of the day, the view that came into focus didn't give him any reason to cheer.

He looked out on the saddest strip of buildings he'd ever seen, stretched along the dirt track that stood as the town's road. No two shacks along it were alike. One house, if that's what it was, was constructed entirely of rough wooden pallets with a flat square of corrugated metal for a roof. He compared it to its neighbors and realized it was one of the nicer homes. The one next to it had a mud foundation with walls made of lashed saplings. Across the street was a hut made only of thick cardboard. One side was covered by nothing more than a dirty sheet.

When another cheer rose, Brad followed Luis down the road to its source. A small crowd of men, women, and children stood behind three big pickup trucks with their arms in the air. Two men in each truck's bed passed bags of groceries over the open tailgate to the waiting hands below. As Brad and Luis got closer, Brad could see how much shorter the people on the ground were than the men in the truck.

Luis stopped, took a pack of cigarettes out of his jacket pocket, and offered one to Brad. He shook his head.

"You picked a strange place for a cigarette break," Brad said.

"Not my choice. Our boss say to stop here."

"Why? Who are those people?"

"Campesinos."

"What does that mean?"

Luis just took a drag of his cigarette and kept his sunglasses turned toward the crowd up the street.

Brad was about to repeat his question when a group of the kids gathered around the truck turned and started rushing toward them. It wasn't until they passed by that Brad heard the sound that had drawn them down the road.

Brad had looked at pictures of a Sikorsky S-76 helicopter before, but he'd never seen a real one. And he certainly hadn't expected to find one here. Peter had walked him through a PowerPoint presentation of the choppers that Boston General was considering purchasing to update its medevac service. The BG bean counters settled on a two-bladed, single-engine Bell 206. The sleek, twin-engine, four-bladed beast settling into the field now was the one Peter had in mind.

Something about the Sikorsky's dark green and gold paint job looked familiar. When Brad spotted the Nueva Vida logo on the aircraft's tail, he realized that the man in the white guayabera shirt and tan slacks exiting the aircraft was his new boss.

The kids must have seen this show before. They shouted and waved to Carlos but didn't move from behind the crude fence of two-by-fours and wire that separated the field from the road. When Carlos approached, the children became more excited. They shrieked and danced when Carlos took the pack off his back, then grabbed and hugged him as he reached into the pack again and again to hand out candy and toys.

Brad approached as the crowd of kids reversed direction and ran past him, shouting as they waved their prizes in the air. "An indulgence on my part, I know," Carlos said with a laugh as he shook Brad's hand. "What they really need is the food and medicine we delivered to their parents. But sugar and soap bubbles—that is what children love best, no? How was your trip?" Carlos asked before Brad had a chance to respond. "I trust Luis attended to your needs?"

"I'm fine. He was fine, though I'm wondering exactly why we're here."

"I thought you would be interested in seeing who you'll be helping with the work you'll be doing. Nueva Vida was created to support more than our patients. We help many villages like this."

"They sure seem to need it," Brad said, turning toward the crowd at the other end of the road. "And appreciate it. I couldn't make out their Spanish, but those kids were obviously delighted."

"They weren't speaking Spanish. It was Mayan or, really, one of several dialects of Mayan spoken in Campeche. These people's ancestors have lived here for thousands of years. We do what we can to take care of our own.

"Now, Doctor," Carlos said, resting a hand on Brad's shoulder, "let's see if we can take a bit better care of *you*. Luis will bring your things, but I think you'll be more comfortable if you take the rest of the trip to your new home with me."

It was almost another hour before they got under way. Brad waited while almost every man and woman in the village came to shake Carlos's hand or give him a hug. Many did both. Finally, Carlos said his last goodbye and led Brad back across the field.

Even with the headset on in the Sikorsky, Brad couldn't make himself heard. A few minutes after takeoff, he stopped talking to take in the view. The green canopy below stretched away in every direction. He had a sense of the size of the Yucatán jungle from the view he'd seen at the top of the pyramid in Cobo, but he was twenty times higher than that now, and the view *still* looked the same. After an hour of watching the endless acres of green and listening to the chopper's ceaseless buzz, Brad began to feel like he wasn't going anywhere at all.

Then Carlos's voice crackled in his headset. Brad missed what he said but saw the speck in the distance that Carlos pointed to. He kept his eyes on it as the chopper drew closer. It was easy to do. It was the only thing below them that wasn't green.

As they approached, Brad's eyes grew wider. The aircraft hovered in place for a moment, then descended to the space carved out of the jungle. The glittering cluster of buildings below looked as unlikely as a hotel on the moon.

Chapter Thirteen

Foreign Soil

NUEVA VIDA APPEARED as if in a dream. As Brad followed Carlos from the helipad to the facility's main complex, the view that greeted him shimmered behind a wall of mist drifting from the fountain out front. The structure's cubist design seemed the perfect fit for its jungle home. The trio of white rectangles that formed its center and two wings made no attempt to compete with the colorful chaos beyond its doors. Each facade featured a wall of glass inset so deeply that its shadowy surface revealed only the mirrored world outside.

The blank canvas of the building's exterior made the view inside even more shocking. He followed Carlos through the glass doors that opened as they approached and then slid closed behind them without a sound, sealing Brad and his host in Nueva Vida's air-conditioned womb. The bright pastel walls held a stunning collection of vibrant abstract art. A series of stone planters sporting the same lush vegetation that grew outside were positioned up and down the halls. Simply removing that flora from its wild context turned the plants into living sculptures that complemented the look and feel of the paintings on the walls.

"It looks more like a spa than a transplant clinic," Brad whispered.

Carlos laughed. "Exactly the impression we want for our clientele," he said. "But I think, Doctor, you'll see that we've addressed *your* needs as well." Carlos turned to the young woman with bobbed hair sitting at the round, wood-paneled island that served as Nueva Vida's reception desk. "Augustina, please tell them we're ready," he said. Augustina keyed a button on her headset and spoke a few words of Spanish into her mic.

A minute later, the click of high heels echoed across the polished tile floor. They grew louder as a trim, blond, middle-aged woman in a powder-blue business suit approached. Behind her walked a short Latina with thick-framed glasses, and a tall Latino man with a shaggy head of curly black hair. All three wore white lab jackets with the green and gold Nueva Vida logo embroidered on the breast.

"Dr. Brad Baker, may I present Dr. Kimberly Roke, our chief nephrologist," Carlos said as the blonde woman extended her hand to Brad. "Dr. Roke is based in Manhattan, so you'll see her onscreen more often than in person," Carlos continued, "but these two associates will be here with you every day.

"This is Dr. Manuel Pena," said Carlos, turning to the big man standing between the two women. "Dr. Pena is something of a Renaissance man. He was an accomplished computer programmer before he made the jump to medicine. He was instrumental in setting up Nueva Vida's intranet. It keeps us connected to the network of local hospitals and clinics that provide the cadaveric kidneys our donors receive."

Dr. Pena grabbed Brad's hand in both of his and shook it vigorously while sharing the full beam of his smile. "Please,

I am Manny. You must know my efforts do not match yours, Doctor. I have read much of your work and I am excite to meet you!"

"Excit*ed*, Manny," murmured the small woman.

"Ah, yes, *excited!*" Manny said, turning and placing a hand on his partner's shoulder. "Rosa likes to keep me on line."

"*In* line," Rosa whispered.

"She is Dr. Rosa Chavez, our anesthesiologist."

Brad shook Rosa's hand. He saw her brown eyes flick to his for a second before darting away. He couldn't catch whatever greeting she breathed, but the clutch he received from her hand was so light, it felt less like a handshake than the quick perch of a passing bird.

"Now," Carlos said with a clap of his hands and a smile. "Permit me to take you on a tour of your new home."

Though Nueva Vida's walls were richly arrayed, the facility's floor plan stuck to the same form-follows-function mandate that dictated the clinic's exterior design. Carlos provided the tour's narration as he led the group through the east wing. "All of the door handles in Nueva Vida have biometric locks," he said, pressing his fingertip to the tiny glass circle on the handle of the first door they came to. "You'll have access to many of them. You only need to touch a handle to see which ones open for you."

He showed Brad the pharmacy, the clinical lab, and the recovery room before approaching the substerile room at the wing's end. Then he ushered Brad in to inspect each of the two operating rooms that opened on either side. One still smelled of new paint and had plastic wrapped around its overhead lights, OR table, and anesthesia machine. Every piece of equipment Brad inspected was brand new.

The tour continued through the patient rooms in the west wing and back to the main lobby. A tall orderly in green scrubs pushing a laundry cart stuck to the far side of the hall as they passed. The big man's head stayed down, but his eyes caught Brad's for an instant before shifting to Rosa, then back to the floor. Brad watched the strange way the man pushed his cart and realized he had a limp that made the cart wobble as he made his way down the hall.

"That was Octavio," Carlos said a few seconds later, stopping their tour to address Brad. "We do what we can to employ the locals. Some, like Octavio, find it especially hard to get work."

"That's admirable," Brad said. "Seems like a tough part of the world to make your way in with a disability."

"It is, but that's not why Octavio is here. He had some, let us say, trouble in his village. He was not welcome there after that. But I am a big believer in second chances. If you give a man a second chance—the right man, that is—it can earn you the kind of loyalty that lasts a lifetime."

"And how do you know who the right man is?"

"Ah," Carlos said. "*That* is the question. Perhaps only instinct can answer that. One man may use a second chance to truly change his ways, another may simply use it to continue with his old ones. In any event, I believe only in a *second* chance. Never a third."

"What's in the back?" Brad asked, pointing to the one section of the building that their tour had missed.

"I guess you would call it, maybe, the *guts* of this building?" Carlos said. "Mechanical, waste, loading docks, also administrative offices, and, of course, security. The whole area is secure, but I'm happy to arrange a private tour for you. For now, there's one more room I'd like you to see.

He led the group back to the main lobby, where the three other doctors bade Brad goodbye. The room off the lobby that Carlos led Brad to next required no keypad; Carlos simply pulled on the handle of a large barn door and rolled it back on its stainless-steel track to reveal the expansive dining room and open kitchen inside.

To Brad, the rows of polished wood tables gleaming under the grid of tiny halogen lights overhead looked like they belonged in a five-star restaurant, not a hospital cafeteria. Two huge aquariums anchored each corner of the back wall. As they approached, Brad could see that one was filled with towers of coral circled by the bright flashes of tropical fish. The other looked much more familiar.

He walked over to it and inspected the slabs of granite screened by waving brown kelp fronds. Scattered across the big tank's floor were the same creatures he'd collected from the tide pools near his parents' farm: moon snails, sea urchins, even a pod of tiny lobsters. Carlos came up behind him and looked over his shoulder. "I thought you would like this one. Each tank holds creatures from two separate seas. The Gulf of Mexico is over there," Carlos said with a wave of his hand, "and, of course, this one has your friends from the Gulf of Maine."

"What happens when the lobsters get big?" Brad asked.

Carlos laughed. "The same thing that happens to big lobsters in any restaurant," he said. "But come, Doctor, I have one more surprise that I'm hoping will make you feel even more at home."

Like everything else at Nueva Vida, the housing units for its staff had been meticulously planned. Brad followed Carlos on a winding path fragrant with the fresh smell of the cedars that lined it, learning from his host that even its quarter-mile length had been carefully calculated. That distance provided a five-minute walk to buffer the transition to and from work each day.

The buildings Brad and Carlos approached were tucked deeply in the trees. The largest was the apartment complex that housed most of the clinic's forty-member staff. Carlos showed Brad its small café, store, and clubhouse with a fully outfitted gym. Then he took him outside to inspect the sparkling cerulean waters of a large swimming pool. Brad laughed when he realized that, of course, it was kidney-shaped.

The tour concluded with a series of bungalows. Each was separated from its neighbors by a screen of towering palms. When they came to the last one, Carlos held a key out to Brad.

The place was perfect. Its fixtures had the same spartan look as the building's exterior, but when Brad entered, triggering the lights, he discovered just how many technical luxuries those clean lines hid. Everything—from the shelf-monitoring camera in the fridge to the motion detector on the self-flushing toilet—was wired to serve his every need.

"Amazing," was the only word Brad could think of.

"Yes," Carlos said. "It was harder to find the architect for our IT systems than the one for the buildings that house them. Speaking of which," Carlos said, holding out a sleek black phone, "this is for you. I imagine you'll be wanting to check in with your family."

"Cell phones work here?" Brad asked, taking the device.

"This one does. It uses the local area network engineered for Nueva Vida to connect by satellite. Our communications can be a bit, *bumpy*, I think you would say? But they are good enough to keep us in touch with the rest of the world. However," Carlos continued as Brad studied the phone's display, "there are times when we need a break from our screens, no?"

"Of course."

"Your new home comes with an addition built for that purpose too."

Just before the chopper landed, Brad had seen a flash from a small hole punched into the jungle canopy just beyond

Nueva Vida's main campus. He'd forgotten it when his attention was drawn to the bright white cubes of the main complex, but now he followed Carlos to the source of that sparkle of light: a glass building a hundred feet behind his bungalow. Brad could only laugh as Carlos showed him what the geodesic dome held inside.

"You built a greenhouse in the jungle?"

"A very special one."

For the next half an hour, Carlos showed him what it took to keep an artificial garden of exotic plants nestled in a tropical rainforest cool. The tall trees planted along the inside of its perimeter were one part of the natural solution to the problem. Their broad leaves served to both shade the soil and transpire the moisture that helped cool the air. Another part was a three-thousand-gallon, black-metal water tank that housed goldfish and aquatic plants, providing conductive cooling for the space. A matrix of solar-powered technology provided additional cooling: an underground soil climate-control system, overhead misters and aluminum-cloth shades, automatic vents, and a series of evaporative cooling fans.

Brad pointed to the one empty plot in the place, a large stone planter filled with earth that sat right in the center of the giant dome. "What goes in there?" he asked.

Carlos smiled. "It's already in." He walked over to the potting table parked along the greenhouse wall, retrieved a thick looseleaf binder, and handed it to Brad. Brad scanned the list of notes on the first page, each accompanied by a date, then looked at Carlos. "You planted a corpse flower?"

"Not just *any* corpse flower. Those pages you are holding are its— what is the word…its *pedigree,* perhaps?" Carlos pointed to the empty planter. "The corm that I had our gardener Aldo plant there was three feet wide, sixty pounds, and almost twenty years old. It's already bloomed twice. The second bloom came four years after the first, and it's been three and a half years since then. There's no guarantee, of course, that the next time your titan arum sprouts, it won't just produce another cycle of vegetative growth. But the botanical garden that provided this corm possesses two others from the same seed stock. Each one produced flowers after their first bloom, both blossoming after exactly four years."

"Where on earth did you get it?"

"That," Carlos said, touching his lips with his finger, "is a secret. One of the conditions of sale."

"It must've taken you months to do this," Brad said, "set up this greenhouse, find the corm. I only accepted this position a couple of weeks ago. You did all this on the *chance* I would come?"

"If you hadn't come, Aldo would have been happy to tend your little garden alone," Carlos said with a wave of his hand. "At least until the day I finally did convince you to join Nueva Vida. All good things are worth waiting for, wouldn't you agree, Dr. Baker?"

Brad shook his head and stared into the planter's rich soil, picturing the green tip of a shoot as it broke through the ground. "Please, Mr. Cardoza," Brad said, turning to extend his hand, "call me Brad." He laughed. "Anyone who's gone to the lengths you have to welcome me should certainly be using my first name."

"And I am Carlos, of course," Carlos said, gripping Brad's hand in both of his. "Whether this plant flowers or not, Brad, I know you and I will grow something very special here."

Chapter Fourteen

The Hypocritical Oath

MANNY WAS IN trouble. Brad held his tongue, but Kimberly Roke didn't.

"He can't get it," Roke whispered as Manny struggled to manipulate the pair of jewelers' forceps he held in his gloved hand.

This was Manny's third attempt to work the tiny, curved needle he controlled with the instrument. He was trying to stitch together the thin edges of two veins with a strand of surgical monofilament no thicker than a human hair.

Brad felt his own fingers tense on the retractor he held in response to the nephrologist's comment. He pursed his lips and released a long breath beneath his mask. Roke had spoken nonstop while Brad and she scrubbed in that morning, talking more at him than with him about the upcoming case. She'd been good at sharing the long medical history of Mateo Sanchez, their patient, but she certainly didn't promote the team spirit Brad had cultivated in his surgical crew at home.

Now he willed the woman to keep her mouth shut while Manny tried again. Brad knew her type A personality only too well. He was still surprised by physicians like Roke, people who reached the pinnacles of their careers while still ignorant of the sensitivity needed to manage a surgical team.

Leading a new team after being away from the OR for over a month presented Brad with two challenges. The first was putting thoughts of the last time he stood at the table out of his mind; Sam's death had shaken the confidence Brad had built during the two decades he'd held a knife in his hand.

The second was regaining his rhythm in the OR, the mystical cadence that inspired his finest work and produced the best outcome for his patients. Time, space, and even Brad's sense of self disappeared when he was in sync with his work and team, replaced by the art of practicing medicine in a sublime state of flow.

So far this morning, Manny had performed well. His only deviation from standard surgical practice happened just before he accepted the scalpel held out to him by the surgical tech to make the initial hockey-stick incision on Señor Sanchez's pelvis.

Brad saw Manny close his eyes, touch his thumb to two fingers, and raise his hand. Then, careful not to touch his body, Manny moved that hand through the air, tracing the same path Brad had learned at his mother's side in the church pew: from head to heart, to one shoulder, to the next, making the sign of the cross.

After that pause, Manny started strong; his scalpel cleanly dissected the muscular planes that exposed the retroperitoneal space. He located the common external iliac artery, his index finger finding the vessel quickly by its telltale pulse.

But despite those moves, Roke was right—Manny didn't yet have the skill required to make the series of tight, consecutive stitches needed for the anastomosis.

"You've done well this morning, Doctor," Brad finally said, slipping his fingers from the rings of his retractor and grasping its shaft with his other hand. "Let's switch places for a while."

Manny's hand froze on its way to attempting another stitch. "Sí, Doctor," he answered, surrendering the needle to Brad. Roke finally backed off, taking a step behind Brad as he began to work.

Although Manny wasn't ready for the OR spotlight, Brad's new anesthesiologist certainly was. Brad had worried about Dr. Chavez's shy demeanor when they discussed Señor Sanchez's case the day before. He'd struggled to hear the woman's quiet voice when he asked her about the anesthesia plan. He was especially interested in Rosa's thoughts about the risks of the powerful neuromuscular blocking agent she would use before she intubated Señor Sanchez and connected him to the ventilator that would breathe for him during surgery.

Rosa had ordered succinylcholine for the procedure. "Sux" acted fast and stopped acting almost as quickly, but, like any drug, it had side effects. It increased the level of potassium in the blood, and potassium was often already elevated in patients with kidney failure, like Señor Sanchez. And high potassium increased the risk of cardiac arrest—the OR event that had killed Sam.

During their earlier conversations, Brad had had to prompt Rosa for details such as the pre-op lab report that showed Señor Sanchez's potassium level was within normal limits. But he had no such problem today. She became a completely different person the moment she passed through the OR's door, confidently answering every question he posed during their pre-op time-out. Her hands moved with quick precision as she performed the intubation, deftly passing the endotracheal tube through the vocal cords and into the trachea. After that, she and Brad fell into an easy rapport as Rosa volunteered information to keep Brad updated on their patient's status during surgery.

Now it was Manny who was silent, only grunting to confirm he heard the tips Brad shared on performing the running suture to join the two veins.

Brad tried to lift Manny's spirits, offering a "Hooray!" when the donated kidney pinked up after Manny removed the clamp on the iliac artery. But although the rest of the team echoed Brad's cheer, Manny didn't make a sound.

✦

Brad changed out of his scrubs and found Kimberly Roke parked in the corner of the Nueva Vida cafeteria, wearing a blood-red business suit that, except for the color, was identical to the powder-blue one she'd been wearing when he met her. He studied her for a moment, watching Roke sip at a mug of black coffee while scanning her phone.

"I'm assuming he gave you one of these?" Roke said with a scowl, holding up her cell.

"Looks like the same one."

"Then good luck. I've been trying to send a two-sentence text for ten minutes."

"Mind if I join you?"

Roke waved him to the chair across from her and started rummaging through the contents of the big tote at her side. "They may have put a polish on this place," she said, "but they still need to work out the kinks."

"Yes," Brad said quietly. "I think you and I might need to do the same."

Roke looked up from her bag and stared at Brad, then placed her hands on the table and slowly interlaced her manicured fingers. Brad noticed that she'd changed her nail polish to match the color of her suit.

"I'd appreciate it," Brad said, holding Roke's gaze, "if, in the future, you'd keep your comments about my surgical staff to yourself during surgery."

"If you didn't agree with my comments, why'd you take over?"

"That's not the point. It's my job to correct my staff, not yours."

"And it's my job to ensure my customers get what they pay for."

"*Your customers*, Doctor?" Brad said, raising an eyebrow. "Don't you mean *our patients*?"

Roke shook her head. The corners of her mouth rose, but Brad wouldn't have called the expression a smile. "You're right," Roke said, "Señor Sanchez is a patient. But this place wasn't built for him. I suggest you get with the program."

"What's that supposed to mean?"

Roke opened her mouth, shut it, and started again. "Ask our boss. And as far as my comments during surgery in the future go, don't worry. As Mr. Cardoza mentioned when we met, this is a special visit for me. I leave tomorrow."

Dr. Roke rose and grabbed her tote. As she walked away, she threw her final comments over her shoulder. "I'll send you the background on future cases from my office in New York. After that, do what you want in your OR. You're on your own."

Brad rose to follow her but saw Carlos intercept Roke in the lobby. Brad went to the beverage station along one wall of the cafeteria and poured himself an iced tea, looking up once or twice to see Dr. Roke nodding while Carlos spoke.

The time he'd spent in the OR that morning suddenly caught up with him. Hours of intense focus to perform critical actions while training others to do the same eventually took their toll. Brad returned to the table and collapsed into his chair to revive himself with a sip of his tea. A minute later, Carlos came over and took the seat across from him that Roke had just left.

"Dr. Roke said Señor Sanchez's surgery went according to plan?"

"Yes. Your staff performed well."

"All of them?"

Brad stared into his iced tea and stirred it with his straw for a moment. "You asked me here because you believed I was the right person to train them, correct?"

"Of course."

"That doesn't happen in a day, Carlos. And it's not just about their technical skills either. A big part of a surgical team's success is the trust they build in one another. I'm going to need yours as well to do my job."

"That is reasonable," Carlos replied. "And I'm guessing that job might be easier to perform when Dr. Roke is not here?"

Brad looked up quickly, and Carlos smiled.

"I thought you two might—what is the expression? Bump heads?" Carlos said. "Still, since she'll be referring patients to us, I thought it important that you meet, if only this once."

"Yes," Brad said, "I've got a question about those patients. Just how do they get those referrals?"

"They pay for that privilege."

"And pay to jump the line to get a transplant here as well?"

"Yes."

"And your government permits them to enter the country to do it?"

Carlos stroked his beard. "Not exactly. We play a little game, but they are in on it. Have you heard of Harvard's stem-cell work on kidney disease?"

"Of course. In the short term, they're using stem cells to help heal damaged kidneys. They're also doing research to use them to stop the expression of destructive genes in kidney cells. But the goal is to use them as the raw material for the nanotechnology that promises the creation of artificial kidneys one day. It's an exciting idea but still just a dream."

"That it is a far-off dream does not matter. Stem cell therapy is more expensive and more restricted in the U.S. Coming to Mexico for such treatments is commonplace. It's simply the easiest way to grant your countrymen, who are looking for a transplant, access to Nueva Vida."

"So they cheat as well as pay to play."

"If you want to put it that way," Carlos said with a wave of his hand. "But they also pay for those who can't. The man you operated on this morning was one of them. Señor Sanchez is a farmer. I assure you that he could not pay for his new kidney with his corn and beans."

"Still," Brad said, shaking his head, "after all the research you did on Boston General and me, you must have realized I thought I'd be working for a nonprofit."

"*Nonprofit,*" Carlos repeated. "An interesting term. There is a particular promise, an oath, you might say, suggested by those words."

"What do you mean?"

"They make one believe that Boston General is a charity, yes? Perhaps offering its services in the same spirit promised by the Hippocratic oath."

"'I will come for the benefit of the sick,'" Brad quoted.

"Exactly," Carlos said, "and it speaks to the next line as well: 'remaining free of all intentional injustice.'"

"Yes," Brad said. "I think Boston General honors that Hippocratic oath."

Carlos laughed. "*Nonprofit* is a convenient term for the majority of your country's hospitals that claim that status. It is especially convenient for those who run them. Your CEOs are paid millions, sometimes tens of millions, per year."

"Even if that's true, the hospitals still treat the poor," Brad answered.

"They treat enough of them to hide where the real money goes: to their investment portfolios and the Washington lobbyists who make sure their tax-free status doesn't change."

Brad couldn't think of a response. Carlos looked out the window and said, "We have a saying in Spanish: *Los* árboles *no están dejando ver el bosque.* It means the trees do not let you see the forest."

"We have the same saying."

"Good, then you will understand. Those are the trees," Carlos said, pointing to the distant tangle of green surrounding Nueva Verde's manicured lawns. "Everything and everyone you are working for here is out in the open. We are not hiding behind clever words." Carlos placed the tips of his fingers on Brad's arm until Brad looked up to meet his eyes. "People with money will always have power, Brad. Perhaps the best thing to do is simply to acknowledge that fact, then give them what they want so we can help those who don't."

Chapter Fifteen

A Return to Roots

"THANK GOD YOU CALLED! I forgot the new password for our checking account, and now I'm locked out. And the floor of the gar…in oil. Your truck must…and before I real…tracked it all over the new carpet…"

"Hello, hello? Catherine?"

But the line was dead.

Brad took off his glasses, closed his eyes, and pinched the bridge of his nose. He had been at Nueva Vida for a month, and his calls with his wife were getting progressively worse.

They'd started sweetly enough. Catherine called Brad after the first auto-deposit from Nueva Vida hit their banking account, sure that it was a mistake. When he told her the fat sum that had landed there was correct, she laughed, then cried, then thanked him over and over again for the sacrifices he was making for her and Grace.

But with the big problem of money solved, the little ones seemed to grow. They'd both underestimated just how much more Catherine would have to take on while Brad was away. Catherine already had her hands full with her elderly mother, Grace, and Boston's Best. Brad's absence meant she had to add maintenance of their home, yard, social network, and family finances to that list.

Grace pitched in, but it wasn't enough. The three of them had had one shaky-framed video chat during Brad's first week away when Grace announced that she'd been accepted to both Bates and Bowdoin. After that, Catherine complained that their daughter had developed a serious case of senioritis. The only subject Grace seemed interested in lately was the scruffy six-foot guy she didn't quite claim as her boyfriend. Catherine told Brad that she'd exchanged all of a dozen words with Todd Rossi, mostly because when he came to pick up Grace, he summoned her with a honk from the horn of the rusty Buick he kept idling at the curb.

After redialing Catherine with no success, Brad put the phone down and got ready for the post-work routine he'd resurrected from his past. Just before he'd closed his suitcase in Boston, he'd thrown in an old pair of running shoes on a whim. He'd had no idea then how glad he'd be that he did.

✦

The road was rough. Manny told him it wasn't really a road at all, just a double-rutted seasonal track that sometimes washed out completely when the summer storms swept in. Manny said at times, it took him close to two hours in one of Nueva Vida's jeeps to travel the fifteen miles to the highway that led to Chetumal. "I take this trip one time each five or six weeks to purchase medicine supplies," he'd said with a frown. "You must believe when I say to you that I am happy I do not go more."

But after jogging around Nueva Vida's perfectly trimmed lawns for weeks, Brad was eager for a change of scenery. Now, five minutes into his run, Brad was greeted by much more than a new view. He'd entered an entirely new world.

Running through it was certainly different than viewing it from the back of Luis's SUV. Brad glanced at the shadowy tangle of growth that lined his way; it was easy to imagine the dangers that lay on either side of the narrow lane. Even stopping in the middle of the path was hazardous. One sip from the water bottle on his hip was enough to convince him to keep moving so the swarm of mosquitoes, that instantly landed, wouldn't devour him.

But there was unbelievable beauty to be found in this forest as well. The green background he raced past flashed with every hue in a child's box of crayons. Over the course of a single mile, he was surprised by a swirl of blue butterflies, crimson bursts of bromeliad blooms, and the chartreuse bill of a toucan, the bird peeking from the brush just before it sailed down the trail.

After Brad ran another mile, the world inside his mind revealed its own images as the endorphins rushing through his bloodstream began to work their magic. Scenes of his new surgical life rose. The weathered bodies of his Mexican patients looked so different from the soft ones he saw in Boston, but the glistening red territory pulsing within both was always the same.

As his feet found their rhythm, Brad breathed deeper, enjoying the smell he knew so well. The rich mix of vegetation, soil, and moisture rising from the bed of old and new growth around him had the same scent of reincarnation that revived him every time he entered his greenhouse garden at home.

He ran till the last knots of tension from his long hours in the OR faded, releasing his body to move like the wild thing it was made to be. Finally, in the free flow through that foreign space, almost two thousand miles from all he knew and loved, Brad felt completely at home.

Until—the faint noise that had been teasing just beyond the reach of his ears grew into something that stopped him dead on the trail. The moment he stopped, so did the sound. He stood panting, straining to hear, suddenly wondering just how far he'd run into these woods as the mosquitoes began to alight on his sweat-stained face and bite the back of his neck, legs, and arms. Brad swatted at them with one hand, keeping the rest of his body still while he waited. He didn't have to wait long.

A lone, guttural growl rose, much closer than the muffled cries he'd heard before. Then the sound grew loud, louder, even louder; its deep, throaty vibrato sending ripples of gooseflesh across every inch of Brad's skin, forcing a flush through his gut that threatened to empty his bowels right where he stood.

Somehow, he managed to turn slowly in place. When that rising howl was joined by another, and another, and another still, Brad finally found the will to run.

He ran so hard and so fast that the rush of blood in his ears competed with the savage sound of the cacophony echoing above. He ran till he welcomed the pain in his legs and every hot breath he sucked to escape whatever horror lay behind those doleful wails.

He ran till he finally saw that the light green window in the brush he'd been searching for was more than the distant hope he held in his mind. By the time he could see the white cubes of Nueva Vida in the distance, the only sounds he heard were the gasps of his own ragged breath.

Brad broke from the trees, still sailing in a flat-out sprint, staggered, and dropped down on all fours like whatever beasts he'd fled. Then he heaved and retched across the fresh-cut grass.

"Doctor? You okay, Doctor?"

Brad looked up but didn't see anyone. He dragged the back of his hand across his mouth, wondering if his flight through the forest had taken its toll on not only his body but his mind as well. He tilted his head higher and saw the small man responsible for the manicured lawn he crouched upon, ten feet up the trunk of a royal palm, a machete in his hand.

He'd spoken to Nueva Vida's head gardener only a couple of times. Though Aldo wore the same white shorts and shirt embroidered with the clinic's logo as the rest of his staff, they never quite looked like they belonged on him.

His round face, heavy-lidded eyes, and straight hair made Brad think of the people who had ruled this land for three thousand years—Aldo's ancient Mayan ancestors.

"I'm okay," Brad said, rising slowly. Aldo climbed down the trunk and dropped the dead palm frond he'd hacked from the tree's towering crown. He slipped on the sandals he'd left at the base of the tree, then looked at Brad with an expression Brad had never seen on the man's face before—a frown.

"Sick?" Aldo said.

"No, just—well, I heard something. In the forest, some kind of howl, I guess."

When Aldo's brow furrowed, Brad tried to mimic the sound that had inspired the fastest run of his life.

The old man's mouth opened for a second, revealing his few remaining teeth. Then he shrieked a high-pitched laugh so loud and long that Brad looked around to see if someone could explain the joke to him.

Finally, Aldo palmed the tears from his face and gained enough control over his voice to answer Brad. *"Un mono,"* Aldo managed between the last of his laughs.

"Un mono?"

Aldo bit his lower lip and looked at the ground, then squatted, curled both hands under his armpits, and grunted.

"A monkey?"

"Sí! Monkey!" Aldo said, breaking into laughter again.

"Are they dangerous?" Brad asked. "It—or I guess *they*—sounded big." Aldo frowned, so Brad tried again. "Monkey hurt me? Pain?" he asked, pointing to his chest.

"No, no, no," Aldo said, smiling. "No monkey hurt. *Jaguar, tarántula, serpiente hacen,* hurt. No monkey."

Brad offered a sheepish smile. "I thought I was going to die."

Aldo held Brad's gaze for a long moment. "Is okay," he said, offering his own smile in return.

"What's okay?"

"Die. Is okay."

"It's okay to die?"

"Sí," Aldo answered. "Maya say die okay."

Now it was Brad's turn to frown.

Aldo took a couple of steps closer to Brad. "All," he said, spreading his arms and slowly spinning in a circle, "all die." The old man put his hands in front of him, waved his fingers, crouched down, and let his hands rest still on the ground. "All die," he repeated softly. He paused and then reversed the movement, letting his fluttering fingers rise as he stood. Then he raised his arms high above his head. He spun round and round, waving his arms, ending the lesson with a final shout: "All live!"

After staring at his empty surgical schedule in Boston for so long, Brad had been delighted by the view of Nueva Vida's online system that came up on the new laptop Carlos had given him. He might have had problems with Kimberly Roke's professional demeanor, but he certainly respected her administrative skills. The medical histories of every patient he'd operated on so far were deep and detailed. Each was complemented by an extensive record of the blood typing, tissue typing, and serum crossmatching that ensured the viability of their donated organs. This was especially impressive considering the fact that Roke was gathering this information from the scores of Mexican colleagues who had supplied Nueva Vida with its patients so far.

Brad knew Roke's rich patrons would be coming, but he was glad he had spent the past month extending the lives of people who would never have had a second chance at life without him and his new team.

Now, after recovering from his harrowing run with a long shower and a cold beer, he pulled up his schedule. But instead of lists of names and procedures, he found a string of empty boxes staring at him, just as he had at home.

✦

"You and your compañeros are getting better," Carlos said. Brad had sent him a text about his empty schedule, and now he and Carlos sat on Brad's screened-in patio sharing a few shots from the bottle of Casa Dragones tequila that Carlo had brought with him. "Those dates are free because I had something else planned for you and your team—a stay at our private resort in Cancún."

"For the whole week?"

"Is that a problem?"

"Of course not," Brad said. "It's incredibly generous, Carlos, considering that I've only been here for a month."

"Not at all. *Give and take*—that is the American expression for the secret to a successful partnership, yes?"

"I'm not sure there's quite as much give in America."

"Yet that is what makes things go smoothly. Like this tequila." Carlos raised his glass.

"Best I ever had," Brad told him.

"Its source is Mexican, one hundred percent blue agave. But there is something foreign responsible for this flavor,"

Carlos said, holding the clear liquid so it caught a golden flash from the last of the day's sun. "It is the container it is aged in—an American oak barrel. It requires five years in those casks from your country to acquire this taste. The best of both worlds, no?"

Brad took a slow sip. "I wonder, Carlos, how you'd feel if I checked in with *my* other world next week instead?"

When Carlos looked away without responding, Brad feared he'd insulted his boss, but after a moment, Carlos looked back and gave Brad a nod. "Nueva Vida has kept me from my own family, sometimes for many weeks at a time," he said. "They are used to it now, but my wife and children were very upset with me at first. Perhaps it is the same for you?"

Brad laughed. "My daughter's eighteen. She's already got one foot out the door. But Catherine, yes, it's been a bit difficult for her, adjusting to life alone."

Carlos drained his glass, set it down on the table, and rose. "Of course. Just ask Augustina. She will make all the arrangements. *La familia lo es todo.* Family is everything, no?"

✦

Brad tiptoed along his upstairs hall, hoping to surprise his wife and daughter with his last-minute visit home. When he found nobody there, he slipped back downstairs to see if he'd missed anyone on his way up. Midway through his tour of the first floor, looking for a loved one, he remembered the last time he'd done the same thing. This time, thank God, Murray wasn't lying dead by the back door. But there *was* someone moving in the greenhouse outside.

He watched her for a moment, not quite believing what he saw. Catherine had always been a great mom, nurturing everyone in the Baker family since its beginning. But she was no earth mother—the living things she cared about weren't rooted in the ground.

But now here she stood, in front of a row of orchids, a tray of ice cubes in one hand, Brad's gardening notebook in the other, with her reading glasses perched on the end of her nose as she frowned at the page.

"Three cubes each," Brad said.

Catherine screamed and launched the full tray of ice cubes straight into the air. He had her in a hug before the last one hit the ground.

Chapter Sixteen

New Shoots

THINGS STARTED OUT normal in the bedroom but got strange quick.

Brad was a generous lover, always making sure to take care of Catherine's needs. But part of him often remained distant while they made love, as if he were standing by the bed like he did in the lab, monitoring his performance to gauge its desired effect.

As a physician, he understood the evolutionary role of sex as an undeniable drive that ensured that no matter what toll disease or disaster took on an individual life, life on the planet would always go on. Still, he could never quite reconcile the logic of that biological imperative with his own role in nature's great survival plan.

Catherine had been so happy to see him when he appeared in the greenhouse that all the problems that dominated their phone calls simply faded away. As she lay next to Brad, she murmured the string of worries she'd stored up in his ear. He dissolved each one with a peck to her forehead, an eyelid, a cheek, the nape of her neck. Then his kisses found other places to land.

Later, Brad would wonder just when they made the switch from their regular script. He'd think back on that hour with Catherine, so grateful that they'd had the house to themselves, so amazed at the animals they'd become, remembering the pants and grasps that escalated in a grapple toward gratification that shook the big bed hard enough to send the teacup on the nightstand clattering across its top to crash on the floor.

Through it all, a series of images kept returning to him, scenes he'd barely registered during his blind run through the Calakmul rainforest just days before. And the thought that came in the midst of that montage wasn't really a thought at all. It was a feeling—no, *two* feelings—that left him sweaty and spent in the sheets with his wife, the same two feelings that had sent him sailing down that twisting trail.

Something had changed in the jungle. Changed in him. In the arms of his wife, he felt it rise again, a braided blaze of exultation and desolation—the beautiful, terrible pairing of pure joy and fear.

+

They sat in their robes at the kitchen counter later, eating a dinner of leftover Thai takeout. Halfway through the meal, Catherine asked a question that stopped Brad's hand on its way to the wine bottle: "What's it like down there?"

He topped off their glasses while he thought of how to pack the last four weeks into a reply. "It's a study in contrasts, I guess. I've been operating on some of the poorest people in the world in the best transplant clinic money can buy."

"You used to talk about starting a place like that somewhere in upstate Maine. What do you call it, the country?"

"The county. Aroostook County."

"Right. You said the county would be the perfect place for a first-class clinic that could provide jobs and care for the people up there."

"I did?"

Catherine laughed. "You did. You were as idealistic as I was back then when you were in med school. You were gonna heal the sick. I was gonna feed the poor."

"Isn't that what we've been doing?"

"Maybe. But for me, there's a pretty big gap between the time I spend pitching in corporate boardrooms and my bimonthly stints in the food bank, actually serving the people Boston's Best was built for."

"You serve them best in those boardrooms. You feed a lot more mouths there than you do on those Saturday-night shifts in Roxbury."

"That makes sense on paper, but that kind of service is different from the one delivered in person to those we're trying to help. There was a woman who came in just before we closed last time I was in. She was dressed in rags, literal rags—her pants had more duct tape than fabric—and she had her daughter with her, maybe eight or nine years old. The girl kept her face turned toward the floor the whole time. But the woman and I locked eyes when I scooped a mound of shepherd's pie on her plate. I think she wanted to say something to me. The look she gave was so frightened, so desperate, I thought she might scream. It scared me. But instead of asking if she was all right, I just chirped something stupid to her girl. I should have said something to the mother. I should have helped her."

"You helped her," Brad said, reaching over to take Catherine's hand.

"Not enough. But you get my point. We've grown comfortable with all this," Catherine said with a nod to the big open kitchen they sat in. "It's too easy to forget the struggle most people go through each day just to survive."

"It's not easy down there," Brad said. "Most of the people I've been operating on are dirt-poor. And most of my surgical staff started out that way. Every night in my bungalow, I think about things I haven't thought about in years. I thought I was just homesick, but hearing you talk now makes me realize that most of those memories that have been surfacing are from when I was in med school. Especially that semester I spent back in Maine. You remember that trailer we rented?"

"Of course. We couldn't even scrape enough together for a double-wide."

"Exactly. We didn't have much more than the patients I saw in those clinics up in the county. But when you talk about looking into the eyes of people in real need, I did it then. And in that jungle down there, I'm doing it again."

Catherine flipped her hand to give Brad's a squeeze. "Then, as hard as it is to have you away, maybe this is good for you? Good for us?"

"Maybe it is."

They both jumped at the sound of a bang from the street loud enough to rattle the kitchen windows. Brad leaped off his stool, but Catherine just laughed and grabbed his arm.

"Relax," she said, still giggling. "I was ready to call the cops the first time I heard that too."

"What is it?"

"Your daughter's new boyfriend."

Brad heard the rat-a-tat sound of knocking valves from the engine that had just backfired. It began to fade just as the front door opened and Grace breezed into the kitchen wearing a huge black parka. She stopped in her tracks when she saw Brad.

"You're home," she said. The expression on her face was one Brad didn't recognize.

"Surprise," Brad said, moving in for a hug. Grace's hands barely grazed his back in response. As he pecked his daughter's cheek, Brad caught the unmistakably sweet, heady scent of marijuana.

He drew back and tried to think of which question he should put to his daughter first. Catherine beat him to it.

"What's with the coat?"

Grace looked down and seemed surprised to see the parka she wore. "It's Todd's. I was cold."

"Why didn't you give it back?"

"I forgot."

Catherine slid a glance to Brad. "Seems like you forget a lot of things when you're out with Todd."

Grace frowned. "Why didn't you tell me Dad was coming home?"

"She didn't know," Brad said. "It was a surprise."

Grace turned her frown on Brad.

"What's wrong?" Brad asked.

Grace's face grew darker. She spun on her heels and took a step toward the door.

"Hey!" Brad said.

"What?" Grace yelled, turning back.

Brad took a deep breath, forcing himself to stay calm. "Your mother and I are trying to talk to you. You can't just disappear."

"Why not?" Grace asked, walking away. Brad could just hear her finish the remark as she started up the stairs. "You did."

✦

The more Brad thought about his family's reaction to his visit, the more it made sense. Catherine had always loved surprises. Brad had been springing them on her ever since he tucked a pair of concert tickets for the B-52s into the paperback he'd lent her on their third date. Grace, however, shared her father's penchant for controlling the actions and events in her life. The quick plans for Brad's departure to Mexico hadn't pleased her. It was no wonder she'd been cool when he waltzed back into town.

There was one group Brad had no intention of surprising. When he e-mailed Peter to tell him about the trip home, he'd promised him that he'd handle things differently this time and steer clear of BG. But when an e-mail from Bonnie popped up in his inbox, he couldn't resist asking her to dinner at his home. He knew Catherine would be on board. She and Bonnie had been friends ever since Bonnie had rescued Catherine from a huddle of BG employees talking shop at a company dinner.

Brad extended an olive branch to Grace by inviting both her and Todd to the meal. Still, he was relieved (though dubious) when she told him they already had plans.

Catherine had shooed him and Bonnie out of the kitchen while she made the final preparations for the meal. Now he sat with Bonnie at the dining-room table, each of them holding a stiff negroni.

"So," Bonnie said, chewing on the orange slice that topped her glass, "tell me about Mexico."

"You first," Brad said. "How are things at BG?"

Bonnie put the orange peel on her cocktail napkin and took a slug of her drink. "Weird. Porter's competent, I guess. But the mood in the OR is completely different. He and Miles snapped at each other a couple of times. Miles's fellowship is almost up, and I heard he was talking to a few nurses about joining his team."

"He didn't ask you?"

Bonnie laughed. "People are picking sides, Brad. I think Miles knows where my loyalty lies."

Brad swirled the ice in his half-empty glass. "Maybe you could get in on one of the other teams?"

"I've asked. You know how it goes. They're pretty tight groups, the good ones. Our is the one that sucks now that you left. Porter's been a floater, but I heard he wants to run it."

"He could handle it."

"Maybe. But I doubt they'll add a new one for Miles and keep ours as well. If Miles takes over ours, I'm out."

"Sorry, Bonnie."

"Don't be. I have a friend in HR at Tufts who said she could get me in there if I want to jump ship. I reached out to her when Cindy Butler started pushing my buttons, but Butler's completely disappeared. Do you think Faye Kirby dropped the case?"

Brad swirled the ice in his drink again while he thought about it. "No. Peter would have told me. He's been keeping me in the loop via e-mail. I think Legal may go to bat for me now that Nueva Vida's paying my salary and Peter sold the board on my PR value down there."

"Your turn," Bonnie said. "It must be so different where you are than at BG."

"It is," Brad said, "and in some good ways, I guess. I'm not thrilled about Nueva's pay-to-play model, but my boss seems to be a straight shooter. And there's no one between him and me. I don't have to deal with all the bureaucratic bullshit we wade through at Boston General." Brad laughed.

"What's funny?" Bonnie asked.

"What's funny is the name the Mayans have for the jungle Nueva Vida is in. Given everything you told me, I think it'd make a better name for BG."

"What's it called?"

Brad took a long sip of his drink. "*El reino de la serpiente*—the kingdom of the snake."

✦

He had one day left at home. Brad had hoped to spend it with his family, but Grace surprised them by saying she was cooling it with Todd for a few days while she buckled down to prep for her final physics exam. Brad decided not to push it. Whether she'd locked herself in her room to nurse a broken heart, study, or both, he and Catherine took their daughter's latest move as a win.

As for Catherine, she had a deadline to meet for Boston's Best annual budget. She'd already rescheduled conference calls with two donors twice and couldn't move them again. So Brad spent most of the morning in his greenhouse tending to the long list of tasks Grace had neglected and Catherine hadn't gotten to.

He held his trowel over the soil that covered his titan arum. Three small green shoots of some other plant had seeded themselves in the big pot reserved for Brad's corpse flower. Whatever they were, they looked strong and healthy, each sporting a pair of tiny flat green leaves spread wide open over the translucent chartreuse threads of their stalks. Brad paused, the tip of his tool hovering in the air, wondering about the tiny wisps of growth he was about to terminate. He drew his hand away.

He laid his tool on the potting table and thought about his conversation with Bonnie, then decided to add one last chore to his to-do list before he left home. Though Brad thought it best to let nature take its course in the greenhouse, he couldn't quite adopt that attitude to the world beyond its door.

Chapter Seventeen

House Call

ACORN STREET HADN'T changed much in over two hundred years. That thought came to Brad as he walked along its cobbled lane, eyeing the brick-faced row houses the road ran between. The buildings must have looked a lot like this when the first Europeans came to this land and built them, setting up shop here in the early seventeenth century. Now, this single block on Beacon Hill charmed the millions of tourists who came every year for a quick peek, and the lucky locals, like Peter Webb, who paid dearly for the privilege of living here.

It had been three years since Brad had taken his only other stroll down the street. He'd been a bit on edge, walking arm in arm with Catherine on that April evening. He heard the story of the accident that had left Peter's daughter, Mallory, bedridden years before. Several versions of the story, actually. None of them were quite the same. All of them were bad.

"Looks like spring," Catherine said, pointing to the splashes of yellow daffodils and purple pansies peeking from the window boxes lining their way. When they knocked on the front door of Peter's brownstone, they flushed a tiny wren from the nest it had built in the wreath hanging there.

They were still laughing when Peter's wife opened the door a moment later. Ruth Webb welcomed them warmly, took the bottle of wine Brad offered, and ushered the Bakers into her home. The dark circles under her eyes, however, didn't match her smile.

Throughout the tense evening that followed, the small group of doctors and spouses the Bakers joined did their best to keep the party alive. But every gap in the conversation they rushed to fill only made it more obvious that the thoughts of everyone around the table were on the person sequestered in the bedroom upstairs.

Just two weeks later, Catherine told Brad what everyone else listening to the BG grapevine already knew: Ruth was leaving Peter.

"You should take him up to the condo at Sugarloaf," Catherine said. "He might appreciate a trip with no women around at a time like this."

"Sounds like the women around him will be gone soon enough," Brad answered, surprised by his wife's suggestion. But what really astonished him was that Peter Webb actually accepted the invitation.

Maybe it was the booze. Maybe it was the weather. Maybe it was the six straight hours of skiing with no lift lines that had both men staggering off the slopes at the end of the day. Whatever it was, that first night at Sugarloaf, as they sat side by side staring into the fireplace in Brad's condo, Peter Webb started talking—and didn't stop.

"I know why you asked me up here," he began. Brad could feel Peter's eyes on him, but he kept his own on the fire.

"That dinner party was a stupid idea. Ruth just saw it as one more way for me to bring my work home. I should have cut back my hours at BG years ago to help out more with Mallory.

"Our daughter was a force of nature," Peter continued, his voice brightening with the memory. "Constantly moving. On the soccer field and off. In the classroom, on student council, weekend jobs. Always trying to get ahead."

"Wonder where she got that from," Brad said.

Peter laughed. "Both of us. Ruth was like that too. Once." Peter grabbed the scotch bottle on the table between them and topped off their glasses. "Anyway, Mallory was headed to Bard. Good school, I guess, but she could've gotten into an Ivy. I would've preferred that, and that she focused on something other than English lit. Maybe not medicine, but biochem, engineering—she had the chops for those, and more. She could've gone anywhere. Been anything." Peter paused. When he spoke again, his voice dropped to a whisper. "Until her prom date drove them both into a tree."

In the silence that followed, the fire popped and hissed.

"I heard the boy was killed," Brad said softly.

"Instantly. When we got to the hospital, I didn't think Mallory would make it either. Her GCS score was three."

"Jesus."

"Yeah. *Deep* coma. Totally unresponsive. But after a couple weeks, she came out of it. She was in rehab for a year before we moved her back home. There was some progress at first. She eventually got to level four on the Ranchos scale. But that took her twenty months. You know the stats—that's the usual timeframe for any significant improvement."

"How long has it been since the accident?" Brad asked.

"Thirteen years."

Peter got up and put another log on the fire. Brad watched him poke at it until he saw the edges of Peter's dark silhouette glow gold against the building blaze.

"Ruth's had it hardest," Peter said with a sigh. He collapsed back in his chair. "We've probably been through a couple dozen nurses. Jeannie, the one we have now, she's the best. She does nine to five every day, but Mallory doesn't exactly keep bankers' hours. I do all right with helping her eat and bathe, the physical things. But believe it or not, that's the easy part."

Brad waited.

"She gets upset. A lot. When she does, neither Jeannie nor I can do a thing.

Ruth's the only one who can calm her down. But it takes a lot out of her. No, it took *everything* out of her. She finally got to a point where she had nothing left to give to either of us. She researched some places. I didn't know about it until she spread the brochures across the breakfast table a couple of months ago."

The ice in Peter's glass tinkled. Brad noticed that the hand that held the glass was shaking.

"We've been fighting ever since. I don't blame Ruth. I really don't. I get a break from it when I'm at work, but not her. She hates to leave the house, and she's always got her cell phone with her in case Jeannie calls. Even then, she worries about what state Mallory might be in when she returns."

"Maybe she *would* do better in the right rehab," Brad said.

"*Rehab*'s the wrong word for those places. At least for her. She's never going to get any better."

The silence stretched so long that Brad thought the conversation was over. Then Peter spoke again.

"My father walked out on me and my sister, Penny, when we were just kids. 'My shiny Penny,' that's what he called her," Peter said with a joyless laugh. "She *was* shiny—a bright, bubbly girl. She lit up our whole family. Right till the day he left. Then she changed. We all did, I guess."

For a moment even the fire was silent. The only sound was the wail of the wind across the empty slopes outside.

"I don't even know if Mallory knows who I am most days," Peter said, turning to Brad, his voice breaking. Brad could see the firelight swimming in Peter's eyes. "But I can't do it, Brad. I just can't put her away."

✦

There was no bird perched on Peter's door as Brad approached it now, and the flower box under his window held nothing but a twisted mat of yellow stalks. Brad pushed the doorbell and heard the echo of its chime through the thick glass of the sidelight by the door, but he could see nothing but his own reflection.

The face that gazed back wasn't one he wanted Peter to see. Brad stopped chewing on his lip and tried to force a smile to replace his frown. He'd changed his mind a half dozen times about whether he should show up unannounced, especially since Peter didn't even know he was in town.

His first thought *had* been to let Peter know he was coming, but he'd wanted to surprise Catherine and felt foolish asking Peter not to mention his upcoming visit to anyone. He wound up trashing the half-written e-mail. Now he wished he'd sent it.

Brad considered leaving and took a single step backward, then stopped when he heard the quick patter of footsteps descending the stairs. The door swung open to reveal the face of a young woman he recognized. It took him a second to place it since the woman's flushed cheeks and tracksuit made her look like she was dressed for a run, not nursing duty.

"Dr. Baker?" she said.

"Uh, hi—"

"Toni, Toni Bartlett. Pediatrics."

"Of course, sorry."

"Come in," Toni said. "I'll tell Dr. Webb you're here."

Toni sprinted back up the stairs before Brad could reply. He had a minute in the hall to look around while he waited. The space looked orderly enough, but the slice of kitchen he could see through the doorway revealed a stack of dirty dishes in the sink and a pile of dish towels on the floor. The hall he stood in smelled of Pine-Sol, but the odor of something sour drifted from the kitchen.

Peter's footsteps on the stairs were a lot heavier than Toni's, and though his white hair was disheveled, he greeted Brad with a smile and ushered him down the hall and into his study. "I just wrote you an e-mail an hour ago, and now, like magic, you appear," Peter said.

"Cardoza gave me a week off at the last minute," Brad said as he took off his coat and sat down. "Sorry. I should've called."

"Nonsense," Peter said with a wave of his hand. "But we could've had dinner if I'd known."

"Thanks, but I needed to spend time with Catherine and Grace."

"But not today?"

"They had plans they couldn't change. I fly back tomorrow. Thought I'd catch up with you if you have a moment."

"Sure. It's been pretty crazy here this morning. Mallory's new nurse called in sick. Toni's pinch-hit for me a couple of times before when I got caught like this."

"How is she?" Brad asked.

"Young, but she's got a lot of energy."

"I meant Mallory."

"Oh," Peter said, and the way his face fell made Brad wish he hadn't asked. "The same. How 'bout you?"

Brad took a long moment to scan the wall of framed golf photos behind Peter's desk. More than one featured Peter in the company of celebrities and politicians; there was even one with an ex-president.

"I'm guessing you didn't come here to talk about my golf game," Peter finally said.

Brad felt his cheeks flush as his eyes darted back to Peter's face. "I want you to know that I didn't go by the hospital," he said with a sigh. "But I *did* have Bonnie over for dinner this week. I just wanted to know what was happening back at BG."

Peter smiled but shook his head. "How many e-mails have I sent you to tell you just that?"

"I know, Peter. But you can only fit so much into an e-mail."

"Fair enough. Maybe I can do better."

Peter turned to the PC on his desk and pecked away. A minute later the printer behind him whirred to life and spat out two pages.

"You're not supposed to be able to read this yet," Peter said as he passed the papers to Brad. "Nobody is. I called in some favors to get a copy before it runs."

At the top of the first page Brad recognized the byline of a reporter from the *Boston Globe*. The headline beneath it read: "Boston General Surgeon Brings New Life to Mexican Kidney Transplant Program."

Peter waited quietly while Brad read the rest. It was a flattering story of Brad's role in pioneering Nueva Vida's work. "It runs in the *Globe* on Friday," Peter said. "I was going to e-mail you the article once it came out."

"Thanks. Thank you, Peter," Brad said when he finally found his voice.

"No problem. You're the one down there in the jungle. I think that article might just be the thing that secures your position back here when you're done. But we still—"

"Mmmmm! Aaahhhh!"

The wails that echoed down the stairwell made both men freeze. Peter's eyes went wide before he shot from his chair and ran out of the room. "Sorry, I gotta go," was all he said. Brad heard the thunder of Peter's footsteps racing up the stairs, two at a time. A bump and a crash came next, followed by a scuffle hard enough to shake the chandelier in the front hall.

"Mmmmm! Mmmmm! Aaahhh!" Brad heard again, followed by the sound of Peter's and Jenny's voices, then another round of anguished cries.

Brad stood up and waited with one foot in Peter's study and the other in the hall, trying to decide whether to move toward the door or the stairs.

He listened for another minute and heard those two long-drawn-out syllables again. They were softer this time, more moans than howls. The voices that followed were gentler too. Brad could just make out the sound of Peter cooing.

The silence that settled was so complete that Brad could picture what must have happened next: Peter's gnarled but steady hand slipping the silver thread of a needle into his daughter's arm.

Brad grabbed his coat and left, closing the front door behind him quietly. Halfway down Acorn Street, he hugged his arms across his chest, but the chill that raced up his spine didn't come from any wind. He'd finally made sense of the pair of wails he'd just heard. They came from the lips of a thirty-four-year-old woman struggling to connect the first two sounds she had ever made: *Mmm. Aaa.* In the bed she'd been confined to for the past sixteen years, Mallory Webb was still calling for her mom.

Chapter Eighteen

Operation Uncle

HE'D BEEN AWAY for only a week, but as Brad scrubbed in next to Manny, he realized just how much he missed the guy. After taking over during their first transplant together, Brad grew concerned when Manny moped through their next operation. But after that, Manny bounced back. His surgical skills improved, and though his fingers still moved slowly, by the time Brad had left for Boston, Nueva Vida's second surgeon's sutures were almost as tight and even as Brad's.

Now his young associate was yammering away as usual as the two men scrubbed in before surgery. Brad didn't mind.

"And the grasses around Nueva Vida is beautiful," Manny said. "The *grasses*—that is the word for the place around a building, yes?" Manny asked, stopping mid-scrub to put the question to Brad.

"Grounds," Brad said.

"Sí, grounds," Manny continued. "They are nice, but after so long here, sometimes I want a different look. So I ask Aldo—you know Aldo?"

"I know Aldo."

"He shows me a special place in the jungle. I go sometimes, not too far from here. You run on the road to Nueva Vida, no?"

"I do," Brad replied, switching his attention from the bottom of the arm he'd just finished scrubbing to the fingertips of his other hand.

"There is a big palm with two pieces, a split, no? Not far from the start of this road."

"Sure, I know it."

"Aldo shows me a path right after that palm. It is *sacbe*. In English you say, 'white way,' a road used by Mayans many thousand years ago. This one leads to Calakmul temple, but just a short walk is a place with no trees that Aldo shows me. I think holy place for him, maybe. At the edge is tall stone. Smooth. Plain. But on *other* side," Manny said, his voice growing softer as his eyes widened above his mask, "is carving. You know a stela?"

"Sure. We saw some in Coba."

"Sí, Coba has stela too! But no tourist see this one. On back of *this* stone, if you look close, you see face. Aldo says this is face of snake king." Manny grew silent. When he started speaking again, his voice was lower. "Maybe king like man we operate on today."

Brad stopped scrubbing. "What do you mean?"

"You don't know this man?"

"Sure, you read his history too. Señor Diaz is seventy-three years old and has stage three kidney disease. Pretty close to stage four, actually. His first kidney transplant was fourteen years ago. That organ's failing, and the transplant left him with a CPRA rate of over ninety-five percent. He was *very* fortunate to find a donor. It takes a lot of luck to match a patient with an antibody level that high."

"Or lot of money," Manny said under his breath.

"What do—"

"I say too much," Manny said quickly.

Brad waited a moment before he replied. "It's okay, Manny. I may not like it, but I've talked to Carlos. I knew we were going to get patients like this, the ones who pay for the rest."

"I am glad you know this," Manny replied instantly, sighing beneath his mask. "At first, I do not like it too. But the Church says that to donate kidney is a gift, is sacred, yes? Maybe is so great a gift that is even okay for a person who gets money for kidney instead of giving for free." Manny relaxed back into small talk again, obviously relieved that he hadn't revealed anything to Brad that he didn't already know.

But he had.

Brad just stood and stared at his own raised hands while Manny prattled on. It had been one thing to learn from Carlos that Nueva Vida's patients were paying for priority access to cadaveric kidneys from deceased donors. It was quite another to discover that the clinic he headed was paying live donors for them.

✦

Despite what he'd just learned, Brad did what he always did once he went through the OR doors: he banished everything from his mind except the operation at hand. And though what he'd just learned while scrubbing in hovered like a dark cloud above his thoughts, it soon evaporated under the sunny mood of the team around him.

After returning from his time off, Brad saw what he'd missed in his day-to-day work at Nueva Vida before. The team he led had changed. Their banter and their intense focus had finally found the right balance. Everyone around the table felt it too.

For weeks Brad had watched the same expressions flit across the faces of the nurses and surgical techs that surrounded him. Though they followed his directions, he often saw their eyes shift to Manny or Rosa, the fellow Mexican associates they'd worked with long before Brad arrived. It was the new confidence and poise of this supporting staff, Brad realized, that had transformed the vibe in the room. Once Brad had earned Manny's and Rosa's trust, he had the rest of the team's as well.

It had been a while since he'd enjoyed that kind of faith from his crew in the OR, and it did much more than simply lift his spirits. Señor Diaz's transplant turned out to be one of the smoothest operations he'd ever led. All the information exchanged, every instrument passed, each move to retract, suction, or suture was made with the kind of effortless grace found during any truly creative act. *Operation* was the wrong word for what went on in the OR that morning. The fluid flow of his team's work was more like a medical ballet.

They were done in a little over three hours. Brad ducked into his office afterward to finish up the paperwork on the procedure. In the middle of his report, he heard an angry exchange of Spanish echo in the hall. He poked his head out of his office to see Rosa walking toward him quickly, her mouth in a tight line as she scowled at the floor.

At the far end of the hall, another figure stared after Rosa. He was too far away for Brad to make out his face, but when the looming form noticed Brad watching him, he turned and limped away. Brad knew who it was: Octavio, the orderly. Brad's eyes shifted back to Rosa. As she approached, she whispered something in Spanish, her eyes still trained on the floor.

"Is everything all right?" Brad asked.

Rosa froze, then lifted her face to look at Brad. When her eyes met his, her cheeks flushed red.

"*Es un cerdo,*" she said, her voice still a whisper.

"I'm sorry?" Brad said.

"In America," Rosa said, "women are equal there, yes? Men treat them with respect?"

"Some men. Not all. Did Octavio say something?"

Rosa opened her mouth, then shut it. Finally, she replied, "It is nothing I have not heard before."

"Do you want me to talk to him? Or maybe have Carlos say some—"

"No!" Rosa said, surprising Brad with the fear that flashed in her eyes. "It was a stupid remark, the kind stupid men make, but Carlos would not tolerate it."

"Maybe you shouldn't either."

"I did not. He did not like what I had to say in return to him. I think maybe he will think twice before he speaks to me in this way again. It is okay, Doctor. I am sorry to have disturbed you. Please do not say anything. It is better if I handle this."

"Are you sure?" Brad asked, staring past Rosa down the empty hall.

"I am sure."

✦

By the time Brad reached his bungalow, his thoughts had turned toward a dip in the pool, but the note from Carlos he found on his front door changed those plans. It was taped to a long garment bag: *Please meet me at the helipad at three. Pack an overnight bag and comfortable clothes for two days, but wear this.*

An hour later, Brad walked toward the helicopter in a black tux tailored exactly to his size. The Sikorsky's big blades were already turning. Carlos waited with a smile, then ushered Brad into the chopper and handed him a headset. "Where are we going?" Brad yelled into his mic after he was buckled in.

"It's a surprise, Doctor," Carlos replied as the Sikorsky began to ascend. "You've had a busy day. Try to relax and enjoy the ride."

✦

Ninety minutes later, Brad saw an aqua flash at the edge of the green world below. The white ribbon of the Cancún coast came into focus next. Just before they landed, he saw a figure on horseback at the edge of the waves and thought of Grace.

She had shared only a few meals with him during his short visit home, but he didn't complain. He knew it would be foolish to compete with Grace's new boyfriend for a place in her schedule. Now he wished he'd pushed harder to spend more time with her.

Luis was waiting for them on the tarmac of the private airstrip. He ushered Brad and Carlos into a white limo instead of a black SUV, but he raised the glass partition behind him as soon as Brad was seated, just as he'd done during their previous ride. After the constant roar of the helicopter, Brad found the silence unsettling. He could feel Carlos looking at him. He had a lot of questions for his boss but didn't know where to begin.

"You look troubled, my friend," Carlos said. Brad rubbed a hand across his face. Carlos laughed. "I'm guessing you don't play much poker."

Brad shifted in his seat to face Carlos. "Who is the man I operated on today? Did he pay someone to give him a kidney, the one I put in?"

Carlos waited a few seconds before he replied. "Which question would you like me to answer first?"

"Who is he?"

"He is my uncle. I am closer to him than I was to my own father." Carlos reached over and grasped Brad's arm. "Nothing means more to me than my family, Brad. I consider anyone who cares for them—as you did so very well today—to be family too. Now, as for your second question," Carlos said, sitting back to brush the wrinkles from the pants of his own spotless tux, "you saw the high level of antibodies in my uncle's blood when you reviewed his medical history, no?"

"Of course."

"I watched Santiago struggle for years after his first transplanted kidney began to fail, this man who is, in every way, the strongest person I have ever known. I promised him I would not rest until I found another kidney that would be a match. Once we found one, we did what was necessary to secure it."

"I can't work for a clinic that pays people for their kidneys, Carlos."

"Why not?"

"If you have to ask that question, I shouldn't be working for you."

Brad watched the manicured lawns and trimmed shrubs outside his window in the silence that followed. For a moment, he felt as if he were passing through his own neighborhood back home on some sparkling summer day.

"Do you think alcohol should be illegal?" Carlos asked softly.

Brad turned from the view outside. "You're changing the subject."

"I am not. Please bear with me."

"Maybe better regulated, but illegal? No."

"What about birth control?"

"Of course not."

"Interracial marriage, then?"

Brad frowned. "What kind of question is that?"

"They were all illegal in your country, Brad. All crimes that you could be convicted of and sent to prison for."

"We're a different country now, Carlos."

"Yes, and tomorrow you will be different once again."

"Those examples you're citing are of laws that changed along with our culture, a culture moving forward. Allowing people to sell their organs would be a big step backward."

"That is spoken like a man who would never have to consider doing so. One kidney can change more lives than just that of the person who is paid for it. The money from such a sale is enough to end a lifetime of poverty, not only for the seller but for his children, grandchildren, maybe even generations to come."

"Money paid by the rich to exploit the poor."

"Brad," Carlos said patiently, "haven't we spoken about this? The rich are always going to get what they want."

"We were speaking about cutting to the head of the donor line the last time we had this conversation, not about cutting into healthy people for cash."

Carlos gave a deep sigh. "You can either close your eyes to what is already happening or work to ensure that those who do sell a kidney receive fair compensation and competent care. The black market for these organs is only going to get blacker as the need for them continues to rise. Of course the idea of receiving money for a kidney is distasteful. But you need to ask yourself: What serves the greater good? Twenty people on your country's OPTN donor list die each day waiting for a kidney. In Iran, the success of legalizing paid donations eliminated the need for such a list eleven years ago."

Brad chewed on his lip. "Your argument may be good, as far as it goes. But it still feels wrong, Carlos."

"To someone like me," Carlos said, "or to anyone who is not a surgeon, what you do each day feels wrong as well. To hold a knife and slice through the flesh of another human being goes against every instinct for moral action that a person may possess. But I know that a man like you can see past that naive perspective to do what needs to be done, a man who has the wisdom, the compassion, the *courage* required to heal the suffering of so many in our world."

Brad sat back in the limousine's plush leather seat and closed his eyes, searching for an answer that never came. When he heard the tinkle of glass, he opened them to see Carlos offering what he usually did to conclude a pitch to Brad.

It was a long moment before Brad took the cut-glass tumbler that Carlos had filled from the limousine's small bar.

"I'm not done with this conversation, Carlos, but I'm tired," Brad said, taking a quick slug of the whiskey. "Let's stick to simpler questions for a while."

"Of course."

"Where are we going?"

Carlos filled his own glass and clinked it against Brad's. "Drink up, my friend. We are going to a dinner party, and you are the guest of honor."

Chapter Nineteen

Family Matters

WHEN BRAD WALKED onto the terrace, fifty people stood and cheered. Their applause was so loud that Brad had to take a step back to steady himself. It wasn't just the smiling faces on the sea of tuxedoed men and gowned women that overwhelmed him; the garden he'd just walked into, tucked into the back of a restaurant, looked like an illustration from the pages of some Mexican fairy tale.

Strings of lights twinkled between the crowns of potted palms spaced throughout the cozy patio. Their round bulbs glowed gold against the purpling sky and were reflected as tiny moons shimmering in the pitchers of sangria on the tables below.

The applause went on and on. Finally, the blasts of a trumpet sent the crowd scuttling for their seats, revealing a brass band at the back of the terrace, its members silhouetted against a sea glowing orange from the setting sun.

The band began to play. Carlos took Brad by the arm and led him to a table facing the dance floor the crowd had just retreated from. Carlos bent close to Brad's ear and said something Brad could just make out as the music began to swell. "Now you will feel the true spirit of my homeland, Brad. This is the *jaranas yucatecas*."

The trombone, clarinet, and saxophone picked up the beat laid down by a bass drum, then its tempo was echoed by the audience's clapping hands. A dozen dancers appeared, six men in white suits leading six women in long white dresses embroidered with rainbows of flowers. The women turned as they glided through the crowd to show off the white fedoras on their heads and the long red scarfs around their necks.

The dancers wound their way through the audience to the dance floor. Then the men dropped back to let the women form a chorus line. As they high-kicked, Brad saw that the eyes of each smiling face were trained on him, then felt his cheeks flush.

A cheer went up from the crowd as the women stepped back to let the men take their place. The men repeated the dance, mirroring the women's movements, then disappeared through the crowd to let the women solo again. After that, the men returned, each carrying a small wooden platform and two brown bottles of beer. They found their partners, each man offering a woman one of the bottles in his hands.

The women stepped onto the platforms the men had spread across the floor before every dancer placed a beer bottle upon his or her head. Brad watched in amazement as the ensemble began to high-step, the bottles rising and falling over dancing legs without a single sideways sway.

When the song ended, the dancers smiled and bowed as the crowd rose to their feet with a roar. When the hoots and whistles finally ended, the dancers disappeared, and the band segued into a softer melody that settled the crowd down.

Brad remained standing, replaying the swirling pageantry in his mind while he stared at the vacant dance floor. His eyes drifted to the band and he took a deep breath, catching a trace of the sea air just before closer smells drifted in. As they did, his mouth began to water from those savory scents. He reached for the back of his chair to steady himself before he sat down.

"The dance, the music, it was—amazing," Brad managed.

Carlos responded to Brad's comment with a smile and turned his attention to the rest of the table.

"Dr. Baker, allow me to present your dinner companions," Carlos said. He first introduced his raven-haired wife, Julieta, and his four freshly pressed but jostling children. Next, he gestured to the gray-haired woman opposite Brad, whose eyes were as bright as her silver and turquoise jewelry.

"This is the wife of the man whose life you saved today," Carlos said, "my aunt Carmelita."

Carmelita rose and extended a veined hand. Brad rose in return, surprised to see the woman's lower lip tremble and her eyes begin to fill. She grasped Brad's hand in both of hers, tilted her head down, and pressed her lips to it.

When Brad froze, Carmelita seemed to sense his discomfort. She gave his hand a pat, bowed her head to him, and sat down.

"And everyone else here?" Brad asked Carlos after he found his voice. Still standing, he waved to the crowd of people around them who were now being served.

"They are family too," Carlos said.

"*All* family?"

"Most by blood. The others I have, you might say, adopted. But yes, tonight is *only* for family, my friend. That is why you are here."

Brad sensed the waiter at his elbow and sat down as their food was served. The other guests began eating, but Brad took a moment to study the unusual dish placed before him. Carlos's laugh finally broke the spell.

"It is *cocobichuela*, a specialty here. I think you will enjoy it. Like much in the Yucatán, there is more to it than meets the eye."

Brad looked at the big green coconut sitting in the center of his white china plate. Its top was sheared to reveal a hole capped with a golden slice of pineapple showered with white sprinkles of shaved coconut. He dug his spoon in to sample the dish, releasing the spicy scent of curry. When the mixture of lobster, shrimp, and tropical fruit greeted his tongue, he closed his eyes to savor the flavor. It was perfect for this place, as rich and exotic as the performance he'd just seen.

Platters of gingered mushrooms, chicken enchiladas, beef fajitas, and more came next. When the guests had eaten their fill, the dishes were cleared away so the waiters could serve dessert. Each plate they set down bore a dark chocolate pyramid. When Brad hit his with a spoon, it cracked to release a creamy stream. The taste of chocolate and amaretto was almost too good to bear.

Just when he thought he would burst, Carlos asked if he would like some Mayan coffee to top off the meal.

"Coffee is about all I can manage," Brad told him. Carlos signaled with a nod. A minute later, a waiter rolled over a small cart filled with liqueurs, coffee, and ice cream. Then the final performance of the evening began: The waiter filled a snifter with coffee and ice cream, ignited the liqueur in one of the two silver gravy boats, and poured a stream of blue fire back and forth between the two pitchers. He finally spilled their contents into the snifter and placed the blazing drink in front of Brad.

Brad's mouth dropped open, and Carlos started to laugh until Brad did the same. When the flames died, Brad took a tentative sniff of his drink. Carlos gave Brad's back a pat and left to speak to his other guests. A moment later, Carmelita came around the table and took Carlos's seat. When Brad put his drink down, she took his hand in hers again.

"I prayed, Doctor," Carmelita began. "I prayed to the Virgin Mother for my Santiago each night, prayed for years. You, what you do today, was *un milagro*."

"I'm happy for your husband, Señora Diaz, but I think Carlos is the one to thank, not me," Brad said. "He found the kidney your husband needed. *That* was the real miracle."

Carmelita shook her head. "Carlos loves Santiago, but even Carlos's powers go only so far. He could not do what you do…" Then Carmelita's voice broke, and the words that came next came in Spanish. But the look Carmelita gave Brad while she shared them required no translation at all.

The evening went on and on. Brad gave in to it completely. The food, the drink, the dancing; they all took him to a place far from the one he'd left a few hours ago. One of Carlos's nieces dragged him out on the dance floor and coached him through a series of quick salsa steps. By the time the song was over, his head was spinning in a world he'd never known before.

Later that night, after he'd finished his last cocktail and had been introduced to every single one of Carlos's relatives, the names of whom he would never remember, Brad looked out from the balcony of the suite Carlos had reserved for him. Over the black expanse of the invisible ocean, Carmelita's beaming face came to him. Then, that face dissolved into the night to be replaced by another. But that countenance held none of the joy that had shone from Carmelita's eyes.

When Brad finally drifted off in the middle of his king-size bed, the image began to fade. And when Faye Kirby's face finally disappeared, Brad slept but did not dream.

Chapter Twenty

Dead End

BRAD PICKED UP the ringing phone from the night-stand by the hotel bed and heard Catherine crying.

"Cat?" Brad asked. Catherine's response came in waves, muffled between the pulses of blood in Brad's ears that throbbed in time with the pounding headache he'd earned from the night before.

"Why didn't you answer your cell?" Catherine asked.

"Battery died," Brad answered, laying his head slowly back down on his pillow. "What's wrong?"

"I couldn't get you! I had to call Nueva Vida three times! That chirpy little bitch finally gave me your number. Why didn't you tell me you were going to Cancún?"

"Carlos surprised me with the trip. Now, will you tell me what's wrong?"

Catherine's voice dropped to a whisper: "It's my mother."

Brad waited. "Is she okay?"

"No."

"Catherine?"

"I don't want to say it."

"Just tell me, Cat."

"Pancreatic cancer. She has pancreatic cancer. Stage four pan—" Catherine broke down again.

"Shhh, Cat. It'll be okay." He let her cry a minute longer. When he heard her take a deep breath, Brad tried again. "Can you tell me what her doctor said?"

"That's another thing," Catherine said with a sniff. "It's some kind of rare form of cancer. Lucky Mom! Squashed cell or something; I wasn't really listening by then."

"Squamous cell carcinoma?"

"I guess."

Brad closed his eyes.

"He talked about putting her in a clinical trial for immunotherapy," Catherine continued. "I have no idea if Medicare will cover that. I did some Googling. Some of those drugs cost, like, ten thousand dollars *per dose*."

"You're getting ahead of yourself. We'll figure it out."

"I wish you were here."

"Me too."

When he asked her to send him her mother's doctor's e-mail address, Catherine began to calm down. By the time he hung up a half hour later, she'd even managed a rueful laugh. He felt good about relieving some of his wife's concerns, but Catherine was right to be scared. The diagnosis was bad, and the uninsured costs for treatment could easily spiral out of control.

He used the bathroom and made the mistake of glancing in the mirror when he was done; he winced at the pair of bloodshot eyes staring back at him. "Physician, heal thyself," he whispered, then dug three aspirins out of his toiletry bag and went back to bed.

His headache settled down, but his mind didn't. After inventorying what he knew about pancreatic cancer, his thoughts ping-ponged between last night's party and the concerns he'd carried onto the chopper on his way there. When the latter got the best of him, Brad decided to make a call of his own.

✦

"Sorry, did I wake you, Peter?"

"Hey, Brad. Never went to bed. Mallory had a bad night."

"Sorry, if it's a bad time—"

"No, Toni's here. She's the nurse du jour. She seems to know what she's doing. To tell you the truth, I could use a break. What's up? You sound kind of…off."

Brad managed a weak laugh. "Carlos surprised me with a party. I'm in Cancún."

"Sounds fun."

"I'm paying for it, but that's not why I called. I learned that the kidney I transplanted yesterday came from a donor who had been paid for it."

Brad waited. It took Peter a few seconds to respond. "I guess that doesn't surprise me."

"Well, it sure as hell surprised *me*. You don't condone it, do you?"

"No. But I understand it."

"What's that supposed to mean?"

"You know the stats. There's an escalating supply problem driving the demand for what we do. Maybe one in five U.S. patients on the donor list gets a kidney. The others make do with dialysis or die. Often both. Those odds are certainly a lot worse down there. Eventually, the need for organs is going to make paid donations commonplace. Looks like Carlos is trying to be first to market with that solution."

"You sound like you're defending your MBA thesis."

"Frankly, if I'd known I'd end up in management, I would've gotten that degree before my MD."

"'First, do no harm'—remember, Peter?"

Peter sighed. "I guess I'm really not done training you."

"I don't need to be schooled in bioethics."

"I'm not so sure. Ten percent of all organs transplanted every year come from paid donors. You want to do no harm? Try providing *those* patients with the surgical and post-op care they're certainly not getting from the back-alley butchers operating on them now."

"You sound just like Carlos."

"I should. We're both administrators. We're trained to see the big picture. And I hate to tell you this, Brad, but as his chief of surgery, you're supposed to see it too."

Now it was Brad's turn to pause and consider his response. His answer surprised even him: "I'm pretty close to resigning that position."

"I urge you to take some time to think about that. Your job back here hasn't exactly been secured."

"What about the *Globe* article? I though you said it'd do just that."

"I said it *might*. You didn't hear this from me, but the vote to cut you loose at the last board meeting was split right down the middle. And that was *after* the *Globe* article ran."

"Jesus, Peter. I'm completely isolated down here. I was hoping for more support from you."

"Hey, Brad, whose side do you think I was on in that board meeting? As soon as we've got the votes to bring you back, I'll let you know. Just try to hang in there for a bit longer. You can make your decision then."

✦

Back in surgery a week later, everything that could go wrong, did. As the team was prepping, a new nurse responded to the head nurse's question in Spanish instead of English. When the head nurse answered her sharply, the new nurse burst into tears and ran out of the OR, leaving the team stranded for the next half hour until a fresh recruit could be found to scrub in.

Then the surgical tech brushed his elbow against a table, sending a shower of sterilized instruments clattering to the floor. Even Rosa's concentration seemed off. Every time Brad looked over at her, her eyes seemed to be on the room instead of her monitors. Somehow, the entire team had lost their balance. It wasn't until Brad turned his attention to the surgeon at his side that he realized the cause.

Manny had barely said a word since he'd made his first incision on Señora Molina. Brad had been glad they were operating on another pro bono case, satisfied that the kidney they'd be transplanting into the sixty-year-old Mexican woman didn't come from another poor farmer who'd cashed in on his spare. But now Brad picked up on what everyone around his table seemed to have known from the start: Manny was off. And as soon as that thought came to him, Brad's eyes went to Manny's hand. What he saw was subtle but unmistakable. The scalpel it held, poised to expose the preperitoneal space, was shaking.

"Stop, Doctor," Brad said, quietly but firmly.

Manny's hand froze; the eyes above his mask met Brad's. Manny's eyebrows arched for an instant, then settled again. He surrendered the blade in his hand to Brad, took a step back from the table, and walked out of the OR.

Now Brad and everyone around him froze. Rosa broke the silence a second later by calling out the patient's vital signs, bringing Brad back to action. He called the surgical tech over to take Manny's place. For the rest of that long morning, Brad tried to restore some sense of order to his team. Despite years of training to keep his emotions outside the OR, he struggled to keep his anger at bay. For four long hours, the only words spoken were the snippets of information traded to get the job done. And the silence between those exchanges only made it harder to ignore the elephant who had left the operating room.

When Brad finally scrubbed out, he wanted nothing more than to take a run to clear his head. But he wouldn't permit himself that luxury until the day's last duty was done. He checked the doctors' lounge, the cafeteria, and Nueva Vida's apartment complex but couldn't find Manny anywhere. "Might as well kill two birds," he muttered to himself back in his bungalow and suited up for a run.

Ten minutes later, he gave the sky a glance as he started jogging down the jungle road. It was still only the beginning of May, but the purple crowns of cumulus clouds he'd spotted before ducking under the forest canopy promised the arrival of one of the rainy season's first storms.

A half a mile down the road, Brad spotted the big split palm at its edge. When he approached the path beyond it, his pace slowed. As his feet hit the faint white trail, he found himself hoping that his detour would lead to nothing more than a dead end.

But there was Manny, right in the dirty pair of chinos and a guayabera, his face screened by the mosquito netting hanging from his big floppy hat. Manny's head turned toward Brad. The only other move he made was to lift the edge of the netting so he could take a long swig from the half-empty tequila bottle he held in one hand.

As usual, the mosquitoes started in on Brad as soon as he stopped running. He stood swatting as he tried to catch his breath and think of just what to say. But Manny spoke first.

"My duck is cooked, no?"

It took Brad a moment to decipher Manny's slurred speech, then another to decode the botched idiom.

"It's goose, not duck, and I guess that's up to you. You can start by telling me what the hell is going on."

Manny gave him a long look and took another pull from the bottle, but when Brad went over and held out his hand, Manny surrendered it to him.

"I could be wrong, but I do not think so," Manny mumbled.

Brad gave the sharp sting on his calf a slap. "Either you start talking or I start running," he said.

Manny peeled back the net and rubbed a hand across his face. The eyes that gazed up at Brad were bleary, but they finally focused on him. "Do you remember meeting, you and me, a first time?"

"Of course. You were one of the first people Carlos introduced me to."

"He spoke of my programming, the system that connects Nueva Vida to hospitals across the Yucatán."

"I remember."

Manny struggled to his feet, reaching out to steady himself against the stela as he did. Brad saw a mosquito hover and land on one of Manny's flushed cheeks. Manny made no move to brush it away, either too pickled by the tequila or too lost in his story to react to the pain.

"I never complete this system. Mostly I build *puentes*—eh, bridge, yes?—bridge between it and databases in the hospitals and clinics in the Yucatán that Carlos gives me access to. Every week, two week, three, I add another. But then Carlos brought in others. They take over. I try to log into the system the day after Señor Diaz operation, but my password, it does not work."

"Is that so strange?"

"No. What is strange is *reason* I want to log in. It starts with what you say as we scrub in for that operation."

"What was that?"

"You say Señor Diaz, his antibody level is very high. I am ashamed to tell, I miss this when I prepare for this case. But I think much about it after."

"And?" Brad asked, giving the back of his neck a slap as another bug began feasting on him.

"You say it takes much luck to find a match."

"So?"

"Do you not think it is luck *two* times? First, to find match and second, to find donor who does match and then agrees to sell kidney? That seem like too much luck to me. I could not use Nueva Vida's computer system to find out more. I use my phone instead."

Brad felt a sting on his forearm but barely brushed the insect away as he waited for Manny to say more.

"I call many IT technicians, the people I work with at hospitals to make our donor system. Some would not speak to me because of security, but most would. They know me. I am, perhaps, a friendly person? I think that is why many speak to me. But when I ask about organ-donor records, I am surprise to find that more than one say they now have HLA tissue typing as part of bloodwork for incoming patients."

"For all incoming patients? Why? Those are specialized tests. They're almost always ordered only for organ donors and recipients to determine the chances for a match."

"Of course. I know this too. But again, more than one of the people I talk to tell me that this is new protocol. They are technicians, so don't know why. I think maybe Nueva Vida convinces their bosses to run this test."

"So you were looking for the donor with the profile that matched Señor Diaz's needs."

"That is exact. I get my own luck then. Most of these technicians, I know only from the phone, but I met Francisco Blanco in person at San Pedro Hospital. When I call, I have him run Señor Diaz's HLA profile through system. He gets HLA match from a patient in his system that is very close. But I do not think Francisco would give me more than that if we had not met. After we did, we go out and have many drinks. It was very good time. So when I ask him for name and phone number of the patient in his system, he gives it to me. His name was Hector Vázquez."

Before Brad could stop him, Manny grabbed the tequila bottle out of Brad's hand, tipped it up, and nearly drained it.

"I call number. Señor Vázquez not home." Manny stopped for the cough his quick slug had ignited. "But his wife, she is home," he continued. "I must say I lie to this woman. I tell her I call from San Pedro Hospital to confirm detail of Señor Vázquez's medical record. But when I tell her this, she will cry."

At that, Manny's own eyes teared. "She tell me he is killed by robber coming home from his job one night. 'We are not rich people,' she say to me, 'why they rob my poor Hector?' I try not to believe it," Manny went on, his voice breaking, "but I think they…we…maybe Nueva Vida, they kill him."

Brad stared at the big man who stood shaking and sobbing before him as the mosquitoes buzzed in his ears, and his brain began to spin. Every slap of his hand brought a new thought, his mind jumping from the faces of recent cases to donor statistics to snatches of conversations with Carlos, Manny, and the rest of his team.

"You think this is true?" Manny blubbered.

"I don't know. I need time to think. I can't do it here."

"Okay," Manny said, taking in a huge gulp of air that seemed to settle him down. "We go to your bungalow now, yes?"

"No."

"No?"

"Do you still have access to a jeep?" Brad asked.

"Sí. Carlos, gives me key for when I drive for supplies to Chetumal."

"Good," Brad said. "Go back to your apartment and pack. You and I are leaving Nueva Vida tonight."

Chapter Twenty-One

Night Lights

PERHAPS ONLY A physician would tap into the most recently evolved sector of the brain, the neocortex, to try to understand the unconscious urges born in that organ's most ancient part. Brad lay in bed doing just that. His review of the problem Manny presented inspired the memory of the poster of the triune brain model—a popular theory at the time—tacked to the wall of his fourth-grade classroom. His nine-year-old eyes had drifted to it often as he tried to discern how his own neocortex, limbic system, and reptilian complex could conjure the mix of thoughts, emotions, and basic survival functions known as "Brad."

His thoughts returned to his conversation with Manny a few hours ago. Brad's decision to leave Nueva Vida tonight certainly hadn't been an analytical one. That choice was entirely emotional; his impulse wasn't to think but to run.

He went over the reason not to do so again. Logic told him that before he did anything, he should talk to Carlos, a man whom Brad didn't always agree with but whom he respected. Every time Brad had gone to him with an issue about Nueva Vida's operations, Carlos had delivered a cogent argument while voicing his respect for Brad's concerns. Now Brad was poised to turn his back on his calm and reasonable employer to respond to the hypothetical fears voiced by his hysterical—and drunk—trainee.

But there was an evolutionary reason for the gut instinct that spoke loudest to Brad now: survival. So, after lying in bed listening to the steady beat of rain for hours, he got up, grabbed the two duffels he'd packed, and headed out the door.

He walked quickly, glad for the storm that let him pass by the bungalows next to his without being heard. Then a flash of light exposed him, followed by another. He cursed himself softly for forgetting the motion-sensor spotlights posted over his neighbors' doors.

Brad veered from the sidewalk and left the cover of the trees to walk in the street, looking over his shoulder to see the spotlights switch off. He glanced at his watch, satisfied that he'd be arriving to meet Manny at the satellite parking lot that held the clinic's three jeeps at exactly two a.m., the time they'd set for their rendezvous.

But as he passed Nueva Vida's apartment complex, Brad saw Manny bustling behind one of the jeeps. He unloaded a large carton from it, placed it on the small portico at the front of the building, and was reaching for another when Brad spoke to him.

"What are you doing here?" Brad asked, trying to speak just loudly enough to be heard over the rain.

"The jeep. Someone use it to get supplies. It is still loaded. I think to leave supplies here."

Brad shook his head and swung the tailgate closed slowly until it latched. Then he grabbed Manny by the arm and led him to the passenger door. "Get in," he said.

"I do not—" Manny began.

Brad got into the driver's seat. "Quiet," he said.

Brad started the jeep, switched on the headlights, and pulled away slowly, adjusting his grip on the wheel to turn toward the jungle road. In the next instant he heard Manny suck in a sharp breath. He looked up to see Aldo, caught in the glare of the headlights, standing shirtless in the pouring rain on the sidewalk with his mouth and eyes wide open.

✦

Brad was grateful that Manny stayed quiet as Brad got used to the jungle road. He hadn't planned on driving, but after Manny's recent lapses in judgment, he didn't trust him with their escape—if that was what this was.

"You go too fast," Manny finally whispered. "You think we are follow?"

"Only if your worst guess is confirmed."

"Maybe I am wrong."

"Maybe."

Brad gripped the wheel tightly, trying to concentrate as he divided his attention between the road ahead and the rearview mirror. He half expected to see a bright beam pierce the black world behind them.

He soon discovered that driving a jeep over a jungle road in a downpour was a lot different from racing his BMW down Storrow Drive. When he pushed the vehicle too fast over uneven ground, it bottomed out, sending another spray of muddy water streaming across the windshield. On the flat stretches, the jeep's tires still caught rocks big enough to threaten a blowout, and the vehicle often slipped sideways in the mud. After a while he found the right rhythm, braking before hitting the roughest patches, goosing the accelerator when they were in the clear, and downshifting to climb the rises in the road revealed between the sheets of rain falling from the drenched forest canopy.

In some places, the road completely disappeared under the small streams that had sprung up from the storm. Each time he came to one, Brad gritted his teeth, held his breath, and gunned the engine to blast through. Manny stayed silent, but more than once Brad caught him making the sign of the cross.

The going was steady, but rough. Too rough, it turned out, for Manny. "I am sick," he finally said, throwing the back of a hand to his mouth. "Stop. Please, stop."

Manny shot out the door the instant the jeep halted. Brad could hear him retching into the bushes over the sound of the pouring rain. He waited with his hands clenched on the wheel as he thought of the bottle of tequila Manny had drained the afternoon before. Each time Manny grew quiet, Brad gripped the stick shift to prepare for his return, only to hear another round of retching begin.

As another silent interval stretched, Brad looked into the rearview mirror and saw something that threatened to make him sick as well. At first, he hoped it might be a flash of lightning that had found its way through the trees. A moment later, there was no mistaking the two perfect yellow circles that grew larger in his mirror until the jeep's interior was bathed in light.

The vehicle behind him screeched to a halt. When Brad saw it was another jeep, his mind began racing through excuses, trying to find some story to sell to whoever had chased them down from Nueva Vida. He cracked open the jeep's door to get out, but Manny appeared in the next instant, grabbing the door to stop him.

"It is Aldo," Manny said. "It is maybe best I speak to him."

The wait this time was worse. Brad could just make out Aldo behind the wheel; Manny went around to the passenger side of Aldo's jeep and got in. Brad drummed his fingers on the empty seat beside him, looking again and again in the rearview mirror, but the scene never changed. At last he heard the slam of the jeep door behind him and saw the vehicle jockeying back and forth in tight turns to reverse itself. It disappeared into the dark. Manny opened the back of their jeep, put something inside, then slipped into the passenger seat beside Brad.

"Well?" Brad asked when they were under way again.

"He sees the box, the medical supplies we do not take after we drive away," Manny said. "I am sorry, but I guess I wake him when I pull up in the jeep. He tells me that he thinks we go to emergency because we leave in the middle of the night. It has happen before. Carlos sends a doctor to a woman in a village when her baby is breach. Aldo brings supplies because he think we forget them."

"What did you tell him?"

"I tell him what he think is right. We go to emergency. I say to help children. Children that may die."

"Did he believe you?"

"I do not know. Someone like me, I do not lie well. My tongue is not in it, you would say?"

"Not your tongue. It's your *heart* that isn't in it, Manny."

"Yes," Manny answered softly. "My heart. It does not like a lie."

After they wrestled with the miserable road for almost two hours, Manny let Brad know that they were getting close to Highway 186, the straight paved route that would take them all the way to Chetumal. Then they went over the plans they'd made during their walk out of the jungle the afternoon before.

When Brad found out that Manny had a valid passport with him, he'd offered to buy him a ticket to Boston so they could both sort things out from there. "This is kind," Manny had answered, "but I fly to my parents' home in Mexico City. Maybe is better we go two places?" he said, and Brad agreed. He ordered tickets for both of them on his computer and printed them out that night.

As soon as they reached the highway, Brad hit the gas, eager to get out of the jeep and onto a plane. As the miles clicked by, he began sketching out what he'd do once he reached Boston. Peter could help him dig deeper into Nueva Vida's operations to see if there was any truth to Manny's fears. But even if they were groundless, Brad decided that he was done with Nueva Vida. With or without the support of BG's board, he'd take his chances with whatever career he could salvage at home.

Home. The very thought of it brought a lump to Brad's throat. For the past six weeks he hadn't allowed himself the luxury of picturing himself there, putting that hope aside every morning to turn to the work that needed to be done in this wild and foreign land. Now that he was headed back to Boston, the faces of his wife and daughter shone in his mind. He was still a gifted surgeon. If BG was done with him, he'd find another way to use his talents to support those he loved.

Not far from Chetumal, Manny dropped off to sleep. Brad looked over to see the big man's head lolling to one side as he snored softly. At that angle, with his round cheeks, full lips, and crown of thick black curls, he looked like a sleeping child. Brad caught his own smile in the rearview mirror as he sped toward the glow on the horizon that promised the start of a new day.

A moment later, he saw a different light in his rearview mirror, one that had his eyes flicking to the jeep's speedometer and lifting his foot from the pedal.

The flashing blue lights came up fast, but when Brad braked to pull over, the police cruiser veered around them and sped past in the other lane. Manny roused at the jeep's decrease in speed just in time to see the cop fly by. "I think we have too much excitement tonight," Manny said with a sleepy laugh. "I am glad we do not have more."

"Agreed," Brad said, returning Manny's grin.

But Brad's smile faded when another set of flashing blue lights appeared in his rearview mirror. He saw that the police car ahead had slowed and pulled into Brad's lane. Its blue lights flashed in time with the ones of the second cruiser, now close behind. Brad pulled over to the shoulder and killed the engine.

"I will talk," Manny said.

"I've got it," Brad replied. "I wasn't more than ten kilometers over the limit. I'll take the ticket and pay the fine."

"They may ask for money, not give you ticket," Manny said.

"Then I'll pay the bribe. In either case, I'll pay, and we'll be on our way."

A Mexican federal police officer stepped out of the cruiser behind them and approached with a blank expression on his face. Every inch of his uniform was black, from the cap on his head bearing the big gold star right down to the tips of the tightly laced high-top boots that clicked across the gravel.

Manny already had the registration out of the glove box. Brad took it and pulled out his license and had both waiting at the window when the cop walked up. The officer took them, gave them a glance, and uttered a single word:

"Pasaporte."

Brad turned to dig the document out of the backpack he'd parked between the seats as the door to the cruiser in front of them opened. The cop that got out looked like a supersized version of the one standing by Brad. He walked up to Manny's window and gave it a sharp rap with the butt of his flashlight. When Manny rolled it down, the cop barked something in Spanish to him.

"They want to search jeep," Manny said softly.

Brad looked at the other cop. He stood silently by Brad's window and with the back of his hand to Brad, waved him out of the car.

Brad gave the cop his passport, and he and Manny got out and followed the smaller cop to the side of the road. While they stood there, the big cop went to the back of the jeep and started pulling cartons and luggage out and tossing them to the ground.

The two cops spoke to each other in Spanish. Brad turned to Manny for a translation, but as soon as Manny began, the larger cop yelled something at him.

"He say we are not to speak," Manny whispered.

After the jeep was unloaded, the smaller policeman came over to Brad. "Why do you have these supplies?" he asked, pointing to the boxes of gloves, dressings, and gauze piled on the ground.

Brad recovered quickly from his surprise at the man's flawless English. "As it says on my license and passport, I'm a doctor. I work for a medical clinic."

"Which clinic, please?"

"Nueva Vida. Near the ruins in Calakmul."

The cop stared at Brad. Brad turned to see the big cop drop to his knees, flip onto his back, then inch forward under the jeep, switching on the flashlight in his hand.

"You work for a clinic, in the jungle?" the smaller cop asked. Manny started to answer, but the cop held the flat of his palm up to Manny to silence him. The cop's eyes stayed on Brad.

"Yes."

"Forgive me if I find that difficult to believe."

The big cop shouted something in Spanish. When he crawled out from beneath the jeep, he was holding a small box covered in duct tape. After he gave the box to the smaller cop, his hand went to his holster and Brad's mouth went dry. The cop slipped the gun out and pointed it at Brad.

"Do not move," the smaller cop said quietly.

It took the officer a couple of minutes to peel enough duct tape off the box to remove the lid. He examined its contents for a few seconds, then turned it toward Brad.

Brad read the labels on the rows of small vials. The tiny type on each one was the same: *Fentanyl.*

"I find it hard to understand," the policeman said as he grabbed Brad's shoulders to turn him around, "why a doctor would need to carry narcotics taped to the underside of his car."

As Brad felt the cold steel of the handcuffs bite into his wrists, he wondered the very same thing.

Chapter Twenty-Two

Graft Versus Host

BRAD KNEW THREE things: he was alive, alone, and in trouble.

The last time he saw Manny, he was being put in the big cop's cruiser. Manny hadn't uttered a word when he was cuffed and led away. But when his eyes met Brad's, they said everything.

At first, the panic they telegraphed moved Brad to try to summon Manny's courage. Brad had raised his head, clenched his jaw, and nodded to his friend.

It was that moment of crisis that revealed that Manny was, indeed, a friend. At some point during their weeks standing together over the operating table, they'd crossed the boundary between mentor and trainee. The sight of Manny's shackled wrists as the big cop marched him away pierced something deep within Brad, revealing the strength of the bond they'd formed.

But when the small cop put Brad in the back of his cruiser and placed a black hood over Brad's head, the alarm Brad had seen in Manny's eyes inspired something other than courage. In the darkness that descended, the memory of Manny's gaze sparked Brad's own fears.

Those fears threatened to grow to terror; Brad tried to quell them with the techniques he'd developed to master other crises in his life. After a few minutes of deep breaths, he felt the jackhammering carotid pulse in his neck settle enough to give his mind a chance to come up with a better plan than the instinctive response to flee or fight.

But there was no way to think himself out of being bound, blindfolded, and whisked away to some unknown place in a foreign land. The best he could do was concentrate on the steady hum of the cruiser's wheels. Mile after mile, he tried to hold on to the sound so he wouldn't lose his mind.

He had no idea how long he'd been doing that when the cruiser came to a stop. The door beside him opened with a pop. "Stand up," the cop said. His hands guided Brad out of the car and walked him a few feet before Brad heard another door open with a squeak. He was guided into the back seat of what felt like a different type of vehicle. When it started moving, there was no humming mantra for Brad to lose himself in this time. And the longer they bounced and rocked along a far rougher road, the darker Brad's visions became of where and how this ride might end.

He had a long time to consider those fears. When the vehicle finally stopped, Brad heard a new voice. "Get out," it said. Brad stood, and a hand took his arm to guide him. "Step up," the voice said, and the hands ushered him over a threshold where a blast of air-conditioned air sent a chill down his sweat-covered spine. Then the hands led him down a corridor where their footsteps echoed. They walked and turned and turned again. When they stopped, Brad heard the jangle of keys, then felt the cuffs slip from his wrists. The hood was whisked off his head just before a steel door swung shut behind him with a bang. His hands flew to his ears to muffle the hollow echo ricocheting through the tiny space he stood in.

Brad spun in a slow circle to examine the six rectangles that confined him in an eight-by-eight-foot cell. Everything in it was white, from the concrete floor to the cinder-block walls to the ceiling high above, which was inset with a flat fixture that splashed cold light across the room. Brad traced the ceiling's outline to find the tiny white cylinder of a security camera staring down on him with its single glassy eye. The only other items in the space were a concrete bed with a thin mattress and a steel sink-and-toilet combo, both painted white as well. There was no window, only a small ventilation grate high on one wall.

He turned in place a few more times before spotting one final feature: a single recessed panel at the bottom of the door. Like every other surface in the room, there wasn't a single mark on it. The cell and everything in it looked like it had never been used.

He gave another long look at the video camera before moving toward the bunk. He stayed standing when he reached it, struck by the feeling that sitting on the bed would be the final act required to make his predicament real. So there he stood, once again trying to quell the rising sense of panic in his gut by engaging his brain.

He thought about the first part of the long silent ride that had brought him here. Now he realized just how strange that silence was. Didn't Mexican police use radios to stay in contact with one another? The one in the cop's cruiser never made a single squawk. Brad's eyes stayed fixed on the rough surface of the concrete floor under his feet as his mind started examining the other curiosities of his arrest.

Why had two cruisers pulled them over instead of one? And why had the second cop thought to look under the car?

Drug trafficking was a fact of life in Mexico, of course, but Brad found it hard to believe that dispatching pairs of police cars to pull over and search every speeding vehicle was standard procedure, even here.

Even stranger than the drug bust was the place it had landed him in. He'd had plenty of time to envision what a Mexican jail might look like during his long ride. He supposed he should be happy that there were no cutthroat cellmates in this clean, quiet room. But it was still one more unsettling surprise in a day that had completely upended his world.

Then there was the question of the cached fentanyl. Anyone at Nueva Vida could have been motivated to steal the lucrative stash of opiates the clinic kept on hand to treat severe post-op pain. Brad had only glanced at the carton's contents that the cop flashed at him, but there might have been as many as fifty vials nestled there. Their street value could easily total a hundred grand, maybe more. He found it hard to believe that either Manny or Aldo was a drug smuggler, but *someone* had stashed the clinic's drugs to sell them on their next trip with the jeep.

He stood and stared, going over every other detail of the past few days, looking for some clue as to what had brought him here. But thinking only inspired more questions. Finally, Brad did the only thing he could: he lowered himself onto the bunk, stared at the wall, and waited for answers to come.

+

Maybe he slept. He must've slept because he found himself lying down. But with no window and no break from the artificial light, no sound seeping through the walls, no phone, no watch, no visitors, no variables at all in this prison, it was hard to tell what time it was—or if time was passing at all.

He stood up and used the toilet, trying not to think about the camera aimed at him from above. The moment he turned on the water in the sink to rinse his hands, he heard a swift swish followed by a clatter. He spun around just in time to see the small panel in the bottom of the door slide shut behind a bowl of food resting on the floor.

He carried the bowl, which held some type of stew and a spoon, to his bunk. He was at once ravenous and cautious about what he was about to consume. He took a tentative bite, then another. There was something bitter mixed in with the bits of meat and vegetables, but he was so hungry he ate it all.

An hour later Brad's stomach flipped. He rushed to sit on the toilet, then stood up slowly when he was done and steadied himself against the sink as he washed up. He returned to his bunk and sat motionless, waiting for the dizzying waves of nausea to die down. The queasiness passed, but the woozy feeling grew stronger.

Brad crossed his arms over his chest and hugged himself tightly while he tried to clear his mind. He pursed his lips and concentrated on controlling his breath to slow the rush of blood in his head. As he stared at the horizontal grid of cinder blocks on the wall, things began to change.

The lines in the grid wavered, settled, then wavered again. After a moment, Brad saw that the periphery of each block expanded slightly as he inhaled, then settled again with each exhale. He took a deeper breath and watched as the grid of lines curved even wider, then slowed his breath and saw them settle at the exact same speed with which he exhaled. The room was breathing. It was breathing with Brad.

His eyes raced over the wall, looking for some part of it that wasn't moving, someplace stable he might rest his eyes and mind. He spied a spot of green in the corner; he climbed off the bunk and crawled across the concrete floor for a closer look.

A single sprout of clover had somehow struggled through the seam between the wall and floor. Brad inspected the delicate network of veins radiating from the point where the plant's leaves joined its stem. The pattern shimmered, then expanded, filling Brad's field of view as it grew larger and larger until he was looking down on a scene he knew well. It was one he'd surveyed often as a boy, nestled in the upper boughs of the ancient oak tree that stood behind his childhood home. The soft mottled texture of the clover's surface had reformed and resolved into an eagle's-eye view of his father's coastal farm.

Brad's mouth dropped open at the sight of a thousand emerald fronds flickering and waving under an invisible sea breeze. Far off in the corner of the field, a spot of crimson bloomed like a dormant ember ignited by a ghostly wind. The speck began moving steadily in a straight line across the green.

Brad's eyes filled as his nose caught the scents of soil and tractor oil; his head spun with the power of the memory of the red flannel shirt his father always wore. Then tears spilled down his cheeks as Brad watched his father making his way through the corn.

He reached for the scene, but the tips of his fingers destroyed the lie of its scale, making it vanish in a flash to reveal the small, single plant, its sharp green outline clear against the blank white canvas of the floor. Then he noticed the shapes of the clover's leaves that he had missed before: three tiny green hearts joined at the tips to the thin green filament of the plant's stalk that made them one.

He sat back, sucked in a breath, and closed his eyes. Catherine's face, then Grace's, and finally his own appeared, painted on the inside of his eyelids in the same triple pattern as the clover's leaves, each chin pointed toward the other pair. The trio of portraits began to rotate, picking up speed as they spun.

Brad's eyes flew open as he crab-walked backward from the dizzy vision, now desperate for the respite of his featureless room. He stared at the cinder-block surface opposite him, relieved to find the grid of lines between the blocks had settled. He rubbed his eyes, then rested his vision on that steady white field.

At first he found its whiteness a comfort, like waking to the surprise of snow that had fallen during a long Maine night to promise the peace of a quiet winter day. But the more perfect he found that immaculate expanse, the more impure he felt, as if he were an antigen—a foreign body in a place he didn't belong, the graft the host was bound to discover, attack, and finally, destroy.

With that thought, the lines of mortar between the cinder blocks faded along with the pebbled white texture of the wall. The surface of the featureless plane glowed even brighter, then receded behind a shadowy rectangular frame that zoomed in like a reversed telescopic lens. When it stopped, it revealed a shining altar.

Brad scuttled farther until he'd backed into the room's far corner. He felt busy fingers fluttering over his groin. He brushed, then slapped his hands against his crotch, again and again, but those fingers would not stop.

Weeping freely, he opened his mouth to scream but made no sound. His stymied wail grew in his gut until it threatened to explode. But his tongue froze fast with the secret of his shame.

Brad turned his face to the square in the ceiling, seeking salvation from the light above. A string of familiar words began to play in his mind, drifting across the years from his place in the pew where he sat nestled against his mother's side.

"Lord, I am not worthy that You should come under my roof; speak but the word, and my soul shall be healed."

The litany played over and over in Brad's mind until the thoughts in his head manifested as sound, the prayer now sung by his own ten-year-old tongue. The light above grew stronger, but Brad drew away.

Over the next few seconds, or minutes, or hours, Brad turned to a refuge other than the one that beckoned above. Growing smaller and smaller, his arms wrapped around his legs as he hugged his knees to his chest, he tucked his head, and collapsed into a ball.

There, in the corner of that small, sterile cell, he retreated to the only place—the only one—he had ever placed his faith in. Brad clung to himself, and himself alone.

Chapter Twenty-Three

Thirteen Bowls

THERE WERE THIRTEEN bowls now. They lay in a line, each one the same shape, size, and color. White, of course. Brad had started washing them after bowl number four. They didn't really smell bad, but it gave him something to do.

It had taken him a long time to even think about eating from bowl number two. It had hovered in his hand, right over the toilet, filled with the same stew that had sent his body, mind, and soul spiraling the first time he ate it. But some stronger sense of self-preservation stilled his hand. If the only thing he could count on in this small, square nightmare was something to eat, did he really want to risk losing the one thing keeping him alive?

He set bowl number two down beside bowl number one, hoping his door would slide open again to reveal the choice of some other fare. He waited as long as he could and finally surrendered when his appetite outgrew his will. He gobbled the cold contents of bowl number two down before he could change his mind.

There was no bitter taste, no terrifying tour through his persona and past this time. It had taken him a while to piece together enough of his muddled mind to realize that he'd been given a hallucinogen along with his first meal. He took some comfort in knowing that the psychedelic experience came from a drug. During that horrific journey, he'd lost confidence in the power of his analytical skills to save himself. But he didn't lose his mind.

All the meals that followed bowl number two were the same: bland and completely benign. He had no idea how often the meals came or, more important, *why* they came.

Why was he here? What did whoever was behind this madness want? He'd been offered no chance to face his captors. No one had visited his cell or taken him someplace darker for an interrogation. He'd reached the point where he wondered if a beating would really be so bad. At least there'd be some human contact, some assurance that there were other people out there, walking and breathing, living their lives beyond the confines of this tiny room. Maybe he could even find some-one to bribe or bargain with. Or beg, if it came to that, if that was his only hope of getting out of this cage.

But nobody answered his calls, his yells at the door, his screams at the camera. (Had he *really* screamed?) Nothing changed except the number of bowls he kept company with. He'd spent—how long? Certainly hours, probably days (the possibility of *weeks* really scared him), stacking, sliding, spin-ning, and playing with them until he finally quit. Other than fingering the short whiskers of his new beard, it was the only game in town.

Finally, he'd set the bowls on the floor and arranged them to mirror just how small his life had become, putting them down one after the other, each identical and empty, stretching to take its place in a long—maybe endless?—line.

When the end did come, Brad was denied even the chance to put a face to his fears.

Under the ceaseless glare of the room's artificial sun, he'd lost all sense of circadian rhythm. He simply drifted off and drifted back with no memory of deciding to go to sleep, no awareness of when he awoke, or why the time for rest was done.

This time, it was different. This time he woke in darkness with the grip of strong hands around his neck.

"Turn over," he heard, and he could've cried—then did cry—at the welcome sound of another human voice.

The hands retreated when Brad turned onto his stomach, an instant before the hood slipped over his head. It was no surprise at all when he felt the cuffs clutch his wrists again.

✦

Life was running backward. He took the same blind trip down the winding hall, the same stumble over the threshold, felt the same shock between the cool of the building and the blast of heat from the tropical sun, the same slip into the back seat, the same long, bumpy car ride. But there was no change of vehicles this time before the sudden switch to a smoother ride. But eventually, the sound of the ride did change. The soft crunch of wheels rolling over crushed stone was comforting—at first.

As more miles rolled by, Brad began to understand that he was not being taken to the place he'd started from.

His pulse picked up. The sound from the car's wheels came in waves, their low rumble punctuated by the staccato throb of blood in his ears that seemed to echo within the confines of the hood. No breathwork could stop it this time. The man who'd had that capacity had been whittled away. The fragile core that remained had no such control. Brad could only listen in the darkness to the drumbeat of his own rising fear.

The car stopped with a skitter of gravel. Brad walked a wordless march and then was ordered to stop. Beads of sweat pricked his face and neck, ran in small streams down his legs and arms. He stood there, trembling, imagining that he was standing next to some shallow grave scratched from the earth. The faces of his family flashed in his head. He scraped enough sanity together for a single thought, perhaps his last: Would he hear the gun fire before the bullet pierced his brain?

✦

A thin wind whistled. A crow croaked its ragged caw. The tinkle of keys came with a click as the cuffs slipped from his wrists. The crunch of footsteps drifted away. An engine coughed and caught. Wheels faded to the whisper of his own breath, the only sound around.

Brad fumbled with the cord at his neck and slowly peeled the hood from his head. He turned to see an ocher-colored land of nothing but dry dirt and rock, dotted here and there with a few wisps of brush drained to the faintest green. All was set beneath the haze of white clouds that blocked both sun and sky. It was the most beautiful thing he had ever seen.

Then his parched throat grew tight as he did what he'd done so often in his cell, the thing he'd done so rarely in the life he'd lived before.

Brad wept.

✦

It might have been only a few minutes. He didn't know. Time was still new. At some point he looked down the rocky path that stood for a road and saw the black speck of a vehicle growing larger as it moved toward him.

It was still far off when he identified it. And with that recognition came an epiphany. And as it did, he realized it had been nibbling at the edge of his awareness ever since his capture. He'd retreated from the revelation, one that would expose him as a fool, the man Sam claimed he was in that Harvard pub years ago: the doctor drunk on playing God, too blinded by power and prestige to ever believe he could be a pawn in another man's game.

The SUV pulled up. The back door opened. Carlos stepped out.

His spotless white suit sparkled against the dull land. His face was blank, but his eyes were sharp as he walked over to stand in front of Brad. They regarded each other for a long moment. Brad couldn't think of a single thing to say.

Now that Brad was here in the light of day under an open sky with the possibility of tomorrow before him, the full weight of his capture, confinement, and unknown fate hit him hard. His knees buckled. Carlos moved quickly, catching Brad in a hug to keep him from falling to the ground.

The part of Brad that wanted to punch and kick and bite the arms that held him flashed once, grew fainter, and disappeared, as if extinguished in the fall down some deep and distant well. As Carlos led him to the car, Brad looked down to see his own feet shuffling through the dust, moving like the zombie he'd become. Then he lay down in the back seat and slept the sleep of the dead.

Chapter Twenty-Four

Recovery Room

H E WOKE WONDERING why he couldn't hear the sea. It took Brad a moment to realize that he wasn't in his childhood home and another to figure out why he'd thought he was: it was the scent of fresh-baked bread that had drawn him from his dreams, a smell he hadn't woken to since he was a boy.

He pushed the satin sheets aside and sat up to scan the kind of room he'd never find in Down East Maine. Its bright red walls fairly glowed against the dark brown timbers of its ceiling beams and door and window frames. The Mission-style architecture was complemented by the colorful fabrics spread throughout the room. All of them, from the heavy floor-length curtains to the plush bedspread and hand-woven rugs scattered across the terra-cotta floor, bore the bold geometric patterns of traditional Mayan designs.

His eyes drifted to the bathroom doorway. The hazy memory of standing under a stream of warm water in its walk-in shower floated back to him. He seemed to recall someone putting a stethoscope to his chest, maybe even feeding him something before he was tucked into this big bed.

He lay back down and watched the large carved blades on the ceiling fan turn as his thoughts spun through pieces of the past few days: the timeless time in the cell, the jarring blind drive, the shaky seconds waiting for death, the dizzy vision of the black SUV drawing near as his mouth went dry. Stress and dehydration might explain the lapses in his memory between those shaky mental snapshots—but they didn't explain why he was here.

He got up and went to the window for a glimpse of the world outside. The midday sun lit a sprawling yard surrounded by high stone walls. The short-cut grass glowed neon green against a bushy border of tropical blooms. At the far end of the lawn stood a sparkling fountain raining down in the center of a clear blue pool. Behind it, a small white gatehouse stood guard behind a tall black fence.

A flicker of movement drew Brad's attention to the far edge of the property. A distant figure walked briskly, his head swiveling from side to side. It took Brad a moment to recognize that the thing poking over the man's shoulder was the long barrel of a rifle.

A soft knock brought Brad away from the window. The heavy wooden door swung open, and Carlos came in carrying a tray of food. He gave Brad a quick nod and smile, placing the tray holding eggs, fruit, and a basket of golden-brown baked goods on the coffee table in the sitting area.

Carlos took a seat in one of the two armchairs and motioned Brad to the other. "I'm sure you have questions," he said. "But perhaps you would prefer to eat first? You are lucky," he continued, picking up the basket and tilting it to show Brad the sugar-glazed loaves nestled inside. "Julieta made *campechana*, a sweet bread she will bake only for special occasions."

Brad approached but remained standing. "Why, Carlos?" was all he said.

Carlos let the basket hover in the air. "A small word that holds *many* questions, no?"

"Then let me start with one: Why did you imprison me?"

"Why did you steal my jeep and run off with my surgeon?"

"Because you killed Hector Vázquez, then lied to me about it."

Carlos put the basket down and shook his head slowly. "I have never lied to you."

"Another lie. You said you'd paid for the kidney I put into your uncle."

"I did not. I said that I did what was necessary to secure it. However, we did offer to pay Señor Vázquez—on several occasions, in fact. He had three chances to give me a call."

"Then you killed him."

Carlos spread his hands.

"And used your clever words to deceive me."

"My words were true. You believed what you *wanted* to believe. But I understand that, Brad. You are an American. Like most of your countrymen, you have more invested in the stories you tell yourself than in the truth."

"I know you're a murderer. That's no story."

"And I know that there are many stories that stand between you and your own crimes. For a surgeon, you are remarkably ignorant of the blood on your hands."

"I've never killed anyone."

"Not directly. But you've profited from the murders done by others, and I think that is much worse. The only difference between your crimes and mine, Dr. Baker, is time."

Brad could only stare in response.

Carlos walked to the window and pulled back the curtain. Julieta and one of Carlos's young sons raced onto the lawn.

Brad could hear their distant laughter as they chased a soccer ball across the grass.

"Tell me what you see," Carlos said.

"I see a beautiful family in a beautiful home that was probably paid for with the blood of innocents." If Brad's words shocked his host, Carlos gave no indication of it.

"Let me tell you how I came to have this family, this home," Carlos said, turning away from the scene. "My father, and his father, and his father before him, they were all farmers, growing corn and whatever other crops they could scratch out of the dirt to feed their children. They worked in fields not far from the resorts where the rich came to feast and play with their families. As a child, I worked alongside him, plowing and planting, weeding, gathering the harvest. It was hard work, but honest, you would say. Your own father, he was a farmer, yes?"

Brad nodded.

"So you know. But my father wanted to do more than just feed us. Little by little, he managed to put a bit of money away with the hope that me and my brothers and sisters, or at least some of us, might someday have a chance for a better life than he had. I have heard that aspiration called the American dream, but really, it is one that parents everywhere share.

"But my father's chance, our family's chance, for that life was destroyed. When I was a young man, our president—a man who lied about the election he lost to retain that position—accepted the North American Free Trade Agreement in a bid to hold on to his power. It was his way of trying to make Mexico a first-world country."

Carlos laughed. "But the results were quite the opposite for my family and many others like ours. NAFTA opened the gates for cheap corn to flow south from the U.S. Suddenly, our crops were worthless for anything but feeding our pigs and ourselves. My uncle Santiago saw what was happening. He tried to persuade my father to do what others were doing: grow the marijuana that your rich, bored countrymen were so hungry for. He saw it as the only way to survive the ruin of our economy.

"But my father was afraid. He did not have the will to do what needed to be done. I did. I left him and went to work for Santiago so I could do more than just survive."

"You went to work for a drug cartel," Brad said. "That's where you got the money to start Nueva Vida, to find the kidney that could save Santiago. But now that you have Nueva Vida, I'm guessing the murder of"—Brad laughed—"your *donors* isn't going to stop."

Carlos spread his hands. "I have the lives of my children, my grandchildren, and their children to think of, Brad. I am at the same point that your forefathers were when they came to America. They saw a land of endless opportunity for themselves and their progeny, but that dream was paid for with the murder of the Native Americans living there and the Africans they captured, enslaved, beat, raped, and killed. You have never had to think about what it cost for you to live the privileged life you lead."

Carlos pointed out the window again. Brad saw Julieta and her giggling son collapse onto the ground. "Like me, you watch over your beautiful family in your beautiful home. But make no mistake, like me, you have paid for all of it with the blood of innocents."

Julieta and her son got to their feet to resume their game. Brad frowned, searching for some way to take control of the conversation again. "Why'd you have me drugged?" he asked. "What reason on earth could you have for wanting me to lose my mind?"

"So you could find it, of course."

"How was taking away my sanity supposed to do that?"

"By replacing it with something different. Some would consider the experience you had a great gift."

Brad laughed and turned away, but Carlos continued. "Mayans called the land Nueva Vida is now on 'the Kingdom of the Snake' for good reason. They believed serpents represented the entry of divine forces into the small slice of reality that you and I consider the real world. For them, the trip you took would have been the equivalent of transubstantiation, the manifestation of God as flesh and blood that any good Catholic celebrates in the Holy Communion. The Mayans simply used hallucinogens instead of bread and wine. And, in my opinion, to much greater effect. The Catholic Church counts on the masses to blindly accept what they're told about the power of the world beyond our own. You had the privilege of seeing it for yourself."

"So, let me get this straight," Brad said, looking Carlos in the eye. "You threw me in a cell to free my mind?"

"To change it, at least."

Though Brad had woken feeling well rested, this conversation left him completely exhausted again. He sat down in the chair next to Carlos, put his head in his hands, and stared at the floor. "How long do you plan to hold me here?"

"You are not a prisoner. You are a guest in my home. You may come and go as you wish."

"Go where?"

"Anywhere."

Brad looked up. "And Manny—where is he?"

"Like you, Dr. Pena has been given some time to consider the terms of his employment."

"Have you freed him?"

"Not yet."

"What will happen to him?"

"That depends on him and on you. We have a long list of patients waiting. Your defection has upset a lot of powerful people. But if you're ready to get back to work, perhaps we can convince Dr. Pena to join you."

Brad chewed on his lip and, despite himself, glanced at the food on the tray. Like every other important conversation he'd had with Carlos, he found himself talked into a corner. He knew it was impossible to change Carlos's point of view, so he changed the subject instead.

"Can I call my wife? I'm sure she's frantic." Then Brad asked the question he should have asked first. "How long have I been gone?"

"One week," Carlos answered. "Your wife has called Nueva Vida several times. To her, I must confess, I *did* tell a story instead of the truth. I told her that you were called away on a medical emergency." Carlos laughed. "But I thought there was maybe some justice in telling her the same lie that you yourself told poor Aldo."

When Brad stayed silent, Carlos took a sheet of paper from his jacket pocket. "You've been through much, my friend. I think it best if you remain here as my guest for a few days more. Take some time to eat and rest until you feel like yourself again. When you do, you have many decisions to make, ones that will affect people other than you.

"After that, you may fly back to Boston if you wish. But I must tell you, if you do, there are other stories I am prepared to tell. Stories that will certainly follow you home and seal Dr. Pena's fate here."

Carlos unfolded the paper in his hand and laid it on the table beside the tray. "If you leave us, this is the first one I will share with my friends in the press. Do you remember what I told you on your first tour of Nueva Vida when we passed Octavio in the hall?"

Brad thought for a moment. "You said you believed in second chances. But never a third." Carlos smiled and nodded. When he was gone, Brad picked up the piece of paper and read.

Prominent Boston Surgeon Arrested for Drug Trafficking

Dr. Bradley Baker, senior transplant surgeon at Boston General Hospital, was arrested last week in Chetumal, Mexico, for the alleged theft of fifty vials of fentanyl, a synthetic opioid fifty to a hundred times more powerful than morphine. The street value of the drugs seized in the arrest by Mexican federal police is estimated to be over 100,000 USD. Police report that Dr. Baker was stopped for speeding while he and Dr. Manuel Pena, a fellow transplant surgeon at Nueva Vida, the Calakmul clinic where both physicians are employed, were on their way to the Chetumal airport. Federal officers said both men had airline tickets in their possession when arrested. Dr. Baker has been employed in Nueva Vida since taking a leave of absence from Boston General last March following the death of his patient, Reverend Samuel Kirby, who died during a kidney transplant that Dr. Baker performed. The death is currently under investigation and is the subject of a pending medical malpractice lawsuit over Dr. Baker's alleged negligence.

Chapter Twenty-Five

See Flower Be

BRAD'S CELL PHONE came calling the next morning. The last time he'd seen it, it was sitting on the dashboard of his getaway jeep. Now, when Brad woke up on his second day in Carlos's home, here it sat, parked in the same spot Carlos had left the news article that threatened to put Brad out of a job and into jail.

He picked it up and pushed the tiny button on its side. The screen flickered to life to show that the battery was low, but the signal-strength display showed every bar full. For the first time since he'd received the phone, Brad took a closer look at the small black rectangle he used so often.

When Carlos first gave it to him, Brad registered its sleek frame and glass face as just another iPhone knockoff. Now he toggled the phone off and on to see what logo flashed. None did. He flipped it over and found no markings on the phone's back either.

He turned it over again, thinking that he knew nothing at all about the device. Then he muttered a soft "shit" as he realized every call, text, and e-mail he'd sent or received on it had probably been seen or heard by someone in addition to the person it was meant for.

The same had to be true of his laptop, of course. And what about the communications *not* sent through those devices? Was all of Nueva Vida bugged? Snatches of conversations from the past three months began playing in Brad's mind. Instructions to his team in the OR, casual conversations in the cafeteria and halls, maybe even his talk with Manny in the jeep during their late-night flight, Carlos—and others—may have heard them all.

He looked at the phone again. It felt heavier. It was a long time before he finally moved a finger to dial Catherine's number.

Grace answered. "Dad?"

"Hi, honey. Sorry, I meant to call Mom."

"You did. Now she'll really be pissed she forgot her cell. She's been trying to get you for, like, a week."

"I know. I'm sorry, I—"

"Your boss told her what happened. She calmed down after that. He called her every day to tell her what you were doing. She would've totally freaked if he hadn't."

"I was, okay."

"Yeah, well, Mom didn't know that. You should thank the guy. 'God bless Carlos,' that's what Mom kept saying."

"Well, thank *you* for the update."

"How are those kids?"

"What kids?"

"The kids in that village. The ones that came down with the fever?"

Brad stayed silent as he tried to figure out Carlos's story.

"Dad?"

"Better. We, uh, we took care of it. How are you? How's Todd?"

Grace didn't respond.

"Grace?"

"We broke up."

"I'm sorry, honey."

"No, you're not. I could tell you didn't like him."

"How could I not like him? You didn't give me a chance to get to know him."

"You weren't home long enough to get to know him."

"Don't you think I'd rather be at home with you than here?"

"Then why aren't you?"

As the silence stretched between them, Brad tried to think of how to respond. He had more answers than ever to Grace's question, and more reasons than ever not to share them over the phone.

"I'll tell Mom you called," Grace said, and the line went dead.

✦

For the next two days, the only sign of Carlos that Brad saw was Carlos's family. Brad was free to come and go as he liked around the estate. He noticed other armed men in addition to the guard he'd spied patrolling the perimeter, but they steered clear of him.

Most of the other people he saw were women and children. Julieta welcomed entire families—probably extensions of her own, Brad realized—into her home. Every time her path crossed Brad's, she would smile and invite him to join them for dinner. And every time Brad declined, he'd find another tray delivered to his room.

The sound of a helicopter woke Brad on his final morning at the Cardoza estate. As Carlos ushered him aboard the chopper, Brad caught sight of Julieta in the window waving goodbye. As the helicopter rose to reveal the full size of the huge property, Brad wondered how much Julieta knew about just what it cost to keep her family in their handsome home. There was no way she could be completely ignorant of the life her husband led, but Brad knew that when the truth gets in the way of what people want, they tend to believe what they want to believe. And as soon as Brad had thought about Julieta, he remembered Carlos saying the same thing about him.

✦

A day later, Brad was back in surgery at Nueva Vida. For a moment, when he'd first spied the line of jeeps on his way into the clinic, he had the crazy thought of running again but discarded the idea as quickly as it came. Carlos might not wait until he reached the highway next time. It would be so easy for him to write another news story. Perhaps this one would be an account of his head surgeon's final rainforest run. In the jungle, there were so many ways to die.

So Brad did what he was trained to do and focused on the one thing he could control: the scalpel in his hand. And though that hand didn't betray the thoughts in Brad's head, he'd never been so glad to have a mask covering his face.

His new second in command at the table certainly seemed steady. Raúl Molina was Manny's complete opposite. The dyed-blond hair peeking out from under his surgical cap was straight and short, and Raúl was younger, too. So young that Brad had assumed the slight man in his OR that first morning was a new surgical tech until Rosa introduced him.

Brad had Raúl assist him and watched his new trainee carefully while they worked. Raúl spoke perfect English, and Brad could see the promise of good tissue sense in the long slender fingers of the man's steady hands. He answered every question Brad asked quietly but quickly and accurately. And though he was younger than any transplant fellow Brad had ever known, Brad saw no sign of trepidation in his eyes. If anything, they showed the hunger of a junior surgeon just waiting for the chance to take the knife in his own hand.

Raúl and everyone else in the OR knew that he was auditioning for that role. Brad could feel it in the tense mood that had settled over the team. Any doubts about Raúl's trial status were confirmed by the surgical schedule that Brad scanned. Over the past few months, he'd learned there were two sources for Nueva Vida's patients. The high rollers came from Kimberly Roke's New York City practice. The local patients were referred by a handful of doctors across the Yucatán. Despite the backlog of rich patients that Carlos mentioned, it was obvious that he wasn't about to start sending them to a brand-new team. Now Brad saw his poor pro bono transplant recipients for exactly what they were: practice dummies for the premium customers Nueva Vida was built to serve.

Brad's boss may have betrayed him and imprisoned his former second-in-command, but Brad felt there was one person whom he could still rely on. Most of his team lapsed into the same tentative performances that marked their first few weeks of surgery, but Rosa did everything she could to rally them. She was quicker than ever with her responses to Brad's questions and always delivered them in a tone that left no doubt that he was in charge. With every exchange, Brad felt the team inch a bit closer to the *esprit de corps* he'd worked so hard to instill in them.

During Brad's first week back, Rosa helped make surgery the one place in Nueva Vida where he could relax and lose himself in his work. After he scrubbed out, he looked for other distractions. He took longer runs in the jungle, tiring himself to the point where his exhaustion outweighed his worries so he could catch a few hours of sleep. Even then, there was no way to banish the demons that haunted his dreams.

Finally, after one particularly trying case, Brad walked to his bungalow and spied the faint path by its side that promised him a refuge other than the one he'd made of surgery. When he entered the greenhouse, he found the fertile world inside the glass dome looking even healthier than the one beyond its door. The large stone pot in the center was the only container in the place that didn't have green shoots and leaves spilling over its sides.

He went over to the potting table and started rummaging through the packages on the bottom shelf, reading snippets of Spanish before he found a bag of fertilizer. He grabbed a trowel, dropped the bag at the base of the planter, and started raking the top layer of soil. After a minute, he had the sense that he wasn't alone. He turned toward the door and sucked in a quick breath at the sight of Aldo standing there.

Aldo laughed, then pointed to the trowel in Brad's hand. *"No rastillar,"* Aldo said.

"Rastillar?"

Aldo mimicked Brad's raking of the soil.

"No raking?" Brad asked.

"Sí, no rake."

"I was going to add in a bit of fertilizer," Brad said, pointing to the bag at his feet. "I thought it might help prompt this thing to sprout." He pointed to the pot. "Nothing else in here seems to have a problem growing."

"No necesita fertilizante," Aldo said.

Brad frowned. "There must be *something* I can do to get this thing going."

"No do. See."

"Sorry, Aldo," Brad said. "I don't understand."

Aldo came over and held out his hand. Brad realized what Aldo wanted and handed him the trowel. Aldo grabbed the fertilizer too, put them both back on the potting table, then returned to Brad's side. He didn't say a word, just stood there with his face turned toward the big empty pot.

"Now what?" Brad finally asked.

"Now stop," Aldo replied. "No work. Stop. See flower, be flower."

"See flower, be flower?"

"Sí," Aldo said, laughing at the repetition of his rhyme. "See flower, be flower."

Brad gave the gardener a puzzled frown, and Aldo laughed again. Then the man's expression grew serious; his eyes narrowing as he looked intently into Brad's.

"No do," he said again. "See. See flower be. *After* see, *help* flower be."

Chapter Twenty-Six

Business Plan

THERE WERE A lot more holes to dig. Brad and Sam had cheered when the first clouds rolled in on that hot August afternoon. But the cool breeze had turned into a brisk wind. Every gust lifted more of the dirt at their feet and showered it down on them. It took all they had to keep their fifteen-year-old hands on the handles of the power auger they clutched as it chewed through the dry ground.

When Brad switched the auger off to give them a break, Sam spat on his palm and wiped at the fresh spray of dirt peppered across his cheeks.

"You're only making it worse," Brad said with a laugh, but Sam didn't laugh in return.

"Maybe we should stop," Sam said, tipping his head toward the graying sky. "I don't think we're going to finish before this storm starts."

"You heard my dad. He expects us to be done by the time he and my mom get back from Portland tonight. He wants to put the fence in tomorrow. We don't get paid if the holes aren't dug."

"It was sunny when he said that. We got *most* of it done. He wouldn't mind if we stopped because of the rain."

"He wouldn't, but I would," Brad said. "Now help me lift this son of a bitch. We hit another rock. It's your turn with the digging bar."

The two boys grunted as they heaved the machine out of the hole and laid it on the ground. Sam grabbed the long steel pole lying beside it but stopped before placing it in the hole.

"It's at least a mile to your house from here," Sam said. "Maybe more. We should check on my sister. That vegetable stand is farther from the house than we are. If I know Barb, she'll still be painting it even after it starts to pour."

"You worry too much, Kirby," Brad said, grabbing the pole from Sam's hand. "I'll dig this one out, but the next two are yours."

But Sam had been right. Midway through the next hole, a crack of thunder sounded so loudly that it dwarfed the auger's incessant whine. When the second boom came, the boys froze to stare at each other for an instant, then dropped the machine and ran.

For the next ten minutes, they sprinted across the open field, slitting their eyes against the stinging rain. When they reached the house, soaking wet and panting, it was empty. They ran back out to the porch just as Barb came in sight at the end of the long dirt road. They got her in the kitchen and toweled her off, but Brad had to find her a dry change of clothes to get her to stop shivering.

Brad's chiding of Sam for his caution that afternoon was a familiar refrain between the two friends. But now, as he sat in his bungalow in Nueva Vida and thought back to that distant summer day, Brad wondered what living a life driven by ambition had cost him. And Sam.

"I've spent my whole life chasing ideas on how to get ahead," Brad said, surprising himself by speaking the words aloud. He didn't speak his next ones, but they sounded louder in his mind: *You followed your heart, Sam. I should have done the same and stayed with you instead of rushing out to catch that plane.*

✦

When Brad saw he'd missed yet another call from his wife, he finally pushed the tiny green phone icon by her name.

"You had three chances to give me a call—" Catherine began.

"I know, I'm sor—"

"No. *I'm* sorry, Brad."

"*You* are? Why?"

Catherine laughed. "I wasn't sorry before. I was ready to rip every plant out of that goddamn greenhouse of yours when I couldn't get a hold of you. But then Carlos called to fill me in on where you were, and I felt horrible. When he told me how you'd diagnosed those kids when nobody else could, how you saved them…" Her voice broke. "I felt so *small*, Doc. And so proud of you."

Brad said nothing.

"Doc?" Catherine said.

"Thanks. It was no big deal," Brad said, hating himself—and Carlos—for the lie.

"I bet their parents thought differently."

"How's Grace?"

Catherine waited a beat before she replied. "Why do you do that?"

"Do what?"

"Change the subject when I'm trying to tell you how much I think of you."

"Sorry. It's this place. It's just—it's hard to stay in sync with you when I'm so far away," Brad said.

"You sound it."

"Sound what?"

"Far away. What's happening down there?"

Brad chewed on his lip and tried to think of any words that might sound better than the soft crackle of static stretching between Boston and the Yucatán.

"As far as Grace goes," Catherine said slowly, "I never thought I'd say it, but I miss Todd."

Brad laughed, grateful for the change in subject. "That bad?"

"At least she and I were talking when she was dating that dipstick, even if it was just to argue about him. Now I'm lucky if I get a dozen words out of her at dinner during the few nights she deigns to eat with me."

"It's probably for the best," Brad said. "I can't quite see Todd fitting in with the kids at Bowdoin."

"Yeah, well, it'll be a long, hot summer till then. Classes end next week."

"When's graduation?"

"Two weeks later, June twentieth. Any chance you can make it home?"

"I'll try, Cat. The—that trip to treat those kids, it put us pretty far behind."

"Sure. I know, Doc, it's just that it'd mean a lot to Grace. And I have to say, I could use a house call too. Especially a bit of that bedside manner of yours."

Brad's jaw clenched and he felt his face flush as he wondered who else was hearing this call. "I'll see what I can do," he finally said.

"Promises, promises."

✦

The long list of surgeries Brad performed over the next few days kept thoughts of his family far away. One morning, however, he woke with something Catherine had said in their last call playing over and over in his mind: *You had three chances to give me a call.*

He felt a fresh stab of guilt, but when he followed the feeling, he realized that wasn't why Catherine's words troubled him. On any other morning, he would've simply pushed the thought aside to get ready for another busy day. But as he lay there, Brad realized that busy wasn't getting him anywhere any longer. Aldo's strange suggestion in the greenhouse came to him: After *see,* help *flower be.*

"There was no flower to see," Brad mumbled. But maybe that was Aldo's point—he had to pause long enough to observe what was happening instead of rushing in to follow some plan mapped in the mind.

He turned over in bed to gaze out the window that faced the green thicket outside, peering deeper into it as he tried to find the secret he sensed hiding in Catherine's call. A small yellow bird broke from the brush as he stared. In the next instant, Brad realized that the message he was searching for hadn't come from Catherine; it came from Carlos, who had spoken the same words.

On Brad's first morning in his boss's home, Carlos told him that Hector Vázquez "had three chances to give him a call." Brad sat up straight in bed with the memory. He still didn't understand why those words were important, but by the time he scheduled his first meeting with Carlos since his return to Nueva Vida, he did.

✦

They were way past small talk now. Carlos simply gestured to the seat across from his desk when Brad walked into his office the next afternoon. Brad started talking the moment he sat down.

"It took me a while, Carlos, but I get it. I know how Nueva Vida works now."

Carlos motioned to someone standing in the doorway. Brad turned around to see one of the waitresses from Nueva Vida's cafeteria hurry in. She placed a tray with two cups of coffee on Carlos's desk.

"Thank you, Alma," Carlos said. "Please close the door."

When the door clicked shut, Carlos picked up a cup, and turned the tray to offer the other one to Brad. "So," he said, "how do you believe Nueva Vida, as you say, *works*?"

"Your partners want to make money—at any cost," Brad said, ignoring the coffee. "But I'm guessing you're the voice of reason among them. The one who points out the *true* costs of the business you do."

Brad looked at the closed door behind him, then leaned closer to Carlos and said in a low voice, "I'm guessing offering to pay Hector Vázquez for his kidney was *your* idea. You were the one who kept upping the price in those three chances you gave him to accept those offers. But that was before others decided there was a different way to get a kidney from him."

Carlos took a sip from his cup, placed it on his desk, and raised his eyes to meet Brad's. "You can speak freely in this office, Brad. But only in this office and perhaps a few other rooms in Nueva Vida designed for these kinds of conversations. Now that you have, shall we say, moved into upper management, I can share the details about our clinic's security protocols with you."

"Understood. That makes things easier."

"Good. Now, why don't you tell me exactly what you have to say."

Brad poured a hit of cream from the small pitcher that Alma had left next to his cup, gave it a stir, but still didn't drink. "I think," he said, setting the spoon down carefully, "that you have a longer view than your partners do of just how profitable Nueva Vida could become. Killing for kidneys is cheap in the short run. But it's risky. What if I told you that there's another way to get all the donors you need by supplementing your cadaveric kidneys with a steady supply of paid live donors as well?"

Carlos gave his beard a stroke. "I'm listening."

"The first thing you showed me when I came here was the kind of pro bono work you're doing to keep the locals happy."

"That's a very cynical view."

"Do you deny that you're investing in those communities for the PR value?"

"What I deny is the polarized perspective that is so typical of you Americans. Those people are my countrymen. Is it so hard to believe that I want them to profit along with Nueva Vida?"

"If that's true, there's a way you can put your working capital to better use by doing both."

"Go on."

Brad looked at the door again, then pulled his chair even closer to Carlos's desk. "Concentrate all your current pro bono efforts in one area and increase the budget. Establish medical clinics throughout the Yucatán. It wouldn't take a lot of cash to set each one up. I know how to do it from the clinical rotations I did in rural Maine as a medical student."

Carlos pursed his lips for a second. "I see the benefits to the poor and to our public relations, Doctor, but certainly not to Nueva Vida's bottom line."

"It may take time, but it will come."

"How?"

"From the database you'll build from every single patient who walks through those clinics' doors."

Carlos took another sip of coffee, and when he did, Brad could see that he saw Brad's vison too.

"Their blood," Carlos said as he set his cup down again.

"Their blood," Brad echoed. "You supplement the potential donor data that you've tapped into in the major metropolitan hospitals with a network of smaller facilities. But this time, you'd build the network and run it. I'm guessing your government partners would grant you a lot of leeway in your clinics' patient protocols in exchange for their free health care. You could start with HLA testing, maybe even eventually move to a model where you freeze samples for cross-matching against potential organ recipients to test for antibody response. I could work up the model for the database, but I'd need programming help, preferably from someone with a medical background. Manny would be—"

"Given the right directions, the programmer would not need to be a doctor. But I think you know that, Brad. Your concern for Dr. Pena is admirable, but I have to tell you, negotiations for his continued employment are not going well."

"Let me talk to him. If he knew that this plan would end the kill—"

"It would take a lot of time and money to set up such a system across all of the Yucatán," Carlos said.

Brad opened his mouth to steer the conversation back to Manny, then shut it again. Every part of the plan he'd laid out so far benefited Nueva Vida. He knew Manny's role in it wasn't critical, and Carlos had called him on it.

"It would take a while to set up the whole system," Brad began again, slowly, "but you'd be profiting from it long before it was completed. You'd keep costs low by providing only the most basic health services to patients in each facility."

"And with enough patients," Carlos said with the slightest of smiles, "the supply of matching donors willing to sell their kidneys would certainly rise."

"High enough to convince your partners that they don't need to take the risk of killing them," Brad said. "You know it's the right move, Carlos, one that'll reduce the likelihood of murder charges that you're risking now and pay huge profits in the end. A plan like this could even pave the way for this place to go completely legitimate one day. If the rest of the world follows Iran's paid-donation model, Nueva Vida would be positioned to be its leader when it did."

"Perhaps," Carlos said. "I don't expect you to believe me," he continued, swiveling in his chair to glance at the neatly trimmed grounds outside his office window, "but nothing would make me happier." He turned back to Brad with a question. "And what would make you happy, Brad?"

"A flight home. But there's only one way I can see that happening."

"And that is?"

"Promote me."

Carlos's eyebrows rose, but Brad stayed silent.

"Promotions are based on job performance," Carlos finally said.

"How's your uncle doing, Carlos?"

"Very well, thanks to you. But you have already received a bonus for that job."

"What bonus?"

"Your life."

"I want more."

Carlos laughed. "What is more valuable than that?"

"My family's future."

"If you want more, you'll need to give Nueva Vida more in return."

"I just presented a plan to do that."

Carlos's eyes narrowed. "Some of my partners might not be willing to wait the length of time it takes for that kind of investment to pay off."

Brad finally took a sip of his coffee as he got ready to conclude his pitch.

"I have more to offer," he said. "Something that will yield an immediate increase in the quality of organs available for transplant."

"Cadaveric organs?"

"Yes."

Carlos stayed silent for a moment before he replied. "Even with your perfusion drug, the paper you presented shows that a cadaveric kidney treated with ReNovus is, at best, at least three years short of the twenty-year life span of a live-donor organ. Our customers want the best kidneys money can buy."

"That paper was based on older data, not the latest trials I was running just before I came to work for you. Even Peter Webb hasn't seen those results. He likes to be updated only on confirmed ones."

"So you're sure about the extended life span?"

"I am. I ran the trials enough times to be sure. I wanted to do one final run before I shared the results with Peter and Boston General, but they're solid. I'm certain that we've got a drug that makes the life span of a cadaveric kidney good for twenty years, at least,—equal to a live donor's organ."

"That may be good for Boston General, but how does that help us?" Carlos asked.

"We make Nueva Vida the sole licensee of ReNovus. We do the first phase of clinical trials here on a broad body of transplant patients, capitalizing on the wealth of cadaveric organs Mexican law has made available."

"Boston General will never agree to that."

"They will if I sell it to them. Half the board wants me out because of Sam Kirby's death. I'll tell them I'll resign if they sanction Nueva Vida's initial proprietary use of ReNovus. BG grants you an exclusive license while we prove the drug's value down here. They get me off their hands, capitalize on the public relations value of helping a developing country, and still rake in the profits once the exclusion on the license ends. And when it does, we ensure Nueva Vida still has rights to its use—at no additional cost."

Carlos's eyes locked on Brad's in a gaze so intense that Brad felt like Carlos could read every thought in his head. But Brad stared right back. He had nothing to hide.

"And I'm supposed to simply trust you? Give you a smile and a wave as you hop on a plane and hope you'll talk to your board and not a federal agent?"

"Of course not. Before you send me off, you bring me all the way in, Carlos, way past upper management. You hold a press conference. We make the kind of noise that can be heard clear back to the States. You announce me as Nueva Vida's new chief operations officer, double my salary, and throw in triple as a signing bonus. Then you introduce me to your government and health-care associates. We take lots of pictures of me smiling with all of them while I shake their hands."

Brad stopped to let his boss take in his words. Carlos stared past him at the wall, but Brad knew what he was really looking at: the vision of just how rich, and powerful, Nueva Vida could become.

"Your raise and bonus secures your family's future. Your promotion secures ours," Carlos said.

"Exactly. Once your money is in my bank account and my picture's plastered in the papers, nobody will believe I wasn't a willing partner in all that's happening here, even if I was crazy enough to talk about it."

Brad's eyes drifted to a picture on the desk of a beaming, much younger Carlos in a tux, one arm around the waist of his new bride. "But what I'm hoping," Brad continued, "is that, in a couple of years, when the first clinics are set up and the ReNovus pipeline is in place, you'll allow me to spend more time with my family."

Brad faced Carlos directly to say what came next. "But I know I'll need to return here whenever you want me, Carlos. Like you said, the rich are always going to get what they want. I'm just trying to do the same."

"As I mentioned," Carlos answered, "even if I agree to all of this, I'm not sure my partners will."

"You were able to convince me to go all in on this place," Brad said, rising to leave. Convince them."

Chapter Twenty-Seven

Data Scan

THE TIME FOR moral arguments was done. Brad ignored the screen in front of him in his new office in Nueva Vida, mentally reviewing the business plan he'd shared with Carlos. He sat back in his chair, satisfied that it was based on cold calculations alone. More kidneys from more clinics and cadaveric organs perfused with ReNovus yielded higher profits at lower risk than killing donors did. He hadn't bothered to mention the humanitarian value of sparing lives. He finally understood that, here in the jungle, the innocent were the first to die.

So far, his pitch to Carlos hadn't gotten a response from the cartel, but Brad had received a change in his schedule. Two days after they'd met, he logged onto Nueva Vida's intranet to see that Dr. Antonio Garcia had taken his place in surgery. Brad had yet to meet the guy. And every time he spotted members of his team in the cafeteria or anywhere else on the campus, they avoided his gaze.

Except for Rosa. She met his eyes as she walked down the other side of the hallway in Nueva Vida one morning, staring so intently at Brad that he'd stopped and waited for her to speak, but she never broke stride. Brad watched her as she continued past him, padding down the corridor in her white sneakers and green scrubs until she disappeared around a corner.

He saw Rosa again one evening, surprised to find her in her office hours after the rest of the surgical team was gone. "What are you doing here so late?" he asked.

She kept her eyes on her screen and typed. "I'm always here at night."

"Don't you get tired after a full day in surgery?"

"I take a nap afterward. I don't need much sleep. And it's quiet here at night, nobody to bother me while I'm trying to get work done."

Rosa kept typing without looking up. Brad got the message and left.

Another thing that changed after Brad's talk with Carlos was his access to Nueva Vida's digital world. After Carlos gave Brad a quick tour of some of the rooms in the back part of the clinic that had been off-limits before, he led him to the new office where Brad sat now.

Carlos introduced him to Felipe, the chunky twenty-something Mexican computer geek who was at Brad's disposal to help him navigate Nueva Vida's intranet. Brad's job, for now at least, was to familiarize himself with the existing system. That was the first step before he added his proposed clinics' potential paid donors into Nueva Vida's cadaveric-kidney database—*if* Carlos's associates green-lighted Brad's plan.

On the first day in his new role, Brad found it almost impossible to concentrate. Felipe kept popping in to check on him, though Brad had learned all he needed to know from the chatty guy during the digital tour of the system Felipe gave him in their first hour together. Even more distracting were the ambient sounds of a working transplant clinic that seemed to be getting along just fine without Brad at the helm.

After a sleepless night following that first long day, Brad stopped by Carlos's office to see if he could change his hours. "It is for you to decide when and how you work, Brad," Carlos said. "You have almost the same clearance that I do to come and go around Nueva Vida. Your fingerprint will now unlock most doors on campus, and most of our computer network is open to you as well. You can see what we do, just as we can see what you do. There is really no need for us to keep secrets from each other now. Wouldn't you agree?"

So here Brad sat, at ten o'clock on a Monday night, his brain percolating from the second cup of coffee he just drank as he tried to concentrate on the rows of data before him. Though he was well-versed in reading medical charts, he had two challenges in interpreting these: First, they were imported from dozens of hospitals and clinics, each using its own format for organizing information. Second, they were in Spanish.

His Spanish had improved a bit during his three and a half months in the Yucatán, but he still spoke a pidgin version that brought more laughs than responses from his peers. His skill in navigating the human body just didn't seem to translate into unlocking the secrets of foreign tongues. He knew where the neurological key to doing that lay: the Wernicke's area, the region of the brain responsible for speech comprehension. But try as he might, he could never get the neurons packed into that small portion of his left temporal lobe to fire up his fluency.

The translation software Felipe installed helped. After a week using the system, Brad was getting quicker at locating a patient's gender, race, age, and blood type in their medical chart. Some even had the HLA tissue-typing records Manny had told him were now being included at Nueva Vida's request—or demand. Brad had no doubt that more would follow as the cartel continued to pressure the medical institutions it had infiltrated to include those blood tests in their admissions protocols.

But tonight, Brad was venturing into new digital territory, and doing so carefully. He knew at least one of the tiny video cameras posted all around campus was probably watching him. And he suspected that his digital journey through Nueva Vida's database was being tracked, click by click, as well. So instead of scanning for specific information, he began a full chronological review of all of Nueva's Vida's reformatted records from day one. If questioned by Carlos, he would say he was simply reviewing the database to find ways to streamline it.

Nueva Vida's medical charts were easier to evaluate than the mishmash of imported records he'd scanned before. Each entry was consistently formatted, and after a few entries, Brad knew exactly where the information he was looking for would appear. Though there were no names attached to the donor data, the words and numbers that presented their biological portraits were easy to identify.

There were a lot more records in the database than he'd expected to find. The names of the surgeons changed often. Almost all the patients appeared to be Hispanic, and Brad wondered how many of these guinea pigs were still suffering from the post-op complications caused by unskilled hands. How many had never made it off the table at all? And would any of the well-to-do patients who walked out of Nueva Vida smiling at the brighter future that now dawned for them ever know how much pain and death their new lives had caused?

Finally, Brad reached the record he'd wanted. He felt his pulse quicken when he saw Santiago Diaz's name, but he kept the pace of his scrolling consistent. And though Hector Vázquez's name wasn't on the record, the donor data that identified him was.

Brad kept his eyes on the screen, but his thoughts lay far away, on the dim hope that the data he'd just scanned had inspired. Here was proof that Carlos's uncle walked off the operating table with Hector Vázquez's kidney. And when he did, Santiago Diaz carried something else within him as well—the DNA fingerprint that proved his new lease on life had been paid for by the murder of another man.

Chapter Twenty-Eight

Double Dose

THE JUNGLE CLEARING made for a pretty poor office. But it was private, so Brad hunched over a sheet of paper with a pencil in his hand and worked on a draft of the e-mail he planned to send. After every two or three words, he swatted a mosquito. A thin thread of blood from the last one he'd nailed marked the middle of the page.

While his eyes were on his note, his ears stayed alert, straining to catch any sound different from the buzzes and birdcalls drifting through the humid air. When he finished the last line, he read the message three times, struck a match, and watched the paper collapse in a curl of ash and flames.

An hour later in the shower, he went over the note in his mind again, letting the cool spray refresh him after his long run. Even here, with the water running over his face in the bathroom of his bungalow, he was careful not to move his lips as he went over the note in his head. By the time he toweled off, he had the message down.

He went to the fridge and grabbed a beer, the final prop for his scene. Ever since returning to Nueva Vida, he'd lived every second of his life as if he were on camera, never knowing when he actually was. He'd been surprised how easy it was to act cool once you got used to the idea of someone watching you. It was hard only when you had something to hide.

He set the brew by his laptop, took a sip, and began.

Dear Peter,

Sorry it's been a while. Work backed up after I was called away to treat some children with dysentery in a village not far from here. Azithromycin and IV fluids did the trick. All recovered well.

There were some staff changes while I was away, but all in all, I've been impressed by my team's skills. The standard of care here is quickly rising to match the one we've set at BG.

Since it looks like it might be quite some time till I get back home, I wanted to ask you to check in with Stevens on the latest numbers from the lab. Data was trending toward some pretty exciting results before I left. As usual, I wanted to verify them before I shared them with you. Stevens should have conclusive stats by now.

We're getting close to matching live-donor-organ life spans with ReNovus's latest formulation. I think Nueva Vida may be the best place to scale up clinical trials before we publish results again. I have ideas about how that might work and look forward to discussing more with you when I make it home. You might even want to feel out a few members of the board about that idea.

Thanks for your thoughts on this plan. In the meantime, send some of that glorious Boston June weather down to us,

*will you? It's godawful hot here in the jungle, but the work
is going well!*

Best,

Brad

He sent the note and took a longer pull from his bottle,
allowing himself to actually enjoy the beer this time. Then he
squared his shoulders, looked at the screen, and started pecking again. Writing to Catherine would be easier. And harder.

He'd had no reason to practice this message. His notes to
Catherine were a lot shorter now. Though his wife had always
been more comfortable than him in pouring her heart out on
the page, Brad tried his best to answer in the same vein.

But not now. Not when others were reading every word
he wrote. He did the best he could to warm up three short
paragraphs before hitting Send. Grace hadn't responded to his
last e-mail. He hated to admit it, but he was glad.

A birdcall floated to him from somewhere in the jungle,
the same strange rising, chortling squawk he always heard
this time of the day. He'd asked Aldo about it, finally resorting to imitating the call. Aldo did his own interpretation, a
much more accurate one. "Is chachalaca," he said, laughing.
The bird's call had become Brad's alarm clock. Now it echoed
again. He closed his laptop and headed to work.

✦

By now he was used to the night noises here in Nueva Vida,
what few there were. The buzz of the floor polisher as an
orderly worked the hall, the walkie-talkie's squawk as security made their rounds, the constant hum of the AC—they all
faded into the background as Brad started another shift before
his screen.

Tonight, he was working on a draft of standard operating procedures for the new clinics, even though he still wasn't sure they'd ever break ground. With his surgical schedule cleared and no word on the business plan he'd pitched to Carlos, Brad had begun to worry that maybe the cartel was making other plans for him.

Long runs in the jungle and deep dives into work were the only things keeping him sane. Sketching out a patient-intake protocol was the form the latter was taking now. But it was hard to stay focused on the task. After a few seconds, Brad realized that it was because his concentration had been broken by a different kind of sound.

It was distant, but sharp—a crack followed by a thin tinkling. He walked out of his office and tilted his head toward the far end of the hall. No crack and tinkling this time, just a squeak of rubber on tile, then a soft whoosh, like something being dragged across the floor.

Later, Brad would think back on the seconds that followed, wondering why he'd crept so cautiously toward the noise, why he'd opened the door to the doctors' lounge only an inch at a time, why his body seemed to know it needed to move so slowly and carefully.

It took him a second to register what he was seeing in the lounge. At first, he thought someone had simply dumped a pile of scrubs beside the remnants of a broken drinking glass, its bottom half intact, the broken rim jagged.

An instant later, the pile of scrubs resolved into two bodies: a small woman just barely visible under the sprawling hulk of a very big man.

Brad began to ease the lounge door closed again, convinced he'd stumbled on a tryst. Then he remembered there was a couch inside. Why on earth would the lovers choose the hard tile floor for their bed? He inched the door open again.

The bodies had shifted in those few seconds. Now Brad had a clear view of the smaller one. His eyes moved up from the woman's waist until he found himself staring straight into a familiar face—with an unfamiliar expression. Brad's eyes opened as wide as hers, as Rosa's fear ignited his own.

The man on top of her had one hand on the waistband of Rosa's scrubs, pulled low to reveal her thigh. The guy was big—much bigger than Brad. Brad couldn't see his face, but he knew there was only one person on Nueva Vida's staff who was that large: Octavio.

Brad was about to look around for some kind of weapon when he saw that Octavio had one in his hand. It was so small that if Rosa hadn't turned her head at just the right moment, Brad might not have seen the silver flash of the scalpel's blade at her neck.

Now Brad moved even slower as he closed the door and began to back away. His mind raced as he turned in a full circle in the hall, willing the security guard to appear. He didn't.

He moved toward the fire extinguisher on the wall with thoughts of snatching it, running back, crashing through the door, and bashing it into the back of Octavio's head. Then he stopped, thinking just how easily the blow could drive the man's hand forward to bury his blade in Rosa's neck.

Brad stared into space, imagining how long it might take to find help and everything that could happen—would happen—to Rosa in that time. Then he focused on the sign posted by a doorway down the hall. He took a dozen quiet steps away from the doctors' lounge and then broke into a dead run toward the surgical suites.

He'd had more than one conversation with his team about the need to keep the OR organized. As he ran into OR 1, he hoped the surgeon who'd replaced him wasn't quite as concerned with squaring away supplies.

But the room was clean. There was no scalpel lying about that Brad could use. He was just about to sprint to the other OR when he saw the anesthesia cart. Resting on its top lay a tiny vial. He rolled the container with the tip of his finger. The liquid in the 10-milliliter syringe sparkled. The label read SUCCINYLCHOLINE. Brad knew sux paralyzed more than just a patient's airway muscles. It performed that same trick on every single muscle in the body.

The sounds from the doctors' lounge were louder as Brad ran toward it. Just before he reached the door, he heard Rosa yell, *"¡No! No te—"* Her words cut off by the sharp slap of skin hitting skin. Brad stopped, willing his hammering heart to slow down. He inched the door open.

The bodies had shifted again. Rosa was still flat on her back, but her head was turned away, probably due to the force of Octavio's huge hand.

Octavio had dropped the scalpel and was kneeling over Rosa, his palm pressed to her throat, his knee planted high between her thighs. His other hand pulled at the waistband of his scrub pants. Rosa still wore her top, but her own pants were gone.

Now Brad drew on the skill he used to prep for surgery: visualizing every step he would take, down to the slightest move.

It would be harder for Brad to make his move now since Octavio no longer had his back to him. Brad kept a steady eye on his target and drew in a deep breath, shifting his eyes for the second it took him to pop the cap off the syringe in his hand. In that instant, he saw the spot where the needle could do its job quickly.

With his next breath, Brad charged through the door. He was three steps inside before Octavio's head swiveled toward him.

Octavio froze. That moment was all it took for Brad to close the distance to him. He swung, stabbed the needle into the side of Octavio's neck, and sank the plunger halfway down before Octavio moved.

Octavio rose and roared. Rosa crab-walked backward the instant she was free.

Octavio brushed the syringe from his neck and came for Brad, grabbing the back of a metal folding chair along the way.

Octavio swung the chair. Brad dropped to the floor, feeling a rush of air on the back of his neck as the chair just cleared his head.

A bright spike of pain bloomed in the back of Brad's calf at the same time that he felt a warm stream of blood flow from his nose. Octavio grabbed Brad's leg tighter and began dragging him. Brad twisted onto his back and kicked with his free leg until the heel of his shoe connected with Octavio's hand.

"Puta madre!" Octavio screamed, releasing Brad and curling his hand against his chest. Brad twisted to all fours and crawled toward the table in front of an alcove at the end of the room. When he reached it, he slipped under it and popped out on the table's far side.

Octavio took a half dozen lurching steps toward him, grabbed the end of the table, and spun it 180 degrees. Brad was surprised by the expression on Octavio's face: the giant on the other side of the table was smiling at him.

Then Brad saw why his attacker grinned. Octavio had cut off any chance of escape from either side.

Octavio spread his arms, gripped the table's edge, bent his knees, and, in one swift motion, flipped it onto its side; the sharp sound of cracking tile and splintering wood echoing off the walls. For an instant, all was quiet. In that moment Brad caught a glimpse of Rosa. She was perched on the back of the couch on the far side of the room, her eyes and mouth open wide.

Octavio dropped, put his shoulder against the underside of the table and drove it forward like a linebacker as Brad retreated toward the wall.

Then—Octavio stopped, stood up, and froze.

When the two men's eyes met, Brad no longer saw a smile on Octavio's face. His mouth opened and closed like a fish gasping for air.

One of Octavio's hands rose palm forward, the fingers curling and flexing like a child waving bye-bye. His other arm shot out and up, then fell with a spastic jerk.

He stood there wobbling in place, for a moment, looking like the monster that he was: the skin on his face rippling with the fasciculations the sux had ignited in the muscles below. Octavio's expression then flashed from one grotesque contortion to another, like the horrors seen in some mad, psychedelic dream. He just managed to get a palm to his chest before his legs crumpled and he dropped to his knees, then fell sideways to the floor.

Rosa was up in the next instant. She scooped up her scrub bottoms and ran toward the door.

"Rosa!" Brad yelled, stopping the woman in her tracks. "Get an Ambu bag!"

Rosa turned to look at Octavio, now quivering violently on the floor. Octavio's lips were already turning blue, signaling that hypoxia was setting in. "Now!" Brad yelled, then dropped to his knees beside Octavio.

As Rosa ran out, Brad wondered if she'd be back. For the next few seconds, he felt paralyzed too, caught between the instinct to save his own life and the impulse to save the man who'd just tried to end it, now suffocating in front of him.

Just as Brad moved into position over Octavio to start mouth-to-mouth resuscitation, he heard the quick patter of Rosa's feet as she ran back into the room. In one hand, she held the Ambu bag; in the other, a cell phone. She dropped the bag and uttered a quick stream of Spanish into the cell. "Carlos is coming," she said.

Brad placed the device's mask over Octavio's nose and mouth and began squeezing the bag attached to it to breathe for the man. Incredibly, instead of leaving, Rosa was walking slowly around the debris-strewn room with her eyes on the floor.

"What are you looking for?" Brad asked.

"This," she said, dropping to one knee. She picked something up and brought it over to Brad: the syringe, intact and still half filled with sux.

"Si ese hijo de puta hace un movimiento," Rosa whispered through gritted teeth as she motioned toward Octavio with the needle, *"le daré lo demás."* Brad didn't understand her words but could guess what they meant.

After Brad had bagged Octavio for a couple of minutes, Octavio's eyes fluttered, then opened. He coughed and thrashed, then lifted his head. He seemed about to try and sit up, but Brad lunged, planted both hands on the man's chest, and pushed him back onto the floor. Octavio's head hit the tile hard. He winced and moaned. Brad didn't care. He didn't start bagging him again, since Octavio could breathe, though that was about all he could do.

When the sound of running footsteps echoed in the hall, Rosa ducked out. A few seconds later, Carlos and Luis entered the room. Octavio's eyes were now open and alert, but after they spotted Carlos, they were the only part of him that moved. Carlos said something softly to Luis that sent him away, and Carlos knelt beside Brad.

Carlos held up the half-filled syringe that Rosa had given him. "Good thinking, Doctor," he said with a nod to Brad.

Luis rolled a gurney to a stop in the hallway a minute later and came to Carlos's side. "I think it will take all three of us to lift him," Carlos said, moving behind Octavio and positioning himself under one arm. Brad moved to the other side. When Luis was at his feet, they hefted Octavio onto the gurney.

"OR two," Carlos said to Luis, and he and Brad followed Luis as he pushed Octavio to the operating room. As soon as the gurney was under the surgical lights, Luis grabbed one of Octavio's arms, slipped a zip tie from his jacket pocket, and secured the arm to the rail on the gurney's side. When Octavio tried to turn toward him, Carlos grabbed his shoulder and pinned him in place until Luis came around with another zip tie and strapped the other arm down.

By now Octavio was completely awake. He said something in Spanish, but Carlos cut him off with a "Shh," giving the arm he'd just restrained a pat.

He smiled. "You've come a long way from El Claro, Octavio," Carlos said. "You worked hard at Nueva Vida. You earned your own apartment and a few days off every month, and I even heard you managed to send some money home to your dear mother. You remember what I said when I hired you?"

After a moment, Octavio responded, his voice low. *"Mi pasado está muerto."*

"That was the first part, yes," Carlos said. "Your past is dead. But the second thing was that it was only what you did in the future that mattered to me. It is you, Octavio, who decided what that future will be."

Before Brad could blink, Carlos jabbed the syringe of sux into Octavio's neck.

"Don't!" Brad yelled, lunging at Carlos, but Luis stepped in and grabbed Brad from behind. It took Brad a moment to realize the hard finger pushing against the back of his neck wasn't a finger. It was the barrel of Luis's pistol.

"There will be no Ambu bag this time," Carlos said as Octavio thrashed against the restraints. Carlos's hand stayed steady. He pushed the plunger down slowly until the syringe was empty.

Octavio's eyes went wide. Then they relaxed—but the fear they flashed remained. A slow stream of saliva spilled from the corner of his mouth.

"What happens in the next few minutes should be familiar to you now," Carlos said. "Once again, you will feel every muscle fail, including those in your chest, just before your lungs fail you too.

"But don't worry, Octavio, your mind will not be affected by the sux at all. You will see it all. Hear it all too—each breath we take as you struggle for your own, while we wait together in this quiet room. Then the sharpest sting will come, the sting of surprise, when you realize your own body has betrayed you—just as you betrayed me.

"All this will pass in a short time for us. But for you, I believe, it will be different. For you, Octavio, I think it will seem like a very long time before you die."

Chapter Twenty-Nine

Cell Call

IT TOOK OCTAVIO five minutes and nineteen seconds to die. Brad knew this because his eyes were on the clock on the wall of OR 2 the whole time. Neither Carlos nor Luis said a word, but Luis's gun never moved from the back of Brad's neck. So Brad's eyes stayed fixed on the clock's second hand. And for the first time, he noticed that hand didn't make a clean sweep around the dial. It jumped and stopped, jumped and stopped, a thin red line twitching between the present and whatever came after its end.

Somehow, when he got back to his bungalow, he managed to sleep and kept right on sleeping through most of the next afternoon. When he finally rose, he could barely move. His fight with Octavio had lasted only a few minutes, but Brad felt like he'd been in a battle that had raged for days.

He skipped his run, then decided to skip work too. After sixteen hours of sleep, he was still beat. He was so tired of it all. Tired of staring at a computer screen all night. Tired of running the same up-and-back lap on a road to nowhere in the jungle every afternoon. Tired of trying to convince himself that the plan he'd floated to Carlos had a chance to earn him anything other than a bullet in his brain. He went back to bed and listened to the chachalaca's call die with the day until sleep finally took him again.

+

The greenhouse was a mess. Brad was on his hands and knees there the next morning, scooping up piles of mud. He'd spent the first hour of his day tracking down the source of the leak from the big water tank that kept his indoor garden cool. When he'd first entered the dome-shaped building, his eyes went to the same spot they always sought every time he opened the door. But instead of the tip of green he hoped to see emerging from the circle of dirt in the pot, he found an inch of water on the floor.

He was just cleaning up the last of the slop when he heard the door open behind him. He turned, expecting to see Aldo, but it was Carlos. He was dressed in a freshly pressed business suit instead of the guayabera and chinos he usually wore.

"I thought you were Aldo," Brad said. "He usually keeps this place spotless."

"Aldo has gone to his grandson's to help him on his farm for a few days. If he'd been here, I assure you, it *would* be spotless."

Brad stood up and smacked his dirty palms on his shorts, trying to think of something to say. Then he realized thinking might not be the best way to determine how to handle the murderer who stood before him, so he followed the instinct that told him to treat Carlos as if this were any other day.

"The guy must be, what, seventy years old, and he's doing farmwork?"

Carlos laughed. "Yes, that is Aldo, and he is closer to eighty than seventy. I offered to send some money to his son so he could hire another man to help him, but Aldo said no. He would rather haul piles of dirt and pull weeds on his knees himself. It is the best way he knows to show his love for his family."

"Where are you going?" Brad asked, giving Carlos's polished shoes a glance.

"I have appointments scheduled with our associates for the next three days, all across the Yucatán. Please wash up, pack your suit and tuxedo, and meet me at the helipad at noon. You're coming with me."

✦

It all happened just as Brad had planned. Carlos had his pilot make a stop in Chetumal for a meeting with the CEO of a medical center that first afternoon. After a night in a four-star hotel, they headed north and spent the next three days choppering all over the Yucatán. They hit the resort towns of Playa del Carmen and Cancún first, even making a short hop to the coast of Cozumel to meet a medical-supply tycoon for lunch on his yacht. The next day they moved inland and hit two hospitals in Valladolid and a clinic in Tizimín before flying to the town of Progreso on the west coast of the peninsula.

Brad met dozens of doctors and medical administrators, but Carlos saved Yucatán's biggest city for the final day of their tour. They hit three hospitals in Mérida and capped off their trip with a black-tie charity ball for a diabetes foundation. When Carlos accepted an award for Nueva Vida's support at the highlight of the event, he used the occasion to call Brad up on the stage.

The cameras flashed and the audience clapped as Carlos announced the promotion of his new chief operations officer to the audience. Even after seventy-two hours of glad-handing strangers and fielding endless questions about Nueva Vida's plans, Brad made damned sure to muster up plenty of smiles and *thank yous*, then left the stage to work the crowd.

When they finally boarded the Sikorsky for the flight home the next morning, Brad was tired but grateful for the breakneck speed of their tour. He'd been accepted into both of Nueva Vida's worlds now, the public and the private. Staying busy in the former gave him a welcome respite from the latter.

But as Brad looked out of the chopper, he found no place to hide from the thought that found him in the open air; the private world of ruthless ambitions was the one he really served. If his plan failed to sate his employers' greed, the cartel would find another way to feed it.

✦

On Monday morning, Carlos texted Brad to meet him in his office. Brad found Carlos standing by his office door with an envelope in his hand.

"What's this?" Brad asked.

Carlos waited for Brad to take the envelope before he answered. "My part of our deal."

Brad lifted the envelope's flap and withdrew a slip of paper—the record of a huge deposit made to Brad's bank account that morning. Also in the envelope was a first-class plane ticket.

"Tomorrow?" Brad asked, reading the departure date.

"Meet Luis in the parking lot at six a.m. He'll drive you to Chetumal. You'll be in Boston in time to have dinner with your family. You've got one week. I trust you'll be able to arrange a meeting with Boston General's board to discuss the license for ReNovus in that time?"

"That shouldn't be a problem."

"I'm sorry I couldn't get you home last weekend to attend your daughter's graduation, but I was still in negotiations with my partners about your trip. Please convey my congratulations to her on the completion of her studies. I'm sure Grace has worked just as hard as you."

Brad opened his mouth to ask how Carlos knew about the event, then shut it when he remembered that he and Catherine had spoken about it over the phone. It took another moment for him to manage a weak "thank you" to a man who no longer even tried to hide the fact that he was privy to every single detail of Brad's private life.

Carlos nodded, then fixed Brad with a stare. His eyes narrowed slightly as he spoke. "I must tell you, Nueva Vida's board was split on whether or not to go with your plan. I cast the deciding vote. Can you guess when I did that?"

Brad thought for a moment. "After what happened to Rosa?"

"Yes. The morning after her attack. I'm not sure you understand how significant your actions were that evening."

"I'm glad I stopped Octavio but not that I got him killed."

"Octavio is responsible for his death, not you."

"You could have—"

"Do you know how Rosa came to work for me?"

Brad frowned, confused by the conversation's turn.

"Santiago and I had many competitors," Carlos continued, "when we first tried to establish our business. There was a rival…*company* that we eventually put out of business. Rosa was one of their assets at the time."

"What kind of asset?"

"They ran a prostitution ring. She was fourteen years old."

"Jesus," Brad whispered.

"She was a very, you might say, *broken* person then. Julieta and I took her into our home and raised her as our own. I could tell from the first time I met her that she was very smart. After she'd spent a year with us, her grades at school showed that.

By the time she graduated from high school, they were good enough to get her into college, then far beyond. That is how she came to be your anesthesiologist."

"I had no idea."

"Of course not. She is a very private person. It took me a long time to earn her trust. I failed her by extending my trust to Octavio.

"But still," Carlos said with a tight-lipped smile, "each man must be judged on his *own* merits, no?" Carlos took Brad gently by the arm and steered him down the hall. "So I am trusting you with this trip, Brad. But before you go, I'd like you to meet with Luis to make sure its conditions are perfectly clear."

When they came to the intersection of a hall leading to the back end of Nueva Vida, Carlos stopped. It was the one section of the building that Brad had never been in before. "Please go to room 302," Carlos said, pointing down a short corridor. "That door is open to you now. Luis is waiting for you."

Carlos left, and Brad looked in the direction he'd pointed. Only a series of small emergency lights lit the way ahead. The space looked more like a tunnel than a hall. After he took a few steps, however, motion-sensor lights flickered on, providing enough illumination to see the small room numbers stenciled on each steel door.

He followed the lights down the hall, taking two turns before finally reaching room 302. He put his thumb on the small blue screen of the biometric lock, heard a soft click, twisted the handle, and took three steps into the room. The door swung shut behind him, and Brad froze.

A wave of nausea rose from his gut as his knees buckled. He would've hit the floor if Luis hadn't been there. He caught Brad and pivoted his body so that Brad landed on the bunk instead.

The same bunk. On the same concrete floor. Facing the same white cinder-block walls he'd stared at for the longest week of his life.

Luis went over to the steel sink and ran the tap, then offered Brad a glass of water. Brad only stared. "Is best to drink," Luis said, holding the glass in front of his face for so long that Brad finally grabbed it. He took the sip he needed to speak because his mouth had gone completely dry.

"All that time?" he managed. "Here?"

"Is easier to have you here," Luis said, pointing to the camera in the corner of the ceiling. "*Muchos ojos*—eh, many eyes—to watch in Nueva Vida."

Luis sat on the bunk next to him. Brad drew away.

"But in America," Luis continued, "your trip, not so many eyes there. So we have a talk here first, then you go. I have a thing for you to listen." Luis took out his cell phone and placed it on the bunk between them. "Your Spanish is not so good. But I think you know whose voice."

All Brad heard was a murmur. Luis fiddled with a button on the phone until it grew loud enough for Brad to decipher the buzz as words. And though he couldn't understand the Spanish, Luis was right—he knew that voice, although it rose and fell in a way he'd never heard Manny speak before.

There were other Spanish voices as well. He'd never heard the loud one. The other was soft. He couldn't be sure if it was Luis's or not. He heard a softer sound next—a single sob perhaps. Then, a different, louder sound. And though Brad had never heard Manny make that noise before, he knew the screams were his.

Luis switched the phone off as the last of Manny's cries echoed in the small room. "He is still alive, Doctor," Luis said. Then he put his hand in his suit jacket. He drew out his closed fist slowly and held it in front of Brad. "If you give us reason, this is for Manny too," Luis said, rotating his fist and uncurling his fingers to reveal the syringe of sux in his hand.

Luis made his soft chuffing laugh. "Is funny, you find this for Octavio. I like this drug. I use it many time. Very hard to, eh, *detectar*—what is English word?"

"Detect," whispered Brad.

"Yes, detect," said Luis, raising the syringe. "And fast. Fast enough," Luis continued, getting up and wagging the syringe at Brad like a finger as he talked, "that maybe is just what a man need one night when he go into house. A house not *his* house. House of someone he go to—*para estudiar*. Eh, study? Yes, study. But maybe dog bark that night. Bark to tell owner of house that man is there." Now Luis held the syringe up in the air between them and slid his finger on the end to mimic pushing the plunger down. "That dog bark one time. He bark two. But no three time. That dog, he no bark again."

Luis went to the door and paused, keeping his back to Brad as he said, "Stay here if you like, Doctor. No lock this time. I meet you tomorrow to take you to plane. But you think on this room. You think on Dr. Pena. You think on your dog. You think on your family. You think on all, when you go home."

Chapter Thirty

A Haven at Home

I'M FREE.

The thought didn't come to Brad during takeoff. And it didn't come when the 727 broke through the bank of gray clouds he'd woken up to that morning, bathing the cabin in the lemon-yellow light of the late June day. It didn't come as Brad settled in for the first good sleep he'd had in weeks, his thoughts dissolving in the engines' white noise while the weight of all he'd carried aboard lifted with the plane.

The thought bloomed later, at Logan, amid the bustle of the baggage claim. *I'm free*, Brad thought when he spied a Red Sox cap turned backward on a kid's head at the same moment the woman ducking in front of him to grab her bag left a trace of the same perfume Catherine wore.

The feeling lasted all the way to Belmont. But all it took was one look at his big Victorian house from the cab window to remind Brad of just how far he'd traveled during the past four months. The peace of mind he'd been blessed with for the previous few hours faded as fast as a dream, the kind you rise from without remembering its story, only the sense of joy it sparked, making you wish you could return to the dark bliss of sleep instead of facing the harsh light of the waking world.

The place looked good. Catherine had complained about the price of a paint job when she'd started getting quotes at the beginning of May, but now the clapboards shone bright white, and the rotted board in the kitchen window frame that Brad kept meaning to fix had been replaced. The freshly trimmed lawn glowed in that chartreuse shade found only in early summer, and the beds around each bush and tree were topped with perfect circles of dark brown mulch.

The scents of cut grass and cedar that greeted Brad as he trundled his luggage up the driveway brought a lump to his throat. He'd thought of these two tidy acres of ground almost every night, the place where he and Catherine had realized their big dreams for their small family. But now that he was here, walking into his house, it didn't look like home needed him.

A half hour later, he discovered the one part of the property that did. When he first saw it, he gave a joyless laugh at the irony of his find—after cleaning up his greenhouse in Mexico, he'd found the same job waiting for him in Boston.

There was no leak here, though. A leak would have been welcome. Everything in the place was bone-dry. Nothing but brown husks filled the pots, and a faint smell of rot lingered in the dead air. The recirculating fans in the ventilation system were still, and the sprinkler system had given up the ghost as well. A flick of the switch on the wall revealed that the lights were dead too. A trip to the basement showed that the circuit breaker had tripped, obviously not recently.

He reset the circuit, went upstairs to change, and headed back to the greenhouse. Only then did he think to check on the big pot in the middle of the room. But when he dug his finger below the surface, he found the soil there was wet. *Too wet.* He pushed his finger deeper. The dirt below was even wetter. He sighed and closed his eyes.

He grabbed a hand trowel from his potting table and turned back to the pot, but waited a moment before deciding to dig. He abandoned the trowel after a few minutes and went into the garage to grab a shovel. It didn't take him long to discover just what he'd hoped he wouldn't find. The corpse flower's corm was completely rotten. So much of it had decomposed that he almost missed the last of its pulpy remains.

"I'm sorry," Catherine whispered from the doorway.

Brad turned from the pot and forced a smile. "It doesn't matter."

"Why didn't you tell me you were coming home?" she asked, ignoring his dirt-stained sweatshirt and jeans as she grabbed him in a hug.

"You'll ruin your dress," he said, but he returned the embrace.

"I don't care." She nuzzled closer. "I wish you could have made it home for Grace's graduation," she said, whispering the words into the nape of his neck.

"Me too. I'm sorry. Carlos surprised me with the flight yesterday. I'm here to make a pitch to BG to use ReNovus at Nueva Vista."

Catherine held on to him but drew back, her lips pursed. "Carlos," she said, looking over Brad's shoulder as if she were picturing the man standing there. "I can't decide if that man is the best thing to ever happen to us or the worst."

Brad's kept his own lips shut.

Catherine's eyebrows rose; she searched Brad's face. "Tell me you're here for a while?"

"Only a week. Carlos needs me back."

"*I* need you back!" she said, her eyes beginning to fill.

He pulled her toward him. She resisted at first, then collapsed against him and buried her face in his chest. When she pulled back a moment later, he kissed her wet cheeks and she laughed. They both lowered their arms but kept them circled around each other's waists. Catherine let out a long sigh and looked around the sorry space they stood in.

"I got so busy. My job, my mother. Then one morning I came in here and nothing was working."

"The circuit breaker tripped."

"The basement thing?" Catherine asked with a frown.

"Yep."

"Well, the next time I got back in here, everything had just *died*," Catherine said, waving at the pale stalks around them.

"It's okay."

"But I watered your corpse flower. Every day. Why'd you dig it up?"

"You watered it to death. Like I said, I don't care."

"But I thought—"

"You got the house painted," Brad said.

Catherine blinked, then knit her brows. "I shouldn't have. I just got the bill for part of it. It's twenty thousand, but he's still got trim work to do in the back, so it'll be more. Grace's tuition is due in two weeks, and that goddamned insurance company still says the cost for Mom's infusions are under review, but I know they're not going to pay. Then there's the plumber."

"What plumber?"

"The one I called to fix the leak in Grace's bathroom."

"How much?"

"Sixty-four hundred. But the wall still needs to be fixed." Brad winced.

"But he guaranteed it wouldn't leak again."

"I bet."

"Well, what was I supposed to—"

"It's okay, Cat," Brad said, offering her a smile.

"Why is it okay?" Catherine asked, her eyes narrowing.

"You want the good news first or the bad?"

Catherine broke the embrace, closed her eyes, then rubbed them with a thumb and finger. "Are those my only choices?" she asked when she opened them.

"The good news is *very* good."

"Why do I think the bad news is going to be *very* bad?"

"There's plenty of money," Brad said.

"I checked our account two days ago. Your paycheck doesn't show up for another week. We emptied checking. It drafted from savings three times."

"I got a bonus," Brad said, pulling his cell from his pocket. He fiddled with the app for his bank account, looking up once to see his wife's frown. When he turned the phone to show her the balance on his screen, her eyes and mouth popped open at the same time.

Brad laughed, and Catherine's face settled. Then her frown returned.

"What's the bad news?" she asked.

"I'm Nueva Vida's new chief operating officer. I'm gonna be there for a while."

There was so much more Brad wanted to tell her, but so much he had to lose if he did. After Luis had revealed that he'd been here, in Brad's home, Brad had to assume that the cartel had eyes and ears everywhere.

In a world where every action and conversation could be captured by miniature electronic devices or snatched from wireless waves in the air, Brad would have to take a long, naked walk in the woods with his wife before he'd believe the words they exchanged were theirs alone.

But there was a bigger reason Brad couldn't share the truth about Nueva Vida with his wife. If Catherine knew the danger Brad was in, there was no way she'd let him get back on a plane. And even if going public did manage to shut Nueva Vida down, Brad knew it was a many-armed beast, one that would kill Manny and had the power to reach beyond Mexico as well. If Nueva Vida disappeared, it would simply shrink back into the jungle like a wave of black smoke, biding its time until the day its claws reached out to strike him, and everyone he loved, dead.

✦

Catherine and Brad were halfway through his welcome-home dinner when Grace walked in. She was talking on her cell, but the hand holding the phone dropped to her side when she saw Brad.

His daughter looked better than she had in the few glimpses Brad had caught of her during his last trip home. Her hair was longer, pulled back in a loose ponytail that draped over shoulders bronzed from long runs under the summer sun. And though Catherine said that things were still tense between the two of them, she said she thought their daughter's senioritis had given way to a new sense of purpose. Grace had picked up a part-time job at a local health-food store, didn't smell like weed when she came in, and even asked for Catherine's help in figuring out what she'd need for her dorm room at Bowdoin.

Brad expected to pick up with Grace right where they left off. As she stared across the kitchen at him, he put down a forkful of rib eye and rose from his place, expecting a storm. One came but not the one he'd been bracing for.

Grace's lower lip trembled. Then his little girl ran to him, sobbing, just like she had one morning when she was seven years old and found her pet hamster lying still in his cage.

Brad held her close as she cried, looking over her shoulder to see Catherine's eyes fill for the second time that day. "It'll be all right, Gracie," he said, resorting to her childhood nickname.

"Are you home for good?" Grace sniffed, keeping her face buried in his shirt.

"Only a week. But let's make the most of it," he said. He'd had an idea riding back here in the cab, when this day had been brightest for him. He glanced at Catherine as he shared it.

"Let's go to Maine."

Chapter Thirty-One

Empty Nest

TRADITION WORKED WONDERS to rebuild the bonds of the Baker family. All three of them fell into their old routines the next day, running between the basement, garage, and town to stock up on vacation gear and supplies.

They were on the road early the following morning, chattering about all they wanted to do in the next four days. By the time they crossed into Maine, Grace and Catherine were gossiping about work and school and went on talking until they'd passed Portland. Grace finally curled up against her pillow in the back seat. Not long after, Brad and Catherine shared a laugh at her soft snores.

"I thought you two weren't getting on that well," Brad said just loud enough to be heard over the hum of the road.

"We weren't. That's the longest conversation we've had since you've been away."

"What changed?" Brad asked. When Catherine didn't answer, he risked a look away from the road to find her staring straight at him with an eyebrow raised.

"You're kidding," she said.

"What do you mean?"

"'What changed'?"

"Yeah, with you two."

"Nothing. What changed was that you came home."

✦

There was one ironclad rule the Baker family followed for every trip they took to the Pine Tree State: they always took the long way to their Maine home. And though their vacation getaway on the Schoodic Peninsula was a five-hour car ride from Boston, "home" was still how Brad thought of the place where he'd grown up, or what was left of it.

His father began selling off pieces of the hundred-acre spread when Brad went to medical school to help pay for tuition. By the time Brad's mother died, only ten acres were left. But they were the best ten, the ones perched along the western arm of sparkling Goldsboro Bay.

The short way home was to skip the first turn onto Route 186, the horseshoe route that looped two-thirds of the way down the peninsula and back, to take the other end of the road a few miles farther east on Route 1. But Brad would never think of veering from the tradition his father had instilled in his only child. Though the trips Brad and his parents took south had been few, on every return, his father always took the *first* turn on 186, veering off at the bottom to drive along the Schoodic Loop Road, which ran along the end of the peninsula known as the "quiet side" of Acadia National Park.

On each of those drives home, Perry Baker would slow the pickup down when they broke from the trees at the very tip of the peninsula to give the family time to take in the view of the Atlantic crashing against the long granite finger of land poking into the Gulf of Maine.

Now, as Brad drove, he, Catherine, and Grace looked out at that view framed by the BMW's windshield. Brad said the same words to Grace that his father had said to him every time they took this drive: "Look where you live, Gracie, on the edge of the best damned piece of ground on the planet."

"We don't live here, Dad," Grace said with the eye-roll Brad caught in his rearview mirror. But he kept looking long enough to see the smile that followed it.

✦

Early next morning, Brad dragged his kayak out from under the back deck and checked the weather one more time. The columns of lupines closest to him shimmered in pink and purple waves, but he lifted his eyes and saw that the rest of the hill they covered was as still as the flat blue plain of the distant sea.

Grace was busy with her own boat on the far side of the lawn, eyeing the items in her carefully arranged piles and choosing what to stuff into each drybag.

Catherine stood on the deck above Brad, still in her robe, her hands cupped around a mug. She closed her eyes and raised her face toward the rising sun.

Brad looked at the single kayak left under the deck. "Are you sure you won't come with us?" he called. "We're only here for three more days."

"Remember what I said before you bought that third boat?" Catherine asked.

"You called yourself a landlubber."

"And I still am," Catherine answered, opening her eyes to offer Brad a smile.

"Then maybe Grace and I should stay," Brad said.

"No," Catherine said. "Grace needs time alone with you."

They pushed off from Prospect Harbor later that morning for their overnight trip. Brad and Grace had taken the ten-mile, three-hour tour around the tip of the peninsula once before, when Grace was still in middle school. Their course would take them south, then west to skirt the low bluffs of Schoodic Point, then north for the final two-mile stretch through the Mount Desert Narrows to their campsite for the night, the tiny bare rock known as Little Crow Island.

After ten minutes in the boat, Brad felt comfortable again, his body falling into the familiar rhythm that moved a kayak best: the total torso twist that provided so much more power than his arms could alone. But though his craft slipped through the calm water easily, it couldn't quite match the speed of the one he chased. When he saw the distance between his boat and Grace's increasing, he quickened his pace till he came close enough to call out to her.

"Where's the fire?" he yelled.

"Inside me!" she yelled back, resting her paddle on the lip of her cockpit while Brad caught up to her. "I feel like I could paddle to France on a day like this."

"Raft up," Brad said as he came alongside her. They grabbed each other's boats to float there for a minute as Brad scanned the coast, then turned to the open ocean. He felt almost dizzy with the sight of so much blue around him after months sequestered within the jungle's green.

Then a memory rose on the salty scent of the sea: Brad as a young boy standing next to his father in the back of a lobster boat in these same waters on one of the many days his dad had picked up work as a sternman to help make ends meet on the farm. "All the people from away are over on Mount Desert Island tripping over each other," his dad would say, pointing the herring he was holding east like a silver finger before stuff-ing it into a bait bag. Then Brad would smile and give him the line he was waiting for. "Thank God," he'd say, laughing just as hard as his old man at their tired joke.

"What's so funny?" Grace asked, surprising Brad, first with the question and second with the grin of his own reflec-tion he found mirrored in the sunglasses Grace wore beneath her new Bowdoin baseball cap.

"Just thinking about my father. C'mon, I know the per-fect place for lunch."

His landing wasn't as smooth as Grace's, but Brad man-aged to beach his boat without tipping over on the tiny pocket of gravelly beach he guided them to at the peninsula's south-western end. He grabbed their lunch from a hatch and led Grace past a picnic table and onto the road that followed the peninsula's edge.

"Where are we going?" Grace asked as they followed the road to the top of a hill. Brad ducked into the thin stretch of scrub that separated the street from the sea before he answered. "My dad's spot."

Thirty yards down a stony slope, Brad stopped on a frac-tured granite ledge just wide enough for the two of them to sit on. He handed Grace her sandwich and ignored his own to take a bite of an apple. "He loved this place," Brad said. "There's a spur off the loop road most people take to Schoodic Point to check out the sea from the peninsula's tip. Not many people know about this lookout."

"Kind of dangerous," Grace replied, craning her neck to peer over the ledge at the white plumes of waves rising from the rocks below. "What's it called?"

"Blueberry Hill. And it *is* dangerous, at least down there," Brad said, tipping his head toward the surf. "You can see why that landing we made was so tricky, even on a calm day like this. I only had us stop here because it's close to slack tide. The end of the peninsula gets ripped by the current when it's closer to ebb or flood." Brad laughed. "That's why your grandfather loved this spot. He worked that damned farm hard every day of his life, but in his heart he was as wild and raw as the sea."

"Sounds like you," Grace said.

Brad stopped chewing. "It does?"

Grace turned away to gaze across the water. "I never would have said that before you took off for Mexico. The hardworking part, yeah, but not wild." When she turned her face back to Brad, he was surprised by the tears in his daughter's eyes. "I was so mad at you. You just left. You never asked me what I thought about you going away."

Brad swallowed the bite of apple, forcing it past the lump in his throat. "I'm sorry, Gracie. I told you about the lawsuit. I didn't have a choice. There was no other way."

Grace palmed her eyes dry and turned to the sea. "I wonder if that's really true," she said softly. And as Brad followed her gaze, so did he.

✦

He kept wondering as they paddled around the tip of the Schoodic, thinking of all the arguments he could make to defend his move to Mexico. But somewhere in the middle of the Mount Desert Narrows, Brad lifted his eyes to see the long, low silhouette of the peak those waters were named for and realized he needed to take a different view.

He'd made his decision. He'd lost the chance to spend the last few months with the daughter who'd soon be leaving her home and childhood behind for good. So, later that evening, after they'd beached their boats and pitched their tent and were waiting for the water on the camp stove to boil under a purpling sky, Brad decided Catherine had been right. He had to make the most of what little time with Grace he had left.

"Are you excited about Bowdoin or nervous?" he asked. The question stopped Grace's hand on its way toward the camp stove. A moment later, she fiddled with the knob to adjust the flame. "Both, I guess. I traded e-mails with my roommate. She seems pretty different from me, a bit ditzy. But I checked out the syllabuses for my courses, and *they* seem like a good fit."

"When do you have to declare a major?"

"Not till spring of next year."

"Still undecided between theater and medicine, or are you thinking of other options?" Brad asked. He grabbed the two bags of freeze-dried chili by the stove, tore them open, and set them by the pot.

"No, it'll be one or the other."

Brad laughed. "You're one of a kind, Gracie."

"Why?"

"Because they're such different careers."

Grace turned the stove off and poured the hot water into the two bags, then closed them up to cook. "I've been thinking about that," she said, "and I'm not so sure. They're both about control. As a surgeon, you've got a patient's entire life in your hands. As an actor, you've got that same power over your audience, at least for the couple of hours they're watching you."

"Granted," Brad replied, "but it can be pretty hard to keep yourself going once you step away from those footlights. You'd eat better as a doctor."

"Is that why you became one?"

"No," Brad laughed. "I guess I was just as idealistic as you."

"And now? Aren't you still dedicated to your patients?"

"Of course. But it can be hard to balance their interests against your own sometimes."

"Or your family's?" Grace asked with an expression on her face that gave Brad no room to reply with anything but the truth.

"Yes," he said, meeting her eyes. He reached over to take her hand. "But whatever path you take, Gracie, I hope you know I'm with you, even if I am two thousand miles away."

Grace turned to watch the lone lobster boat making its way past the island. "Thanks, Dad. I know that. But I'm not the one I'm worried about. Our nest is gonna be pretty empty for Mom with *both* of us gone."

Chapter Thirty-Two

Heart Murmurs

THEY GOT HOME the next afternoon to find a note from Catherine on the fridge: *Gone to Ellsworth for groceries. Back by four.*

"We dropped three hundred bucks at Whole Foods," Brad said, shaking his head. "What could she *possibly* need?"

"It's in her blood, Dad."

"What is?"

"The need to feed. She works for a nonprofit that feeds the hungry, remember? Wanna join me on a run?"

Brad shook his head and smiled. "We just paddled ten miles. You go ahead."

Twenty minutes later, he was sitting in his favorite place on the farm with a book in his lap, looking out at the sea. He'd had the contractor take the home his father built down to its stone foundation and then build the farmhouse his mother had always dreamed of. But he never touched a single nail in the big oak barn behind it that he sat in now.

He took a long breath, closing his eyes and drawing in the sweet, earthy scent of the place: grassy notes of hay mixed with ancient animal smells, all of it buffeted for years by the constant offshore breeze. A few more breaths left him more relaxed than he'd been since he'd stepped off the plane in Logan. The feeling was so foreign that he opened his eyes to pinpoint the source of this newfound peace, just the thing he'd hoped to find here in Maine.

It was this place, this building, that put him at ease. As he traced the long beam of sunlight angling through the dark depths of the barn, Brad realized that even on this secluded stretch of Maine's wild coast, part of him still worried that Carlos's reach could extend to this sacred place. In his mind, he could see Luis (or another nameless cartel soldier) driving through the fog some dark, damp night to plant a bug in his farmhouse. But he doubted anyone would ever bother with the barn.

He turned his gaze from the farmhouse outside to the weathered gray boards around the hayloft's window that framed that view. The words, dates, and pictographs carved into those pine planks sketched a quick history of his childhood. The first entry in the bottom corner was from Brad's sixth birthday, when his father had given him the Swiss army knife that still rested on the sill. His father had carved a rectangle, representing a birthday cake, around the date, then guided Brad's hand to inscribe six lines that stood as candles on its top.

From then on, Brad was old enough to use the knife alone. The dates he noted recorded events both big and small: a Christmas blizzard, a night lit bright by the northern lights, the birth of a litter of kittens, the death of a goat, the Sunday morning Brad broke his arm in a fall. Even after all these years, he could distinguish which of those memorials his own hand had carved by the sure, straight cuts that pointed to his future career. Other markings wavered in the wood with less certainty, recording dates and events not so easily read. But those softer scratches made by Sam's hand reflected something of his nature as well.

Brad closed his book and decided to take a short run after all.

It was just over a mile to Sam's sister's cedar-shingled saltbox house. The Kirby family home had been razed years before by a restaurateur from Ohio who went bankrupt before he could rebuild, and the foreclosed property was now a Christmas-tree farm. But when Barb Kirby's marriage failed, she took some of the money from her divorce to build her own warm-weather refuge nearby; most years she flew in from Florida with the rest of the snowbirds to roost in Maine from Memorial Day to Labor Day.

When Brad jogged up, Barb was on her hands and knees with her back to him, pulling weeds from a flower bed. She got up with a grunt when he hailed her, but when her blue eyes met his, they crinkled and shone under the gray sheaf of bangs peeking from the red bandanna on her head, just like they had when she was a little girl.

"Come around to the back deck, BB," she said after greeting him with a hug. "I'll wash up and we can catch up over a beer."

A few minutes later, Barb handed him a cold bottle and settled into the wicker chair next to him with one of her own. When she asked him about Mexico, Brad fed her just enough details to answer her questions and turned the conversation to her.

She eyed him for a long moment. Brad worried she'd dig deeper, but Barb took a long pull of her beer and then shared the kind of longer story he sensed she'd been waiting to hear from him. She skipped the details of her divorce, shining most of her light on her artist daughter in Delaware and the son who was now somewhere between New York and Vermont, hiking the Appalachian Trail.

When she finished by mentioning the funeral service for Sam, Brad tried to apologize for missing it. But Barb grabbed his arm and shook her head. "You were with him when it mattered—at the end," she said. "And there was nothing you could have done to change that, no matter what that bitch he was married to said." Her eyes went wide at her own words, and she laughed so long and loud that Brad had no choice but to join in.

"I could never understand why he married her," Barb said, wiping her eyes, and though she was still laughing, Brad wondered about the source of her tears.

"They had God in common, I guess" Brad said.

"Not *Sam's* God. His was always more merciful than Faye's. And he was less sure, somehow. Even though he was a minister, he was honest about the doubts he had. Faye didn't seem to have any. It was all heaven or hell with her—you were either inside God's grace or out." Barb frowned and shook her head again. "If that's the way it is, I'd rather spend eternity with all those who didn't get into the same club as her. Where is she with that stupid lawsuit, anyway?"

"My old boss says that the tribunal that'll judge its merits hasn't met yet."

They listened to the shrieks of the neighbor kids playing and the hiss of a sprinkler for a minute. Even after all these years, Brad was comfortable in the quiet company of this woman, who was now his oldest friend.

"Maybe Faye will think about what Sam would have wanted and drop it," Barb said, picking up the conversation again. "You think she'd learn a thing or two from a husband whose favorite homilies were on forgiveness."

"That sounds like Sam."

"Why'd *you* stop going to church?"

Brad slipped a fingernail under the edge of the label of his beer bottle and dug at it gently, then pinched its corner and began lifting it from the glass. "It just wasn't my thing, all that chanting and kneeling."

"But it *was* your thing. I remember you telling me once that church reminded you of the foghorn at Prospect Harbor. You said you forgot about it most of the time, but when you heard it, it made you feel better just to know it was there."

Brad kept his eyes on the label he was working. "I did?"

"You did."

He could feel her studying him as he rolled the bottle slowly. When he pulled the label free, Barb got up. "Wait here," she said. "I've got another bottle for you."

"I've had enough beer, thanks," Brad answered, but Barb walked across the deck, pulled the slider open, and called over her shoulder, "It's not a beer."

She came back and held out an old green glass Coke bottle. Brad eyed it for a second, then took it from her hand and ran his fingers from the sculpted flutes at its bottom, to the lettering circling its middle, to the cork stuffed in its top. He raised it higher and inspected the ring of cracked wax circling its neck, then turned it to get a better look at the yellowed curl of paper inside.

"Open it," Barb said.

The cork was new and pulled out easily. The original cork the wax had sealed must have been lost long ago. He spilled the tube of paper in his hand and unrolled it gingerly to reveal the dollar bill inside. The blue ink on the paper was faded but still legible.

"'If you find this,'" he read aloud, "'you can keep the dollar, but please write your name and address on this note so we know where this bottle landed and mail it back to Barbara Kirby.'" Below that was the Kirby's old address. Brad looked up at Barb with a puzzled smile.

"You don't remember?" she asked.

"No," he said, but as soon as he spoke the word, he did. "Guptill Point?"

"You told Sam and me that if you hit the tide right when you threw it in, the bottle could be taken out of Goldsboro Bay and into the Gulf of Maine. Maybe even make it—"

"To France," Brad said with a laugh. "We talked with French accents that whole day."

Barb smiled. "But we promised not to tell our parents."

"Why'd we decide whoever found the bottle would send it to you?"

"I was the one who had the dollar."

Brad tucked the bill and note gingerly back into the bottle. "Did someone actually mail it to you?"

Barb laughed. "Of course not. Sam and I found it on the beach when we were playing there a few days later, close to where you threw it in."

Brad smiled and held the bottle out to Barb, but she shook her head. "Keep it," she said.

"Why didn't you tell me it came back?" Brad asked.

"Sam wouldn't let me. I remember his exact words: 'Don't tell Brad,' he said, 'he needs something to believe in.'"

✦

They had lobsters and mussels, corn on the cob, and blueberry pie—all the fixings of a classic Maine summer meal. Catherine had driven all the way to her favorite bakery in Ellsworth just to get the pie. Brad and Grace were also doing their best to make their last evening in Maine perfect. Grace had put the antique ice cream maker that served as part of the kitchen decor to use while Brad uncorked the bottle of Chablis Grand Cru he'd been saving for a night like this.

They ate it all on the back deck, watching the day fade as a breeze blew in from the sea. A few stars lit the sky, but the forecast promised a long, wet drive back to Boston the next day.

Whatever wall had stood between Catherine and Grace while Brad was away seemed to be completely gone now. The two carried on like schoolgirls through most of the meal, retelling the stories that had been shaped into Baker family legends, taking turns teasing Brad for his role in most of them.

Brad filled Catherine's glass for the second time and reached for her hand; he got a soft squeeze in return. But she only held his hand after that, as if another squeeze might break a bond still fragile after all the months he'd spent away.

The long paddle, run, and sun got to Grace first. After the last bite of her pie, she hugged Catherine and Brad and slipped off to bed.

Later, in bed, Brad found the Chablis had been worth its price; casting a muzzy glow that let him and Catherine ignore what they had to say to each other and give into their bodies' desires instead. But there was no feral jungle romp tonight. They made love slowly and tentatively, as they had in those first days in his dorm room, when they grew still and held their breaths till the sound of passing footsteps faded down the hall. Brad felt as if he and Catherine were strangers again, drawn by the excitement of foreign flesh yet still wary of the pain that could come from a partner you did not yet trust.

For a few blissful minutes, their passion proved more powerful than fear. They rode that wave to finish together. Then the conversation they'd avoided came.

"What's going on?" Catherine asked, her breathing still settling as she curled herself into the crook of Brad's arm.

"What do you mean?"

"Down there. In Mexico."

He waited to let his own heart slow. "I told you, we're building clinics—"

"Not your job. You."

"I don't understand."

"Yes, you do. Something's wrong. And you changed the rules too."

"What rules?"

Catherine shifted away from him and sat up against the headboard to hug her knees to her chest. "*Six months*, you said. You might be down there six months, *at most*, till the lawsuit went away. It's going on five, and it sure doesn't sound like you'll be home by Labor Day."

"I know, but things changed—"

"I haven't. Remember me? Your wife? The person you seem to have forgotten when you accepted a job that would keep us apart for, what—I don't even know how long, and I'm guessing you don't either."

Brad let out a sigh. "With the money I'll make, we—"

"I don't care about the goddamned money. We'll sell the condo as Sugarloaf, or even the house, if it comes to it. I'll get a better-paying job while you find another one. And there's not going to be a *we* if we're living our lives in two separate countries."

He wanted to tell her. Tell her everything. Turn to this woman he'd loved for so long, the one he counted on to counter him, to balance his propensity to run his life like he did his OR, scrupulously following a plan that considered every contingency with the same practices that ensured the best possible chance for success. Catherine was the one who reminded him how unpredictable life was and helped him to revel in its glorious mess.

But one word about what was really happening below the border would lead to another and eventually to the truth that could cost Brad everything and everyone. So he kept quiet, and so did she. They lay in the dark, together and apart, listening to the whisper of the tide's return to the sea.

Chapter Thirty-Three

Staff Infection

DONNA WARD HAD a nickname that Brad doubted she'd ever heard. She had risen to the role of Boston General's CEO on her talent as a bean counter, earning her the nickname "the Calculator" among hospital staffers who bristled at her passion for slashing expenses.

Some said Ward would rather save a dollar than a life.

That passion often put her at odds with another member of the BG board. Peter Webb and Ward had gone head-to-head more than once about decisions that pitted BG's mission against its profitability. During the past few weeks, Peter had e-mailed Brad to say he would do all he could to support Brad's proposal to license ReNovus exclusively to Nueva Vida. But they both knew Peter would need to sell Ward on the idea to get enough votes from the board.

Now Brad sat stuck with the rest of the commuters in a Monday morning traffic jam on Storrow Drive, trying to review his pitch without losing his mind. During his Maine getaway, he'd pushed his BMW to 90 the moment he got north of Portland, relishing the only strip of I-95 on the northern half of the East Coast empty enough to get away with that speed. But that stretch of road was miles away from the one he was trapped on now. While the engine idled, his heart raced with worry that he might miss the most important meeting of his life.

He was only five minutes late when he walked into Boston General's conference room, but Ward still threw him a sharp glance. He smiled and nodded; the CEO returned to her opening remarks.

Brad scanned the room. The wall of glass on the opposite side of the table framed a picture-postcard view of Boston Harbor, but the morning sun blinded Brad to the faces in front of it. When his eyes adjusted to the light, his mouth dropped—he'd never expected to find Miles Riker here.

Ward droned on. Brad shot a glance at Peter, who sat at the opposite end of the long table. Peter looked from Brad to Miles and back again and lifted his shoulders an inch to answer Brad's unspoken question.

"Your presentation, Dr. Baker?"

Brad turned to see Ward's raised eyebrows. "Thank you," he mumbled, collecting himself. He moved to an empty chair and began passing out printed copies of his pitch. "I'm sorry," he said as the stack of documents made their way around the table, "I prepared only enough copies for the board members. I didn't realize Dr. Riker would be here today."

"He's here at my request," Ward said, her eyes fixed on Brad's document. "I thought it appropriate to have a member of the local team that's working on ReNovus weigh in on your plan."

"I see," Brad said, though he didn't. He resisted the urge to look at Peter again after hearing mention of Miles's involvement with the drug Brad had pioneered.

Over the next twenty minutes, Brad laid out the merits of his plan, making sure to look at the faces of the board members he knew would be sympathetic to the charitable nature of his mission. His proposal concentrated on the less fortunate people ReNovus could save, like the poor farmers who spent every day—long before succumbing to the effects of their renal disease—struggling to keep themselves and their families alive.

But when he pivoted to the PR value of that story, Brad addressed Ward and her allies. He focused on the numbers for them, projecting stats of the increased funding that would come to an institution that put the needs of some of the world's poorest people before the profits of their new drug.

It was hard to read the reactions that played across those faces, but as Brad wrapped up, his gut told him his pitch had been well received. Then, Miles Riker spoke up.

"Let me get this straight," Miles said. "You want *this* hospital, which has spent, what, seven years and tens of millions of dollars developing this drug, to waive its rights to recoup those costs as well as its right to use the drug on American patients just so you can use it in some jungle clinic you're running down in Mexico?"

Brad clenched his jaw so tightly in response that it took him a second to open it enough to reply. "Perhaps you've forgotten that this hospital is the institution that sent me to Nueva Vida, Dr. Riker."

"Oh, I remember," Miles said. "We sent you to deliver a paper—not a drug."

"*You* didn't send me anywhere, Doctor. You were working under my supervision when I shared the results of work done in a lab you never set foot in. And you—"

"Yes, well, things have changed since you've been away."

"Evidently," Brad managed. "But—"

"And perhaps," Miles cut in, "*you've* forgotten the events that led to your employment by Nueva Vida?"

Brad could only stare, trying to reconcile the deferential young surgeon who'd walked into his OR on the first morning of his fellowship with the snake who sat across the table from him now.

"Events," Miles continued, "that have exposed this institution to a multimillion-dollar lawsuit and jeopardized the reputation everyone around this table has worked so hard to protect."

"You were in that OR with me," Brad said, his eyes narrowing. He planted a palm on the table, leaned forward, and thrust a finger at Miles. "You know goddamned well that—"

"Thank you for your presentation, Doctor," Donna Ward interrupted.

Brad kept his eyes pinned on Miles, unable to believe the expression that just flicked across his face. It was subtle, but it was there—a smile.

"I'm going to call for an executive session of this board to convene now to discuss the merits of your proposal," Ward said. "Thank you, Dr. Baker and Dr. Riker, for your presence here today. You are both excused."

Miles got up immediately, thanked the board, and left the room. By the time Brad had done the same, Miles was out of sight. Brad realized that was probably fortunate since strangling Miles with his bare hands in the hall probably wouldn't have helped his position with the board.

He found a seat in an alcove down the corridor in sight of the conference-room door. When the board members began filing out of the room a half hour later, Brad ducked around the corner, took the elevator to Peter's office, and intercepted him in the foyer.

"We need to talk," Brad whispered as he eyed Peter's receptionist.

"We will, but I've got to scrub in to monitor a new recruit. What time's your flight tomorrow?"

"Not till two."

"I've got an early meeting. Meet me here at nine a.m. I'll fill you in then."

Brad's last night in Belmont was a lot different than the family's final one in Maine. Grace picked up on the tension between him and Catherine and tried to bridge it with cheerful banter about the weekend behind them and the trip to college that lay ahead. But halfway through her chicken cacciatore, Catherine stood up, wiped her eyes, excused herself, and went upstairs.

"It'll be okay, Gracie," Brad said, trying to salvage their last few hours together.

"Sure, Dad," Grace said. He doubted she had any more faith in those words than he did.

He left early the next morning, allowing time for a run by the Charles River and a quick shower in the doctors' lounge before meeting with Peter. He hoped his jog might grant him a clearer head by the time he came home to try to patch things up with Catherine before she drove him to the airport.

They'd spent the entire night talking, trying to bridge the physical distance that would soon separate them with words that failed to do the job. For the last hour of that long night, they simply held each other in silence.

Maine had been a blessing. But ever since Brad left Mexico, the ghost of Nueva Vida had shadowed him at home, denying him the relief from stress he'd hoped to find there. He'd considered meeting Bonnie for an early breakfast somewhere downtown, far from any of Carlos's electronic ears or eyes. But even if he was willing to risk being tailed to such a meeting, he wasn't willing to risk drawing the nurse, who'd proved to be such a loyal friend, into Carlos's tangled web.

As he drove along Concord Avenue, Brad realized there was another part of his world that was not so easy to infiltrate—the one he was headed to now. For the first time since he got into the car, his hands relaxed on the wheel. He'd been so cautious in every e-mail he'd typed to Peter over the last few weeks that he'd forgotten this was his one chance to speak to him alone. Any move against the cartel was a risk, but Peter had always helped Brad navigate the threats that came with the powerful position Peter had helped him secure.

Brad hit the gas and shot onto the Fresh Pond Parkway. He'd made up his mind: He'd tell Peter about everything happening at Nueva Vida, then hop on the plane, hoping his mentor would find a way to bring him home.

He looked up and caught his own smile in his rearview mirror—then watched it fall as a police cruiser veered into his lane. A moment later Brad pulled onto the shoulder. He stopped the car but not the shudder that came with the memory of what had happened the last time he'd seen blue lights flash behind him.

No Mexican federale approached this time. But the Black cop who walked up to his driver's side window was just as big as the one that had pulled up in front of Brad in Mexico. And he had the same kind of slow, deliberate gait as the cop who'd come up to Brad from behind. Brad had his window down with his license, registration, and proof of insurance in hand when the cop reached him. "I think I was only five miles over, Officer," Brad said.

"Wait here," the cop said, grabbing the documents. He walked back, ducked into his cruiser, and returned a few minutes later. "I had you fifteen over," the cop said, presenting Brad with all his documents and holding out a ticket in his other hand.

Brad was about to argue the point when the cop flipped the ticket over to reveal a Post-it note and a business card. Brad took the ticket and the card slowly. The handwritten words on the note were penned carefully, but it still took Brad a moment to make sense of what he read.

For the safety of you and your family, do not react to what you read below. Do not say a word.

You are in danger. Nueva Vida has bugged your house and car. Meet me at the Beacon Bean coffee shop on Revere Street, now. I will share information that can protect you and those you love.

Brad's eyes flicked to the business card:

Dennis Day, Special Agent

U.S. Drug Enforcement Administration

The cop waited until Brad's eyes met his, then he nodded and walked away.

✦

He made it to a side street near the coffee shop in twenty minutes, but it took Brad another five before his hands stopped shaking long enough for him to unlock his door. When he walked into the Beacon Bean, he found the morning rush in full swing. It took him a moment to locate Agent Day, now changed out of his cop uniform and into a pair of jeans and a windbreaker. He sat on a stool at the end of the counter drinking a cup of coffee and scanning a newspaper, looking like any other worker about to start his day.

When Brad approached, Day put his coffee and paper down, caught Brad's eye, tilted his head toward the hall behind him, and left. After a few seconds, Brad walked down the hall, turned, and caught up to Day, who stood in front of an unmarked door. Day punched a code in a keypad and the lock gave a click. He opened the door wide enough to let Brad slip in and let it close behind him.

In the cheaply paneled room, there was a single metal table lit by a pair of bare bulbs overhead. In the middle of the table was a big Mac computer like the one Brad used at Nueva Vida. The screen was blank, and the cord lay unplugged on the table. Next to the Mac was a pad of yellow sticky notes, a pair of USB headphones, and two small bottles: Bayer and Excedrin.

Day took the folding metal chair on the far side of the table and made a motion for Brad to sit down in the one opposite him. Brad remained standing.

"You might as well sit, Doctor," Day said. "We've got a lot to talk about and not much time."

"I have an appointment I need to get to," Brad said, still trying to reconcile Day's note with everything that had happened.

"No kidding. That's why I stopped you. We're gonna go over every word you're going to say. That way, when Peter Webb repeats them to Carlos Cardoza, you might just make it back from Mexico alive."

Chapter Thirty-Four

Double Duty

THE THIRD GIN and tonic was a mistake. But the buzz from the second wasn't enough to blunt the fact that Brad was two hours away from Mexico. So when the flight attendant in first class whisked his empty cup away and suggested another, Brad returned her smile with a nod. He studied the fresh drink she left on his tray table for a moment while the woman in the seat next to him dug a paperback from her bag. As soon as she put her nose in the book, Brad drained the glass in a single gulp.

Just as he reached for the metal buckle in his lap, the stupid seat-belt sign lit up and the captain's voice came over the PA to warn them of the bumpy air ahead. Brad took his hand from the buckle and looked out the window at the sea of white clouds below, trying to think of anything but his empty glass and full bladder.

The alcohol worked quickly, turning his thoughts from the days ahead to the ones that had just passed. The shock he'd felt when Agent Day revealed Peter's betrayal in that dingy room returned as their conversation began to play again in Brad's mind.

✦

"Why's the DEA involved with a black-market-transplant clinic?" Brad asked.

"Nueva Vida's only one of Carlos's enterprises," Day answered. "His cartel moved away from marijuana once it started being legalized in the States. They diversified into black-tar heroin, but Nueva Vida may be the best way to bring them down."

"So why haven't you?"

"Carlos and his boys are smart. Not as smart as they think they are, but smart enough to keep their most sensitive secrets out of e-mails and phone calls. They've got 'em locked on the servers in the local area network they built down there in the jungle. They spent a ton on IT, but any system can be hacked. We haven't figured out a way to get into theirs remotely, but there *is* a way we can get in from the inside—with someone's help."

"You don't mean me?"

"Of course I mean you."

Brad shook his head. "You have no idea what the place is like."

"We know a lot."

"How?"

"Like I said, they're not as smart as they think. They use coded language when they communicate with people on the outside via e-mail and cell calls. The code words they use in those conversations are pretty good, but they've been using them too long. Every time they do, we get a better sense of the context they're used in. We've cracked enough to decipher a lot of what's going on. Like we know that you now have access to imported patient data and maybe other info on their servers as well. Can you see any financial records?"

"No way. All I can see are internal coms about small stuff, like the OR schedule. And the patient data is anonymous."

"But specific, right?"

"Yes. Why?"

"Because that's the key to bringing them down."

Brad's eyes drifted away from Day and rested on the fake wood grain of the paneled walls. "Hector Vázquez," he said softly.

"What?"

"I saw a record of someone I know they murdered," Brad said.

"Could you pull it up again?"

"I could, but I won't."

"Why not?"

"Because I'm sure they're tracking everything I'm doing digitally. I'm supposed to be building a database, not scouring charts of individual murder victims. If that chart comes up on my screen again, I'll be the next one."

Day was silent for a moment. "Think there are others?"

"Yes."

"Us too. That's why we have this," Day said. He grabbed the set of headphones on the table and pulled the USB plug off its end.

"What's that?" Brad asked.

"The headphones are just a cover for this," Day said, holding up the USB plug. "It's a special flash drive our tech guys cooked up. They call it a bloodhound—you know, since we use it to sniff out the data we want." Day turned the Mac sitting on the table around to show Brad its back.

"You simply plug it into one of these USB ports on the back of your Mac when you start working," Day said, slipping the device into one of the four tiny slots. "Then take it out when you're done. Any chart you pull up on the screen gets copied to it. Do it every time you log in, and eventually, we're bound to get another patient with donor data in their chart that matches that of a murdered donor. Hopefully, more than one. They tell me that a patient's HLA markers are almost as good as a fingerprint."

Brad shook his head. "Bloodhound's a good name for it. They catch me plugging it in and I'm dead. It's not like I can pretend there's music I'm listening to on the computer. They control everything on those machines."

"We know that. The headphones are just to mask the bloodhound while you're carrying it. As far as them catching you goes, don't let them. You got any of these down there in the jungle?" Day asked, peeling a yellow sticky note off the small pad lying on the table.

"Sure, why?"

"Write a note to yourself on one—*Call the wife* or *Get more coconuts*, whatever's plausible down there in the jungle. But do it on the rectangular three-inch-wide ones like this, not the tiny ones. And change the note every few days."

Day reached over and placed the sticky note on the monitor's bottom right-hand edge. "Put the note right here. One inch to the left of it will be where the USB ports start. You just need to stick your hand in to the left of the note and you'll hit one of 'em. It'll take you only a few seconds to seat it, and it'll be even easier to pull out."

"Even if that thing doesn't raise any flags from a log of my computer activities," Brad said, tilting his head to see the tiny device Day pinched between his thumb and forefinger, "they've got cameras all around the place."

"Only one in your office. It's at eight o'clock as you face your computer, and you block the Mac when you're standing.

You slip it in quick when you get there, right before you sit down. When you stand up to leave, do the same thing again. And they're not gonna be watching you the whole time you're sitting there or screening hours of video afterward. If the security guards at Nueva Vida are like most of the ones I know, they'll be watching movies on their phones or napping when the boss isn't around."

Brad shook his head again. "You're going to get me killed."

"I'm not saying this isn't gonna be risky, but you got yourself into this situation, Doc. We know you weren't bargaining on getting involved with murder, but you're the COO of a company that trades in it. We'll keep an eye on your family while you help us crush the cartel. Really, what other choice do you have?"

Brad stood up and took a lap around the dingy room, trying to find an answer. A moment later, he took his seat again with a sigh. "How do I get that thing to you?"

"Not thing—things," Day said. "You gotta put a new one in every time. We don't want all the eggs that could crack the cartel in one basket, you know?"

Brad laughed. "No way I'm taking more than one. If I do this—and I'm not saying I will—you're going to have to find a way for me to exchange the filled drives with new ones."

"Way ahead of you. You make the drop during those long runs in the jungle you take every afternoon."

Brad closed his eyes briefly, realizing that he'd had *two* organizations watching his every move in Nueva Vida.

"We need a spot for the swap," Day said when Brad met his gaze, "someplace our agent down there can find."

"There's a split palm on the edge of the dirt road about a mile from Nueva Vida," Brad said. "A trail paved with crushed white stone leads from it to a clearing not far away. There's a flat stone sculpture on one side."

"That's perfect," Day said. He grabbed the two bottles from the table. "These bottles are special—they're reinforced with plastic seals inside to protect the bloodhounds. They look just like regular ones. Dump out the pills in both before your first run. You dig a hole behind that sculpture, put them in, and place a rock on top. Every day during your run, you put the used bloodhound in this one," he said, holding up the Bayer bottle. "Bayer—*B* for 'Baker data.' And Excedrin—the *E* is for the new empty bloodhound we'll leave for you when we take the one you filled. You with me?"

Brad nodded. "Of course. But it's fifteen miles from the highway to that spot, over a rough jungle road," Brad said. "You plan on having someone make the pickup every day?"

"Every *night*. I got a local down there. We've used her before. She's a marathon runner just crazy enough to love this kind of job."

"I must be even crazier to even consider this," Brad said. He looked at the back of the computer again, leaning in closer to get a better view of the bloodhound in the USB port. "I might be able to reach under the front of the Mac to feel that thing and slip it out quickly. But how the hell am I supposed to slip it *in* blind?"

Day looked at his watch. "You're meeting Webb at nine?"

"Yes."

Day pulled the device out and swiveled the computer around to face Brad.

"You got an hour," he said, setting the bloodhound on the table. "Practice."

✦

A rumble of turbulence turned Brad's attention away from the memory and back to his bladder. He slipped out of his seat and into the lavatory just in time to relieve himself. When he stood and filled the metal basin by the toilet, the jet jumped again, sending a stream of cold water straight from the sink to the crotch of his white linen slacks.

Brad closed his eyes and shook his head. He grabbed a wad of paper towels and mopped at the mess, then wet his hands in the inch of water left in the basin and rubbed them over his face. In the cubicle's thin light, he studied his reflection in the mirror. The lines around his eyes and the gray threads in his hair seemed to have multiplied, and a faint web of veins had bloomed across each cheek. He wondered where the guy this stranger had replaced had gone.

The face he showed Catherine before he left was of a surgeon obsessed with his new position, hiding that of the husband returning to Nueva Vida to protect his family, not his career.

The one he'd turned on Peter yesterday was that of a grateful friend nodding away as he fed Peter the lines he'd rehearsed with Agent Day about the business they'd bolster between Nueva Vida and BG, doing his best to keep the words coming so he didn't throw up.

The face he was composing now was the one he needed to show his boss when he landed, a countenance that could convince Carlos that Brad didn't know that Carlos knew everything Peter had reported to him about Brad's meeting with the board.

But perhaps the saddest face he wore was the one he put on for his daughter before he left—the thin mask that tried to show her that her father had everything under control.

He held his jacket in front of him as he returned to his seat, but the guy across the aisle saw Brad's wet crotch when he sat down and laughed. Brad closed his eyes as his head began to pound from the drinks he'd downed. Just before he passed out, he thought about Agent Day's parting words: *So, Brad, are you ready to be an agent for the DEA?*

Chapter Thirty-Five

To the Dead

"SO, DR. BAKER, HOW did it go?"

Brad took a seat on the other side of the desk from Carlos, ready to play the game. He spent the next five minutes detailing Miles Riker's surprise attack on Brad's licensing plan for ReNovus, though he was sure Peter Webb had told Carlos everything by now.

When Brad finished, he resisted the urge to return Carlos's frown with a smile. For the first time in their relationship, Brad felt like he was a step ahead of his boss. The feeling didn't last long.

"How long until you complete the new patient database?" Carlos asked. Now the frown was on Brad's face as he was forced to play catch-up with Carlos yet again.

"I've still got a ways to go. Why?"

"Exclusive access to ReNovus was half the plan you pitched. I want to know if the other is going any better."

"ReNovus isn't dead yet. The board hasn't made its decision."

"How long?" Carlos repeated.

"It's taking some time, Carlos. The translation software helps, but it's not great."

"Isn't Felipe assisting you?"

"He tries, but he doesn't have a medical background." Brad paused, weighing his next words carefully. "Manny built the system I'm basing the new one on. I'd get it done a lot faster with his help."

Carlos looked at Brad for a moment, then turned to the small planter on the side of his desk and stroked one of the long, spiky leaves that rose from it. "You're a gardener, Brad, you know this plant, yes?"

Brad chewed on his lip as he adjusted to Carlos's latest pivot. "Aloe vera," he said.

"Yes. Most people who notice it think I have it here because of its medicinal properties. What better houseplant is there for a medical clinic than this?"

"Sure, I guess."

Carlos continued to stroke the leaf, running the tip of his finger over the series of small spikes that ran along its edge. "The truth is," he said with a laugh, "despite the fact that I grew up on a farm, I am a terrible gardener. This plant is almost impossible to kill. The easiest way to do that is by watering it too often."

Carlos released the leaf and turned back to Brad. "It is best sometimes not to give some things *too* much attention. I'm afraid that was the case with your friend Manny. We tried everything we could to convince him to return to Nueva Vida."

Brad's stomach dropped.

"But Dr. Pena wasn't interested in continuing his employment under the terms we offered for his return. His contract with Nueva Vida has been terminated."

Brad closed his eyes. In the darkness, he didn't see so much as feel the scene of Manny being led away. The space that opened between them on that strip of highway now grew to an empty ache—a gulf between him and the friend he couldn't save, as wide as the distance between this world and the next.

When he opened his eyes, Carlos continued. "Since securing the rights to ReNovus seems to be a problem, at least for now, I'd like you to focus your work on the other part of your business plan. My partners are eager to break ground on our first clinic."

Somehow, Brad managed to pick up the thread of their conversation again. "But the patient database is the key to getting the bigger donor pool we need."

"There are more urgent items on the agenda. We need your ideas on the physical layouts for these facilities. It will be quite an operation to get them up and running in the remote areas you presented in your plan. We need to know what equipment each should stock, the qualifications of its staff, protocols for patient intake—all those things you told me you learned of in your clinical rotation in Maine."

Brad studied the aloe for a moment. With its fanning spiral of tapered triangular leaves, it really was a beautiful plant. It was easy to miss the thorns that waited, ready to pierce the skin of anything that got too close.

"Can I work on the clinic plans and the patient database at the same time?" he asked, forcing himself to meet Carlos's eyes.

"Do you still plan to work at night?"

"Yes. I focus better when it's quiet."

Carlos pushed his seat back and stood up to end their meeting, so Brad did the same.

"Focus on the clinic," Carlos said as he walked Brad to the door. "Limit the database work to an hour or so each evening.

Our partners are getting restless, Brad. We need to show them proof that your ideas for Nueva Vida's increased profits are more than just a clever plan."

✦

Brad waited a couple of nights before slipping the bloodhound off the end of the headphone cable and into his pocket as he left his bungalow. "Get started right away," Agent Day had told him. But Day wasn't the one walking into the lion's den every night, wondering when the beast he was toying with would catch on to his game.

By now, Brad was attuned to not only the night noises of the clinic, but their timing too. Carlos ran Nueva Vida the same way Brad ran his OR; he trained his staff in the regimented tasks that optimized efficiency. But the same regularity that kept the housekeeping, maintenance, and security teams sharp presented an opportunity for Brad. He knew every ebb and flow of the off-hours schedule, and the slack time between both as well.

He didn't plug the bloodhound in right away. He wasn't sure Carlos knew about the running domino game the security guards had going, but Brad walked by their station often enough to recognize the soft click of their tiles. Those sounds came during Brad's own routine, the nightly stroll he took at exactly ten o'clock through the halls around Nueva Vida's perimeter.

So at 9:55 that evening, when he stood, stretched, and bent forward to inspect his monitor, he slipped his hand below the edge of the sticky note at its end. The move wasn't exactly smooth, but after two or three seconds, the tip of his middle finger found one of the USB ports, and with a flick of his wrist, he slipped the bloodhound home.

He was glad for his walk after that. It took him the full length of one long side of the clinic for his pulse to slow down.

There was only one guard at the security station. As Brad approached, he gave the man a nod, but the guy had his eyes on the row of screens below the counter. Brad's heart started racing again as he imagined the guard replaying the move in front of the monitor Brad had just made. Then the guy looked up and offered his own nod as Brad passed by.

Toward the end of his lap, Brad saw Rosa walking toward him. This time, when she saw Brad, she not only met his eyes but stopped and spoke to him.

"I never got to thank you," she said, extending her hand.

Brad took it and smiled. "I figured you would have had enough of night work after…well—"

"That animal is gone," Rosa said. "Would you like to join me for dinner? I have tamales. They are warmed in the microwave, but they are homemade."

Brad's eyebrows rose. "In the doctors' lounge?"

Rosa met Brad's eyes. "Of course," she said, and when the corners of her mouth rose, Brad froze. It was the first time he'd ever seen Rosa smile. Although her teeth were white and even, he'd never seen canines as sharply pointed as hers.

"We have a saying," Rosa said. "*A mí la muerte me pela los dientes.* In English it translates to 'Death peels my teeth.'"

"What does it mean in Spanish?" Brad asked.

"That death cannot do a thing to me."

Brad followed her into the lounge and sat at the same table that Octavio had bulldozed during his charge. He fidgeted while Rosa tended to the microwave as he replayed his battle with the huge man again.

Rosa moved calmly, even gracefully, as she took the tamales from the oven, arranged them on two plates, and carried them to the table. She went over to the sink, filled a couple of water glasses, and put one in front of Brad. Then she flashed her sharp little smile once more and raised her glass. "To the dead," she said.

Chapter Thirty-Six

A Small Green Spear

BRAD'S MIND RACED while he ran. Unlike his first jogs at Nueva Vida, however, the things that scared him most were not in the jungle he sprinted through. They lay within the walls of the sleek glass building he'd just left.

The screeches and buzzes, the treetop howls, the slithers, and growls—he no longer feared these unnamed, untamed things. He welcomed the rush of blood that came now as the first beads of sweat broke out on his forehead in the daily ritual that let him flush the fears that shadowed him, trading the worries in his mind for the pain he pushed his body to produce. Here in the wild, he'd learned that moving fast was the best defense against any beast. He was less sure that it was the best way to defeat a man.

He'd been moving fast for the past month, slipping a new bloodhound into his Mac every evening in three or four seconds, then, later, removing it in one. And when he loaded patient data, he pulled page after page onto his screen quickly too.

A note he'd found at the drop spot near the split palm two weeks before had prompted that speed. The new bloodhounds had appeared daily in the empty Excedrin bottle, just like Agent Day said they would. But that afternoon, Brad found a single strip of paper and a miniature lighter waiting beside the blank drive inside. *We need more records,* read the first line on the slip. *Burn this note,* read the second.

So Brad increased the number of patient profiles he scanned. One night, he pulled yet another one up, then stopped, aware of how comfortable he'd become with his new routine. That was what really scared him, because letting his guard down was the surest way to get caught.

The one bright spot was his nightly dinner break with Rosa. They took turns bringing in the meal, and though Rosa's were much better, she was always gracious about whatever Brad managed to prepare. He wondered why he felt so comfortable with this strange woman. But one night, as he lay in bed replaying one of their recent conversations in his head, he realized it wasn't *what* she said but *how* she said it that put him at ease.

Rosa spoke the same careful language that Brad had learned to adopt within Nueva Vida's walls, always aware that every word could be heard by unseen ears. Their exchanges were distinguished mostly by what they *didn't* discuss. Neither of them mentioned Manny, let alone the shadowy members of the cartel pulling the strings behind every move the two of them made each day. But somewhere between the spaces of the words they did share, Brad felt the fragile promise of a bond beginning between two people wary of trusting anyone else.

As the split palm came into view, Brad slowed his run to a walk, then made the careful moves he always did: he turned his body to snake through the branches of brush that fell over the faint path to the stela, careful not to disturb the cover that grew over the thin trail leading to the drop spot. He made a final prickly pirouette to remove the last thorny branch in his path, then looked up and sucked in his breath.

His legs tensed to run before his eyes made sense of what he saw. Then the big mud-splattered man in the red Hawaiian shirt and cargo shorts standing in front of his dirt bike removed the cigarette from his mouth and gave Brad a wave.

"Hello, Doc," Agent Day said.

When Brad could find no words to reply, Day flashed him a smile. "I know. If I saw me here, I'd freak too. Had one hell of a ride on the way in. I used to have one of these," he said, pointing his cigarette at the motorcycle before taking a drag. He exhaled and patted his paunch. "About thirty years and forty pounds ago."

"Why are you here?" Brad finally managed.

"I'm a tourist with a taste for adventure, of course," Day said, spreading his arms to show off his attire. "At least, that was gonna be my cover if I met anyone. Tried to avoid that, though. Every few minutes on the way in, I shut my engine off, ready to pull into the bush if I heard another one." Brad continued to stare, and Day held out a bloodhound. "Trade ya," he said. Brad came closer, shaking his head. The men exchanged the drives. "I'm here to tell you that you need to put a lot more records on these things if we're going to stand a chance of finding the ones that'll bring Carlos down."

"He has me working on setting up clinics now. I only have an hour to look at charts at night."

Day took a final drag of his cigarette, dropped it, crushed the butt with the heel of his boot, then pocketed it. "An hour a night's not gonna cut it. Can you push it to two, maybe even three?"

"I have been pushing it. I pushed it in the first place to ask for an hour," Brad said. "If you'd seen the look Carlos gave me when I did, you wouldn't be asking me to try and get more."

"Listen, Brad, this is a race. Nobody wants you to get killed before you finish it, but I got a whole team of analysts trying to help you cross the finish line. They've been going over reports of every suspicious death down here for the past two years, ever since Nueva Vida opened, just to cross-reference them with whatever medical records we can get on our own from Yucatán hospitals and clinics, as well as the ones you feed us. It's all about the data. We need more to increase the chances of getting a match."

Brad threw up his hands. "I'll try, but we need other options, Agent Day."

"Dennis."

"Huh?"

"I think you've earned the right to call me by my first name. The agency and I appreciate what you're going through down here. And you're right about other options. We're all about contingencies. We've worked up one for when you make it home again. Till then, you need to do all you can to help us here."

"*If* I make it home again," Brad said.

"Okay, *if*," Day said. "Till then, I gotta ask you: How far are you prepared to go to stop this thing?"

Brad shook his head and kicked at the dirt. "How far? Haven't you been listening? With your headphones in your vans or satellites or however you've been monitoring the things that have been happening down here? I've been doing everything I can to stop it. The clinics, the access to ReNovus, it's all designed to stop it by making more of the only thing the cartel cares about—money."

"Even if that works, what about the people they already killed?"

"I can only do what I can do."

"You can help bring their murderers to justice. Think about the people those victims left behind, the families that have been broken. And you might think about your own family while you're at it."

Brad fixed Day with a stare. "You said you'd protect them."

"We have, and we will. But this cartel has a long memory and a long reach. Your best chance for protecting Catherine and Grace is to bring it down."

Brad laughed. "Funny. You didn't mention that in our little tête-à-tête in the Beacon Bean."

"Did I really have to? You know these guys better than I do."

Brad waited for Day to meet his gaze before he replied. "To answer your question—how far am I prepared to go? When it comes to my family, *Dennis,* I'd give my life to protect them. Wouldn't you for yours?"

"No question," Day said. He looked at his watch. "How long does it take you to finish your run?"

"About an hour."

"Good." He went over to the bike, grabbed the backpack next to it, removed the soft-sided cooler inside, and took out two cans of beer. "One of the perks of playing tourist is packing like one," he said. "Have a cold one, Doc. We have a lot to talk about before your run is done."

Brad's mind was still spinning from his conversation with Agent Day when he got back to his bungalow. He kept trying to make sense of a "contingency plan" that felt like pure fantasy. He showered to clear his head, but when he sat down at his computer, he got the day's second surprise. He had two e-mails, one from Catherine, the other from Grace. He shook his head; he'd completely forgotten, but his wife and daughter hadn't. The subject line on both notes was the same: *Happy Birthday!*

Lately, Catherine's e-mails had become more frequent as she attempted to bridge the growing distance between them. However, the longer her messages grew, the shorter were Brad's replies. Telling her how he felt while he knew others were listening—and she didn't know—felt like a worse betrayal than not sharing his feelings at all.

She called him a couple of times, and that was even worse. After that, their exchanges deteriorated into perfunctory chats about finances and schedules.

Brad's birthday, however, had inspired Catherine to redouble her efforts to bring Brad close again. Her e-mail spoke tenderly of the time in college when their love had first bloomed. She went on to sketch a portrait of the early days of their marriage when Grace was a baby, so quiet and easygoing that they could simply tote her with them to their favorite burger joint in the city, pop the baby carrier on the table, and share beers and talk of their day.

Then her e-mail took a turn: She asked Brad where that man—the man he used to be—had gone. Reading those words on his screen, Brad thought of all he wanted to say to calm her fears, and wanted to voice his own as well, to share the vulnerability that was the secret to a marriage that endures.

Instead, he pecked a few lines about his work and the weather, feigning indifference to her to shield their intimacy from those who'd read it and use it like a weapon, all the time knowing how his curt reply would wound the woman he loved.

It was even harder to answer Grace's message. Her e-mail was long as well; offering up her hopes and fears in an appeal so open that Brad was tempted to respond with words that came straight from his heart. But his instinct to protect her by shielding their conversation from prying eyes trumped his desire to respond with the tender guidance his daughter so obviously sought.

So even though he knew the window for his paternal counsel was closing, with Grace about to leave to start college and life on her own, he simply thanked her for her note, wished her good luck, and signed off with *L., D.*—for *Love, Dad.* Then he shut his laptop, poured three fingers of tequila into a glass and carried it out the door.

He couldn't lose himself in his work in the greenhouse behind the bungalow the way he had in the one back home. Under Aldo's vigilant care, other than the water leak that sprung when Aldo was away, the plants within it were always perfect. Brad walked in, slumped down on the seat of the greenhouse's bench, drained half his tequila, and closed his eyes.

The thing that bloomed deep in his chest next didn't come from the drink in his hand. And it was different from the familiar fear that had been skittering inside him ever since he stepped off the plane. This was sharper. Stronger. A fire sparked by the man who'd forced Brad to turn cold to his wife and daughter. He tipped back the last of his drink, warming to the white-hot heat of his anger. Then he fed it, adding one thought after another of Carlos, of Luis, of Santiago, of all the other nameless, faceless members of their corrupt cartel. And as each one kindled his contempt for them all, Brad relished the sweet sting of its burn.

He got up from the bench and took a stumbling step to the big pot in the center of the space. He steadied himself there, one hand on its red clay rim, as the tequila threatened to make a return trip past the back of the hand he'd plastered across his mouth. When the nausea passed, Brad spied some tiny thing wavering in the center of the circle of soil. He swept the sweat from his eyes, and there it stood: a small green spear breaking from the depths below.

Chapter Thirty-Seven

The Night Shift

THE HATE HELPED a lot. Brad had been surprised by its bite during his last visit to Peter's office. (Dear God, he hoped it was his last.) He'd walked in that morning after being prepped by Dennis Day, convinced he could keep his game face on throughout the charade of the conversation he'd scripted with the agent. Then, five minutes into their exchange, Peter asked about Grace. Brad turned to look out the window, certain that this man whose hands had cradled his infant daughter at her baptism would see the rage blazing in his eyes.

Somehow, Brad managed to keep his voice level and make it through the meeting, but his knuckles went white on the wheel during the drive home. It took half an hour in the shower before he could look at his hands and not imagine them around his mentor's neck.

Like any new drug, the second dose of hate was easier to metabolize than the first. Brad knew exactly how to prescribe it to himself. Specific pictures seemed to work best. Each night, as he walked toward his computer, he'd conjure up images of who he was risking his life for. One night, it might be the butterfly-shaped birthmark on the nape of Catherine's neck. On another, the quick wink of Grace's left eye that came just before she laughed. Even the memory of Murray's nose peeking through the crack of the front door as Brad opened it when he returned home each evening did the trick. All those memories had the power to fuel him with the anger he needed to put the bloodhound to work.

He pushed his chart review to an hour and a half the first week after his jungle rendezvous with Agent Day. When he saw Carlos waiting at his workstation the following Monday night, Brad couldn't stop the gooseflesh that rippled across his arms. Tonight, it was the image of Grace bent over the camp stove that kept his gait steady. He clung to the vision, recalling Grace's silhouette on Little Crow Island as she reached to take the pot of boiling water off the stove at the end of that magical day, the flame below illuminating three golden arcs tracing the edges of her chin, her cheek, the tip of her nose. By the time he reached Carlos, Brad was able to offer him a small smile with his nod.

"Your plans for the clinic have paid off," Carlos said, returning Brad's grin. "We've found the perfect place for the first one. Please take tonight off. Luis will drive you to the village of Salvación tomorrow. The road there is long and rough. You should get some sleep tonight."

Brad stifled a sigh of relief, then thought of the companion he'd be stuck with for his trip. "Couldn't I just drive myself?" he asked.

Carlos shook his head. "I'm afraid you would not get very far. There are many twists and turns on unmarked roads no GPS can find to reach Salvación. You will stay with Miguel López there for the rest of the week. He treats the medical needs of the locals and also has the nicest house in town." Carlos laughed. "But sadly, in Salvación that is not saying much."

"Is he a doctor?"

"Of sorts. He is very excited to meet you. Señor López has reminded me that a man of your gifts belongs in front of a patient, not a computer."

"But I'm not done with the database."

"You'll have one more week to work on it when you return. I'm afraid Felipe and I will have to muddle through with it after that. The groundwork you laid on our tour of the Yucatán a few weeks ago has generated a lot of new interest. Dr. Garcia does the best he can with the locals, but the patients who keep us in business want only the best, and that is you. We have quite a backlog." Carlos laughed again. "I may even have to hire someone else as good as you."

✦

Luis didn't say a thing as he drove. That was fine with Brad. After their talk in his former cell, Brad had done his best to steer clear of the little beast. If he had to be trapped in a jeep with him for three hours, the side of the man's face was about all he could stand. The ride was every bit as rough as Carlos had promised. After an hour, Brad wondered why his boss hadn't arranged for one of the clinic's helicopters to ferry him to the village.

He knew the choppers were expensive to run, and serving a place as far off the map as Nueva Vida kept them in demand. But as Luis took yet another turn that brought the scratch of brush and pop of rocks, Brad thought of another reason Carlos might have sent him on a drive with a killer down a nameless jungle road. He shuddered as Carlos's last words echoed in his head: *I may even have to hire someone else as good as you.*

They were the longest three hours of Brad's life. But they weren't his last. They finally broke through the trees and drove past a field where men in straw hats worked among rows of ripening corn. A few minutes later, they pulled into a village of oval huts with tall, thatched roofs. When Luis got out and started unloading the cartons packed in the back of the jeep, Brad jumped out and pitched in. As soon as the last one was unloaded, Luis got into the jeep without a word and drove away.

Brad stood among the cartons, casting nervous smiles at the few villagers who made eye contact. Almost all of them were children. One shirtless young boy dared to approach him, but a man called out and the boy ran away.

From the villagers' small stature, darker skin, straight black hair, and heavy-lidded eyes, Brad thought they were probably Mayan. The person closest to him was a woman wearing a long white tunic with colorful embroidery. She stood bent over a small wooden table in a patch of bare earth in front of a hut, slapping out a stack of tortillas with a steady whack. She didn't give Brad a single glance. While she worked, chickens ran past her and between the huts, their clucks mixing with grunts from pigs rooting in pens nearby.

It didn't take long for the grapevine to get word to Señor López that Brad was in town. Brad heard a stream of excited Spanish and turned to see a tall, potbellied man running toward him. Brad held out his hand, but the man ignored it and gripped him in a bear hug instead. Then he turned and yelled in a language that must've been Mayan to a couple of men nearby. A minute later, a battered pickup pulled up. The two men inside hopped out, loaded the cartons in the back of the pickup, then hopped into the truck's bed with them. Señor López ushered Brad into the passenger seat, got behind the wheel, and took off, sending a flock of chickens flying as he sped down the dirt road that wound between the huts.

His host talked excitedly during the entire ten-minute drive to his house. Señor López's English was as bad as Brad's Spanish, but that didn't slow the man's monologue. They managed to exchange first names, but that was the extent of the information the two shared before Brad's garrulous host screeched to a stop in front of his cinder-block home.

Somehow, those first names and their pantomimed communications worked well enough to allow them to treat the endless line of locals that waited outside of Miguel's home over the next three days. Brad saw patients with everything from the common cold to cancer come through Miguel's door. He felt best about the things he could treat immediately, like splinting a broken finger or dispensing a dose of Stromectol to cure a roundworm infection. The best he could do for those with advanced diseases was give them some pain meds from the stock he brought with him and make a plus sign next to their names in the battered notebook Miguel used to record their visits. The notation indicated that they needed to be seen in a real medical facility, but Brad doubted many would ever make the trip.

When Luis pulled up in the jeep on Sunday afternoon, every box of supplies they'd brought was empty. The fears that had chased Brad on his drive to Salvación were replaced on the trip back by an emotion he hadn't felt for so long that it took him a while to identify it: gratitude. *His* gratitude for being able to heal people who paid him only with their murmured blessings and shy smiles.

+

A few nights later, as Brad sat at his computer, his warm thoughts of Salvación began to fade. He thought of the trusting faces of those he'd treated, knowing each would soon be cataloged as another potential donor he'd pull up on his screen. He tried not to think of the awful decision those patients might face if they popped up as a match for someone in the database he was building—weighing the price of surrendering to a surgeon's knife against the money that could grant their children a better life.

On his first run after his return, he'd found a new bloodhound waiting. Since he'd disappeared for a week, he doubted there'd be another waiting the next day. But there it was. As he tipped it from the Excedrin bottle into his hand, Brad thought again of Agent Day's mysterious trail runner, this phantom woman who ran thirty miles a day to drop her tiny payload into this hole. He had only two nights left to work on the database and was determined to put as many patient records as possible on the drive before his last chance to bring Nueva Vida down was gone.

After two hours of transfers, he knew he'd pushed his window for the work as far as he could. He stood up and practiced one of the variations on the ritual he'd perfected over the past few weeks. Tonight, a back stretch would block the camera before he bent over and slipped the bloodhound out. He took his time with the stretch, then removed the drive quickly and slipped it into his pocket as he turned around.

Staring directly at the hand that had been holding the bloodhound was Rosa. Brad's eyes flicked from her face to the clock on the wall behind her, realizing that, for the first time, he'd missed their nightly dinner date. He looked back to find her dark eyes locked on his. He opened his mouth, but no words came. It didn't matter. She was already walking away.

Chapter Thirty-Eight
God's Garden

HE COULDN'T SLEEP. He couldn't eat. He couldn't call his wife or daughter or the mentor he'd thought was his best friend. He couldn't concentrate long enough to read a book, surf the web, or even finish a bottle of beer. So he did the only things he could do: Brad worked. And Brad ran.

Both helped him steer clear of one of the things that could get him killed: his own fear. He knew if he felt it, Carlos would sense it. And if that happened, Brad would be one step closer to lying on a gurney with a needle stuck in his neck this time. But though he might be able to control his own emotions, he couldn't do that for the other person who held his life in her hands.

Ever since Rosa caught him with the bloodhound, Brad had weighed the chances of her turning him in over and over in his mind. No matter how he shuffled the possibilities, it was impossible to solve; would the woman he'd rescued from being raped hand him over to be killed by the man who'd saved her from the same fate years ago?

Rosa had disappeared from the night shift the evening after she caught Brad. Every squeaking door or click of footsteps had him holding his breath, wondering if he was about to learn that Rosa had turned him in.

Brad didn't touch a single patient chart after that night. He decided then and there that his ill-suited role as a DEA agent was done.

On his last evening on the night shift, Brad did the best he could to keep his mind on his work. When he walked out of Nueva Vida, as the sun was coming up the next morning, he felt the same sense of nervous expectation again. But this time he found himself listening for sounds other than the approaching footsteps that might mark his end.

His ears were tuned for more distant noises as his mind swung from his fears to a far more dangerous feeling: hope. No matter how many times he pushed the thought away, it returned, the notion that one of the bloodhounds he'd dropped into the hole in the dirt was the magical key to his release.

In his mind, he saw its contents pulled up on some distant screen, saw it launch the calls and commands that would send a stream of unmarked vans rumbling down the jungle road and a Black Hawk helicopter dropping from the summer sky. Then the army of black-uniformed federales and blue-jacketed DEA agents would swarm over Nueva Vida to bring his nightmare to an end.

But for now, there was only the distant buzz and caws from the jungle as Brad shuffled from the clinic, his mind blank, his senses numb. Too tired to run and too wired to sleep, he walked past his bungalow and onto the path, where he saw a man slip into the greenhouse ahead of him.

Aldo stood still next to the plant that Brad had completely forgotten about since he'd first seen it sprout. The small spear he'd spotted three weeks before had grown into a seven-foot-tall tapered stalk. But the real prize peeked from the plant's top. Emerging from the tight wrap of the corpse flower's dark green spathe was the telltale tip of the yellow-green spadix that held its inflorescence—proof that the years of vegetative growth the titan arum cycled through had come to an end.

"It's blooming," Brad whispered, unable to take his eyes off the plant.

"*Me allegro,*" Aldo said, "*verte sonreír.*"

"Sorry. *Sonreír?*" Brad asked, still whispering, as if his voice might break the vision before his eyes. When Aldo stayed silent, Brad glanced at the gardener. "What's *sonreír* mean?"

Aldo turned the corners of his mouth down, then reversed them into the smile Brad usually found on the man's face.

"Smile?" Brad asked.

"*Sí,* smile. *Siempre te preocupas.*"

"*Preocupas?*" repeated Brad, trying to understand.

Aldo showed the frown again, raising his eyebrows and putting his hands to his cheeks while he rocked his head from side to side.

"Worry?" Brad asked.

"*Sí,* worry!" Aldo said.

Then he went through a series of other pantomimes while keeping his expression fixed. "*Cuando te veo corriendo,* worry," he said, jogging in place as he frowned. "*Cuando te veo trabajando en el jardín,* worry," he continued, miming the raking at the base of the plant he'd urged Brad against months before.

Finally, Brad got the man's meaning. "I'm paid to *preocupar,* to worry, Aldo. At least when I'm performing surgery. I guess I find it hard to shut it off at other times."

"*Por qué* worry?" Aldo asked, raising his white eyebrows. "Ah K'in worry."

"Who worries?"

"Ah K'in."

"Who's Ah K'in?"

Aldo's face grew solemn. "*Todo es* Ah K'in," he said. "Ah K'in," he repeated, walking over to place his hand against the stalk of the corpse flower, then moved on to touch an orchid, saying the words again. "Ah K'in." He went on to caress a lily, a begonia, the frilly edge of a fern, strolling around the perimeter of the greenhouse to let the tips of his fingers brush the blossoms and leaves of the other plants flourishing in the fertile dome, saying the word as softly as a prayer each time he did.

When Aldo returned, he extended two fingers and tapped Brad gently on his chest. "Ah K'in *está aquí*," he said. "Ah K'in," he repeated, tapping his own chest this time. Then he raised his hands high above his head and lowered them slowly, keeping his arms spread wide as he repeated his lesson. "*Todo es* Ah K'in.*" For a moment, his eyebrows knitted. Then his face relaxed when he found the word he was looking for.

"All," he said. "All *es* Ah K'in. Ah K'in worry. No you."

"You're talking about God," Brad said.

"*Sí, Dios.* God." Aldo fixed Brad with eyes so open and full of guileless compassion that Brad was tempted to look away but didn't. "Ah K'in," Aldo repeated, reaching out to lay the flat of his palm on Brad's chest for a moment. The old man's eyes closed, then opened. He smiled, tipped his head toward Brad, and left.

Brad let his gaze rest on the corpse flower again. With his vision fixed on it, he backed away from the plant until he reached the greenhouse's bench and sat down. He stared, his eyes pinned on the marvelous manifestation of all his gardening dreams.

After so many sleepless nights, so many hours of the draining dance between his fears and their distractions, Brad drifted there, his eyes heavy but open, floating through that nameless place between sleep and the waking world. Aldo's words faded into those from long ago. Somewhere, the gardener's fractured English turned to snippets of Brad's childhood conversations with Sam. No words came with that lost language, only feelings, but the ones that rose in Brad were different from those distant days.

For as long as he remembered, any talk of God from Sam had caused Brad to distance himself from his friend. But when he'd heard that deity referenced now, by another title, another man, in another place and time—the most desperate time of his life—Brad's eyes opened to the possibilities tied to that name.

"Ah K'in," he whispered. Then again. He said it over and over, murmuring it like a mantra as the plant before him blurred into a shimmering green tower stretching between earth and sky. He sat and he chanted. It was no appeal he offered. No prayer sent to heaven above. It was—surrender. And though he knew that concession to the limits of his power might not save him, it did comfort him. For those few minutes, Brad found peace in accepting the truth that there were things in this world that were simply beyond his control.

Chapter Thirty-Nine

D.I. 39

IT WAS A big breakfast. Even after Brad ate four eggs, three pieces of bacon, two slices of toast, and an entire mango, his step was light that morning as he walked the path to work. Carlos had been off-site for a week on a business trip. Though nothing would change when he came back, Brad took comfort in his absence and on losing himself in the demands that came with his return to surgery.

For weeks, he'd seen names like Torres, Gonzalez, and Ortiz on the surgical schedule. Not today. He found he'd been assigned his first American transplant candidate. Clayton Price was the sixty-two-year-old owner of a dry-cleaning chain that stretched from Arkansas to Arizona.

Brad spent the last four days training his new team for the tycoon's transplant. That task had been particularly challenging without the one doctor who'd been his best ally in the OR. Though Rosa was scheduled for the procedure today, Carlos had granted her rare request for a few days away, and Brad wasn't sure she'd make it back.

Now he sat down at his computer in his office to pull up Price's medical records to prep for the pre-op check-in with his team. The story he'd scanned earlier was a typical one: years of smoking, obesity, hypertension, and the genetic wild card of familial kidney disease had finally brought Mr. Price to Nueva Vida's door.

Brad shook his head at one particularly troubling aspect of his patient's history. The anemia caused by the man's end-stage renal disease had resulted in a long series of blood transfusions. For a nephrologist, it was always tricky to weigh the immediate benefit of the red blood cells that raised a patient's hemoglobin levels against the antibodies they triggered, knowing the latter reduced the chances of future donor-organ compatibility. But as Brad looked at the long list of transfusion dates, he questioned the wisdom of the physician who authorized them. With a body primed to fight so many antigens, Clayton Price had been very lucky to find a match for the kidney he'd be receiving today.

Brad made some final notes and headed toward the OR. Ten steps down the hallway, just as he was beginning to visualize today's procedure, he stopped. He stared into space, ignoring the curious glance of a passing orderly as Manny's voice echoed in his head: *Do you not think it is luck two times? First to find match and second to find donor who does match and then agrees to sell kidney?*

A minute later Brad was back in his office, going over Price's chart again. He scrolled slowly, heeding the gut instinct he'd ignored the first time. He realized now that there had been something in Price's chart he didn't understand, and that was not a good way to go into surgery.

He went line by line until he found the entry toward the end of a page that had made no sense to him, under the anonymous donor data. He'd reviewed thousands of patient charts over the past few weeks, becoming fluent in every acronym and data key the database used. But the single entry here still didn't make sense. It read *D.I. 39.*

He stared at the code, if that's what it was, and had the sense that he had seen it before. When he realized where he'd seen it, the surge in his stomach made him regret his big breakfast.

Could you pull it up again? Agent Day had asked about that record. Every instinct for self-preservation drove Brad to refuse that request. But now, heading into the OR—charged with a surgeon's solemn vow to preserve a life other than his own—he had no choice but to learn everything he could about the man he was about to approach with a knife in his hand.

He threw in a few fakes before zeroing in on his actual target, pulling up random patient histories to cover his tracks in the event that the record of this morning's search found its way onto Carlos's desk. He could see Carlos's unblinking eyes in his mind as he tried to spin the thin cover story his boss would instantly see through. With a sigh, Brad quit the charade and moved his mouse to click on the icon for the San Pedro Hospital database.

It would have taken him a long time to sift through the histories of the hundreds of patients in those files to find Hector Vázquez's since the man's name had been redacted like all the names in all the other incoming records. But scanning for the code made his search easy. He found the only chart containing D.I. 39. When Brad started reading, he knew instantly that he was looking at the history of the man who had been murdered so Carlos's uncle could live.

And at that moment, Brad knew something else as well: If he was foolish enough to expose his actions further by doing a system-wide search for D.I. 39, he'd find other hits too—the same code that let him know he was about to transplant a kidney into his patient that Nueva Vida had killed someone to get.

Brad had seen Rosa only twice on campus since the night she'd caught him with the bloodhound. Both times, she'd refused to meet his eyes. Now, here she sat at her post behind her anesthesia cart as Brad strode into the OR in his street clothes, ignoring the stares of his team.

"Shut it down," he said. "Mr. Price won't be getting his kidney today."

✝

He'd been running farther and farther down the jungle road. Brad's five-mile runs in Boston had grown to six or seven in Mexico. Now, with an unexpected morning off after walking out of the OR, he'd decided to push himself further, waiting until his watch beeped to mark eight miles before turning around to complete the second half of his run.

The workout did a good job of distracting him from imagining Carlos's reaction to the cancellation of Mr. Price's surgery. As he stood in the shower in his bungalow, a flood of post-run endorphins calmed his fears about the consequences of his actions long enough for him to consider his options.

He dried off and left for the one place he'd felt anything close to hope. It had been over a week since he'd met Aldo in the greenhouse. Now Brad walked in to find the corpse flower had grown another foot. It towered eight feet high; its long, tapered spadix was now taller than the spathe that embraced its base. The swollen shape and frilled edges of that protective sheaf let Brad know it would be only a few days until the spathe unfurled to reveal the corpse flower's bloom.

As he looked over the burgeoning bud, he wondered what his own future held. He knew that Carlos had invested in him a lot of what the cartel prized above all other things: money.

But he sensed that what mattered even more to Carlos was the faith he'd placed in him.

As he listened to the soft hum of the greenhouse's fans punctuated by the short hiss of the misters spraying through the air, Brad played out a dozen ways the conversation with Carlos might go after Carlos found out that Brand refused to operate. None of the exchanges he ran through his head ended well for Brad.

He turned to the option that had come to him during his run. It relied more on wishes than wits, but still might be his best play. With Manny gone, there was no way to steal a jeep this time. He was certainly tired from the sixteen miles he'd just run through the jungle. If his life depended on it, however, he knew he could do another seventeen. With a headlamp on and his passport and wallet in his daypack, he could make a nighttime run and hit the highway at dawn. After that he'd pin his luck on his thumb and the hope that some stranger's goodwill and the cash in Brad's pocket could get him home.

With Carlos due back anytime, tonight might be his only chance. As desperate as the plan was, when Brad left the greenhouse, he'd decided it was his best hope of making it home alive.

Back in his bungalow, he moved quickly with his new sense of purpose. He set out his next day's running gear and grabbed a fresh T-shirt to conceal the two items he kept stashed at the back of his dresser drawer from some hidden camera's eye.

Brad had gotten pretty good with sleight-of-hand maneuvers after all his bloodhound exchanges. The only reason he couldn't slip his passport and wallet under his T-shirt now was that they weren't there.

Chapter Forty

Full Flower

THE ARTERIAL CLAMPS came off. The stitches connecting the two arteries looked good. The other clamps were removed to perfuse the transplanted kidney. After several seconds, the organ began to pink up.

A moment later, a single drop of blood beaded at the suture where the two arteries were joined. The call for suction came as more drops of blood appeared and merged into a stream.

The call for suction came again. The tip of the aspirator moved over the suture, but the blood flowed so fast that it began to pool in the peritoneal cavity. As the space filled, the kidney turned from pink to a rich red.

The aspirator's tip sank below the surface of the small crimson lake now lapping at the organ's sides. Just as the kidney began to disappear in the rising tide, a whiff of something foul corrupted the OR's purified air.

The smell grew stronger. Now only the top of the kidney glistened over the rising red sea. When the kidney's crest turned from maroon to black, the stench of rotting meat filled the room. As his stomach turned, he clenched his teeth. The bile that rose within his throat raced against his stifled scream.

Brad sat up in bed, shivering in a sheen of sweat, his heart still racing from a dream that wouldn't end. He searched the dark and picked out the white line of a curtain edge, the blue glow from his watch. Everything looked normal. But nothing smelled normal.

The stink from his dream hung to the waking world. He sat, staring, sniffing, then holding his breath, trying to make sense of the putrid scent. Finally, he understood.

The end of the path glowed with the light spilling from the greenhouse's open door. There was a figure standing there, his back to the entrance. Brad drew closer and saw that it was Carlos, wearing a black silk robe, with his hands on his hips, his head tilted back to view the eight-foot-tall flower that bloomed while the rest of the world slept.

"It is magnificent, no?" Carlos asked in a whisper, his eyes fixed on the flower. Brad didn't answer but had to agree.

The plant's spathe had unwrapped from the tapered chartreuse tower of its central spadix to reveal the four-foot-wide inverted skirt of the corpse flower's dark burgundy bloom. The smell was much stronger here, forcing Brad to breathe through his mouth as his eyes explored the depths of the spathe's vase-shaped surface. He flinched when something buzzed by his ear.

"Carrion beetle," Carlos whispered, shaking his head. "Look." He pointed to the bug, which had landed on the wall of the spathe and started to crawl toward the bottom. "It is— what is the expression? Eating the bait?"

"Taking," Brad said. He watched the beetle disappear into the spathe's base, searching for the rotting meat that wasn't there.

"Of course. *Taking* the bait to pollinate the real flowers at the bottom. He is tricked into serving the plant's purpose instead of his own."

"I know just how he feels," Brad said.

Carlos turned to look at him. "And how have I tricked you, Brad?"

"With your lies."

"Cite one."

"It's called a lie of omission, Carlos," Brad said, turning to face him. "And there have been many."

Carlos smiled. "You had only to ask if you wanted to know more about Nueva Vida. But you didn't, did you? Your salary, your status—those were the things you cared about when we first met. Can you deny that's why you came to work for me?"

"Things changed. Maybe I changed."

"You did, Brad!" Carlos put his hand on Brad's shoulder, but Brad brushed Carlos's hand away and took a step back.

Carlos laughed. "You've come so far, yet still you resist."

"What are you talking about?"

"When you first learned we were using paid donors, you were shocked. Why didn't you leave Nueva Vida then?"

Carlos waited, but Brad had no answer. Finally, he said, "I tried to leave after I learned you were killing people, but you put me in a cell and later killed my friend, remember?"

"Manny had the same choice you did. And that is the difference between him and you. Jesus said, 'Unless you change and become like children, you will never enter the kingdom of heaven.' Manny had that kind of faith, the faith of a child. Now he is with his God. But you are a man, Brad. Like me, you know you cannot afford such simple beliefs."

"I don't believe in murder."

"And yet when you discovered that Señor Vázquez was murdered, what did you do? You stayed."

"I stayed to find a way for you to get donors without murdering them. But you still do." Brad's head grew light. He couldn't tell if it was because of the smell of death in the air or the question on his lips that could earn that fate for himself. "What is D.I. thirty-nine?"

For the first time, Brad saw surprise flicker across Carlos's face. "Is that why you called off Señor Price's surgery?" he asked.

"What I can't figure out," Brad said, "is why on earth you would keep a record of the donors you've murdered."

Carlos gave Brad a long look. "Shall we sit?" he asked. He headed over to the bench, sat, and took a cigarette from a case in the pocket of his robe, burning its tip with a small silver lighter. "I think I would like to smell something other than our flower for a moment. I found it very difficult to give up smoking, but on special occasions like this," Carlos said, pointing to the corpse flower with his cigarette, "I still permit myself the pleasure." Brad followed him to the bench but remained on his feet.

"To answer your question, D.I. thirty-nine is a simple code. It indicates those who've benefited from the deaths arranged for the donors who had the organs they needed."

Brad's brows knitted. "Why implicate Nueva Vida with that record?"

"Because we implicate the transplant recipients as well. Anyone wanting to prosecute us will have many powerful people in their way. Those people pay us well, but their value goes far beyond their transplant fees. They come here on their own for illegal operations they pay for through banking transactions that we record.

"Who is to say what they do or do not know about the source of the organs they've conspired to obtain? They have much to lose—their businesses, their homes, their spouses, and families.

And, of course, their freedom. A man who is accustomed to five-star hotels and summer homes finds it particularly hard to imagine life in an eight-by-eight-foot cell." Carlos laughed. "You of all people, Brad, should understand that."

Carlos waited till Brad met his eyes before he went on.

"Most of them don't know that they carry the evidence that can link them to these crimes within their own bodies. Learning that the DNA of their donors can be detected in their blood for years has proven to be enough to earn their silence, and often more."

"More money," Brad said.

"Sometimes. But usually favors. We cannot run Nueva Vida in isolation, despite our jungle home. We need friends in business, medicine, and government to clear the financial and regulatory hurdles that prevent our growth. That is why we use the code you found, to mark these…*benefactors*, I think you might call them. Do you know why I chose the number thirty-nine?"

"Does it matter?"

"To me, yes. D.I. stands for *donante involuntario*—'involuntary donor.' The number after it reminds me why it is necessary, sometimes, to trade one life for another. My father thought himself too good to do the things he needed to do to earn a better life for our family. He died digging a row of corn with a hoe in his hand at the age of thirty-nine.

"When I abandoned him to work with Santiago, it was a difficult decision. But when I stood over my father's grave, I knew I had made the right choice, knowing my children would never suffer his fate.

"But we all must make choices about whom we serve. Manny made his choice to serve his God. You called him your friend. I asked another friend of yours to make a difficult choice, but I think you know that, don't you, Brad?"

Brad had enjoyed surprising Carlos a moment ago but now found himself a step behind his boss again. Carlos laughed.

"I heard the recording of your last conversation with Dr. Webb. He was convinced you knew nothing of our relationship." Carlos drew on his cigarette, winced through the plume of smoke he exhaled, and continued. "I still do not know how you figured it out. But in the recording of your conversation with Dr. Webb, I heard something in your tone, or perhaps it was in your choice of words, that told me that you knew he was in my employ."

"He was my friend," Brad said simply.

"And he was truly distraught about betraying you. But he had so very much to lose. It was he whom we originally picked to head our program at Nueva Vida. But when we learned of the cocaine addiction he'd developed to try to stay sharp in surgery, we found a better way for him to serve our needs; we funneled funds to Boston General through donors that Dr. Webb was credited with securing, *and* promised to keep the secret of his drug use safe. Please do not judge him too harshly, Brad. He did it all for his daughter. It was either lose everything and let Mallory Webb spend the rest of her life locked away in an institution or help me secure a much better chief of surgery."

"Me."

"You. I was far from certain that you'd accept the position, but then, perhaps, God stepped in." It took Brad a moment to catch up.

"God didn't kill Sam Kirby," Brad said.

"And neither did you, though there are some who think you did. No, I am speaking of God's decision to call home a man killed in a car crash. A man whose kidney was the perfect match for your friend." Carlos took another long drag on his cigarette. He held the smoke in for a moment, pursed his lips, then puffed out a perfect smoke ring.

"Did you notice anything unusual in the autopsy report on Señor Kirby that Dr. Webb sent you?"

Brad frowned. "Partial blockage of the coronary artery, just as I suspected. There was nothing in it that would make anyone accuse me of malpractice."

"What about his potassium level?"

"I don't remember the numbers, but he had end-stage renal disease, so I suspect it was high."

"Yes," Carlos said, "it was *very* high."

Brad tried to figure out where Carlos was going with this, but the mingled scents of the corpse flower and the cigarette smoke finally got to him, and the world began to spin. He stretched out his hand to steady himself, and Carlos stood up and guided Brad to the bench. Brad sat down, leaned forward, and closed his eyes, breathing through his mouth to avoid the stench. Carlos sat next to him and remained silent until Brad opened his eyes.

"You weren't the only one who jumped into action when you received that phone call from Sam. There was someone other than Peter Webb we'd been speaking with at Boston General, though Dr. Webb did not know about those conversations."

Brad turned to meet Carlos's gaze.

"He was a low-level employee, just a lab technician," Carlos said. "But a small man with very large debts. Luis met with him the week before you came to Cancún."

Brad looked down and shook his head.

"Someone had to die on your table to convince you to work for me, Brad. I'm sorry it had to be your friend. But when we intercepted your call from Sam in the early morning of the very day that you and I were supposed to meet, I took it as a sign. I've found that when you work long enough for the things you believe in, the right doors open for you."

"How did he do it?" Brad asked, still staring at the floor.

"The lab technician?" Carlos laughed. "I can tell you; he was probably more upset than you to be woken by a call that night. But what I said to him got him moving fast. He got to the hospital in time to inject twenty ccs of potassium chloride into one of the units of blood you ordered. That single shot erased his gambling debts and—"

"Killed Sam," Brad said.

"It was a difficult decision. For most men, the amount of money I offered you would have been enough to secure their services. But I didn't want most men. I wanted one who'd committed his life to medicine, not money. I wanted you.

"A moment ago, you said that maybe you changed from someone tempted by the salary and position that brought you to Nueva Vida, but I don't believe that to be the case. In the beginning, Sam's death made you vulnerable to those temptations. But I think, in the end, the money was not why you stayed. It was your position you were not willing to sacrifice. It came with the thing Nueva Vida was named for; a power that people like you share with God—the chance to grant new life to those facing its end.

"Which brings us to another decision you must now make." Carlos stood, dropped his cigarette butt on the ground, and crushed it under his slipper. Then he walked over to retrieve a large manila envelope from the potting table. He turned to face Brad, tapping the envelope against his leg as he spoke.

"Your business plan for Nueva Vida really was brilliant. And I hope you do take comfort in knowing that the increase in donors it will bring may eliminate the need for some involuntary ones, though not all.

"But my partners are just as eager to secure the exclusive use of ReNovus you promised. We will require another physician of your stature and talents to handle the increased workload I'm sure we'll enjoy as a result of your plan. We need your help in convincing the one man who is key to both to join us down here."

It took Brad a minute to respond to the murderer standing beside him. It was one thing to mete out justice to a rapist caught in the act, but the needle Carlos had stuck in Octavio's neck with his own hand was far less maleficent than the one he'd coolly ordered to be placed in a bag of blood half a world away. The light tapping of the envelope against Carlos's leg finally broke Brad's spell. Its soft and steady pats sounded as ominous as a ticking bomb.

Brad replayed Carlos's last words in his head: *We need your help in convincing the one man who is key to both to join us down here.* Brad frowned. "You want Riker?"

"Dr. Webb assures me that Dr. Riker is the one person standing in the way of the board approving our use of your drug."

"We're not exactly friends, Carlos. I can't imagine him agreeing to grant Nueva Vida the ReNovus license, much less coming down here to work with me."

"Dr. Webb is doing what he can in Boston to promote what Nueva Vida can do for Dr. Riker's career. The money we're offering him has him close to accepting the position, but there's something else he wants before he comes to Nueva Vida."

"What?"

"An apology."

"From *me?*"

"It seems he was quite upset by the way you spoke to him in front of the board. For him, your apology is what might be called…a signing bonus? Though Dr. Riker didn't put it quite that way."

Brad shook his head.

"It's the last thing you need to say to the man before you get him on a plane," Carlos said. "Once he's here, I can convince him that it is in his best interests to work with you."

"By putting him in a cell?"

"Why don't you leave the negotiations to me?"

"I won't do it," Brad said.

"As I said, it is your decision to make. But I must say, I think it is easier than the choices I presented to Dr. Webb and Dr. Pena. You don't have to choose between protecting your daughter or your friend or between losing your soul or your life. Your choice is to save either the man who betrayed you or the people you love."

Carlos held the manila envelope out to Brad. It hovered there in the putrid air for a long moment. When Brad finally took it, Carlos left.

Brad's hands shook as he fumbled with the small metal clasp on the envelope's back. He withdrew a stack of glossy white papers, then flipped it to reveal the top photo in the pack.

The shot was of a handsome brick building with a tall tower. The photo lying under it showed a circle of young people standing on a sunny lawn, the yellow disk of a Frisbee frozen between them in midair. Brad couldn't place the location of those scenes until he saw the third photo. When he did, he realized the photographer was a very patient man. His lens must have been trained on the dorm window for a long time before he found the face he was looking for. And when he did, his shutter clicked just in time to capture Grace's smile.

Chapter Forty-One

Glass Houses

BRAD MADE THE decision somewhere over Virginia. After that, everything was simpler. And much, much harder.

✦

He had the cab from the airport drop him off in town. He'd call another one later to take him home. For now, he wanted only a cup of coffee. But he spent three hours inside the Beacon Bean.

✦

"Jesus," Catherine said with a gasp when Brad walked into the kitchen.

"Nope, just me."

"Why didn't you tell me you were coming home?"

"I only found out I was coming last night. I tried calling you from the airport, but your voice mail was full."

She was standing there in a blue blazer and panties, holding a gift bag with a wine bottle peeking out of its top in one hand and a can of cat food in the other. He tried not to laugh but failed.

"You think this is funny?" Catherine asked. Then her face flicked through so many expressions that Brad didn't know what to expect from her—certainly not the next thing she said next. "You can't just keep showing up here."

"Why not? I live here."

"Since when?"

Catherine's cell phone chirped on the table behind her. "I have to take that," she said, and held the can in her hand out to him. "Here, feed the cat."

"What cat?"

"I got a cat."

"You got a cat?"

She put the can on the counter, scooped up the phone, and walked into the dining room. Brad took his laptop bag off his shoulder and placed it on the floor next to his suitcase, then took the can to the electric opener. When he pressed the button, he heard the soft patter of paws coming down the stairs. A moment later he felt something brush up against his ankle and looked down to see a calico kitten. Catherine came back in as he dumped the contents of the can into the bowl the tiny creature was circling around on the floor.

"Why'd you get a cat?" he asked.

"To keep me warm at night. Listen, I've got to go."

"Go where?"

"Patty Dilworth's bridal shower."

"Who's Patty Dilworth?"

Catherine frowned. "Our receptionist," she said, waving a hand in the air as if to brush the question away. "She's new. Brad, why are you here?"

"I didn't know I was coming home until—"

"Wait. Wrong question. I don't really care *why* you're here. The only thing I want to know is, are you here for good?"

He looked at her for a moment before his eyes found a safer place to land on the cat.

"Because if you are," Catherine continued, "I'll forget about stupid Patty Dilworth's shower. I'll forget that you replied to every long e-mail I sent you with your cold comments about our checking account or the weather. I'll forget all the fears I had about what you've been doing down there in Mexico every day or who you might be sleeping with at night—"

"Cat—"

"I'll forget it all," she said. She pointed to the bottle in the gift bag she'd left on the counter. "And you and I can sit down right here, right now, share this bottle of wine, and start all over again."

He reached out his hand, but she wouldn't take it. "Not till you answer me," she said.

He stood there. Even now, with everything falling apart between them, he wanted nothing more than to take her upstairs to bed. He loved everything about her—the long legs above her slightly pigeon-toed feet, the single cowlick by her ear that refused to get in line with the other curls, the way she tipped her chin up right before she started to cry, like she was doing now. The cruelest thing he could do was tell her the truth. So he didn't.

"I'm going back," he said.

Now the cat was winding between Catherine's legs. She picked it up and held it to her face, whispering into its fur. "You're so selfish."

Emotional recall. That was the term Grace used when Brad asked her how she'd been able to actually shed tears over Romeo when she'd played Juliet in the high-school play. He didn't feel angry now, but by remembering the times he had, he sum-moned that emotion easily.

"*I'm* selfish?" he said. "Look around! This house, your mother's apartment, her medical bills, Grace's college,—I pay for it all."

"It takes more than a check to pay for it!" Catherine said, her eyes narrowing as the tears started to spill. "Who do you think keeps it all going while you're down there running around in the jungle? Who cleans the house, pays the bills, feeds our daughter? Remember her? Who waited up every night while Grace was, who knows where, with Captain Cannabis, wondering if she would come home wasted or pregnant, or if she'd come home at—"

"You think I wanted to be down there? I was—"

"Yes! Yes, I do! I think the bigger part of you did. Does! Playing the martyr, *the good doctor*, sacrificing himself to save lives. Well, guess what, Doctor—you forgot to save your marriage. I'm done with it."

Catherine's face crumpled as she started to sob, burying her face in the cat's fur again. She whispered her last words as she ran out of the room, but Brad heard them clearly: "I want a divorce."

He went over to the kitchen table, turned a chair around, and dropped into it to view the world outside. It was that golden time of day: just before it ends, the sunlight slanting between the long shadows of the houses and trees, the last calls of birds mixed with the sounds of children playing their games. He watched the day fade as he heard Catherine getting ready above, kept watching as he heard her heels click downstairs and tap quickly behind him across the kitchen floor. The clicks didn't stop as she spoke to his back on her way out. "I'm not coming back tonight," she said. Then she was gone.

The kitten had followed her downstairs. Now it jumped into Brad's lap. He reached for its head with his eyes still on the world outside. His fingers found the small nub of the animal's chin and scratched beneath it. As it began to purr, he realized he didn't even know the thing's name.

Later, he laid out his business suit on the king-size bed upstairs and thought about the meeting he'd packed the suit for. Carlos hadn't granted him any extra time for this visit. Brad had a nine-a.m. appointment with Miles in Peter's office tomorrow and two first-class tickets lying on his bureau for a flight from Boston to Cancún the following day.

His gray pin-striped jacket and pants looked flat and empty there in the middle of the white coverlet spread across the big bed. He turned away and almost stepped on the kitten, which had crossed the room's deep pile rug without a sound. When he headed down the stairs, the little animal trailed after him, more like a dog than a cat.

From the liquor cabinet over the stove, he grabbed a full bottle of Glenfiddich, broke the seal, took a long sip, and set the bottle down in the middle of the kitchen island. He opened the back door and looked out as the night began to fall. It was warm for Boston, but much cooler than the evenings he was used to now. He noticed a firefly spark nearby and felt the kitten brush past his leg. It bounded onto the lawn and jumped, clapping its small paws at the spot where the bug had disappeared. Brad went after the cat, but it ran away toward the greenhouse.

The door had been left open wide enough for the kitten to slip in. When Brad flipped on the wall switch, he was glad to find the lights worked—until he saw the view inside. It hadn't changed that much since the last time he'd seen it, but some-how the place seemed deader now. Even the rotting scent he'd smelled during his last visit home would have been welcome. Now there was no smell at all; the straw stalks and curled leaves around him had gone as dry as the cracked surface of the broken earth in the big pot he looked at, the one he'd fretted over for so many hours. He went over and put his finger in the soil. It was hard as bone.

He found the cat under a shelf and carried it back to the house. It let out a mew when he put it down. He gave it a pat on the butt to shoo it away from the door so he could shut it before he ducked back outside. As he did, he thought of the last pet he'd found here, then finished the door's swing with a slam.

He headed to the garden shed outside the greenhouse but stopped before reaching it. A flickering constellation of fireflies floated in front of its door. He stared at them for a while, watching the pattern of tiny yellow stars shift and swirl as they winked on and off in the dark.

The big plastic bucket was right where he'd left it, in the corner of the shed, still half full of the river rocks he'd used to edge the flower beds by the patio. He hefted it with both hands and carried it into the greenhouse.

He shut the lights off in the greenhouse and threw the first rock, holding his breath as the sharp crack of glass echoed inside. It wasn't as loud as he'd feared, but still, nothing good ever came from that sound. He worried that a neighbor's call might come from the other side of his wide lawn or, even worse, that he'd see a flash of headlights wash across it as some cop rolled up to see what was going on.

After three or four throws, he knew he was in the clear. No yell floated over the fence. No bark came from some distant dog. All the sounds were ones he made, and they were different with every throw. Sometimes it was a tinkle. Other times a crash. Still others, nothing but the skittering whisper of glass across the stone floor. He waited for the silence that followed each one before he grabbed the next stone. At last, his hand sank into the pail to find nothing but air.

Chapter Forty-Two

The Silent Sea

BRAD DIDN'T SLEEP. He spent the night moving from one room to another in his empty home, carrying the scotch with him. He put the bottle to his lips often during his tour.

He started in the garage, looking over the used green Subaru Outback that he and Catherine had given to Grace for her graduation present. He certainly hadn't seen the small brown rust spots at the bottom of the driver's side door when he found the car online. But the rest of the vehicle looked in good shape. The Bowdoin sticker Grace had put on the back bumper made him smile. Though freshmen weren't allowed to have cars on campus, she'd obviously been excited to share her passion for her new school.

Brad got into his F150 and turned the key. The only sound it produced was a click. He wasn't surprised. Grace rarely used the truck and Catherine wouldn't touch the thing.

Someone had certainly been in his BMW. The car's bright red finish gleamed under the bare bulbs in the garage, making him wonder if it had been both washed and waxed while he was away. When he got in and pushed the icon on his key fob, the marvelous machine purred to life instantly.

He popped the hood and grabbed a pair of jumper cables to get the truck going too. He warmed it up and shut it down. It'd probably be dead the next time someone tried to start it, but he felt better knowing the thing could still run.

Halfway through the kitchen, he stopped to stare at the fridge. Grace had drawn a silly "Gone to College" cartoon of herself on the magnetic board the family used to write their grocery list on. Catherine had yet to wipe the picture away.

The den they'd used as a dog room had evidently become the cat's domain. The kitten was fast asleep, curled upside down in a bowl of potpourri on the windowsill, ignoring the plush new cat bed Catherine had parked on the floor.

Brad took a half-hearted spin through his basement gym before finally going upstairs. He spent most of the rest of the evening lying on Grace's canopy bed, scanning the posters of boy bands she'd lost interest in long ago. The line of dolls she'd collected as a child seemed to stare down at him from where they sat on a shelf. He couldn't tell whether it was disdain or indifference that he read in their glassy eyes.

On his way out of her room, he spied the edge of a red cookie tin peeking out from the closet. He got down on his hands and knees, opened it, and smiled to see the cache inside: a rainbow of sea glass fragments, three tiny pinecones, a white sand dollar, a small blue feather, and a collection of stones and shells that Grace had picked up from the beach near their home in Maine. He took a periwinkle shell and put it in his pocket, hoping she wouldn't mind.

When he got to his bedroom, the only thing he wanted was a shower. He took his time shaving after that. The reflection of the bed caught his eye in the medicine cabinet mirror just as he was wiping a streak of shaving cream from his chin. He went over to Catherine's side and bent over the faint impression left by her head on the pillow. He drew closer, shutting his eyes as he breathed in a trace of her perfume mixed with the sweeter scent of her skin.

He put on a pair of jeans and his favorite Tufts sweatshirt, left the suit on the bed but took the scotch bottle with him.

In the kitchen, he fed the cat and gave it a pat, then left for work like it was any other day. The only difference was, he wasn't dressed for it and was starting it five hours earlier than usual.

At one a.m., Brad had Common Street to himself. At the intersection with Concord Avenue, he brought the BMW to a stop. He thought about how many mornings he'd taken the right-hand turn that brought him to start another shift at BG.

He'd had his sights set on Boston General ever since he first visited Sam there as a child. The BG doctor had diagnosed the diabetes that Sam's Maine physician had missed and was treating him for the diabetic ketoacidosis that had come on with frightening speed. Now, as Brad sat with his engine idling in the dark, he thought about the irony of that first visit to the hospital he'd called home for so long. The doctor who'd saved Sam's life had inspired Brad to follow in his footsteps. Yet, in the end, Brad failed to do the same thing.

He took his foot off the brake and turned left. Twenty minutes later he was on I-95 north with the cruise control set to 75. After that, he kept his hands on the wheel, his eyes on the road, and his ears tuned to the hum of his tires. Every time a thought popped into his head, he returned to that hum. He didn't want to think. He only wanted to drive.

He made his way through the early morning, eventually rising over the curve of the Piscataquis Bridge to see the small green sign welcoming him to Maine.

Even in the wee hours of the morning, there'd been some sparse traffic on Interstate 95 and islands of light winking from the buildings and streets the highway rose over. But now, as he descended the other side of the bridge, he saw nothing but the dark forest that had earned the Pine Tree State its nickname.

His eyes flicked to the clock on the car's digital display. It would be six hours before Miles made it into Peter's office for their meeting. Part of Brad wanted nothing more than to walk in with a smile for both of them and offer Miles his hand. Carlos had picked up on traces of duplicity in Brad's voice during his last meeting with Peter. But Brad was a quick study. He could do better next time.

As he drove, he imagined how good it would feel to get Miles on that plane, knowing the conversation Carlos would have with the ambitious young surgeon once Brad delivered him. It would be such a satisfying game to land Miles in the same "jungle clinic" Miles had mocked Brad for running. But he'd made his choice. He was playing a different game now. And the stakes were higher.

An hour later, he turned onto 295. When he saw the low, blocky skyline of Portland come into view, he thought of his wife. Portland had been their getaway city ever since the first weekend he'd taken Catherine there as a surprise. He'd been a med student then, pinching pennies to pay for a single night's stay in a room tucked into the turret of the Regency Hotel. The early Christmas gift he gave her the next morning cost a lot more. For the rest of that day, she kept holding up that diamond ring on her third finger as they strolled along the city's cobblestoned streets.

He crossed Tukey's Bridge, looked west, and caught the silvery plain of Portland's Back Cove out of the corner of his eye. He remembered the snowy walk he and Catherine took around its perimeter during that magical weekend, then did the math on how long it had been since then.

The number of years he came up with triggered another date in his mind: he realized that the last day of this month would be their twenty-fifth wedding anniversary—and that Catherine would be spending it alone.

With Portland in his rearview mirror, Brad drove on into the endless miles of forest blanketing the rest of Maine. With no traffic at all now, it was easy for him to spot the thing he'd been looking for ever since he took the left on Concord Avenue.

It was too early for most people to be on their way to work, and almost all the commuters would be heading *toward* Portland in a few hours, not away. It could have been a trucker making the long haul to Augusta, Bangor, maybe even Canada. There were a thousand reasons for the vehicle about a quarter of a mile behind him to be on the road.

He started varying his speed, pressing lightly on the gas pedal, then easing off for a mile or two, then accelerating again. All the time, the headlights behind him stayed right where they were, never coming closer, never drifting farther away.

When Brad saw the exit for Brunswick, his pulse quickened. He imagined taking it, parking on some dark side street, sprinting across Bowdoin's manicured lawns, and standing outside of Hyde Hall, calling for his daughter over and over just to see Grace's face for a moment behind a distant window.

But he kept his hands steady on the wheel and passed the exit. His attention drifted from the road to trace a string of memories, starting with the night of Grace's birth, and ending with that last evening on Little Crow Island. They'd had so many days together, good days, the kind he could only hope for when he stood over her crib that first night Catherine and he had brought her home from the hospital. Why didn't those days feel like enough? Why did they all feel so far away from that place in the future where his daughter might go?

Brad drove on. Past Augusta. Waterville. Pittsfield. He passed a few cars going south. A few passed him going north. But the pair of headlights behind him remained.

He made his move ten miles south of Bangor. Every mile after that, he began to goose his speed. He was doing 90 by the time he spotted a big vehicle under a streetlight on the rise ahead.

A few seconds later, he could see that it was a logging truck cruising along in the right-hand lane as it approached the exit for Route 395. Brad pushed his foot to the floor. The headlights behind him began to close in.

Just as he passed the logging truck, he turned the wheel sharply to the right. A deafening blast blared from the trucker's horn. Brad hugged the wheel at the sound, which was followed by a long, piercing screech and the stink of rubber burning on the road.

He hit the gas again, looked left, and saw a black sedan whiz by in the passing lane just before he cut the wheel right to turn onto 395.

By the time he got to Ellsworth, he had to slow down as the fog rolling in from the coast grew thicker. It was still a half hour until sunrise, but the day's first light made the gray mist more confusing as pockets of light and shadow strobed across the car's windshield.

It was quiet here, where Route 1 twisted and turned along the coast. The only car he saw as he drew closer to Hancock came from the other direction and then disappeared into the darkness behind him.

Just north of Goldsboro, a pair of headlights winked in his rearview mirror. They came up fast, then drifted back until Brad could make out a faint glow trailing him as he approached Route 186.

If he hadn't driven that loop road around Schoodic Peninsula for most of his life, there was no way Brad could've made the turn onto the narrow lane at the speed he was going. The car slipped sideways as he tried to keep its wheels glued to the road's curve.

A few minutes later, he rolled down the window to breathe in the salty tang of the sea, speeding south as the first rips in the gray clouds revealed scarlet strips of dawn.

His father's smile flashed in Brad's mind, with white teeth flashing so bright against the black stubble of his beard that Brad felt he could actually *see* his father's face reflected in the windshield, flickering among the shadows cast by the past and the line of passing pines.

Just before he reached the tip of Schoodic Point, another relic of the life he'd lived appeared in his mind—this time as sound. As a pale disk broke the clouds to shine silver on the sea, Brad heard Sam's laugh echo over the waves.

And in the midst of the terror rising in his chest, Brad felt the bright blue spark of hope flare. Hope for another chance. Another start. Another life, promised by the coming day.

Moments later, the red BMW crested the top of Blueberry Hill. An osprey was the only witness to the car's race to its end. A shriek of metal and crack of glass exploded below the big bird, startling it out of its dive to send it back into the sky. For a long moment, the vehicle flew too, then fell with a single splash that sent a plume of white to bloom among the distant waves. When the water settled, the car's wheels faced the sky.

By the time the two men in a black sedan had parked and were peering down on the wreck, the tide had taken the car far from the shelter of the shore. The car made a slow half-turn, listed to one side, and slipped into the silent sea.

Chapter Forty-Three

Post-Op Care

AM I ALIVE?
Am I dead?
Am I…at all?

The smell sparked the first thing that might be called a memory. No, the smells. There were many, layered one upon the other. The bite of antiseptic. A soapy perfume. The faint tang of bleach. Underneath it all, something darker. Ranker. The animal scents from the human body that those other odors might mask but could never hide.

The sounds were familiar too. Distant beeps. Regular. Steady. A swish of soft clicks—a curtain? A door opening. A door closing. The squeak of sneakers coming and going accompanied by distant voices that spoke without words before trailing away.

There were no sights. Only darkness. Then, a thought: *Open your eyes.* But the cloud he'd tried to rise from beckoned. He followed that call instead. So much easier to fall back into that abyss than to try to rise.

+

"How are you feeling, Mr. Gorton?"

"Who's…Gorton?" he asked, his voice cracking as his eyes fluttered open. He raised his hand and touched the thick pad over his nose and winced. When his fingers went to a gauze pad taped over his cheek, another hand came, gently closed over his, and moved his hand away.

A face fluttered in and out of focus between his slit eyelids. A woman laughed softly and the tip of a straw touched his lips. "Drink, Mr. Gorton," the voice said. "Your ride is waiting. It's almost time to go home."

Where's that? he wondered. By the time he was dressed and being wheelchaired to the hospital door, Brad was pretty sure he didn't have a home.

Dennis Day got out of the gray Ford Explorer waiting at the curb, grabbed Brad's duffel bag from the orderly, and steered Brad into the car. Brad shivered, surprised by the cold. In the passenger seat, he slumped back and let Dennis buckle him in. "How ya doing, Mr. Gorton?" Dennis asked as they pulled away.

Brad shut his eyes. "I forgot I was Gorton when the nurse called my name."

"I'm sure she's heard stranger things from a patient coming out of surgery. How you feeling?"

"Like I just went ten rounds with Mike Tyson."

"Shit, you could take Tyson these days."

"Not like this," Brad said, waving a hand at his bandaged face.

"I told you not to do it."

"I remember," Brad said. And as the last clouds of anesthesia cleared from his muddled mind, Brad started to remember everything.

✦

He'd laughed right in Dennis Day's face that afternoon in the jungle when the agent laid out his contingency plan. "The DEA's just gonna fork over a hundred grand to buy a BMW they might never use?" Brad asked.

"They'll only be out the cash it takes to fit it with the automation system," Day said. "If we don't use it, they'll just take it out and sell it again."

"And if you do?" Brad asked. "What then? The car won't be worth much after they pull it out of the Gulf of Maine."

"If we do that, we'll have your car to keep."

"Oh," Brad said. "I didn't think of that."

"We did," Day said.

On the plane ride home from Cancún a month after that surprise jungle meeting with Day, Brad realized he had three choices: He could take Miles back to Mexico and help him transplant murdered donors' kidneys for the rest of his life; he could make a run for it with his family that would probably get them all killed; or he could try Dennis Day's Hail Mary plan.

So the first thing Brad did after landing at Logan was walk into the Beacon Bean, punch the code into the keypad by the door in the back, and wait for Day. An hour later, Brad listened closely as Day gave him details of the plan. As ridiculous as it still seemed, Brad began to appreciate the difference between himself and the man sitting across from him. Brad had never been able to stay a step ahead of the cartel, at least not for long. But with the full force of the federal government, Dennis Day sure had. Day and his team planned the whole thing to a T, knowing that *they* controlled the clock for when their game would begin—the moment Brad's BMW, carrying the bug the cartel had planted under it months ago, deviated from the route Carlos expected him to take.

"Leave your house at one a.m.," Dennis Day told Brad as the bang of pots and pans from the Beacon Bean's small kitchen echoed on the other side of the thinly paneled walls. "That'll get you to the Schoodic around dawn. The peninsula should be deserted, but we'll have a state trooper posted in a cruiser to pull over anyone who tries to get on 186, just in case. You said you're a good driver?"

"I think I am."

"Good. Keep your eyes on your rearview mirror. At some point, you'll see the black Lexus we've been tracking carrying a couple of the cartel's crew. One of them will probably be your buddy Luis."

"Great."

"Play a bit of cat-and-mouse with them once they start following you. Make 'em think you're nervous. Remember your part in the story. You can even try to lose them, since they'll be tracking the bug, but let 'em catch up to you again. Eventually they're gonna figure that you're headed for your house in Goldsboro. The trickiest part will be the peninsula itself."

"Why?" Brad asked.

"You need to buy us some time. Drive like hell once you're on 186. We'll need to do the switch as fast as we can, then put things in play when they get close to that spot. When you reach the turnoff for Schoodic Head, don't take it. Stop in the middle of the loop road. We'll have the rigged BMW right there. You haul ass and run toward the van we'll have standing by. Meanwhile, my guys will remove the bug Carlos's boys attached to the undercarriage of your car and plant it on the rover so they can do their thing."

"The rover?"

"Yeah. That's what they call the BMW they rigged up to drive itself up the road and off the cliff. They've already practiced taking it to the edge a couple of times."

"They can really do that?"

"The technology's been around for more than thirty years. There's over a thousand self-driving cars on the road right now, going a lot farther than the half a mile we'll pilot the rover between the turnoff to Schoodic Head and Blueberry Hill. You picked a good spot. It's a long straight shot down the Schoodic before there. The hill's not that high, but with nothing but rocks and surf below, it's high enough. But the best part is that it's smack-dab in the middle of the sharp curve around the tip of the peninsula, the perfect place for a loser, who's rushing to his childhood home to lick his wounds, to lose control, especially with a bottle of scotch in him."

Brad fixed Day with a stare. "You think that's what I am?"

"It doesn't matter what *I* think. It's what the rest of the world believes. Especially Carlos, after he watches you sipping Glenfiddich all night long from the cameras he planted in your house."

Brad frowned. "What about my body?"

"What about it? It's all paperwork: the accident report, the death certificate, the coroner's findings, the toxicology report that pegs your blood alcohol level well over the legal limit. It's amazing what people will believe when the news comes from the authorities, and we got the ones we need on our side. The Nueva Vida bust is gonna make the careers of some pretty powerful people."

"Like you?"

"No. I'm talking about the head honchos way above my pay grade. They know how to work the system, and the few people they need to help them do it will fall in line."

Brad stood up and pushed his folding chair back from the table in the dingy little room. He shook his head as he looked around, wondering why a federal agency with access to the billions of dollars seized from drug kingpins couldn't rent a better place to hatch the plots that would bring them down.

"What about Catherine?" he asked, raking a hand through his hair.

"What about her?"

"She's not part of your…system. She might demand to see my body."

"She might, but there won't be one."

Brad's mouth opened, but no words came out.

Day laughed. "I told you," he said, "it's all about contingencies. We thought about that one, and we're going to beat her to the punch. The accident report will say you were thrown from the car. We'll wait a week or so, then send an agent posing as a Massachusetts state trooper to tell her they found your body washed up on a beach in Frenchman's Bay a few miles from the crash."

Brad shook his head and looked at the floor. "That'll be a bad day for her. And Grace," he said softly.

"I'm sorry, Brad—"

"She's stubborn, Dennis. She might still demand to see it."

"Again, there's a plan. There are plenty of John Does in the world. If we need a badly decomposed body, we'll get one. And I can promise you we won't have to unzip much of the body bag before your wife asks us to close it up again."

"Jesus," Brad said. "I hope it doesn't come to that."

For all of Dennis Day's plotting, one of the best twists in the tale of Brad's demise didn't come from him. It was only a few hours after Brad left the Beacon Bean that Catherine asked him for a divorce. Lucky was the last thing Brad felt when she hit him with that request, but as he sat alone in his big empty kitchen after she walked out, he realized how perfectly the news fit their plan. And every stone he threw in his greenhouse helped complete the portrait Dennis Day had begun to paint: the picture of a man who'd run away from his troubles to save himself in the jungles of Mexico, only to come home and find he'd lost everything.

Chapter Forty-Four

Laid Up in Limbo

"HOME SWEET HOME," Dennis Day said when he pulled into the Loon's Nest motel just outside of Minneapolis. It had been a half-hour ride from the hospital, but Brad was still shaky when he got out of the car. He accepted the agent's help as Day ushered him into one of the two rooms he'd booked for them. Brad lay back on a stack of pillows before Day positioned ice packs around Brad's swollen face.

Dennis laughed softly. "Hard to believe it, but the nurse told me you're gonna look even worse tomorrow."

"Rhinoplasty isn't exactly a walk in the park," Brad replied, his eyes closed.

"I won't say I told you so."

"Good. Let's not go there again."

They'd had plenty of time to discuss the procedure on the long drive to the safe house outside Chicago the day after the crash. "The witness protection program is no joke," Dennis told him. "We're working on setting you up with a completely new identity. Everything will be new—your job, the town you live in, the story of the life you lived before. But you gotta do your part to make it work. The key to that is the three Ds."

"Which are?"

"*Distance, distract,* and *disguise.* We want you far away from Boston, but that's the easy part of *distance.* Luis and his buddy spent a long time on that cliff after the rover went off. They had just enough time to pull out a camera with a telephoto lens and take shots of the BMW before it sank. Then Luis's partner stood on the cliff scanning the sea with a pair of binoculars for almost an hour while Luis went down the road and walked back and forth across that little scrap of a beach doing the same thing. We intercepted their communications with Carlos after that. They all think you're dead, Brad. But if you make contact with Catherine or Grace or anyone from your past life, they'll know you're alive."

"Understood."

"Good. Now, as far as *distract* goes, that's mostly a mental thing. The most important person you need to sell your new identity to is you. You gotta commit to it completely. If you believe it, others will too. That's the best way to distract your new neighbors from any suspicions they may have about the new guy in town."

"And *disguise*? You got a fake mustache for me or what?"

"Don't knock that idea, but not a fake one. Everything's gotta be as real as you can make it. A beard would be a good start."

Brad was quiet for a moment. "What about plastic surgery?"

Dennis laughed. "You've seen too many movies. We hardly ever do that. It's expensive and not that effective."

But when they got to Chicago, Dennis gave Brad two things that eventually helped Brad change Day's mind: a new laptop belonging to Brad Gorton and lots of time. Brad did some online research and learned that a nose job was the plastic surgery procedure that could make the biggest difference in a person's appearance. He was convinced that a particular surgeon in Minneapolis was the best man for the job.

Dennis tried to talk him out of it, but Brad showed him a series of before-and-after shots on the surgeon's website that Dennis had to admit made the subjects pretty hard to identify. But he was still resistant to the idea until Brad gave him another reason for wanting the surgery.

"You said I needed to commit to my identity to pull this off, right?" Brad asked.

"It's the only way it'll work."

"I'm a surgeon. I know exactly what will happen once they put me under. They're going to take a knife, slice the tip of my nose open, peel the skin back, dissect the cartilage beneath it, and muscle it into its new shape. If that doesn't show my commitment to my new identity, I don't know what will."

Two days later they were on the road to Minneapolis.

✦

They cooled their heels in the Loon's Nest for a month, waiting for Brad's facial swelling to go down enough to erase any trace of the surgery. Dennis fussed over him for the first few days until Brad shooed him away. Then the agent came and went from the DEA's local field office while Brad struggled to find ways to fill his days.

The TV got old fast, and though the plastic surgeon had told Brad he'd have to knock off running for at least a month, Brad began walking a bit farther each day. After three weeks, he was up to a dozen miles, leaving the watch he'd always worn to check his progress during his runs on the nightstand in the motel. He sifted through every memory of the events that had led him to this lonely limbo, losing himself for hours as he strolled, his mind adrift in that space between his past and whatever future he might find.

A week before Brad was scheduled to start his new life, Dennis walked into Brad's motel room while he was eating breakfast and dropped a newspaper on the table in front of him. The headline read: "Illegal Transplant Clinic Raided by Joint U.S.–Mexico Task Force."

Brad put down his blueberry muffin and raced through the article while Dennis waited on the twin bed opposite him. Then he read the piece again, much more slowly.

"They only mention Peter's arrest," Brad said when he finally looked up.

"Field office said Webb tried to bluff his way out of it for all of five minutes. He's out on bail for now, but that won't last. But I heard the ex stepped in to take care of the daughter."

"They didn't get Carlos?"

"Only his lieutenants. Someone must have tipped him off. We had twin raids timed for Nueva Vida and his villa. He and his family were gone. They might still get him, but the cartel's big, Brad, and its roots go deep down there—in law enforcement and just about everything else. Even if we do find him, he's got a big family. And lots of friends."

"What about *my* family?" Brad asked.

"The DEA will hold up our end. We seized a lot of Nueva Vida's assets, though it looks like there are plenty we'll never get our hands on. We got our cover story set. Catherine will get a visit from one of our guys in a few weeks, just like I said. He'll tell her he's an agent from the insurance company that you took a second life insurance policy out with.

"So," Day said, getting up from the bed to pace around the tiny room, "now that you know your family will get the money and you've gotten your new nose, I want you to reconsider the place you're so intent on going and what you're going to do once you get there. I told you how important distance was for keeping you safe, distance in both your location and career."

"It's a completely different country, Dennis."

"Canada's not that different. And New Brunswick's too close to Boston, not to mention your roots in Maine. And not being a surgeon anymore is not enough. If you try playing doctor again, there's a very good chance your cover will be blown. And when Carlos finds you next time—you're dead."

Brad waited until Dennis had calmed down and settled on the other bed again. He stayed quiet until the agent finally met his eyes. "Dennis," he said. "Nothing you can say is going to change my mind. I'm giving up everything—my family, my career, everything I owned, or, maybe, everything that owned me, I guess.

"Down in Mexico, I told myself that everything I was doing was for my family's sake. Catherine called me on that. She said that I'd done it for myself. We were both right, I think. But even doing it for my family was wrong."

Day leaned back on the bed and cocked his head to one side. "How can taking care of your family be wrong?"

"Carlos taught me how. You never met a more committed family man than him. With his kids, he was as gentle as the gentleman he pretended to be. He loved them fiercely. *Too* fiercely and at the cost of anyone who wasn't his family. All the money, all the killing, it was all for an empire he was building to protect them."

"Protect them from what?"

"The same thing I've been working most of my life to protect *my* family from. All the things that might happen that none of us can control. And the more desperate I was to be their savior, the easier it was for me to ignore the needs of everybody else. To the point that I could see the path from the man I was becoming to the kind of man that Carlos is."

"So this is about making amends for all of that?" Day asked.

"No," Brad answered. "It's about caring for people, people other than my family. In the end, I think maybe the best way to serve those we love is to serve the wider world."

Day sat up and rested his arms on his knees. "It's your life, Brad," he said, "but if you do this, if you risk exposing your past by practicing medicine again, it could be over quick."

"It's already over, Dennis," Brad said. "I died once, remember? I'm not afraid of doing it again."

Chapter Forty-Five

A New Bloom

BRAD RAN THE razor over his scalp one last time. By now, he could do it by feel. He finished up while reading a post on his phone about how to build a cold frame for hardening off seedlings. He rinsed the last of the shaving cream from the back of his neck, toweled off, and took a moment to study his face. Like the ranch house and everything in it, the mirror over the sink in the bathroom was small. It made the twelve miles between Brad and his nearest neighbor feel even farther away.

He'd been shocked when the stubble he'd been shaving from his face for his entire life came in pure white, although after he thought about all he'd been through before he'd come here to New Brunswick, he wasn't that surprised. He grabbed his glasses from the top of the toilet tank and settled them on his face.

Dennis Day had visited him here only once after he'd dropped Brad off. He'd come three months later for a final check-in. When he saw Brad's bald head, white-whiskered chin, and the thick black glasses perched on Brad's new nose, he finally admitted the rhinoplasty had been a good idea. All those things anchored an identity that no longer felt new after almost four years here on this remote stretch of Canada's eastern coast.

On the mornings when he shaved his head, the tingling sensation across his scalp reminded Brad of how important it was to pay attention not only to what he *thought* but to what he *felt* as well. It was easy to do that in a place where he could go an entire weekend speaking to no one but the squirrels and jays on his back lawn. When he went into town, his glasses seemed to sharpen his view of what was happening to others, to the hardworking farmers, fishermen and quiet people who visited the small clinic where he treated them and their families. And with every breath through his new nose, he appreciated the smells that came from this place, scents he'd known since his earliest days—the good clean earth and the wild, raw sea that reminded him so much of his father's farm. Though he was living in another time and place, whenever he took a big breath of that air, the distance from both seemed to disappear.

But today would be different. If Dennis Day had known about the trip Brad had in mind, he would have stolen the passport right out of Brad Gorton's dresser drawer, just like Carlos had years ago. Brad took the two-hour trip to St. John's a couple of times a year to pick up supplies, but that was the extent of his traveling. He was looking forward to going a lot farther today. It would be his first trip back to the U.S.A. And probably his last.

He put on his winter jacket and stepped outside to warm up his truck. The sun had just come up, and even now, at the end of May, the morning still had the cold bite of winter. It was one of the things he liked best about being up here, that it was so different from the jungle. The chill that greeted him each day only made him more aware of the warmth of his own beating heart.

He goosed the gas to rev the truck. When he was sure it wouldn't stall, he jogged back inside, slipped a plant out of the grow tent he'd set up in the corner of his kitchen, tucked it under the flap of his jacket, and hurried it into the truck. And for the next seven hours, as Brad drove south, he let his mind wander to all those places he'd tried to keep it from for so long.

✦

It was a ticketed event, but there was no gate around the rows of chairs on the bright green lawn. He got there an hour early and took a seat in the last row on the aisle, where he'd have a long, straight view of the stage.

The ceremony finally started, and the speakers came and went, giving speeches full of platitudes about hard work and distant dreams. The better ones shared personal stories that let the audience make those connections for themselves. The whole thing went on for far too long, but when the procession started, Brad knew he wouldn't have to wait long until the B names took the stage.

He stood up, slipped a pair of tiny binoculars out of his pocket, and trained them on the figures marching up to the lectern. Each one extended one hand for a shake and the other to receive the piece of paper recognizing the past four years of work. Brad had the face he sought centered in his sights for only a minute. But he'd never seen Grace smile so brightly or walk with such sure steps as when she crossed that stage.

He waited all the way through the Zs and through the long round of applause that followed. He waited after, as the sea of black-gowned students broke to flow among the families in the crowd. After a minute, he saw Grace run down the aisle. For one crazy second, he hoped—then feared—that she had recognized him. Then she turned to duck into one of the rows ahead.

He caught Catherine's profile for only a few seconds before her face disappeared behind Grace's raised arms. Behind them stood a taller figure. The man waited for a moment as mother and daughter celebrated, then moved in to embrace them both. Brad watched them and felt his heart rise, and fall.

+

It was a big parking lot. The last thing he wanted was for someone to call security about some guy snooping around between the rows of cars. So Brad walked quickly, scanning the vehicles to find the ones that were green. As the first members of the audience were just approaching the last line of cars, he spotted the one he was looking for.

The rust spots on the bottom of Grace's Subaru had grown bigger since he'd first seen the car. A crop of new bumper stickers had blossomed around the one for Bowdoin: NO JUSTICE, NO PEACE, read one. THERE IS NO PLANET B, read another. LOVE IS GENDER-BLIND, read a third. Brad realized he had no idea where his daughter was headed. But he was surer than ever that wherever Grace was going, the world would be a better place once she got there.

He laid his hand on the car's hood for a moment, then set down the small clay pot he'd been cradling. And on the long drive north, and for so many days after, Brad thought about all the hopes he'd pinned to the small red rose he'd left blooming there.

Acknowledgments

Every writer knows the role research plays in shaping stories that can take the reader from the page to the place where the world the author creates becomes real. Information gleaned from the internet can start that journey, but it takes people to pull it off. That was certainly the case for *The Corpse Bloom*, a book I could never have written without the generous support of the cast of characters noted below.

Mary Kay Moyer, CRNA, was the first medical professional I interviewed for the story. Her position as a nurse anesthetist granted me my initial peek behind the operating room's door. Mary Kay had the skill to distill the details of what happens in the OR and the roles of those within it. She gave me the knowledge I needed to lay the foundation for my story.

Two other anesthesiology experts let me build on Mary Kay's lead with specific knowledge about the pharmacological tools of their trade and their ingenious ideas on how to use them to add a dose of intrigue to my plot. David Andrews, MD, served as the sux specialist who shared the literal inside story on the biomechanics of succinylcholine. His notes on sux's effects inspired ways to describe Octavio's death that were far more bizarre than anything I could have dreamed up on my own.

Daniel Landry, MD, gave me details on another drug that became the key to bookending Carlos's role at the story's start and end. It was Dan's idea to use potassium chloride as the cause for Sam's unlikely heart attack in chapter one, then have Carlos reveal his hand in arranging for the injection of that substance in Sam's transfused blood near the story's end.

Roxanne Taylor, RN, MSN, CCTC, provided a wealth of information needed to build the clandestine organ-procurement network at the heart of Nueva Vida's brutal business model. Roxanne's in-depth view of the science of donor-recipient matching gave me the insight I needed to design the medical database the cartel used to identify potential donor-victims, the same system that Brad bugged to try to bring the cartel down.

Other professionals outside of the medical world were no less instrumental in helping me bolster the book's plausibility and plot. Brandon Tam's expertise as an orchid specialist gave me the botanical understanding I needed for the symbol I planted at the heart of my story. His notes on the nature of the *Amorphophallus titanium*, and the timeline for its maturation, grounded the subplot that let the corpse flower serve as the metaphor for many aspects of the story, including Nueva Vida's birth, growth, and deadly intent.

Internationally bestselling author, Tess Gerritsen, played a seminal role in my story's start. Tess used her award-winning talent for discerning potent plots to suggest the initial idea of using illegal kidney transplants as the malicious medical malpractice that could cause Brad's life to derail. Award-winning mystery writer Bruce Coffin used his keen eye for plot twists to suggest one when I shared my initial story outline with him. It was Bruce's idea to turn Brad's trusted mentor Peter Webb into a traitor.

Heidi Hammond O'Connor provided the red pen required to create the grammatically and contextually correct Spanish used in the novel. Heidi's linguistic skill in parsing and perfecting my meaning for all the Spanish-language words helped translate the idioms, actions, and emotions I tried to convey.

Acadia State Park law enforcement ranger Chris Wiebusch helped me solve a plot problem critical to creating a plausible climax for those readers who know my home state well. Chris made multiple stops on his regular beat around the Schoodic Peninsula to photograph possible locations for Brad's "supposed" car crash into the sea, which led me to the perfect spot for that drop on Blueberry Hill.

The Pinecone Writers' Den was meeting monthly in my home four years ago when I first waded into this story. The feedback from this trusted tribe of scribes helped me sharpen both individual scenes and the overall structure of my narrative in the early stages when I was trying to turn a ten-page outline into a novel that could keep readers engaged and guessing to its end.

Both Tracy Roe, MD, and Heidi Dorr were instrumental in giving this book the objective editorial eye that brought my final draft up to the high standards of the traditional publishing industry. Tracy's dual careers as copyeditor and urgent-care physician provided a unique pair of insights to copyedit the story from an editorial and medical perspective. Heidi's generous guidance from our first e-mail exchange led me both to Tracy and to my education of the intricacies of top-tier editing. That process ended with Heidi's meticulous proofreading that put the final professional polish on this book.

Finally—last, but hardly least—*The Corpse Bloom* owes both its birth and completion to Lee Thibodeau, MD. As a writer leaning toward the genre of literary fiction, I would never have attempted to write a medical thriller if Lee hadn't convinced me to tackle this tale. His global oversight of the medical narrative, and the network of professional peers he made available to me, were major factors in allowing me to make the leap to the dynamic style of storytelling this work demanded. Lee's most valuable gift to the book, and to me, however, was his steadfast belief that I could pull it off. I remain profoundly grateful for his faith in me.

Author's Note

Thank you so much for reading The Corpse Bloom. Book reviews are the lifeblood of authors like me who seek to strengthen their relationships with the readers we write our stories for. Please consider sharing a review on Goodreads, Amazon, and/or the website where you purchased the book. Recommendations to your friends and family on social media are also greatly appreciated! I invite you to sign up for my newsletter at brywig.com/newsletter to be kept updated on my future novels as well.